LIZZIE'S WAR

LIZZIE'S WAR

| *A Novel* |

Tim Farrington

HarperSanFrancisco
A Division of HarperCollins*Publishers*

The book is a work of fiction. References to real people, events, establishments, organizations, or locales are intended only to provide a sense of authenticity, and are used fictitiously. All other characters, and all incidents and dialogue, are drawn from the author's imagination and are not to be construed as real.

HarperCollins books may be purchased for educational, business, or sales promotional use. For information please write: Special Markets Department, HarperCollins Publishers, Inc., 10 East 53rd Street, New York, NY 10022.

HarperCollins Web site: http://www.harpercollins.com

HarperCollins®, 📖®, and HarperSanFrancisco™ are trademarks of HarperCollins Publishers, Inc.

FIRST EDITION

Library of Congress Cataloging-in-Publication Data is available.

ISBN 0–06–056234–X

05 06 07 08 09   RRD(H)   10 9 8 7 6 5 4 3 2 1

For my father, Major F. X. Farrington, USMC (ret.),
with love and gratitude

Let every man abide in the same calling wherein he was called. . . .
Brethren, let every man, wherein he is called, therein abide with God.
1 CORINTHIANS 7

PART ONE

Nothing that is worth doing can be achieved in our lifetime; therefore we must be saved by hope. Nothing which is true or beautiful or good makes complete sense in any immediate context of history; therefore we must be saved by faith. Nothing we do, however virtuous, can be accomplished alone; therefore we must be saved by love.

REINHOLD NIEBUHR

CHAPTER 1

JULY 1967

DETROIT WAS BURNING. The midsummer sun that had made the Ohio turnpikes the usual ordeal seemed suddenly uncertain, caught in the sludge of a smoky sky like a pale orange dime stamped into hot blacktop. In the chastened light, her hometown was ominously unfamiliar. Even the freeway signs seemed ambiguous, inexact translations from the language of her childhood. Elizabeth O'Reilly was disoriented—she refused to use the word *lost*—and she was running out of gas.

There were almost no other vehicles on the road, not even cabs and buses. That was the most unnerving thing of all. She always made these visits to her parents braced for traffic, the proud clogged streets of the Motor City, the mass of good American steel in motion. She recalled glimpsing a newspaper headline the day before, something about riots, but she hadn't taken the news seriously. Detroit was ever volatile, and the newspapers loved to blow a few broken windows up into chaos in the streets. She'd been too busy seeing her husband off to Vietnam to fret about such things.

In the seat beside her, Liz's eight-year-old daughter, Katherine, fiddled with the radio, looking for the Beatles. Since the release of *Sergeant Pepper's Lonely Hearts Club Band* in June, Kathie and her friends had been in an ecstasy of grief, sobbing through a series of candlelit pajama parties over the death of Paul, which was obvious from the rose he was holding on the album cover. Liz found all the preadolescent intensity a little much. But Kathie was susceptible to extremes of poignancy. At Dulles Airport the previous Wednesday, she'd clung to her father and wailed. She was sure that he was going away to die, like Paul. Mike, stiff in his dress greens and self-conscious in public, his beautiful black hair buzzed close to his skull by some fanatic Marine barber, patted her with a pained air and told her it was no big deal, it was just his job and he'd be home soon. He was uncomfortable with emotional extravagance—with any emotion at all, really, Liz thought ruefully. She knew her husband just wanted to get off to his war without a lot of fuss, and she'd tried to rein Kathie in a bit. But her heart wasn't in it; she'd even felt a surreptitious gratitude for the frankness of her daughter's horror. Kathie was wailing for all of them. She was just prepared to be louder about it.

Liz heard something that sounded like gunfire close by. Or maybe a backfire. Surely a backfire, she told herself. She could see no flames, but the smoke was denser now, sifting in sinister threads across the freeway. As Kathie continued to wade through the radio's stations, Liz caught a snatch of feverish news coverage—*". . . in a twelve-block area east of Twelfth Street . . ."*—but her daughter skipped past it blithely. Liz almost told her to go back, then decided not to press the issue. There was no sense getting everyone all worked up.

In the back of the Fairlane station wagon, her other three children occupied themselves with the quiet ease of seasoned travelers. Between the moves imposed by the Marine Corps every couple years and frequent trips to their scattered relatives, they'd spent a lot of their childhoods in cars. Deborah, the youngest at five years old, was reading *An Otter's Tale* for perhaps the fiftieth time, oblivious to the mayhem nearby, her china blue eyes and perfect round face composed. She had already finished the book once this trip, somewhere on the Pennsylvania Turnpike, and had turned back to the first page and started over immediately. As Liz watched her now in the rearview mirror, a siren began to scream in the burning inner city to their right. Her younger daughter turned a page. She had an air of serenity, like a child in a dream.

Beside Deb-Deb, Angus, seven, pressed his face against the window on the freeway side of the car. He had been counting license plates since Maryland and was up to thirty-seven states. The paucity of traffic was the only effect of Detroit's upheaval that he seemed to have noticed so far. Behind him, in the station wagon's rear well, Danny, the oldest at ten years old, had put his biography of Stonewall Jackson aside and turned toward the smoke, his brow wrinkled just like his father's would have been, more in alertness than in fear. He met Liz's gaze briefly in the rearview mirror, his glance both sober and excited, and she felt the weird camaraderie she had felt with him almost from the moment he was born, the sense of someone home behind those blue-gray eyes. It was oddly comforting. And, sometimes, scary.

The children didn't know it yet, but there was a fifth passenger. Liz was six weeks pregnant. It had been a catastrophe of sorts, a classic Catholic mistake. The last thing she wanted. But there it was. She could feel the new life inside her as a hotter place, a burning spot, as if she had swallowed a live coal. And as a weight, tilting some inner scale toward helpless rage. It wasn't something she wanted to feel. She had more than enough guilt and ambivalence with the children already born.

The maddening static gave way abruptly to music. Kathie had finally found a station to her satisfaction.

What would you do if I sang out of tune?
Would you stand up and walk out on me?

"I see a tank!" Angus exclaimed.

"There aren't any tanks in Detroit," Liz said firmly, wondering if it was true.

"That's an APC," Danny offered from the back of the car.

"Wow!" Angus twisted in his seat to get a better look. "Hey, look at all that smoke!"

"God help us," Liz muttered. "What in the world is an APC?"

"An armored personnel carrier," Angus told her, a little condescendingly. Both her boys were fluent in military jargon, Marine Corps brats through and through. She would have preferred them to be up to speed on Wordsworth.

"Something's burning!" Deb-Deb piped up.

Kathie looked up, prepared to be dramatically alarmed. "What?!"

The gas gauge needle was farther below the *E* than Liz had ever seen it, lower even than it had been the time she ran out of gas on the D.C. Beltway at rush hour with all four kids less than six years old and crying for dinner. The Woodward exit was coming up; the exit after that was the Chrysler Freeway. If she didn't get off soon she was going to end up running out of gas on the bridge to Canada or something.

I get by with a little help from my friends,
Ooo, I get high with a little help from my friends . . .

"Do APCs have license plates?" Angus asked.

The Ford's engine hiccuped, unnervingly, and Liz hit the turn signal and lurched toward the exit ramp, trying to remember how to get to Nine Mile Road from downtown. If she could just pick up Gratiot somehow, she was home free. But nothing looked the same when it was burning.

IT WAS A HELL of a way to find out a friend had died. The forklift brought the seabag into the warehouse and dropped it without ceremony onto a wooden receiving pallet. The driver, a teenage corporal with an unlit cigarette dangling from his mouth like a fuse, hopped down and handed Captain Michael O'Reilly, USMC, a casualty ticket and the seabag's tag. O'Reilly initialed the manifest, and the kid took the clipboard back, tossed off a perfunctory salute, and clambered onto the forklift. He threw the vehicle into reverse, pulled a nifty 180, and powered out of the warehouse gloom into bright Okinawan sunlight, the cigarette, still unlit, cocked at a jaunty angle now.

Mike shook his head wryly; it was nice to see a man who loved his work. He held his breath while the diesel fumes dispersed, then turned to the casualty ticket and learned that Larry Petroski was dead.

It was just too weird, like a joke gone wrong. There had to be a punch line. Toward the rear of the building, looming in twilight the color of wet cement, rack after rack of temporary shelving stood loaded with seabags that looked exactly like this one. Mike had received seven bags since lunchtime, certifying each and releasing it to the forklift corporal's deft manipulation. The kid could place a seabag on the highest shelf without even fully stopping the forklift, with a touch as light as an Oscar Robertson layup. The bag would slide off the tongs into its slot, the rickety shelves would rock and settle, and by the time they had stopped creaking the kid would be out the door again, on his way for the next load, the forklift spewing fumes as the engine revved. He could actually get as many as three bags on the narrow rack, and he could shelve the things two at a time in a pinch. He was a fucking genius with that forklift. Given the volume of seabags coming in, Mike had been grateful for the kid's heedless efficiency until now. But this bag was Larry Petroski's.

In the silence of the deserted warehouse, a big Okinawan rat skittered along the wall behind the nearest shelves. Mike let his breath out and read the casualty ticket again. Petroski, L. C. 1lt. 914179 B-1-3.

Larry had been due to make captain soon. He was one promotion cycle behind the rest of their Basic School class because he'd gotten the school commander's daughter pregnant. Larry married Maria Dumar without excessive delay, which accounted for the fact that his career was not scuttled entirely, but the CO, Colonel Rutgers E. "Red-Ass" Dumar, had never forgiven him. To read Larry's fitness reports from that period, you would have thought the guy was smuggling drugs and defacing Bibles. In fact, Larry had been one of the best in that officer class, an effortlessly gifted man, blond, brilliant, and graceful under fire, with a rowdy sense of humor a bit too broad for his own good. He'd dutifully named his first son Rutgers, after his father-in-law, but Larry always called the boy Chevy, for the 1953 sedan in which the kid had been conceived.

Mike heaved the seabag onto the field desk beside the pallet. He was supposed to sort through its contents and make sure there was nothing compromising in it, nothing that would embarrass the slain Marine's family or reflect badly on the Corps. An exercise in post-mortem discretion. It was a tedious, emotionally grueling task under any circumstances, a classic shitty little job for the SLJO, or shitty little job officer, which was what Mike was briefly here at Kadena Air Force Base, Okinawa, while he waited for his papers to be processed. He'd been on the Rock a week, sorting through the seabags of dead Marines and stacking casualty tickets like a funeral home clerk. If nothing else, the macabre duty and the boredom of nights in Camp Hansen's transient BOQ had made him eager to just get on a plane to Da Nang and take whatever came, to start doing what they really paid him for. What Larry had been doing: shooting at bad guys, and getting shot at in return. Putting his ass on the line for God, country, and the commandant of the Marine Corps.

The combination to the seabag's lock was on the second tag, the one Larry had filled out before he caught his own flight to Da Nang six months before. Mike recognized his friend's anniversary with a pang: 9-8-56. Larry had married Maria, who was already showing by then, under the crossed swords of his Basic School classmates at Quantico's Church of St. Francis of Assisi, two days after graduation, on the Feast of the Birth of the Blessed Virgin Mary. His unhappy new father-in-law, suspecting the infamous Petroski irony, had only hated him more for that extra religious flourish. But Larry never really gave a damn.

Mike spun the dial, and the lock fell open. The seabag's contents were the usual mix of civilian clothes, service "A" uniforms, and books unsuitable to a war zone. Larry had apparently meant to get around to reading Dostoyevsky. There was the edition of Kipling's poems, with "If" and "Gunga Din" dog-eared, that Larry had had since Basic School, a how-to book on enclosing a porch, and another on plumbing. There was a spare set of dog tags with rubber silencers and a pair of the ugly black military-issue eyeglasses that no one was willing to wear. And there was the personal stuff, the stuff that broke your heart: a gold necklace in a blue velvet box, probably purchased in Hawaii as a coming-home present for Maria, and Larry's wedding ring, in a plastic bag. No one wore his wedding band in the field; there were too many ways for it to catch on something like a howitzer carriage or a helicopter door and tear your finger off. The wives hated it, they wanted to think of their men wearing the rings every moment they were in danger, but that was just the way things were.

There was a good picture of Maria and the three kids, all boys named for honored ancestors but invariably called by nicknames based on their places of conception—Chevy, Lejeune, and Ramada— all of them with the same cocky Petroski grin. There were some Japanese fans, probably also presents, a small jade Buddha, two boxes of chocolate-covered macadamia nuts that had melted into single lumps, a pair of lacy white, lavender-scented women's underwear, a very old rosary, and a pink rabbit's foot, much the worse for the wear.

There was no question that the underwear was Maria's, and Mike left it among the effects when he closed the seabag up. He took the rabbit's foot out. No sense burdening Larry's wife with superfluous irony.

In the rear of the warehouse, the skewed racks imposed their temporary order on the twilight. They seemed both makeshift and weirdly timeless, like the scaffolding he and Liz had seen once through a dawn fog at the archeological digs at Pompeii. A jury-rigged frame for the lumpen dead.

Mike moved to drop the ragged rabbit's foot into the trash can, caught himself, wavered, and finally put it in his pocket, feeling foolish. It was sentiment, pure and simple, a way of trying to hang on to Larry somehow. The damn thing had already proven itself useless.

AT THE OFFICERS' CLUB, a group of second lieutenants, boot brown bars in crisp traveling uniforms, fresh out of Quantico, had gotten an early jump on happy hour and were singing boisterously from the middle of the bar.

> *Born in the backwoods, raised by bears,*
> *Double-boned jaw, three coats of hair—*

"Schlitz," Mike told the bartender, a weathered sergeant who was making no attempt to hide his disdain for the junior officers.

"Got no Schlitz," the bartender shrugged, and, after a pause long enough to register contempt but deftly short of outright insubordination, "sir."

> *Cast iron balls and a blue-steel rod,*
> *I'm a mean motherfucker, a Marine, by God!*

The off-key chorus dissolved into macho banter. The new lieutenants couldn't wait to get to Vietnam and kick some Charlie ass. Mike glanced at the bartender's name tag, then leaned forward and spoke under the din in an even, quiet tone. "Sergeant Browning, they've had Schlitz on this godforsaken Rock since I ran Third Platoon, Charlie Company, here in 1959, and if you can't get me my goddamned beer, you'd better not still be behind that bar when I come back there to get it myself. I just sent my best friend's seabag home to his wife, and I'm feeling a little testy."

The bartender met his eyes, then let his gaze drift to O'Reilly's chest, noting the Chosin campaign ribbon, Bronze Star bar, and Purple Heart.

"I might have a Schlitz or two stashed away for a special occasion," he conceded, and turned to the cooler. He dug deep and produced two cream and brown cans, which he pierced brusquely with a C-rat tool. He handed one can to Mike and kept the other for himself.

"Thank you, Sergeant."

Browning lifted his Schlitz. "Here's mud in your eye."

Mike took a breath and raised his own beer. "To First Lieutenant Lawrence C. Petroski, Bravo Company, 1/3. 'Your dextrous wit will haunt us long / Wounding our grief with yesterday.'"

"Semper Fi," the bartender seconded. They touched their cans together and drank. Mike took one long pull, and then another, before lowering the can. It made an empty clank as it hit the bar, and Browning got him another beer without a word. Down the bar, the second lieutenants were agitating for more drinks, but Browning ignored them and took his own beer over by the sink, where he busied himself polishing a series of shot glasses.

Through the open doors to the terrace, the sun was easing toward the East China Sea. The breeze stirring the palm trees smelled like frangipani. Across the surface of the turquoise lagoon below, Okinawan fishermen's skiffs skittered like water spiders, making glittering ripples. It was all indecently idyllic. Like Hawaii, Mike thought, only with warehouses filling with the luggage of the dead. He was going to have to write to Liz. Jesus. Should he write to Maria too? What the hell did you say? *Dear Maria, So sorry Larry bought it. He was a helluva guy.* There wasn't really anything to say. It came with the job. That was the thing the women never got. It came with the fucking job.

On the wall behind the bar was a framed cartoon: two vultures sitting on a branch. "Patience, my ass," one of the vultures was saying. "I want to kill something."

The brown bars had begun to sing the "Marine Corps Hymn," but nobody seemed to know the second verse. Mike set his empty beer can on the bar beside the first and took the rabbit's foot out of his pocket. What a ridiculous goddamned thing to hang on to.

"Another one, sir?" Browning asked.

"Thanks, no, Sergeant," Mike said, and rose to go. Much as he would have liked to have his private wake for Larry Petroski, he was almost certainly shipping out tomorrow, and he had to get his own seabag squared away.

"THIS ISN'T THE EXIT for Grandma's house, is it?" Danny asked.

"No," Liz said, trying to sound calm. "Kids, get down on the floor."

Woodward Avenue looked like it had been bombed. Liz had taken a right off the exit ramp, but she was already thinking she probably should have gone left. The street's six lanes were deserted and strewn with debris. Three National Guardsmen with M-14s, the only human beings in sight, stared incredulously at the passing station wagon from the glass-strewn sidewalk in front of a looted grocery store. She could see empty shelves through the gaping window. The next building was a burned-out hulk, and the one after that was too.

"What's happening?" Angus asked.

"It's a riot, birdbrain," Danny told him.

Deb-Deb looked up from *An Otter's Tale*. "What's a riot?"

"Shut up and get down on the floor!" Liz snapped. "Now!"

The urgency of her near-panic had finally leaked into her voice. The children hastily complied. Kathie began to cry. Deborah, seeing Kathie's tears, followed suit. Angus lifted his head to look at Danny, to see whether he should cry too.

"Angus—"

"Danny's got his head up!"

"If Danny jumped off a cliff, would you jump too?" Liz demanded, realizing with dismay that she was quoting her mother. It had come to that. She was turning into her mother, in spite of her best efforts. That seemed worse somehow than Detroit in flames.

"It would depend on how high the cliff was," Angus replied judiciously, after a moment's consideration.

On the radio, the Beatles had given way to the Byrds' sugary version of "Mr. Tambourine Man."

Take me for a trip
Upon your magic swirling ship
All my senses have been stripped
And my hands can't feel to grip—

Liz reached over and snapped the music off, immediately regretting the forfeiture of the last vestige of normality. In the absence of electronic filler you couldn't hear anything but a single siren receding in the distance. The silence of the city was the most frightening thing she'd ever heard.

"Hey!" Kathie protested, raising her head from underneath the dashboard.

"Angus's feet stink," Deb-Deb noted from the floor of the backseat, where she remained crouched obediently. She was the only one of the four who would do something the first time you told her.

"Do not!"

"Do too!"

"We just drove past a gas station," Danny said.

Liz hit the brakes, and all four kids pitched forward. Kathie smacked her head on the dashboard and began to cry again. Angus fell on top of Deb-Deb, who squealed in protest.

"Sorry, sorry," Liz said, peering into the rearview mirror. The tiny gas station was half a block behind them already. She hesitated, but they were the only car on the road, and finally she just put the car in reverse.

"Kathie, go ahead and turn the radio back on," she said as she began backing up. "Angus, for God's sake, get off of Deb-Deb. Danny, keep an eye out and tell me if I'm going to back into anything."

"All clear back here," Danny said, while the other children sorted themselves out. They were accustomed to a certain amount of chaos on rides with their mother.

> *I'm ready to go anywhere*
> *I'm ready for to fade*
> *into my own parade—*

"Everybody except Danny get back down on the floor," Liz said. "I am absolutely serious about this."

It felt outrageous, backing down Woodward Avenue in broad daylight. She found herself keeping one eye out for the cops. But they were obviously busy elsewhere. The two-pump gas station was deserted, but an older black man who looked like the owner was sitting on a chair outside the office door. Liz backed up to the first pump, hearing the heartening little ding-ding as the tires went over the welcome cable. It sounded like the place was in business. From sheer force of habit, she checked her lipstick in the rearview mirror. It was gone, of course, and her hair was a fright. She got out of the car and smoothed her powder blue skirt, blinking in the bright sunlight, smelling smoke.

The owner, if that was who he was, was staring at her in open dismay, but Liz decided that the best thing to do was to just act as if everything were normal. Just another white woman in her best traveling suit, stopping in a burning ghetto for a fill-up.

She unscrewed the cap to the tank and picked up one of the nozzles, but the pump was dead. A National Guard truck rumbled by, with a dozen soldiers in the rear with automatic rifles, all of them looking up, scanning the rooftops for snipers. The building across the street was burning, a quiet fire, weirdly matter-of-fact. All four of her children's heads were up again.

"Mom, I'm hungry," Angus announced, as he had at every gas station since Virginia.

"There are sandwiches in the cooler."

"Can I have a candy bar?"

"I want a candy bar too!" Deb-Deb said.

"We'll see," Liz said. "Now get down. I don't want to have to tell you again!"

The four heads disappeared. Liz hesitated, then crossed the pavement toward the office, noting for the first time that the owner had a shotgun across his lap. The little building's window was shattered, and the glass had been swept up into a neat pile by the door. Inside, the floor was strewn with toppled shelves. A hand-lettered sign propped in the corner of the empty window read, "NEGRO BUSINESS. PLEASE DON'T BURN."

"Jesus, lady," the man said as she walked up to him.

"I know, I know." He had a kindly face, and Liz gave him her best woman-in-distress smile, feeling foolish and very suburban. "I'm afraid I got a little off my usual route."

"I guess you did."

"Your pump doesn't seem to be working."

"Pump's turned off," the guy said. "I'm just tryin' to keep the place from blowing up."

"Would you mind turning it back on, just for a quick fill-up? I'm really in a bind here."

The man looked over at the station wagon full of children, whose heads were all up again. "I guess you are," he said. He hesitated, then shook his head. "I been runnin' this place for almost twenty years, and I ain't never seen the likes of this. There was that riot in '43, but I was overseas then. I was in the damn Marines."

"My husband's a Marine."

"How 'bout that. I was a sergeant. First Negro sergeant in my unit. They wouldn't let me do nothin' but laundry, though. I'da been just as glad to get shot at, after three years of laundry, I can tell you that."

"My husband was a sergeant," Liz said, feeling there was no need to complicate the rapport with Mike's current rank. "In Korea. He just left for Vietnam."

The owner gave her a sharp, more attentive glance. His wide, somewhat sad brown eyes were shot through with streaks of red. She wondered how long he'd been sitting here with that shotgun. He looked like he hadn't slept in days.

"I lost my oldest son in Vietnam," he said. "Just last year. Died in a damn helicopter crash. Can you believe that? They wouldn't even give him a Purple Heart. I said, Dead's dead, the boy deserves his medal. But they got their rules, I guess."

"I'm sorry for your loss," Liz said.

"Thank you, ma'am. I hope your husband makes it okay."

"Thank you."

They were silent a moment. The building across the street continued to burn, but otherwise the neighborhood was eerily peaceful. Angus, his nose pressed against the car window, was making suggestive motions with his hand and mouth, miming eating a candy bar. Deb-Deb's little moon face beside him looked hopeful too. Liz made a fierce quashing movement with her hand, and her children's heads ducked out of sight again.

"I'll pay you double for the gas," she offered. "I'll give you a dollar a gallon."

"There's no need to pay me double, lady," the owner said, offended. He stood up and leaned his shotgun against the wall. "Jesus. I ain't here to make no money off no one's troubles." Still shaking his head, he shuffled over to the pump, fumbling for a key ring as he went. At the pump, he turned a key in the slot and set her tank to filling with the nozzle on automatic.

"God bless you," Liz said as he walked back to her, and the man shrugged.

"God bless us all, I guess," he said, sounding tired. He went by her, into the office, and began righting the toppled racks. Liz followed, tiptoeing amid the wreckage. The floor was strewn with items the looters had rejected: tampons and sugarless gum, Kleenex boxes, packs of cinnamon jawbreakers, and some postcards of Detroit. A bottle of mouthwash had smashed, and the place smelled like Listerine. Scattered amid the debris were several unlikely candy bars; apparently whoever had looted the place had not liked Three Musketeers. Liz retrieved four of the candies and then, after a hesitation, a fifth for herself. She was already craving chocolate, feeding the pregnancy. As a sop to her conscience, she also grabbed a can of Fresca.

Amid the floor's debris, the headline of a disheveled copy of the *National Enquirer* caught her eye: "1200 TO DIE SOON AT KHE SANH."

Liz picked up the paper and scanned the article, wondering where Khe Sanh was. Jeanne Dixon, the psychic, was predicting all manner of mayhem there.

The only place-name Liz knew in Vietnam was Saigon. Mike had not known where he was going to be stationed. All she had for a mailing address was FPO San Francisco 96602. The Third Marine Amphibious Force was operating throughout I Corps, Mike had told her. Whatever that meant.

Not that any of it meant anything, really: who, what, why, where, when. All she really wanted to know was that her husband wasn't going to die.

She took the *National Enquirer* up to the counter, feeling ridiculous, along with the soda and candy bars and a postcard for Mike, who would appreciate the irony. The owner was trying to rehang his overhead cigarette rack. He'd already replaced his framed business license; through the cracked glass, she noted the name in proud roman script: EDWARD JOHNSON, PROPRIETOR. The liquor shelves behind the counter were neatly scoured, as if a cleaning service had come in. The cash register had been pried open, and the empty drawer hung askew.

"Uh, what do I owe you for these?" Liz asked, laying her salvaged goods on the counter, hoping she had exact change.

"No charge," Johnson said cheerfully, giving up on the rack and leaving it hanging tenuously by a single screw. He rummaged behind the counter and found the well-chewed remnant of a cigar. "Just take what you want. Everyone else did."

"Oh, no, I couldn't—"

"Hell, my nephew got himself a color television set the other day." Johnson struck a match and puffed for a moment, getting the cigar butt lit, then blew a circle of fragrant smoke politely away from her. "No antenna, though. I told him, If you're gonna risk gettin' shot for a damn TV, you might as well steal some rabbit ears to go with it. But that boy never had much sense."

"Well, how about the gas?"

He glanced at the pump monitor. "It's still filling. You must have one helluva big tank."

"Eighteen gallons," Liz said. It had been a selling point for the station wagon; she could drive for almost three hundred miles without stopping, if the spirit moved her and her bladder held out. The kids hated it.

"I got you for twenty-five, and counting."

"Well, that's odd."

Their eyes met; then Johnson hurried from behind the counter and out the door. Liz followed, her brain still trying to do the math. Across the dirty asphalt, the air around the station wagon was rippling in the July heat, as if the car were engulfed in its own dreamy atmosphere. It took Liz a moment to realize that the automatic pump had failed to shut off and that gas was overflowing onto the pavement. She could see all four of her kids' faces, alert to the possibility of candy bars, pressed hopefully against the car's windows. Across the street, the building burned on, the flames visible in the upper stories' windows now, licking outward like dragons' tongues. The city was on fire, and her children were sitting in a puddle of gasoline.

"Oh shit, oh shit, oh shit," Johnson breathed. He took a step toward the car and stopped, remembering his lit cigar.

Liz couldn't move. She knew that she should do something, but she couldn't for the life of her think what it was. She felt strangely incendiary herself, as if the electricity of her terror might arc across the pavement and set off the fireball. She felt like a lighted torch.

Johnson spat into his hand and stubbed the cigar out, clenching his fist around the butt to be sure of it. Liz winced. Everything was moving in slow motion now. She could feel the man's pain, like a hot nail's point, in the palm of her own hand. She could feel everything, and everything was clear, like the view through a rinsed windshield. She could feel her overwhelming love and her horror and the specter of her loss, pooled like the gasoline on that pavement, waiting to ignite. But she couldn't move.

Johnson crossed the asphalt like a man walking on ice and sloshed without hesitation into the puddle of gas. He flipped the catch on the pump, turning off the flow, then opened the back door of the station wagon and said something. Angus hopped right out. Kathie, in the front seat, seemed frozen, and Johnson opened the passenger door with a reassuring smile, reached in, and lifted her gently in his arms.

"Angus, come here!" Liz called, and her son trotted toward her. Behind him, Edward Johnson carried Kathie, who was sobbing. In the car, Danny had climbed over into the backseat and was sitting beside Deborah, the two of them engaged in some sort of discussion.

"Danny!" Liz hollered. Her oldest son turned and met her eyes, and she saw his father in his unhurried amusement, in the look that said, Yeah, yeah, calm down, I'm on it.

Angus reached her, and Liz took him in her arms; and a moment later Johnson set Kathie down beside her. In the station wagon, Danny and Deb-Deb continued to speak, and then Danny got out of the car, lifted his sister across the puddle of gas, and set her down. He took her hand, and they walked toward Liz. Deb-Deb seemed untroubled and was even beaming from the attention. She really did adore her older brother.

As her last two children walked up, Liz engulfed them too. Beside her, Edward Johnson smiled his sad-eyed smile, pleased and a little indulgent, absently rubbing his hand. Liz could see the blistered spot on his pale pink palm. The realization that this man had taken fire against his own skin, for the sake of her children, finally made it all seem real. She began to cry, from gratitude and relief. Kathie joined in readily. Deb-Deb looked a little puzzled, and Angus squirmed.

Danny patted her comfortingly.

"It's okay, Mom," he murmured. "It's not that big a deal." It was just what his father would have said, of course. But his father wouldn't have been crying too. Somehow Danny had ended up with Mike's ridiculous toughness and her own big soppy heart.

"It is a big deal, sweetie," she told him. "It's a big, big deal."

Beside her, looking at the broad, spreading puddle, with the flames from across the street reflected in it, Edward Johnson shook his head.

"I don't know what the hell I'm gonna do with all that gasoline," he said.

CHAPTER 2

AUGUST 1967

from: Capt. M. F. O'Reilly
Fri 4 Aug '67
TDO, HQ Bn., 29th Marines
Phu Bai, RVN
c/o FPO San Francisco, Calif. 96602

Dearest Lizzie,

Well, here I am in the garden spot of Southeast Asia. It's really very pleasant if you don't mind dust on everything, an average temperature of about 93°, and 103% humidity. That all changes in the rainy season, I'm assured. They say you can stand up to your knees in mud and have dust blow in your eyes.

The local people are sincere, hardworking, brave, trustworthy, loyal, etc., and till their fields and paddies industriously all day long. At night they shoot mortars at us. We shoot back, of course. I'm not sure when anybody sleeps. Last night our howitzers quit firing about 0300 and the silence woke me up. I think it woke up the local VC too, as they took the opportunity to shoot a rocket in here. One rocket, just for irritation value. I had laundry on the line when the damn thing hit, and it's full of nifty shrapnel holes now. My best dungarees at that. Those VC are malicious little bastards.

There's a lovely breeze blowing at the moment. It keeps the dust nice and fresh. And mere yards away, Boom, Boom, go the howitzers, shooting yet another H&I mission. (Harassment and Interdiction, just to keep them on their toes out there—our artillerymen's way of saying Hi.)

Speaking of laundry, you'd appreciate the system here. You have two choices: you can go to an approved Vietnamese-run laundry, where they will lose your dirty clothes so that you can buy clean ones, or you can use the patented USMC self-laundry system. I prefer the latter. It works thusly: you take your dirty dungarees, throw them in a bucket, add Cold Power Cold-Water All, water (of course), and let soak for a few hours. You then slosh vigorously for thirty seconds, rinse, and hang out to dry. In a couple of hours you've got spotless, sweet-scented clothes with a brand-new, fresh coat of dust. Unless they get hit by a rocket, of course.

I'm on "temporary duty" here at the moment, getting "oriented," which translates into reading a lot of idiotic memos on venereal disease and the various local fevers, sweating, sweating some more, and walking down to Battalion Headquarters three times a day to pound on a desk and demand action. But I've been promised a company, so I can't really complain. No doubt they'll send me out to do something entirely futile. The big buzz in I Corps at the moment is SecDef McNamara's latest brilliant idea: In order to discourage the infiltration of large NVA units across the DMZ, we're going to put up a big fence with little electronic jingles on it and big signs that say Keep Out. We've got about ten thousand Marine bulldozers clearing a quarter-mile-wide no-man's land along the Ben Hai

River, under constant mortar fire, and an equal or greater number of Marines getting shot at while protecting them. The damned thing's called the Trace, possibly because there isn't a trace of common sense in the whole idea. Scuttlebutt has it that some major in division operations at 3rd MarDiv drew a line on a map, more or less at random; it went up through channels, and lo and behold, we're implementing the Trace. An exquisitely conceived project.

Meanwhile, we're in the lap of luxury here at Phu Bai. We even have our own shower set up, a nifty fifty-five-gallon diesel drum full of greasy water, with holes punched in the bottom and a pull string control. If you want hot water, you shower in the afternoon; for cool water you wait 'til later at night.

I don't know where all the wind came from, but it's threatening to blow my hootch away. Visibility is down to a few inches, so I'll secure for now. Give my regards to all hands, and tell them Daddy's fine, just dusty. I'll write again as soon as I excavate my writing gear.

Your
Mike

P.S. Armed Forces Radio mentioned that there was a bit of a ruckus in Detroit last week, apparently while you were there at your parents'. But I figured you had sense enough to stay clear of the downtown.

P.P.S. Larry Petroski, unfortunately, got himself killed last week. Right before I got here. It seems that he and his radioman were the beneficiaries of a command-detonated mine somewhere near Con Thien. The usual unpretty sight, by all accounts: nothing but hair, teeth, and eyeballs. Another happy casualty of Mr. McNamara's Wall. Victor Charlie loves to blow up unit commanders, of course.

*Larry wasn't wearing his bars—we never do in the field—but it's
kind of hard to hide a guy with a radio on his back, dogging your
every step. C'est la guerre, as they used to say hereabouts, circa
1954. He still had that goddamned rabbit's foot he won at the
Prince William County Fair while we were in Basic School. The one
he said would make him bulletproof. You might want to give Maria
a buzz.*

*P.P.P.S. While I'm thinking of it, in the unlikely event that I should
be standing around in front of something and get shot myself, I told
them to notify you but not Mother and Dad directly. I figured it
might shake the old folks up to have some clod amble in and say I'd
been slightly injured when a 60-ton tank ran over my big toe or
something equally silly. Like being in my best fatigues when the next
rocket fills them full of holes.*

THE 122MM ROCKET killed two second lieutenants who hadn't even
been assigned to anything yet. They were sleeping on cots in a shallow
bunker when the rogue rocket landed in the doorway, which they had
left open to the cooler night air. One of the guys was using his nice
new flak jacket as a pillow, but it wouldn't have mattered if he had
been wearing it, as the blast blew his entire face away. The other guy
also suffered massive head wounds; he too had been sleeping with his
head pointed toward the door. The bunker had no blast wall and only
plywood and a single layer of sandbags for overhead cover. A sentry
said he had noticed the glow of two unshielded cigarettes through the
open entryway, about an hour earlier, and one of the lieutenants had
a tape deck playing, against every noise reg and rule of common
sense. The tape was still limping along when they dug the guys out,
playing The Yardbirds super slow.

All in all, the two men had made just about every mistake you could make in the absolute minimum amount of time necessary to die. No one could even remember their names, they had to look them up, and there was some squabbling over who was going to write the necessary letters to their families. As temporary duty officers, they were technically under the command of the battalion, but the CO said he was damned if he was going to write letters to the families of two fucking new guys who hadn't even had the sense to close their bunker door. In the end, they had Mike write them, since he was a captain and probably would have been stuck with the guys as platoon commanders anyway.

He wrote two scrupulous, respectful, sympathetic letters, making what he could of the marginally heroic material at hand; but all he could really think was that now some poor bastard on Okinawa was going to have to go through these guys' seabags. He wondered if that made him heartless. Everyone at Phu Bai was mad at those two idiots for dying so easily and so fast.

"SO, YOUNG MAN, what are you going to be when you grow up?"

"A Marine, Father," Danny O'Reilly said.

Father Winters smiled benignly. But the old priest smiled benignly at everything, and Danny couldn't really tell what it meant in this particular case. Danny had come to the introductory meeting for the new crop of altar boys prepared to be awed, but there was little that was awesome about Father Winters. The man was round, soft, and petulant, with a smile as phony as his hair, which looked like Davy Crockett's coonskin cap minus the striped tail, mashed a little flat. It was hard to take someone with a wig like that seriously, even if he was a man of God. The polyester aloha shirt only made it worse; Father Winters's complacent belly heaped the tropical fruit design into a compost of overripe mangoes and lurid plums. He wasn't even wearing his collar, and he wore white golf shoes with the spikes removed, which made a spectacular clicking, like a herd of tap dancers, on the marble-tiled floor in front of the altar rail.

There were five new altar-boy candidates sitting in the front row of St. Jude's church. Military kids, mostly, erect and well scrubbed, with haircuts that made their ears stand out like radio dishes: the suburban Virginia Beach parish was largely Navy families. The boys all looked intimidated and suitably grave, even Danny's best friend, Percy Killebrew, who sat beside him with his clip-on tie askew, maintaining an uncharacteristic silence. With Father Winters's attention on him, Danny didn't dare glance to his right for fear that Percy would lift an eyebrow and send him into spasms of laughter. Percy had already told Father Winters he was going to be a rodeo clown when he grew up, a put-on so brazen that it had been all Danny could do to stifle his guffaw. But Father Winters just smiled benignly and let the flippancy pass. It was clear he wanted to get to his golf game without undue controversy.

"A Marine," Father Winters repeated now, his tone suggesting that a rodeo clown might have been easier to digest. He floundered for something salutary to add, then brightened. "Weren't you a Marine, Father Germaine?"

"A Navy chaplain, Father," Father Germaine answered, with a trace of stressed patience that suggested he had corrected the misimpression before. He stood behind Father Winters and to his right, slumping unmilitarily in basic black. A strong-jawed man in his midthirties, with wiry hair like a chunk of unrefined coal and eyes of Vandyke brown, Germaine really needed to shave more often. On days that he said morning mass, his five o'clock shadow arrived by early afternoon. "I did spend some time in the field with Marines, though."

"Of course, of course." Father Winters regathered himself. "Well, the warrior's calling is a noble one. In this imperfect world, we will always need dedicated men willing to risk their lives to keep our country safe and strong. And to replace the, ah, casualties we are suffering at present, of course."

The priest's vague blue gaze wandered once more over Danny; finding nothing of further interest, he turned his attention back to the group.

"As aspiring acolytes, you are entering a sacred tradition, one that has endured for millennia. Like Father Germaine and myself, you are now servants of the God of Abraham, Isaac, and Jacob. It is a grave and weighty responsibility, and not to be taken lightly. You will have the privilege of assisting at the celebration of the Mass, the Holy Eucharist, a ritual that has survived virtually unchanged since the Last Supper." He eyed them sternly. "Two . . . thousand . . . years."

The words rang in the empty church. Winters let the silence stretch on. The boys sat rigid, even breathless, motionless under the weight of millennia.

"Two thousand years," Father Winters repeated at last. "And for most of those two thousand years, the Mass has been conducted in Latin. Our Holy Father has recently seen fit to allow Mass to be said in English, but make no mistake: the Latin Mass will be back." He chuckled, indicating humor. "Remember, you heard it here first. Save your Latin lectionaries. The vernacular service is a fad."

Father Germaine grimaced, approximating a smile. The boys uncertainly followed suit.

"We will therefore be requiring you altar boys to learn the Liturgy of the Word not just in its English version, but in the Latin as well. It will be a bit more work for you, but you will be grateful for the effort in the long run. And it will save us untold time when the Church corrects Her course. Some things simply do not change. *In principio verbum erat*, eh, Father Germaine?"

"*Sic*," the other priest agreed, deadpan. "*Atque multorum stulti-tiam perpessum esse.*"

Father Winters blinked: too much of a good thing. "Yes. Well." He glanced at his watch and brightened. "Unfortunately, I have another engagement this afternoon, but Father Germaine will be walking you boys through the rest of your orientation. Unless there are any questions at this point?"

He surveyed the group magnificently; but no one stirred. The boys' stoic faces suggested that they were prepared to die before conceiving a question.

"Good, good," Father Winters said. "Then I'll leave you in Father Germaine's most capable hands. I look forward to serving with you all in the near future."

And, with a hand motion somewhere between a wave and half a benediction, he was gone, his golf shoes clattering on the marble. The church's side door whooshed and thumped behind him. Father Germaine studied the floor at his feet, letting the echoes settle before he glanced up and met the boys' expectant gazes. His look was sober and a little weary, but something in his eyes suggested that they had shared a joke.

The boys relaxed, a palpable loosening as everyone began to breathe again. Danny was conscious suddenly of the quality of silence in the deserted church. It really was an awesome thing to be in the sanctuary without the usual Sunday crowd. The empty pews stretched behind him into dimness like receding centuries. A life-sized Christ, lurid with pre–Vatican II blood, hung by savage iron spikes from a cross as raw as railroad ties. To the left of the altar, in an arched niche lined with chunks of irregular stone, the Virgin Mary lifted an ivory hand over a bank of glittering candles. The quiet was so deep, it seemed to Danny he could hear the whisper of the flames.

"Two thousand years is really not such a very long time," Father Germaine confided, before he got on with the business of teaching them the intricate choreography of the mass. It was hard to tell whether the thought made him happy or not.

ONE OF THE EIGHT THINGS to which a property owner was entitled under the old King's Grant in Virginia real estate law was "the promise of quiet enjoyment." Fat chance, Liz thought, listening to Danny trying to start the lawn mower. It was a sound as painful as a child's racking cough at night. Mike had invariably gotten the thing going only after fifteen minutes of furious labor and volumes of the sort of inspired swearing only a Marine could manage. Perhaps the profanity was some kind of crucial element. She ached to go help Danny, but her older son had insisted on doing the job himself. It was all very Mike-like.

The washing machine's buzzer sounded, but Liz ignored it. The signal always went off halfway through the rinse cycle, and she had long since adjusted to waiting ten minutes after it sounded. It was a Cleaning Monday, and the other children were engaged in chores of their own. Kathie was sweeping the dining room with her pink Suzy Homemaker broom, blowing kisses as she worked and announcing from time to time, apropos of nothing, "I love you all." She was a remarkably cheerful housekeeper. Angus, meanwhile, sat a bit sullenly at the dining room table, refusing to lift his feet for the broom, ostensibly engaged in polishing the silverware. He was still on his first spoon, however. Deb-Deb was in the living room, "dusting" with a big yellow feather duster, an operation that looked more like an Isadora Duncan dance, with much waving and theatrical flourishes.

None of the kids was accomplishing much, but Liz was not overly interested in actual effect. The institution of Cleaning Monday had been a spasm of sorts on her part, a summer program she had imposed during an uncharacteristically fervent attempt to order their lives immediately after Mike's departure in July. It was enough at this point that the kids were going through the motions; she seldom did more, in her own housekeeping efforts.

The lawn mower engine caught at last, sputtered, then settled in to a heartening roar. Liz relaxed as Danny pushed the machine off on an arc toward the lake. With a moment to herself, she considered throwing up. Her morning sickness always unnerved the kids; Deb-Deb was afraid Liz might puke up the baby and refused to be comforted by attempts to explain the mechanics of the process. In any case, Liz was actually feeling relatively good today—her nausea had been easier with every pregnancy and was already tapering off. The downside of being such a seasoned baby machine was that even with a uterus the size of a mere orange, she was already showing; her stomach muscles had long since been savaged into slackness. She was going to have to start telling people soon, which she dreaded. It was hard to imagine accepting the inevitable congratulations with sufficient cheer.

She finished cleaning up the breakfast dishes, then went into the utility room just as the washer was rattling to a stop. She transferred the mass of wet laundry to the dryer, culled a load of whites from the Sisyphean resources of the dirty pile, and set the machine to Hot-Warm. She would add bleach if she could remember to when the machine had filled, but it didn't really matter. The boys' socks and underwear devolved inevitably toward gray.

"Mom, Kathie's not working," Angus complained from the dining room.

Liz glanced into the dining room, and, sure enough, Kathie had parked her pink broom by the window and disappeared. Desertion was a constant problem on Cleaning Mondays, though it was usually the younger kids who went AWOL first.

"Do you want me to go find her?" Angus offered hopefully.

"You just keep your butt in the chair, mister. Why don't you do another piece now? That spoon is shiny enough."

Angus set the very bright spoon aside and grudgingly fingered a salad fork. "Do Marines even use silverware?"

"Of course they do. On, uh, the Marine Corps birthday."

To her astonishment, this actually seemed to motivate her younger son. Angus turned back to his polishing with renewed vigor. At his present rate, Liz thought, he might even have a place setting or two finished by the time the Marine Corps birthday came around in mid-November. Her son stuck his tongue out slightly when he concentrated, just like Mike.

Liz made a quick circuit of the house in search of Kathie and finally found her daughter upstairs in the master bedroom, standing in front of the full-length mirror on the closet door, posing in Liz's wedding dress.

Liz paused in the doorway, surprised by the sudden constriction in her chest. She didn't want to cry. But she was close. Kathie was so radiant, so innocent and happy. What hurt her heart most, Liz realized, was that the main thing she felt at the sight of that long-forgotten white dress was an unexpectedly savage depth of irony. She'd been radiant, innocent, and happy once herself; but apparently she was no more. She and Mike had married in the chapel at Catholic University six months after she'd met him. She'd been eighteen, a drama major, an actress. She'd just played Rosalind in *As You Like It,* and she'd been dazzled and in love. The Old Testament reading at the wedding mass had been from Ruth—*Whither thou goest, I will go; and where thou lodgest, I will lodge*—and it had all been lovely and moving. Certainly Liz hadn't foreseen eventually lodging in the ramshackle Quonset huts and cardboard tenements that passed for officer housing at a series of obscure Marine Corps bases throughout the South. She and Mike had been going to go to New York, and Paris. She'd thought she was marrying a deep, literate veteran who wanted to write novels, who would send flowers backstage after her performances, who would lie around in bed with her on Sunday mornings with the Arts &

Culture section of the *New York Times* spread across the quilt, discussing Ibsen.

They had processed from the church under the crossed swords of a bunch of Mike's old Korean vet Marine buddies, not a starving writer in the bunch, which probably should have tipped her off—*Thy people shall be my people, and thy God my God*—but hadn't, somehow. There were the scars, of course, a glamorous gash along Mike's temple from the grazing of a Chinese Communist bullet, mostly hidden at that point by his civilian-length hair, and a Rorschach mottling of raised white ridges on his back, from a spatter of shrapnel he assured her had been no big deal. But she'd thought Mike was done collecting scars for his country.

And now he was off to this new war, making a career of it after all, in line for a fresh set of wounds or worse. It hurt, strangely, to see that dress, that white scar where her naïveté had been; and it hurt most that it hurt. *Where thou diest, will I die, and there will I be buried: the Lord do so to me, and more also, if aught but death part thee and me.*

Be careful what you wish for, Liz mused, and hated herself for the thought.

She said briskly, to beat the rising tears, "Well, don't you look beautiful."

Kathie turned a shining face to her. She was the only one of the four who had Mike's deep, somewhat mournful brown eyes, which in Kathie took on an air of disconcerting pathos. She looked lost in the huge gown, engulfed in an immensity of silk and taffeta. "How old do you have to be to get married?"

Older than eighteen, Liz thought, but she said, "Probably you should be out of second grade, at least."

"Can we take a picture of me to send to Daddy?"

"Of course, sweetheart." Liz found the Brownie camera, and her daughter posed happily for a couple of shots, wrestling the train around as if she were grappling with a white dragon.

They had just finished the roll of film when Angus appeared in the doorway. "Mom—"

"Angus, what did I tell you about staying in that chair?"

"Danny's hurt."

Liz bolted past him and hurried down the stairs, with the other children following. Danny was in the kitchen, his right leg below the knee awash in an appalling amount of blood. Liz had an awful moment, thinking he might have severed something, but upon examination she saw the lawn mower had just thrown up a rock and gashed his shin.

She hastily ruined a couple of dish towels stanching the flow of blood; Kathie, looking eerily nurselike in the wedding dress, had fetched the first aid kit without being asked, and once Liz had cleaned off the worst of the blood and applied pressure to the cut, she began to relax. There was blood on the wedding dress by now, inevitably, as a result of Kathie's earnest efforts. There was blood everywhere. So much for Cleaning Monday.

"It's like you got wounded," Angus told his brother breathlessly as Liz began to apply the gauze bandage.

Liz rolled her eyes, but Danny brightened. He liked that. A Purple Heart, the height of glamour. A wound like this probably merited only a telegram: *We regret to inform you that your oldest son, Daniel F. O'Reilly, was wounded in action while mowing a lawn in the Virginia Beach province . . .* If he'd lost his leg, they'd have sent two Marines to the door.

Liz cut a piece of tape to hold the bandage in place. Danny's face was still tight with pain and shock, and there were tears standing in his eyes, but he was containing them. Go ahead, sweetheart, it's all right to cry, Liz thought, her heart aching. But he wouldn't, of course: he was his father's son. She hated the goddamned Marine Corps.

CHAPTER 3

AUGUST 1967

FATHER ZEKE GERMAINE awoke alone, as he had for the last twenty years, with his whole body quivering in the dark with a peculiar intensity, like a freshly plucked guitar string. The predawn shakes had begun one day when he was seventeen. It had been terrifying at first. It felt like the skin was being stripped from his nerves each night and had to regrow every morning, and every morning less and less grew back, as if his raw nerve endings were being schooled to some ultimate nakedness. He'd been a promising student, and the condition had ruined him for the usual pursuits. This had distressed him at the time, though it seemed comically beside the point now. There had been a phase of doctors and therapists, and then a phase of diets, vitamins, and faddish agendas, and finally one of philosophies; but in the end every attempt at a solution failed, and Germaine had surrendered to his daily incapacitation. In time it had even come to seem like a kind of tenderness, a mercy, as if the staggering weight of God's presence, bearable in the twilit kingdom of unconsciousness, were being moderated to the flimsicr scaffold of his waking self.

There had even been a seductive quality to the trembling, in the early days. A sweetness, once you were past the death rattle of ambition. Germaine would lie in bed helplessly, waiting for his nervous system to settle, panicked at first and then defeated in panic and finally at peace with defeat; and when stillness finally came, the peace in which he found himself was precious and fierce with an unassailable joy. In the early years of his calling, he had felt the trembling to be unstable ardency, his soul slipping out of the womb of dreams into the day's fresh incarnation like a newborn colt staggering to its unsteady feet, eager for the world. That honeymoon spirituality seemed embarrassingly naive at this point.

There had been a long period in his working priesthood when the trembling had seemed like a side effect of heroic exertion, and then of valiant exhaustion; and then for a time after coming home from the war he had thought it was probably just blown nerves, the anticipation of incoming mortar rounds that would not go away; but these days Germaine knew he woke up shaking from too much alcohol. So much for the hopeful quiver of an infinitely gentle, infinitely suffering thing: he'd solved his mystical dilemmas by becoming a quiet drunk.

The room was pitch-black. Recently enough, waking in such blackness, he would have been surprised to have survived so far into the night, been certain that he still lay blind, blasted, and abandoned in the bomb crater muddy with blood, dying beside a wounded river with a dead man in his arms; that he had dozed, merely, in the precious stillness between the fall of mortar shells, at the hour of his death. But two years in a suburban parish had tempered Germaine's nightmares and retrained his expectations; his terrors now were banality and despair. Though maybe that had always been true.

Through the wall, he could hear the laborious drone of Father Winters's snoring and, from the bedside table, the slightly dyssyncopated ticking of the two alarm clocks Winters insisted his assistant pastor set every night so he wouldn't oversleep for morning mass. Sometimes Winters, reeking of peach schnapps and fraternally disregarding the smell of Germaine's bourbon, would even come into Germaine's bedroom before retiring, ostensibly to discuss some bit of parish business but actually to make sure the clocks were wound and the alarm pegs out. Apparently the previous assistant had been a slugabed, and the older priest had a horror of the handful of faithful old ladies standing outside a locked church in the dark, thwarted in their morning devotions.

Not that Winters ever woke before 8:00 a.m. himself; early rising was for priests on the rise, as he liked to say. Germaine had needed no alarm in the decades since his body began ringing two hours before every sunrise like a struck gong, but he obediently set the clocks every night to pacify his superior. He even found a bitter pleasure in the petty exercise; those twin clocks keeping superfluous time seemed apt enough symbols of his life these days.

He lay in the dark, waiting for his soul to settle in his body as gray began to bleed into the sky to the east. Some days the trembling eased by the time the alarms went off, some days not. Today, not. The jangle of the first alarm, and the clatter of the second a moment later, sent a fresh electric jolt through his nerve endings, but Germaine always let both alarms ring, on the off chance that they would wake Father Winters.

This is the day the Lord hath made, he thought, as he pushed in the knobs and the clamor ceased. Let us rejoice and be glad in it. Was it a sin to long for the way time stopped, in death's arms in that crater? Was it a sin to despise the gratuitous new life that God had given him beyond the bloody footprint of that grave? Germaine swung his feet to the floor and limped off to the bathroom. In the other room, his pastor snored on, and it was certainly a sin to hate him so.

THE AUGUST AIR was soft and warm as the light came up. Germaine walked from the rectory to the church with Venus gleaming above the eastern horizon ahead of him. He was five minutes early, as he always was, to avoid having to make small talk with the old ladies who showed up at 6:00 on the dot, but the new altar boy was already waiting at the locked entrance to St. Jude's, standing patiently at parade rest in the mild rose light, dressed in a new white shirt and black pants.

"Good morning," Germaine said.

"Good morning, Father."

"I'm afraid I've forgotten your name."

"Danny. Daniel O'Reilly."

"You're up early, Danny O'Reilly."

"Yes, sir," the kid conceded. All the military kids said "sir" when pressed. It always made Germaine's heart hurt, though he wasn't sure exactly why.

He said, "This is your first mass, isn't it?"

"Yes, sir."

Germaine hesitated, wanting to say something to mark the moment, but all that came to mind was a snatch of Job: *I have said to decay, Thou art my father; and to the worm, Thou art my mother, and my sister.* He wondered again what God really expected of him now, a ruined man like a rotting fruit in a basket full of innocence.

"Well, then, let's get to work," he said. He unlocked the door and they entered the church together, the boy self-consciously matching Germaine's steps as they paused at the stone font to wet their fingers in the holy water and cross themselves, then walked up the aisle toward the altar.

ON SATURDAY MORNING, Liz piled the kids into the station wagon and made the three-hour drive north to see Maria Petroski. It felt like a suicide mission, the military wives' version of the Charge of the Light Brigade, but there was no way around the duty. Maria on the phone had seemed abstracted, her voice strained thin and high, assuring Liz that she was doing "as well as could be expected." It sounded painfully rehearsed, the party line press release, the noble Marine Corps widow keeping a stiff upper lip, and Liz dreaded getting past that tissue-thin surface to Maria's actual condition. The worst had happened, the thing they all dreaded, and in the end there was going to be nothing to do except sit there with the worst having happened and cry.

In the backseat, Kathie was leading the other children in song, a maddening ditty called "You Can't Get to Heaven." It was a sort of religious "Ninety-nine Bottles of Beer on the Wall," subject to endless elaboration. Kathie had learned the song at the Sunday school she attended sometimes with her friend Temperance; Kathie, the only white child at Lynnhaven Pentecostal, preferred the vivid services there to the stodgy Catholic decorum of St. Jude's and always came home rolling her eyes back in her head and praising the Lord, fired with unsettling zeal for Our Savior, Jesus Christ. The original lyrics to "You Can't Get to Heaven" had long since been forgotten. Probably they had something to do with avoiding sin and vice, with the challenge of actual goodness, but now the kids loved to make up their own absurd conditions for salvation. The only real theological criterion was that it had to rhyme.

"Oh, you can't get to heaven," Kathie sang, and the other children echoed, "Oh, you can't get to heaven!"

In a Chevrolet (In a Chevrolet!)
'Cause the Lord drives Fords ('Cause the Lord drives
    Fords!)
Down the heavenly way! (Down the heavenly way!)

And the chorus, in rollicking unison:

Oh, you can't get to heaven in a Chevrolet
'Cause the Lord drives Fords down the heavenly way.
I ain't a-gonna grieve, my Lord, no more!

It passed the time, at least, Liz consoled herself, as the next verse started up; it kept the kids amused and squabble free on these long drives. And her daughter was in her element, leading the sing-along. Kathie had the makings of a great camp counselor.

Oh, you can't get to heaven (Oh, you can't get to heaven!)
In a psychedelic hat (In a psychedelic hat!)
'Cause the Lord can take a lot ('Cause the Lord can take
    a lot!)
But he can't take that! (But he can't take that!)

South of Fredericksburg, Angus spotted the sign for the Stonewall Jackson shrine and wanted to stop. He had inherited the Jackson biography from Danny, and both of the boys had inherited a perversely glamorous view of the Confederacy from their father. Mike had all three volumes of *Lee's Lieutenants* on his shelf, along with endless analyses by partisan historians of the flanking movement at Chancellorsville and the tragedy of the missed opportunities on the second day at Gettysburg. Born in Yonkers and raised north of the Mason-Dixon Line, Mike identified for some reason with the embattled Rebels. Her husband's weakness for the underdog had led him astray, Liz thought. She often tried to remind the boys that nobility in defense of an inhuman system was nevertheless bloodshed for an ignoble cause, but it was impossible to make much headway with a reasoned abolitionism in the face of vivid images of J. E. B. Stuart dying young with a cavalier feather in his hat and Jackson standing like a stone wall at the first battle of Bull Run, which the boys, like their father—and the rest of the South—called First Manassas.

"We haven't got time to stop," Liz said. "Mrs. Petroski is expecting us."

"Oh, *Mom,*" Angus exclaimed.

"It's probably just some big piece of granite with a plaque on it anyway, Angus."

"No, it's the house where he died," Danny supplied from the back of the car. "The big piece of granite with the plaque on it is at the place where he got shot."

"Well, there you go," Liz said, but Angus had lit up.

"Can we stop at the place where he got shot?" he persisted.

"Some other *time,* Angus."

Her son flopped back against the seat. Danny, to cheer him up, said, "They had to amputate Stonewall Jackson's arm, and they buried *that* outside the field hospital in Chancellorsville."

"Wow," Angus said, brightening.

"Robert E. Lee wrote him a letter that said, 'You have lost your left arm, but I have lost my right.' It looked like he was going to make it, after the operation. But then he died of pneumonia."

"A glorious death in a stupid, ugly war is still just a stupid, ugly way to die," Liz said by way of ending the discussion. She hated these drives through the hallowed battlefields of northern Virginia. The boys had way more fun with Mike at the wheel.

THE CREPE MYRTLES were in pink, white, and lavender bloom at the Petroskis' big colonial home in suburban Dumfries. Trees planted by Larry, Liz couldn't help thinking as she pulled into the driveway beside Maria's station wagon. She was dizzied by a glimpse of how much of mundane life must be painful for Maria now. The garage door was open, and Liz could see the lawn mower, the neatly hung tools above the workbench, and a battered yellow Renault inside. Larry's lawn mower, Larry's tools, Larry's car.

Nailed to the back wall of the work area was the LIVE ORDNANCE AREA / OFF-LIMITS TO CIVILIANS sign Larry and Mike had stolen from the gunnery range at Camp Lejeune in 1959. Liz remembered the night they had brought it home. She and Maria, who lived across the street then, had been drinking coffee in the kitchen of the drafty little house the O'Reillys were renting in Jacksonville when the men came in after a long day firing howitzers, flushed with North Carolina winter cold and adolescent excitement over their trophy, their fatigue jackets smelling of cordite. She and Maria had long since adjusted to the fact that boys would be boys: they'd just laughed with the men— live ordnance, stolen government property, ha-ha—and added Jameson's to the next round of coffee. The sign had hung over the O'Reilly stove for years, but the Petroskis had ended up with it some- how. Maybe when Mike had made captain and Larry had been passed over for the first time. A consolation prize.

A sudden series of explosions just outside the car window jolted Liz back to the present. She flinched as Kathie and Deborah shrieked.

"Incoming!" Danny hollered, flinging open the back door of the station wagon. "Out of the vehicle, Angus! Hit the deck!"

Angus opened his own door, dived out onto the ground, and rolled into a combat-ready position. Cranking her window up, Liz could see movement in the azalea bushes near the front of the house now, and three strawberry blond heads. They had been ambushed by the Petroski boys. The attack was not unprecedented, and not even really unusual, though Liz had expected a more subdued atmosphere this visit, given the circumstances.

A second string of firecrackers arced through the air and landed next to the car. Kathie shrieked again, a little gleefully this time, beginning to enjoy the attention. She and Lejeune Petroski, Maria and Larry's middle son, had had crushes on each other since nursery school, though the courtship manifested mostly as teasing.

The azaleas shuddered as the Petroski kids gathered themselves for a direct assault, after the artillery prep. Danny and Angus were already moving along the shielded side of the station wagon, preparing to launch a counterattack. Visits between the Petroski and O'Reilly clans involved a surprising number of small-unit infantry tactics.

The front door opened, and Maria Petroski appeared in a ragged pink bathrobe. Liz glanced at her watch; it was almost one o'clock. Her friend was normally up with the sun, with her face on and her perky colonel's-daughter outfit of the day in place by the time she cooked the boys breakfast. Liz's languid morning ways had always made a comic counterpoint to Maria's tendency to hit the ground running. But Maria's hair was unbrushed today, unwashed, and unhennaed, with a shocking trace of gray showing at the brown roots. Liz steeled herself to keep her mouth shut.

"Goddammit, Chevy, what did I tell you about those firecrackers?" Maria hollered shrilly.

The bushes stilled. There was a moment's silence as her sons weighed the tactical situation, and then Chevy, the oldest, stood up resignedly, followed by Lejeune and Ramada.

"What did I tell you?" Maria repeated.

"Not to set them off until next Fourth of July," Chevy conceded, studying his Keds. Four months older than Danny, he looked like his father, with the same square shoulders and Dudley Do-Right jaw, the same clear blue eyes on the lookout for trouble, and the same reckless grin, suppressed for the moment but always suggested.

"Is it the Fourth of July?"

"Lejeune threw the second round!"

"Just answer the question, mister. Is it the goddamned Fourth of July?"

"No, ma'am."

"Well, then?"

Chevy met her eyes, with the hint of a characteristic gleam. He was going to make some smart-ass Petroski crack, Liz thought, but Chevy caught himself and shrugged. It was almost sad. Liz couldn't remember ever seeing Larry's oldest son subdued.

"Give me the rest of the firecrackers," Maria said.

Chevy nudged Lejeune, who hastened to hand her a capacious plastic bag.

"*All* of them."

Lejeune glanced at his older brother, who shrugged again and nodded. Lejeune rummaged in the bushes and produced a second, even larger, bag.

"Now you boys take your guests out back and find something to do that doesn't involve explosions."

Relieved, the three Petroski boys bolted around the corner of the house, followed by Danny and Angus. Kathie and Deborah followed more slowly. Things would sort themselves out soon enough, Liz knew, as she got out of the car and met Maria's eye with a smile. The children were as intimate as cousins. The older boys would amuse themselves in a variety of rowdy ways. Kathie would linger near the edge of the scene, flirting antagonistically with Lejeune. Ramada would show Deb-Deb his G.I. Joe and trains, she would show him her otters, and eventually the two of them would settle in and make something spectacular out of pipe cleaners, Popsicle sticks, and glue.

"Jesus, these kids," Maria said as Liz approached the porch.

"Live ordnance area," Liz agreed, testing the range of irony, and Maria rolled her eyes with a heartening resilience.

"Larry bought them six bags of the damn things at some roadside stand in North Carolina, right before he left. They've long since shot off all the bottle rockets. The neighbors are ready to kill me."

"Boys will be boys," Liz said. It came out of her mouth before she could stop it, their old wry refrain. Their eyes met. Maria smiled ruefully, then began to cry. Liz moved to put her arms around her and cried too. There really wasn't anything else to do.

IN THE KITCHEN, a last trace of coffee in the still-heated pot had cooked down to a smoking brown crust. The table was littered with English muffins, variously buttered and smeared with jam and marmalade, each with one bite gone, apparently the jetsam of several failed runs at breakfast. The phone was off the hook, the receiver buried under an embroidered blue pillow that said HOME SWEET HOME, to muffle the distress signal. When Maria stopped crying and went to the bathroom to wash her face, Liz cleared the debris from the table, scrubbed the scorched carafe, set a fresh pot of coffee brewing, and looked for sandwich fixings. But Maria came back with a bottle of Jose Cuervo Especial and some margarita mix and seemed in no mood for solid food. Liz set up the blender and added ice cubes and some frozen strawberries to a conservative ration of early afternoon tequila, but before she could put the top on, Maria took the bottle and tilted it. Watching the tequila go glug-glug-glug, Liz decided to say nothing. Clearly it was no time to think of the long drive home.

The sink was full of unwashed stemware, and the loaded dishwasher hadn't been run. The last clean glasses in the cupboard were Flintstones jelly jars. Liz poured two drinks and rinsed a couple of Slurpee straws that had already seen hard use. They settled in at the Formica table in the breakfast nook, with a view of the backyard. The screen was flickering on a little black-and-white television with the sound turned off that sat on a stool beside the table, and Maria kept one eye on it.

Apparently she had gotten into the soaps. Beyond a battered apple tree drooping with unripe fruit, the children were quiet, huddled over what was probably something dangerous.

"So, how did you hear about it?" Maria asked.

Liz hesitated, then conceded, "Mike wrote me."

"Of course. The good old USMC grapevine. No sparrow falls unheeded. The loving Corps takes care of its own."

"You should have called."

Maria shrugged. "There are a lot of things I should have done. Starting with marrying a doctor and having girls."

Liz sipped her drink, too fast, and her throat froze up. She took several surreptitious breaths through her mouth, trying to thaw the piercing lump of pain, conscious of the beginnings of a headache at the base of her skull.

"So, what had Mike heard?" Maria asked after a moment, apparently oblivious to Liz's distress. She was still keeping one eye on the TV, following the silent twists of *As the World Turns*.

"Not much more than they told you, I'm sure," Liz said, sure that whoever "they" were, they had been more delicate than Mike's terse "nothing but hair, teeth, and eyeballs." For so-called minor wounds, the Marine Corps sent a cryptic telegram, but for major wounds and deaths they sent two somber men in uniform, who sat there in your living room, resolutely vague about the way your man had died or been maimed, full of useless military sympathy.

"They didn't tell me anything. I ran out the back door."

"What?!"

"The damned Marine Corps–green sedan pulled into the driveway on a Tuesday afternoon, and a chaplain and a major got out. I didn't need the fine print read to me at that point. They don't send two guys to tell you your husband cut himself shaving. I told Chevy to lock the front door, and I went out the back."

"Where did you go?" Liz asked, fascinated in spite of herself. She had always wondered what *she* would do if the two Marines, like Death in dress greens, came to her door. It made perfect sense to her that Maria had bolted. She was even envious of such an honest response. Most of the wives she knew ended up serving the guys iced tea, trapped by the social context. You were allowed to cry, but it was considered bad form to faint or scream.

"Does it *matter?*" Maria asked.

"I suppose not."

They leaned forward to sip their drinks, the Slurpee straws filling like thermometers in a heat wave. On the screen, Tommy Hughes had lit up a hand-rolled cigarette and was taking a deep, exaggerated drag.

"Is that what I think it is?" Liz asked.

"The times they are a-changin," Maria said. They watched Tommy pass into a state of sinister bliss. In the backyard, Danny and Chevy had climbed the apple tree and were bombarding Kathie, Lejeune, and Angus with green fruit. Liz considered intervening, but Kathie looked like she was happy being pelted, with Lejeune, and the younger boys were returning fire.

"So what *did* Mike say?" Maria prompted after a moment.

Liz hesitated, reviewing Mike's terse summary of Larry's death, trying to find the bright side of getting blown up by a mine. Was it comforting, or more distressing, that the mine had been command detonated? Did it ease the pain to know someone had killed your husband on purpose as opposed to a random explosion? And where the hell was Con Thien?

Maria's straw gurgled, breaking what had become an awkward silence; her Flintstones jar was empty. She rose and crossed to the blender for a refill.

"Larry made captain the day before he died," she offered. "Had you heard *that?*"

"No," Liz said, duly dizzied by the irony. Or maybe it was the tequila before lunch.

"Finally." Maria upended the blender and shook the last of the pink slush into her glass. "That's probably what got him killed. Those goddamned captain's bars. They love to kill officers."

"Mike said he wasn't wearing his bars. He said they never wear their bars in the field."

Maria perked up. "Oh? What else did he say?"

Liz realized that she had blundered. She tried to put herself in Maria's place. What *would* she want to know? What really mattered? That Larry had not died in vain? By Mike's account, the interdiction campaign that had gotten him killed was wrongheaded. That someone had been there for him in the end, whispering comfort, holding his hand as he bled out? Most likely the poor man had never known what hit him. *The usual unpretty sight.* "You know Mike. It was the same old trenchant macho crap. But I know it tore him up. He loved Larry like a brother."

"The weird thing is, it feels like it was my fault," Maria said.

"Oh, for God's sake, Maria—"

"No, seriously. I mean, if I hadn't gotten pregnant, Dad would never have gotten a bug up his ass about Larry, and Larry would have been a captain long since, like Mike. He wouldn't have been leading a goddamned platoon in the field."

"He would have been leading a company, most likely," Liz said. "Like Mike."

"Company commanders don't get killed."

This wasn't true, and they both knew it. But it was true that company commanders didn't get killed as often as the leaders of platoons. Liz held her tongue. It felt very strange to be defensive over the happenstance that her husband was still alive.

As the two women sat in silence, Ramada and Deb-Deb appeared in the doorway, earnestly allied as always, in search of scissors. Maria roused herself with an obvious effort and rummaged through a kitchen drawer.

"Can I have a Slurpee too?" Deb-Deb asked Liz.

"These are grown-up Slurpees, sweetheart. We'll get you a real Slurpee on the way home."

Deb-Deb took it in stride, which none of the other kids would have done. "We're making angels for Ramada's daddy, and we need scissors to cut out the wings."

"That's wonderful," Liz told her, her eyes filling. The liquid lunch had left her volatile, she noted. But fortunately her younger daughter was having too much fun to notice.

"Do you think blue wings are all right?" Deb-Deb asked.

"I think blue wings are perfect."

"We're using cotton for the clouds."

Maria found a pair of scissors that couldn't do too much damage, and Ramada and Deb-Deb trotted off happily. Maria took the opportunity to mix a fresh blender of margaritas and carried it back to the table. She tipped the pitcher and sloshed Liz's glass a bit too full. An icy pink rivulet eased down the side of the Flintstones jar. Liz intercepted it with her finger and licked it off, tasting nothing but tequila. Maria had made the second batch very strong.

Maria replenished her own margarita and sat down, leaving the blender within easy reach. They both drank, considered their drinks in silence, and drank again.

"They're giving him a big sloppy handful of medals," Maria said at last. "Of course. The booby prizes. 'His indomitable courage, inspiring leadership, and selfless devotion to duty upheld the highest traditions of the Marine Corps. He gallantly gave his life for his country.'"

Liz held her tongue. The wives all hated medals. She had made Mike promise not to be heroic, for all the good that would do when it came down to it. Boys would be boys.

"A Purple Heart," Maria enumerated. "A Bronze Star. The Legion of Merit. And get this: the goddamned Vietnamese Gallantry Cross, courtesy of the grateful Republic of South Vietnam. Like I give a good goddamn whether their pissant little country is run by a right-wing fanatic or a left-wing crank. Like that was worth dying for." She stared at her glass. "They haven't even gotten the body home yet, for some damned reason. No one can give me a straight answer about why."

Probably still looking for the pieces, Liz heard Mike saying in her head. She reached for her drink again and said nothing. The silences were getting longer. She had begun to hope they would get around to crying again soon. At this point, crying seemed like a relief.

A sudden change in the tenor of the child noise from the backyard made both women lift their heads.

"Oh, Christ, they're in the damned water," Liz said, getting to her feet. Danny and Chevy, fully clothed, were entangled in the middle of the Petroskis' small blue wading pool. "Shit. Are those two fighting?"

"Looks like it." Maria sighed and rose resignedly to follow. "I'm betting Chevy started it. He's been hell in school lately."

They hurried out the back door. The two older boys were flailing at each other. Kathie, Lejeune, and Angus stood at the roiling water's edge, shouting encouragement to the combatants. Maria and Liz pushed past them, hollering for their sons to stop, but Danny and Chevy thrashed on, until Maria waded into the pool and separated them. Held at arm's length, they continued for a moment to try to get at each other before settling down.

"Chevy Petroski, you are in *such* deep doo-doo," Maria said.

"He started it!" Chevy insisted, snuffling. Now that the heat of conflict had passed, both boys were tearful. "He just started punching me!"

"Is that true, Danny?" Liz demanded from the edge of the pool. Maria, still keeping the boys apart, was wet to midthigh, and Liz wondered whether she should climb into the water to drag her own son out, in motherly solidarity. But she was wearing a decent pantsuit, while Maria's bathrobe had seen better days.

"He pushed me in!" Danny said.

"Chevy?" Maria demanded.

"We always push each other in!"

This was true. The boys seldom came home dry from a visit between the families; but the inevitable dunkings were normally a gleeful ritual. Maria and Liz hesitated.

"He ruined my watch!" Danny said.

"You were bragging that it was waterproof!"

"It *is* waterproof!"

"If it's waterproof, how could I ruin it?" Chevy demanded.

Danny lunged for him, catching Maria off guard. All three of them toppled over into the water. The other three children started to shout again. Liz sighed, hoping her slacks wouldn't shrink, and waded in. She grabbed Danny by the scruff of the neck and hauled him off Chevy. Her son was weeping again, and she thought she understood. The watch, a grown-up-looking timepiece with the Marine Corps insignia on the face, had been a gift from Mike on Danny's last birthday.

"Go get yourself dried off," she told him. "You know Chevy didn't mean to wreck your watch."

"Dad said it was waterproof," he sobbed.

Liz took him in her arms. She couldn't say what she wanted to say, which was that sometimes men were wrong. That sometimes gadgets failed. Watches leaked and carburetors clogged; M-16s jammed at fatally inconvenient moments and minesweepers didn't beep at every mine. Condoms tore. But that wasn't the kind of thing you told a ten-year-old in tears. Instead, she simply held her son as he sobbed, feeling his wet shudders through her ruined blouse as if they were her own.

WHEN THINGS HAD calmed down, Chevy and Danny made a sheepish peace and went upstairs together to towel off. The other children, sobered by the incident, went to play Ping-Pong in the garage. Maria took Liz to her bedroom to find something dry to wear. They undressed in the master bath and dropped their soggy underwear on the floor. Liz hung her pantsuit in the shower, where it dripped desultorily, the colors leaking out. Maria tossed her own sodden bathrobe in the tub. Liz followed her out into the bedroom, where Maria opened the closet and took one of her husband's shirts off a hanger.

"Take your pick," she said, slipping the shirt on and going to a drawer to rummage for some shorts. "We still wear the same size, don't we?"

"It always looks better on you, somehow," Liz said. She wavered, uncomfortably naked but disconcerted by the wardrobe half filled with Larry's clothes. Maria glanced over at her and exclaimed, "Oh, my God, Liz. Are you—?"

Liz gave her a taut smile. "Going on eight weeks."

Her friend floundered for a moment.

"'Congratulations'?" Liz suggested dryly.

"Well, of course. Sorry. But—"

"Don't bother, sweetie. I just want to lie down and die." Liz turned back to the closet and chose a yellow sundress that she had always admired on Maria. Pulling it over her head and checking herself in the mirror, she marveled at how pale she was, this late in the summer. They hadn't been to the beach since Mike had left.

"That looks good on you," Maria offered, crossing to stand beside her.

"Hah," Liz said. "I'm already fat as a pig."

They stood together in front of the mirror, looking glumly at their reflections. After a moment Liz turned sideways, almost grudgingly, to check her profile. Maria put a hand on Liz's tightening belly, and they smiled at each other.

"Does Mike know?" Maria asked.

"Oh, yes."

"Couldn't he have gotten out of going, then?"

Liz just looked at her. Maria conceded the obvious with a shrug.

"Are you going to have it?" she asked.

"Is the goddamned pope Catholic?"

"Mike wants it?"

"I don't think Mike gives a damn, frankly," Liz said, and surprised herself by beginning to sob. Maria took her in her arms, and Liz buried her face in her friend's shoulder and wept, mortified at having to be comforted by a woman recently widowed. Mike in fact had suggested an abortion—he knew a Navy medic willing to do it with a minimum of back-alley indignities. No doubt he had believed he was being supportive. He knew how much she had been looking forward to the freedom of all the kids finally being in school. She'd been thinking of taking a few classes, resuming the progress toward her abandoned degree, or getting involved somehow in the local theater. But despite her own ambivalence, Mike's willingness to abort the pregnancy had only enraged Liz. It had seemed too much like hideous convenience, a sacrifice to the gods of duty, honor, and country. What she had really wanted was for him to stay home from his goddamned war.

BETWEEN LIZ'S post-tequila headache and the general sobering effect of the Petroskis' loss, the first half of the drive home that evening passed in a subdued silence. By the time they got to Richmond, though, Kathie had the children singing again. She had had a gratifying heart-to-heart talk with Lejeune about the death of his father and was riding high. Deb-Deb was happy too, on the whole, with an array of the blue-winged angels she had made with Ramada spread across the backseat, and Angus couldn't believe his luck: Maria had sent the bags of firecrackers home with the O'Reillys.

In the far back of the station wagon, Danny, dressed in some of Chevy's clothes, which were a little big on him, was quiet. He spent most of the ride home staring out the window at the darkening oak and pine forest that lined the highway, but as they crossed the James River he roused himself to add a fresh verse to "You Can't Get to Heaven."

"Oh, you can't get to heaven," he sang, and the other children, smiling in anticipation, echoed, "You can't get to heaven,"

> *In a yellow submarine (In a yellow submarine!)*
> *'Cause the Lord's favorite color ('Cause the Lord's favorite*
>   *color!)*
> *Is Marine Corps green—*

The kids erupted into delighted laughter at the punch line. "Is Marine Corps green!" they echoed, and everyone chimed in jubilantly for the chorus:

> *Oh, you can't get to heaven in a yellow submarine*
> *'Cause the Lord's favorite color is Marine Corps green.*
> *I ain't a-gonna grieve, my Lord, no more!*

Liz drove on, the headlights blurring ahead of her, glad for the settling darkness that hid her filling eyes. She couldn't really imagine at this point that the Lord would have the nerve to favor anything but the humblest mourners' black. Danny, she knew, was still wearing the ruined watch, doggedly, as if it might start ticking again at any second, despite the USMC insignia barely visible beneath the moisture fogged on the crystal face. And Larry Petroski had been sure that goddamned rabbit's foot made him bulletproof.

CHAPTER 4

AUGUST 1967

MIKE MADE HIS WAY to the 2/29 Battalion command bunker to check in after dinner, as he had every day for the past week. The CP was crowded and unusually abuzz for this late hour, including half a dozen clearly superfluous officers standing around the battalion net radios as if they were listening to the seventh game of the World Series.

"What's up?" Mike asked the nearest lieutenant, an eager-beaver type who looked like a GE College Bowl competitor in the standard Marine Corps–issue black horn-rimmed glasses.

"Hotel's getting the shit kicked out of them," the kid said. "They got hit by at least a battalion, and they're cut off. Hotel-Six is dead."

"Jesus." Mike pictured the Hotel Company CO, a lanky Texan named Daniels. Something Daniels. He couldn't remember the guy's first name, which bothered him. All that came to mind was "Jack." But he knew that wasn't it. He'd liked the man.

"Where are they?" he asked.

"Nobody's quite sure, at this point," the lieutenant replied, a little breathlessly. "Somewhere near the Trace. They're scattered all over the place up there. We haven't heard a word from their First Platoon since midafternoon."

A pogue, Mike decided, resisting a sudden urge to throttle the guy. A rear-echelon motherfucker. Marines were dying a few kilometers to the north, and the kid couldn't keep the high school pep band excitement out of his voice.

"Did we send help yet?" he asked.

"Foxtrot went out in choppers, about half an hour ago, but no one knows where they are now either. I don't think anybody really knows what the hell is happening."

The radio crackled just then, a shaky second lieutenant's voice from somewhere in the darkness east of Con Thien, pleading for something he wasn't going to get that night. The kibitzing lieutenant perked up and returned his full attention to the drama. Mike left him there and crossed the room to the map table, a piece of plywood laid atop some empty ammo crates, where the battalion CO, Lou Whittaker, was bent over a laminated map with a grease pencil in one hand and a handset in the other, half a step away from the battalion net radio operator. Everyone else was keeping a respectful distance, as if the pain of command were contagious. With his shorn skull gleaming beneath the bunker's single electric light, a bare bulb dangling from a wire, Whittaker looked lonely and timeless, like an anguished monk, hunched in penance.

"Skipper," Mike said.

Whittaker glanced up. "Jesus, Mike, Hotel walked into a shit sandwich up there. Daniels is dead."

"I heard."

"Looks like you've got your company, if you want it."

"Yeah," Mike said. "You want me to go now?"

"No, fuck, it's already dark. I just threw Foxtrot in there without enough time to set up a decent night position. Get yourself a few hours' sleep and go in the morning." Whittaker looked at the map, and Mike saw the weariness in the lines of his face; the man had aged ten years in the last ten hours. "Jesus. It's gonna be a long night for those guys. I wish I could get on a chopper myself."

"Any idea what we're up against?"

"I think they must have run into the setup for a major assault before it could hit Con Thien. A battalion, at least. Maybe a regiment." He met Mike's eyes. "The last voice on the radio from their First Platoon was a corporal."

A nineteen-year-old squad leader on the platoon radio meant at least three layers of higher-ups had been incapacitated one way or another, the levels of command ripped away like skins off a damaged onion. Mike said, "I'll get them home, Skip."

"Get your chopper ride lined up before you hit the sack. I want you up to the line of departure by dawn."

"Yes, sir."

"Good luck, Mike."

"Thanks, Skipper," Mike said, but Whittaker had turned to the table already and sunk back into his ruminations, staring at the scrawled grease pencil marks as if they were his own blood smeared across the map.

The eager young lieutenant was still glued to the radio near the bunker's exit, and Mike paused on his way out. The kid reminded him of Angus. Half the Marine Corps reminded him of Angus, at this point in his life. He was definitely getting old. He ducked out through the blackout curtain. It was pitch-black outside already; night came fast in the tropics. He wondered what Liz was doing. To the north, a single flare lit the sky and settled slowly, like a wounded star.

from: Capt. M. F. O'Reilly
HQ Bn., 29th Marines
Mon 14 Aug '67
Phu Bai, RVN

Dearest Lizzie,

Quickest of quick notes—there's literally a helicopter waiting for me and I wanted to get a note off to you before my little jaunt. Friday the 13th came on a Sunday this year for the CO of Hotel Company 2/29 (in the form of a rocket-propelled grenade yesterday) and they're sending me up somewhere southeast of Con Thien to fill the poor guy's shoes. Hopefully his feet are not still in them.

The good news is that I finally got my company. The bad news is that nobody knows exactly where they are. Apparently the plan is to fly me around for a while in the general vicinity, yelling "Yoo-hoo? Yoo-hoo?" until somebody either shoots us down or tells us where to land. Your typical field-type cluster fuck. But anything's better than watching another John Wayne movie with the reels out of sequence here in Phu Bai.

I'll drop you a note after we straggle in from our camping trip, to let you know my new address.

I love you. Remember that. Don't ever forget that. And all my love to the fearsome foursome.

> *your*
> *Mike*

LIZ SET THE LETTER on the kitchen counter and tried to think of what in the world she should do next. The so-called good news boiled down to the fact that Mike was replacing a man who had just been killed by a grenade. Her husband's new job, the longed-for career advancement. Company commander positions available; must be willing to relocate and get blown up. New openings daily. She realized that she was furious. *I love you. Remember that. Don't ever forget that.* What the hell kind of thing was that to say? Why not just come out and say, Honey, I'm jumping into a helicopter and going out to die?

Liz read the letter again, then stuck it into a junk drawer full of dead flashlights, outdated holiday party napkins, and keys to nothing in particular, and went to unbolt the back door. Maybe Maria had the right idea after all, she thought. She'd be damned if she was going to sit around like a good military wife and make iced tea when the moment came. When those two Marines pulled into the driveway, she was out of here.

THE USUALLY PACKED dentist's waiting room at the Oceana Naval Air Station clinic was deserted except for Liz; apparently everyone had cleared out of town for August vacations. The O'Reillys usually cleared out themselves, when Mike was in the right country. But not this year. Instead of a joyful couple of weeks at the beach, Angus was getting something like seventy-three cavities filled and Liz was eating chocolate-covered raisins, a little maniacally, one after another, and thumbing through a year-old *Time* magazine. The cover story asked, "Is God Dead?" Liz hoped not, but she found herself reading the article with a certain suspense. It was better than subjecting herself to the parenting magazines and the women's journals and stewing over all the ways she was screwing up as a mother and a wife.

It was the pretense of routine that was the hardest part, she thought. Going through the motions of ordinary life. When in reality there was nothing ordinary at all, when every instant could be the one in which the whole illusion of normality toppled like a cardboard stage set.

As she sat skimming a sidebar on Nietzsche in *Time*'s consideration of God's demise, the door to the waiting room opened and a tall man in unseasonably dark clothes entered. Liz saw that it was the assistant pastor from St. Jude's, the gloomy one, Father Germaine. She gave him an instant to acknowledge her, but he seemed preoccupied. Maybe it was just as well. Her skin had regressed to a teenager's nightmare, and her breasts felt massive. Mike always loved that; they'd had some of the best sex of their marriage late in the first trimester of her various pregnancies. But Liz always felt like a freak at this point, like Gina Lollobrigida with a bad complexion.

She ducked back into the magazine as the priest went up to the receptionist's window to check in, moving with a trace of a limp. Liz wondered whether he knew how badly his clothes fit him. The black suit looked like it had been cut from a pattern with square corners and stapled into place.

Danny liked Germaine a lot, she knew, though she wasn't sure why. He had always struck Liz as grim and impenetrable, an old-school priest in the bleak medieval mode, ascetic and unworldly. But maybe he lightened up for early mass. Maybe he was a morning person.

Germaine's conversation with the receptionist went on for a while. Apparently he was very late for his appointment. Or possibly very early. From what Liz could gather, he might even have come on the wrong day. But he and the receptionist finally worked out something detailed involving mutual patience; as the priest turned from the window and moved to sit down, the receptionist took the opportunity to roll her eyes at Liz, who smiled back sympathetically.

Germaine settled into one of the plastic seats, his right leg begrudging the bend. Liz touched her hopelessly oily hair to try to settle it, then lowered her magazine and smiled helpfully, but again the priest refrained from recognizing her. He settled into a thousand-yard stare at the wall above and to the left of her head, where a travel poster for the Caribbean hung.

"Hello, Father," Liz chirped, sounding to herself like a Catholic schoolgirl and resenting that. But it was a very small waiting room and she really couldn't stand the tension. Germaine didn't seem like a *Sports Illustrated* kind of guy, and the fascination of that cruise ship poster wasn't going to do the job for long.

Germaine's gaze swam laboriously back from its distance, his unkempt black eyebrows betraying genuine surprise. Liz realized that he really hadn't recognized her. He might not even have known she was in the room. He *still* didn't recognize her.

"Liz O'Reilly, from St. Jude's," she supplied.

"Of course," Germaine said unconvincingly.

"Danny's mother? He's one of your altar boys."

"Of course," he repeated, in exactly the same tone, leaving her to wonder briefly whether he even knew who Danny was. But after a moment, Germaine added, "He's . . . interesting."

"Danny?"

"Yes."

Liz gave him a beat to elaborate, fruitlessly, then prompted, "Good interesting or bad interesting? I mean, a mother wants to know."

"Oh, interesting is always good," Germaine assured her. "Better than good, really. Especially for a kid."

"Isn't that a Chinese curse, though? 'May you live in interesting times'?"

The priest shrugged. "All times are interesting, in that sense. If you're paying attention. That's just the reality of incarnation."

Liz had a sense of the conversation having gotten spectacularly off track in a very short time. She wasn't sure what they were talking about anymore. She wasn't sure if she had known what they were talking about at any point, actually.

Looking to recover some traction, she offered, "He told me you called Father Winters a fool."

Germaine looked alarmed. "Danny said I called Winters a fool?"

"In Latin, apparently."

"Jesus. I really don't recall—"

"Oh, don't worry. He thought it was very cool."

Germaine's eyes drifted back to the travel poster. Liz began to recognize a cognitive rhythm and waited patiently, and sure enough, after a moment Germaine smiled. "Well, like I said, an interesting kid. His Latin is better than Winters's, clearly."

"He just has a good ear. He spent about three hours with my old Dominican High Latin dictionary, deciphering it."

"I'll have to be more careful," Germaine said. "You get spoiled, thinking no one's listening."

LINE OF DEPARTURE, *lock and load,* Mike thought, as the Huey crossed the unpaved track of Highway 9, just west of Cam Lo. He banged the magazine into his M-16, pulled back the bolt, and chambered a round. As an officer, he wasn't supposed to be carrying anything heavier than a sidearm, but that was rear-echelon horseshit. Things got simpler in the field. You rode a helicopter to a strange place for someone else's reasons and people tried to kill you and you tried to kill them back. The creed drilled into every boot Marine recruit at Parris Island finally came into its own: *This is my rifle. There are many like it, but this one is mine.* He clicked the weapon over to full automatic—a hot landing zone was no place for the niceties of controlled fire—and checked the safety. On, soon to be off. *My rifle is my best friend. It is my life.*

He had been sitting on his flak jacket—the most likely place to take a casual round on a chopper ride was up the ass—but he put the jacket on now, unbuckled his helmet and fastened the strap across the back, field-Marine-style, and shouldered his pack. Beside him, the helicopter's only other passenger, an eighteen-year-old PFC with wide hazel eyes, who looked a little like Angus, did the same. The kid had a ravaged moonscape complexion, a stutter further distorted by a Philly accent, and some kind of Polish name with seventeen syllables and two vowels, but he would inevitably be called Ski, if he lived long enough for anyone to learn his name at all.

It was odd to be in such an empty chopper. The light Huey gunship normally carried a squad, seven combat troops—or, depending on whether you were coming or going, three casualty litters, two sitting wounded, and a corpsman. Most of the time, if you got to ride in a helicopter with so much free space, you were dead.

My rifle, without me, is useless. Without my rifle, I am useless.

At the Huey's open hatch, the door gunner, impassive in a black-visored helmet, hunched over his M-60 machine gun, studying the terrain below. They were flying at 1500 feet over the foothills of the northern Quang Tri Province. Somewhere down there, Mike knew, amid knobs and ridges swathed in elephant grass and clumps of gnarled trees, Larry Petroski had died; and the man Mike was replacing, Captain Something Daniels, had died down there the day before. It wasn't something to spend a lot of thought on at this point. *I must fire my rifle true. I must shoot straighter than my enemy, who is trying to kill me.*

The pilot waved him forward, and Mike made his way up to the cockpit and squatted beside the seat. The man pointed to a grease-penciled grid on his map and then to a ridgeline about half a mile ahead of them. From 1500 feet, it didn't look any different than all the other ridges in the area, a curved knuckle of elevation made feature-less by a sea of elephant grass. Mike gestured with his hand—*take it down*—and the pilot, a major in an immaculate green one-piece nylon jumpsuit, shook his head.

"No LZ!" he hollered. And, keying his radio headset, speaking to whoever was on the ground, "Hotel, this is Blue Pete. I have no visual, repeat no visual. Say again your location. Over!" He listened, circling the chopper with one hand and jotting a series of numbers onto the plastic map in grease pencil with the other. Looking over the pilot's shoulder, trying to see exactly where it was in Vietnam that he was probably going to die, Mike couldn't read a single one of the scrawled coordinates. He wasn't sure he trusted this guy's math.

I will keep my rifle clean and ready, even as I am clean and ready. We will become part of each other.

"Smoke!" he shouted above the engine noise, and the pilot glanced at him, inscrutable behind his mirror shades. He was clearly ready to turn the bird around and go home. Never fly with a major, Mike thought. Any chopper pilot who had lived long enough to make major was probably way too careful to be of any use to a grunt. But the guy finally keyed his headset mic and asked for a smoke grenade to mark a landing zone.

There was a pause, and then a reluctant smudge of purple smoke billowed near the crest of the ridge adjacent to the one they had been circling. Mike relaxed. At least he could die on the right hill now.

My rifle is human, even as I, because it is my life. I will learn it as a brother.

The pilot gave Mike a look that said, I hope you're happy, and spoke into the headset. "Hotel, Blue Pete. I've got purple smoke. Over! . . . Roger that. Tallyho!" He pushed the controls forward, and the chopper veered and plunged groundward in a sickening spiral. The guy could fly after all, when he put his mind to it.

Mike groped back to a spot near the door, his stomach feeling like it was half a step behind him. A series of metallic *thunk*s, like a nail gun, stippled the floor toward the rear of the chopper. Ground fire from an AK-47.

The door gunner swiveled his M-60, blasting back, almost certainly at random. The noise was deafening. Spent shell casings clattered everywhere like a flurry of brass crickets. Clinging to a stanchion, PFC

Krzykrewski looked green. The helicopter flared out of its dive with another stomach-boggling whoosh and hovered ten feet over the ridge, the elephant grass flattening below it from the rotor wash. Krzykrewski took the opportunity to throw up on the floor.

Mike moved to the brink of the open hatch, followed by the queasy Krzykrewski. He considered the daunting drop to the ground and motioned to the door gunner, *Lower!* The guy hollered into his headset to the pilot, then shook his head, managing to look embarrassed even through the black visor. The careful major felt that they were low enough, and even his crew knew it was chickenshit.

Fuck it, Mike thought. Anything was safer than wallowing here ten feet off the ground making a target for rockets. Besides, the chopper stank of vomit now. A little memento for the aviation wing, from the guys who got muddy and bled. *Before God I swear this creed. My rifle and I are the defenders of my country.* Mike gave Krzykrewski a let's-go bang on the shoulder and jumped, holding his helmet with his left hand, field-Marine-style, and his M-16 with his right.

WHEN ALL ELSE FAILED, there was laundry. Liz hated the stuff. It fell like snow throughout the house in every season, dumped by the constant storm of children. She had left Detroit on a drama scholarship with nothing in her head but dreams of the glorious stage. She had played Antigone in high school and Joan of Arc as a college freshman, to standing ovations, and now she was the Penelope in an unattended farce, weaving and unweaving the same pile of dirty clothes while waiting to hear exactly how her man had died.

Deb-Deb swam into the kitchen, moving with the distinct sinuous movement that denoted otter locomotion in her little world. She chirped lightly.

"You just had breakfast," Liz said.

Deb-Deb chirped again and held her paws in front of her chest in a begging motion. Liz sighed and gave her a Triscuit, and her daughter turned and undulated out of the room, holding the cracker between her lips. It wasn't about eating, Liz knew. Deb-Deb would swim back into the living room, to the otters' den she'd built out of couch pillows, and store the Triscuit carefully beneath the afghan in the corner, for the coming winter. Liz sometimes feared that she gave her youngest child too much magical leeway. But the fluid, playful world of otters suited Deb-Deb; she lived there more than she did on dry land.

Liz poured the last of the Saturday morning coffee into a mug that had been used only twice and sat down at the kitchen table. The precious moments between the wash cycle and the spin would be her last chance of the day to breathe quietly. She could hear the intermittent thud of a baton hitting the floor upstairs, where Kathie was practicing her trick twirling. She and Temperance were the stars of the school's crew of majorettes, and the ceiling of the girls' bedroom was pocked and scuffed with the scars of overenthusiastic tosses.

The boys were off somewhere burying a turtle. The casualty rate among amphibious pets in the O'Reilly household was tremendous; the latest fatality, in a sadly shriveled condition, had been found under the couch this morning after a protracted search. Liz had been ready to give up after half an hour, but Danny had insisted on finding the body. Marines didn't leave their dead on the battlefield. Angus had cried, but Danny had bucked him up with the promise of a funeral with full military honors. They'd taken their BB guns and were going to give the turtle a twenty-one-gun salute.

In short, the kids were happily occupied. No one was crying, no one was fighting, and no one was in obvious immediate danger. The grocery list was formulated, and the children's dentist appointments were set. Mike's most recent paycheck wouldn't clear the bank until this afternoon, so she couldn't dig into the stack of unpaid bills until tonight. Her gynecologist seemed happy enough with the progress of her pregnancy, and he was much more pleased with the five pounds she'd already gained than Liz was herself. The toilets were clean, within reason, and she had vacuumed less than a week ago. The laundry was in motion and the sink was empty.

Liz sipped her coffee and dunked a cold tater tot in the pool of ketchup on her plate. Maybe it wouldn't be such a bad day after all. Hell, it was almost ten o'clock, and no one had showed up yet to tell her that her husband had been killed.

PART TWO

Sir, the United States Marines: since 1775, the most invincible fighting force in the history of man. Gung ho! Gung ho! Gung ho! Pray for war!

RECITED BEFORE MEALS AT OFFICERS' CANDIDATE SCHOOL, QUANTICO, VIRGINIA

The truth is that the more ourselves we are, the less self is in us.

MEISTER ECKHART

CHAPTER 5

SEPTEMBER 1967

A T LARRY PETROSKI's funeral mass, on Labor Day, Liz threw up. At first she thought her nausea was metaphorical, a response to the God-and-country homily by the complacent priest; and then she thought it was guilt, that she was so appallingly glad it was Maria's husband in that casket and not hers; but as the literal bile surged in her throat, the fine points ceased to matter and she clapped her hand over her mouth and bolted, smacking through a gauntlet of black-clad knees in a blind rush from the pew.

She made it only three steps down the center aisle before she doubled over and the first wave spewed. Liz tried to catch it in her cupped hands, but it was too much, and in any case her stomach heaved again and again. She'd had three cups of coffee, a bowl of Cheerios and a piece of toast, and several of Maria's Bloody Marys at the Petroski house beforehand, and it all came up in wave after splattering, convulsive wave. She was beyond embarrassment; it was more like dying, a truth so absolute that there was nothing to do but surrender to it.

When she came back to herself, she was on her hands and knees on the bespattered tile, smelling sour vodka and tomato juice. Danny was beside her, looking alarmed. The other children, thank God, had stayed in the pew. Liz smiled ruefully at her son, trying to indicate that she was all right, which was ridiculous, of course. This wasn't the kind of thing you wanted your kids to see.

Why did you throw up, Mommy? Well, sweetie, I guess I just can't stomach this shit.

The glib priest had mercifully fallen silent, and everyone was staring at her in degrees of sympathy and dismay. She'd gotten turned around somehow and was facing the front of the church, looking right at the flag-draped casket set before the altar. It seemed like such a formal and tidy package, so un-Larrylike. They'd finally squared the edges off that joyful, incorrigible man and made a standard-issue hero of him in spite of everything.

And what is a hero, Mommy? Nothing but hair, teeth, and eyeballs, dear.

Her stomach convulsed again. Danny put his arm around her tenderly, trying to keep her hair out of the way, as you would try to make a dying man comfortable on the battlefield, not flinching at the splatter. He was his father's son, all right, Liz thought; and he was having to grow up way too fast. She began to cry, she was so ashamed of herself. It really wasn't the kind of thing you wanted your kid to see.

AT THE QUANTICO National Cemetery an hour later, Liz stood across the grave from Maria with two children on either side, the girls closest, squinting in sunlight so bright it seemed perverse. The front of her dress was streaked with the vomit she hadn't been able to sponge off, as were Danny's pants. She felt empty as a ghost, an incidental casualty of the ceremony. Maria, armored in a black wool dress, black pillbox hat and gloves, and black sunglasses, had her own three boys arrayed

in a somber row of diminishing height. She looked implacably composed. She'd told Liz over the Bloody Marys that morning that she
wasn't going to cry, she wasn't going to wail, and she wasn't going to
accept the flag from the casket, that they could take their goddamned
Stars and Stripes and stick it where the sun didn't shine.

Sure enough, when the white-gloved sergeant in his dress blues
brought her the flag, folded crisply into a triangle, Maria sat unmov-
ing, looking at the thing as if it were roadkill dragged home by the
dog. But Chevy, proud and stiff beside her, wearing his new black suit
like a uniform, reached out, and the sergeant handed him the flag
with some relief. Maria glanced across the grave and tilted her sunglasses back on her head, her eyes finding Liz's. A dry, frank look,
spent, and eloquent with resignation: there was no way to beat the
system. First they took your husband; and then they took your son.

Liz met her friend's gaze helplessly; and after a moment Maria let
her sunglasses fall back into place and put her arm around Chevy's
shoulder as he clutched the flag to his chest.

The seven riflemen of the honor guard snapped their M-1s up and
fired, chambered rounds and fired again, and again; and as the echoes
of the shots faded a lone bugler played Taps from a green knoll above
the grave site. Kathie, and then Deb-Deb, began to sob. Liz wept too.
It was poignant almost beyond endurance; but in her heart she
fought the poignancy, for Maria's sake and, finally, for her own. Let
the sweet sad song play on and make its little moment's magic. Tomorrow that same bugle would play Reveille, and everyone would
wake up heedless and duly inspired to do it all again. Except, of
course, for those with nothing left to lose among the living, and those
who rested with the honored dead beneath the clean white stones.

"IS LIEUTENANT PETROSKI in heaven?" Angus asked on the way
home.

"Captain," Danny said. "He made captain before he died."

"Of course Uncle Larry is in heaven," Liz said.

"If Daddy gets shot, will he go to heaven too?"

"Shut up, birdbrain," Danny said.

"Hush, Danny," Liz said and, to Angus, "Of course he will, honey. But Daddy's not going to get shot."

MIKE COULD SMELL the Marines before he saw them. It was a distinctly male, American smell, part locker room and part wet dog, the reassuring stink of troops in the field. The elephant grass was shorter near the hilltop, maybe three feet high, and trampled down, and a hint of Hotel Company's desultory perimeter was discernible in a series of shallow foxholes, where unshaven men in filthy dungarees lounged with their rifles cradled close, their ponchos jury-rigged to create some shade. They all looked hot, tired, and sullen. Almost everyone had their flak jackets unfastened in the heat. The troops in sight seemed remarkably casual, even bored, but it was a deceptive tedium. Somewhere within hollering range, a hundred and eighty armed and edgy U.S. Marines were dug in, ready to fire at anything that moved. Yet he and Krzykrewski had penetrated well inside the company's position before they were challenged.

The good news, Mike thought, was that no one had taken them for bad guys and shot them. The bad news was that nobody seemed particularly well positioned to shoot anyone. Boredom and slack tactics were a particularly lethal combination. The old military rule of thumb, that war was 99 percent dull routine and 1 percent pure terror, applied in Vietnam as well. The uniqueness of Vietnam was that you could get killed here as easily when you were bored as when you were terrified.

Mike, with Krzykrewski still tagging along, headed for a gaggle of antennas toward the center of the position. The Hotel Company command group of nearly a dozen grimy men, none showing any indication of rank, was crouched in a natural hollow in the trampled-down elephant grass. No one had bothered to dig in, and one well-placed mortar round could have taken them all out, but that was life at the top. Most of the men were heartbreakingly young. They eyed Mike and Krzykrewski noncommittally as they approached.

"Where's your Six?" Mike asked the one who seemed to have the most lights on, a gangly radioman with clear blue eyes. The kid jerked a thumb toward two men near the center of the group, an older black man in a sleeveless green skivvy shirt and a self-important young fellow in sweat-soaked fatigues. The older guy had the resigned look of a senior noncommissioned officer containing disgust. The younger guy was a little too bright-eyed. Here we go, Mike thought.

"I'm Captain O'Reilly, the new CO," he said.

The older man spat, barely short of insubordinate, confirming Mike's sense that he was a sergeant. The younger man jumped up and almost saluted, then caught himself. To salute anyone in the field was to make him a target. "Lieutenant Claridge, sir. Welcome aboard."

Mike squatted and gestured for Claridge to get down again too. The sergeant hadn't moved. "Thanks. What's our situation?"

Claridge hesitated.

"Pure cluster fuck," the noncom supplied. He had a Mississippi accent and a tattoo on the meat of his shoulder, a red dragon breathing a stream of flame that said, SIC SEMPER FIDELLIS.

"We've assumed a defensive posture," Lieutenant Claridge said hastily, to which the noncom, with an air of supplying a translation, added, "Our asses are flapping in the wind."

Mike eyed the older man. "And you would be—?"

"Master Sergeant Isaiah Tibbetts." They stared at each other. "Sir."

"Well, Top, why don't you humor me for a minute here and shut the fuck up."

Tibbetts's eyes sparked angrily, but he set his mouth in a firm line and said nothing. Mike turned to Claridge.

"Call the platoon leaders in here, I'm going to want to see them right away," he said. "And after that you and I will make some rounds. Our perimeter is a mess. We're going to need to move some of those positions in and tighten up. We'll send out a squad to mine the path we came in on. We'll need to arrange some reconnaissance. And let's get everybody digging in. Some of these guys haven't even gotten their shovels dirty yet."

Claridge looked pained. "Sir, the men are tired. And, begging the captain's pardon, pissed off. We've been humping these hills for almost a week."

"Better tired and pissed off than dead. Call the platoon sixes in, Lieutenant."

"Aye, aye, sir," Claridge said. His hand twitched, he wanted so much to salute, but he restrained himself and scuttled reluctantly to the radio.

Left alone, Mike and Sergeant Tibbetts squatted for a moment in silence.

"Jesus, Top," Mike said at last.

"Yes, sir," Tibbetts agreed. "Jesus Fucking Christ. Welcome to Heartbreak Hotel."

"So, what's the story, with this company?"

The sergeant hesitated. "The straight shit, sir?"

"Hell, yes, the straight shit."

"The straight shit is we been patrolling this fucking cesspool for the last six weeks with the stupidest fucking rules of engagement you ever heard, and taking casualties almost every fucking patrol without ever getting any back. Yeah, the men are tired and pissed. But they're mostly just sick of getting their asses kicked. They'd like to at least get some back."

"We'll get some back," Mike said. "What about Daniels?"

Tibbetts hesitated. "I'd hate to speak ill of the dead, sir."

"God forbid," Mike agreed, deadpan.

They looked at each other, making their mutual assessments; then Tibbetts shrugged. "Captain Daniels was a nice man. A very nice man. He hated to ask too much of the men, and he wanted everyone to like him. And golly gee, sir, they liked him a lot."

"But—?" Mike prompted.

"But he was a fuckup," Tibbetts said. "And he left you with a fuckup company. And if we keep fucking up, a lot more of us will be dead. Because Lieutenant Claridge is a fucking nice guy too. Sir."

Mike was silent for a moment, then he said, "Well, Top, I have four kids at home, and a wife I love, and I am the meanest motherfucker you will ever meet, because I intend to get home to them alive."

The sergeant met his gaze. He had surprisingly gentle eyes, brown as new coffee. "Aye, aye, sir. I got a little boy myself."

"Let's get to work, then," Mike said.

THE OCEANA NAVAL Air Station PX on the last Saturday afternoon before school started was jammed with harried mothers, their children in tow. Liz pushed a shopping cart up the boys' clothing aisle, tossing six-packs of white athletic socks and BVDs on top of the basketball hoop and the girls' new sweaters and dresses. Everyone had outgrown last year's clothes, lost last year's book bags, and scorned last year's lunch boxes. Danny wanted a "Combat" lunch box this year, which meant that Angus did too, so that would be easy. Kathie had set her heart on a Barbie lunch box. But not just any Barbie, a Negro Barbie. It had something to do with her friend Temperance. Liz had found nothing but blond-Barbie lunch boxes, and one brunette, at half a dozen stores so far. She'd tried to make a case to her daughter for patience, for breaking down the lunch box color barrier with all deliberate speed, but Kathie would settle for nothing less than immediate action.

Deb-Deb wanted an otter lunch box, which was probably impossible. She would have to settle for Baloo from *The Jungle Book*. A mammal, at least.

Fifteen feet ahead of Liz, Danny and Angus skulked along the edge of the aisle with plastic M-16s in their hands, taking cover where they could find it among the racks of children's clothing. They were treating the shopping cart as a convoy vehicle to be escorted through the hazards of the PX.

Danny reached the end of the aisle and checked both ways, then motioned Liz forward, using the standard field maneuver hand signals taught at Basic School. Angus waited, half visible behind a rack of fall skirts, until she had rolled by, then fell in behind her, covering her rear. As Liz turned left, heading toward the school supplies aisle, she ran into Betty Simmons, who was pushing a cart loaded with smart skirts, crisp blouses, and improbable hair ribbons for her two teenage daughters.

"Why, Lizzie O'Reilly, as I live and breathe!" Betty exclaimed in the syllable-adding Richmond accent that made it so hard to take her seriously. But Betty couldn't help herself. It was all real, from the silver-blond bouffant hair stiff with hair spray to the cheeks caked with foundation and the gooseberry-green dress and matching heels.

Liz tugged her T-shirt down in a futile tidying gesture and said, "Hello, Betty," trying to not parody the drawl. Danny and Angus had taken up ambush positions nearby, rifles at ready. Before they could open fire, Liz shooed them on toward the school supplies section and turned back to Betty. "How are you?"

"Same-same," Betty said cheerfully. This meant "wonderful"; Betty's life was in apple-pie order. Her husband was a bird colonel on track for general, and both her daughters were beautiful, bright, wholesome girls, honors students glossy with noblesse oblige and sublimated sexuality. "Yourself?"

"Same-same," Liz echoed, meaning "disordered." There was no competing with Betty's impeccable life, and Liz tended to take refuge in irony. "Just trying to get the monsters outfitted before school starts up."

"They just keep growing out of things, don't they?" Betty agreed. She gave Liz's midsection a frankly appraising glance, then looked up and raised an eyebrow. "Why, *Lizzie,* pardon my big mouth, but I do believe—"

"Yes," Liz conceded, a little resignedly. It had probably been too much to hope her condition would escape Betty's omnivorous attention for long. "A couple of months."

"How wonderful!"

"Yeah, wonderful," Liz said, trying to sound sincere. She had school supplies to buy, for God's sake. She didn't have time to fake the appropriate maternal emotions on such short notice.

"We'll have to throw you a shower, of course."

"Oh, no, there's really no need—"

"Nonsense," Betty said firmly, and Liz decided to let it go. There was no swimming against the tide of Betty's sense of the proprieties in any case.

"I'm sure Mike is thrilled too," Betty went on. "How is he doing over there?"

Liz hesitated, and a wave of dizziness hit her, a darkness swimming with green and purple blotches. *Shit,* she thought. It wouldn't do to collapse in a faint at Betty Simmons's gooseberry-green feet.

She took a deep breath, and the store came back into focus.

"Fine," she said, firming up her grip on the shopping cart. "Last I heard, anyway. I haven't had a letter since Wednesday."

"Well, no news is good news, right?"

Liz shrugged. "Who knows?"

Betty's Maybelline-red lips pinched; such frankness broke the rules of military wife cheerfulness. Liz added, "I mean, he writes almost every day, but the letters tend to show up in batches of three or four, with gaps in between. Something about the way they get the mail out of there." She caught herself, feeling that she was beginning to babble. They both knew that Mike could already be dead and his letters would keep showing up anyway for a week and a half. It had just happened to Maria Petroski. But pointing that out broke the damn rules too.

"When's he due back?" Betty asked, trying to return the conversation to solid ground.

"God, I don't know. I can't think that far ahead. Next August, I think. The eighteenth?"

"Buy yourself a 1968 calendar," Betty advised. "Mark the date. It really helps. An anchor in the future. That's all that got me through while Dick was over there."

"I'm not really a calendar person. I'm more of a one-day-at-a-time type. Like an alcoholic."

Liz had meant it as a joke, but Betty's highlighted blue eyes widened into hurt. Too late, Liz recalled the stories. According to the wives' grapevine, it wasn't just a calendar that had gotten Betty through her husband's tour.

Liz said hastily, "It must be nice, having Dick home safe and sound."

"Oh, it is, it is. The girls are in heaven." Betty hesitated, then confessed, "He's put in for another tour. He may leave again as soon as January."

"Oh, Betty—" Liz trailed off, unable to come up with something sympathetic to say that wouldn't violate the code.

"I've been looking for a 1969 calendar," Betty said. "But they're not out yet."

Danny hurried up just then, clutching a box. "Mom, look at this! They've got watches with the Marine Corps emblem!"

Liz gave Betty an apologetic glance. "Not now, Danny."

"It's only eight dollars!"

"I'll look at it in a minute, hon."

"*Please,* Mom? I've got $17.30 in my bank at home. I'll pay you back."

Betty still looked like she might cry. Liz said, "Just put it in the cart, Danny. Of course I'll buy you the watch."

Danny set the box on top of the sweaters as if it were a soap bubble. "Thanks, Mom."

"You'd better get one for your brother too," Liz said, trying not to think of the week's budget.

"I'm pretty sure this one is waterproof," her son said. He ran off, his plastic M-16 cradled in his arm.

Liz turned back to Betty. "I'm sorry."

"It's all right. Boys will be boys."

"They sure will."

They stood in silence for a moment while all around them military mothers pushed loaded carts and shepherded children.

"Let's have coffee together sometime," Liz said.

Betty met her eyes, a rueful, grateful glance. She'd overpainted her lipstick as usual into a smear of constant smile that gave her the look of a sad clown. "Yes, let's."

AS SOON AS they got home from the PX, Danny rummaged through the bags and dug out the Marine Corps watch.

"What time is it in Vietnam?" he asked as he pulled out the stem to set it.

"I don't know," Liz said. "We'll have to look it up in the atlas."

Her son ran off into the living room. Liz took the heel of a loaf of Wonder Bread and drowned it in Hershey's syrup from a freshly purchased bottle. The chocolate and ketchup diet, she thought rue-fully, rolling the bread up to stuff it into her mouth. She felt like a hypersensitive tank. She'd gained more weight with every pregnancy and had a harder time losing it. Maybe this time she'd just succumb entirely and turn into one of those sprawled, demoralized women with too many kids. Maybe she already was one of those women.

With her craving briefly stilled, she took the shiny "USMC: Tradi-tion of Pride" 1968 calendar out of one of the other bags and tore off the plastic cover.

"Twelve hours, Mom!" Danny called from the living room.

"What?"

"Vietnam is twelve hours ahead of us. It's already nighttime there."

"How about that," Liz said. "I guess your dad's asleep." The calen-dar's illustration for August 1968 was the famous photo of the Marines raising the flag atop Mount Suribachi on Iwo Jima. She looked at it for a long moment, feeling vaguely defeated, before she circled the eighteenth day of the month in red and crossed to the re-frigerator to tape the calendar into place.

CHAPTER 6

SEPTEMBER 1967

from: Capt. M. F. O'Reilly
H Co., 2nd Bn., 29th Marines, 6th Mar Div FMF
c/o FPO San Francisco, Calif. 96602
Sun 3 Sept 1967
circa Gio Linh, RVN

Dearest Lizzie,

Sorry for the gap in correspondence. I've been running around the landscape with the jolly crew of company H, 2/29—called Heartbreak Hotel, inevitably. More like Half-ass, at this point: the usual USMC-issue array of maniacs, morons, stone-cold killers, and fuckups. They'd been sadly neglected, discipline-wise, by their previous owner. With a little drill and butt-kicking, they'll learn to wreak proper Marine havoc, but we haven't had a minute to train.

To keep us amused, confused, and unprepared for actual combat, the battalion brass in their wisdom have sent us to scenic Gio Linh, which is run by the South Vietnamese army out of the saddest shantytown of inadequate bunkers you ever saw. A real four-star resort, this place. The rats actually own it, the ARVN are just renting. On a clear day—which of course never happens—with good binoculars, you can see the Peace Bridge, which is what they call the bridge across the Ben Hai River, which connects North and South Vietnam. On a very clear day you can even see bad guys over there in their nice Soviet-issue Salvation Army uniforms. On any kind of day at all, they try to kill you. But not very hard, and in any case, they are extremely poor shots.

Meanwhile, they fly their flag on their side, we fly the RVN flag on this side, just so nobody gets the countries confused. Remember: North Vietnamese, bad guys. South Vietnamese, good guys.

They've got us running sweeps toward the border every few days, to assess the strength, movements, and combat readiness of the insect population. The bugs are the real winners so far in this war. The bugs, and the vagaries of cultural exchange. I spent several exciting hours in the rain the other night, on our most recent camping trip, trying to decipher information relayed to me via radio by a South Vietnamese lieutenant. Have you ever heard two excited Vietnamese talking over a radio? It sounds like a head-on collision between Fibber Magee's closet and a Ringling Bros. circus train. Only more so. All this during a fierce firefight that turned out to not have any bad guys in it. Four friendlies wounded while we tried to bridge the language barrier. What a way to run a war.

You would like my radio operator, though. He is a cool-headed young fellow named Stinson. The relationship with your RO is sort of like a marriage, without the fights, good meals, or sex. (But picture 180 restless children carrying guns. These half-trained adolescents make the fearsome foursome look angelic.) Stinson is all of twenty, a saxophone-playing music school washout who smokes like a Korean War–vintage jeep and swears in stereo like any good

*Marine. He may succumb to lung cancer before his tour is up, but
meanwhile Juilliard's loss is Hotel Company's gain. The kid has an
ear like a Mozart-loving bat, can sift the sense out of all manner of
static-ridden garble even with people shooting at him, and is fluent
in the Vietnamenglish necessary for survival here in Gio Linh. As he
and I are joined at the hip by the radio, 'til death do us part,
Stinson is also endearingly determined to keep me alive. Definitely
an A+ attitude.*

*Anyway, Alpha Sierra Sierra Romeo Sierra, as they say on the
company net. All Secure, Situation Remains the Same. We're
gearing up for our next jaunt, minutes after returning bloodied
(mostly by the mosquitoes) but unbowed from the previous one. I'm
sitting here in the bunker I share with an ARVN major and 6,000
rats, sipping a cup of hot tea—instant type, complete with sugar, no
lemon, damn the luck. If the letter is a bit sticky, it's because I
stirred the tea with my pen. Usually I'm more civilized, but I didn't
have a knife handy. The only trouble is that now the pen squirts tea
when I retract the ballpoint. C'est la guerre de l'Indochine.*

*I'm glad to hear your puking is easing off. I've been having
sympathetic pregnancy symptoms myself, abdominal cramps
(possibly related also to the fine USMC cuisine) and severe, no
doubt hormonal, irritability, which I take out on the bad guys.
Maybe you should start carrying a gun yourself; it is marvelously
therapeutic.*

*In any case, give my love to the tadpole. If it's a boy, I think we
should name him after Larry.*

*I miss you, darling. Wish I was back in our big happy bed.
Stinson is all very well, as shotgun marriages go; he keeps the
antenna bent down so the snipers don't drill us, and he is faithful,
loyal, true-blue, and concerned for my continued well-being. But he
lacks your wit and your perfect ass. There's nothing in this*

goddamned country that can compete with either of those, frankly. I can't wait to survive this nonsense and get home to you.

Love, your
Mike

P.S. Give my love, as ever, to the fearsome foursome—glad to hear you got them outfitted for school. That's funny that the boys want to take their M-16s. Tell them they can take them, but they can't have a round chambered and should keep the safeties on until they actually see something worth shooting. Oh, yeah, and tell them, firmly, from me, to not shoot their teachers. Or at least to adhere strictly to the rules of engagement and wait until the teachers shoot first.

DEB-DEB WAS HAVING a crisis of conscience over the fact that Mike had referred to the baby as a tadpole. Tadpoles grew into frogs; and otters ate frogs. It was like a lion cub learning her mother was pregnant with an antelope, Liz supposed. You spent your early years learning to eat something, and then you had to deal with the thing as a sibling. At least that was the clearest reading of the situation she'd managed so far. Deb-Deb in tears was not entirely coherent.

Liz was sitting in her ob-gyn's office waiting for her monthly check-in, trying without much success to comfort her daughter, who was sobbing. It was just one of those days. Liz had just had lunch with Betty Simmons at the Officers' Club and was feeling particularly inadequate anyway. She had accepted the invitation hoping Betty would drink too much and commiserate over her husband's imminent return to Vietnam, giving Liz room to complain too, but Betty had apparently regrouped as a model military spouse after her brief moment of humanity in the PX and spent the meal drinking French water and singing the praises of her exemplary family. The older

Simmons daughter, Miranda, a high school senior, had gotten early acceptance and a full scholarship to the University of Virginia. Betty's other daughter, Bernadette, was the something-something of the Honor Something as a sophomore, sported astronomical PSAT scores, and had received a citizenship award from the Kiwanis. Meanwhile, Liz was forced to concede, Danny and Angus were being hauled down to the principal's office for carrying plastic weapons to school and conducting search-and-destroy missions along the unsecured borders of the playground; Deb-Deb's kindergarten teacher was concerned that all her artwork was otter related; and Kathie had burst into tears at her second grade class's most recent current events discussion, when asked what her daddy did for a living. Kathie was afraid to say her daddy shot people, which was her understanding.

Liz had managed to disarm the boys for the moment, and she was resigned to Deb-Deb's watery reality sense, but she had no idea what to tell Kathie. She knew that Mike would have laughed and said, "Better Daddy shoots them than they shoot him, sweetie."

In retrospect, the lunch had been a mistake. Liz could see that she'd been lonelier than she'd realized. She'd even, apparently, been desperate. But Betty sober was no fun at all, even without the relentless gung ho. Liz had ordered a chicken salad sandwich and ignored it in favor of the french fries, triple-dunking every fry in a deep puddle of ketchup and feeling as if she had "I am pregnant and mad for greasy carbohydrates" written on her plate in lurid red. She dreaded having to discuss her maternal ambivalence, but Betty seemed mercifully oblivious. The baby on the way was a good thing, and Betty said all the right things cheerfully and got on with ordering Liz's universe properly. Over her own severe salad, dressing on the side, no wine, she advised Liz to tell Kathie, "Daddy's job is defending our country," but only Betty could pull that off with a straight face. Hence the flourishing teenage daughters on bright tracks into adulthood. The

O'Reilly kids would have to deal with shades of gray: Daddy was a Marine, for better and for worse, but Mommy had married an English major. Mike at twenty-two, just back from Korea and deceptively reticent about his weakness for heroism, had been the smartest, funniest man Liz had ever met, a lean, laconic, deliciously tender man with an unerring eye for the absurdity of human institutions and a beautiful head of curly black hair. He still saw through the human comedy, more keenly than ever; and he was still brilliant, funny, lean, and tender more often than not; but somewhere along the line her husband had decided he was willing to die for the goddamned institutions anyway. She really hadn't seen that coming.

And the hair, of course. The hair was gone.

At the end of the lunch, Betty had frankly pulled Marine-wife rank and grabbed the check, putting it all on her husband-the-colonel's O-Club tab with an initialed flourish. Had Liz known it would come to that indignity, she would have ordered the wine anyway and drunk the bottle alone.

Worse, she had somehow ended up promising to use Miranda Simmons as a babysitter, should she need one. Betty, smarmily sympathetic over the antics of Danny and Angus at school and the imminent pressures of another child, had managed to imply that Miranda might be a helpful influence.

Sitting in the ob-gyn's now, trying to comfort her sobbing daughter, Liz resolved to die before calling on Betty's helpful daughter. Not that she had anywhere to go in the evenings anyway; but she'd rather leave the kids home alone, if it came to that, defending the house with plastic M-16s. Danny was perfectly capable of dialing a telephone if the place started to burn.

"It's not really a tadpole, sweetie," she told Deb-Deb as the latest wave of tears ebbed enough for conversation. "It just looks like a tadpole for a while. Daddy was joking around."

Deb-Deb snuffled dubiously. "Why does it look like a tadpole, not a baby?"

Because ontogeny recapitulates phylogeny, Liz thought, but she couldn't come up with an immediate translation of that and offered instead, "Because my womb is full of water and it's happier swimming around."

"The baby is swimming?"

"Yes. It's more like an otter than a frog, really. I think it has hands already. Little teeny hands and feet."

"How does it breathe?"

"It's connected to me by a tube. Like a deep-sea diver."

Deb-Deb's eyes widened as she tried to picture this, but the image seemed to please her. She considered the situation for a moment, then said, "Maybe I could play with her in the pool when she comes out."

"I'm sure she would love that," Liz said, noting her daughter's assumption of gender but deciding not to fight that battle now. Deb-Deb no doubt felt she had enough brothers.

THE RADIO spluttered in the dark, a whispered "*Alpha Sierra Sierra Romeo Sierra,*" barely audible in the hammering rain. The Second Platoon listening post was the last position to broadcast their midnight check-in, and Mike sat back in the muddy foxhole as the radio lapsed into static. He could relax for an hour or two now. The bottom of the hole had eight inches of standing water in it, and he made a splash as he settled, but wet was wet once you were soaked through, and he'd been soaked through for fourteen hours. It felt good to relieve knees stiff from squatting.

The night beyond the foxhole was impenetrable, a streaming blackness that drowned his usual sense of himself as the spider at the center of the company's web, alive to every tremble of the converging threads. It was unnerving, inheriting total responsibility for a group of armed, demoralized strangers on a moment's notice. It wasn't just that the noise discipline was for shit. There were people walking around with empty grenade pouches because they didn't want to carry the weight; half the squads had food in the ammo cans and no bandoliers, and when Mike had first shown up the mortar crews weren't bothering to carry plates and tripods, though he'd fixed that quick enough and had some helo-ed in posthaste. Hotel was in dire need of about a month of training and reinforcement, but they'd been in the field almost continuously and Mike was still steering the company only broadly and approximately, as if it were a truck on ice, seeing how much control he actually had of this huge and lethal machine. Learning to juggle three or four radios under fire, each with someone screaming for an immediate decision. Getting to know the crucial personnel, the platoon leaders, sergeants, and forward artillery observers who were his eyes in the field, and the radio operators who were his ears, finding out who he could count on and who he couldn't. Learning the ropes of air support and artillery support. Learning who back at battalion headquarters was an idiot and who wasn't.

That, and trying to keep his people from getting killed. Taking over a fucked-up company in the field was like being handed a burning sack of shit with a baby in it. You definitely wanted to get the poor kid cleaned and fed eventually, but the first job was just to get the damned fire out. They'd been lucky so far to not run into anything serious in the course of their wanderings, but luck like that couldn't hold.

To Mike's immediate left, Stinson had fallen asleep the moment Second's LP had cleared, his helmet off, his ear against the receiver in case anything unexpected came through. To Mike's right, the only other upright figure in the foxhole was Doug Parker, the First Platoon commander. Huddled in his hooded poncho, the lieutenant looked like a Buddhist with an M-16, pointed down so the barrel didn't fill with water.

"I'm gonna close my eyes for a minute, Dougie," Mike said. "You okay to stay awake?"

"Fresh as a daisy, Skipper," Parker said.

Mike chuckled appreciatively; they were all spent after the day's slog through the mud, and the lieutenant's humor was the only dry thing left. Parker, a Princeton grad, had the makings of a decent platoon leader in spite of his Ivy League handicap.

"Wake me if the Chinese come into the war," Mike said. He tugged the hood of his poncho over his helmet, adjusted the angle of the runoff to miss his nose, and let his chin drop to his chest. He was finally going to get to dream of home. It was amazing how warm and dry he was in his dreams these days, how utterly happy he was in Liz's arms. The rain drumming against the rubber drowned out the low crackle of the muted radio, but Mike knew Stinson heard things better in his sleep than most men did awake. Besides, the NVA were way too smart to be out in the rain on a night like this.

ON THE WAY home from the doctor's office, Liz stopped to pick up Kathie at her friend Temperance's house, where Kathie often went after school to play. The Williamses lived an easy walk from the elementary school, down a narrow street in the older, presuburban housing on the north side of Little Neck Road. It was a working-class neighborhood of mostly black families, a world away from the two-story colonials and ranch-style split-levels of the King's Grant development on the other side of the school. The houses were simple clapboard boxes barnacled with bedroom additions, flanked by clotheslines laden with laundry and gardens green with edible vegetables. Kathie, glamorized by Temperance's domestic life in general, wanted to put up a clothesline in her own suburban backyard and had acquired a taste for collard greens sautéed in bacon grease, though she remained unenthusiastic about broccoli and spinach.

The driveways were dauntingly narrow, one-car driveways for one-car families, no room for boats. Temperance's mother, Liz knew, walked to her job in the school cafeteria, while her father drove the family's ancient Buick to his job at the Norfolk Naval Shipyard. Liz parked her big Ford station wagon on the road, with the wheels in the mild grassy ditch. Deb-Deb got out of the car with her, still subdued by considerations of the thing swimming inside her mother. The ob-gyn had picked up on her concerns and given her a cheerfully literal lecture on prenatal development and a green lollipop, but Deb-Deb had been so upset by the wave of fresh information that she hadn't opened the candy.

An American flag, its stripes weathered to soft pink, drooped from an angled stick beside the screened front door. Liz knocked once, drew no response, and knocked again, rattling the flimsy frame without producing much noise. There didn't seem to be a doorbell. She could smell something chickeny cooking within the house, and the Supremes' "You Can't Hurry Love" was blaring on a record player upstairs. Liz could hear Kathie clearly, singing along to the grainy 45—the Flo Ballard harmony, she noted with pleasure, strong, dignified, and contained. Temperance was riffing more exuberantly on the melody.

Liz knocked one more time, then called "Hello?" through the screen door. There was an answering call from the back of the house, and a moment later Linnell Williams hurried up the hallway with a wide-eyed three-year-old on her hip and a spatula in her hand. Temperance's mother was a slender, even fragile-seeming, woman of about thirty, lost in a bright red sundress, the skin of her beautiful shoulders poured smooth as a Reese's peanut butter cup. She wore a tiny cross on a gold chain around her neck and battered blue flip-flops.

"Sorry, sorry, sorry," she said, laughing. "Can't hear nothing back there, this house is *way* too big and those girls are singing way *too* loud. How you doin', Miz O'Reilly?"

"Liz," Liz said, as she always did. The house actually seemed painfully small to her, for a family at least as big as her own. She felt overdressed in her go-to-the-doctor skirt and blouse and wished she had worn shorts. "I'm fine, thank you. And who's this?"

Linnell Williams glanced down, giving the little boy an affectionate jounce. "This little hunk o' burning burning love is Dmitri Jay Williams the Third. Say 'Hey,' DeeJay."

"*Heh,*" Dmitri said, readily enough.

"Hey, Dmitri," Liz said. "I'm pleased to meet you. And this little hunk is Deb-Deb."

Dmitri beamed, showing a mouthful of perfect tiny teeth. "Heh!"

"He say he pleased to meet you too," his mother supplied. "Hello, Deb-Deb. Ain't you a pretty little thing?"

"We were at the baby doctor's," Deb-Deb told her.

"No kidding," Linnell said, keeping her face toward Deb-Deb, so obviously being tactful that Liz felt compelled to add as brightly as she could, "Yep. Another one on the way."

Linnell gave her a glance, picking up on something in her tone, but said readily enough, "That's wonderful. Congratulations."

"Thank you," Liz said, and then, frankly rueful, answering the glance, "Life is what happens while you're making other plans."

"I hear that," Linnell said dryly. Liz felt absurdly grateful. It was the most realistic and supportive thing anyone had said to her yet.

"The doctor gave me this sucker," Deb-Deb said. "But I'm saving it for the baby."

"Sounds like a plan," Linnell Williams said. "It's gonna be a lucky little baby, to have such a sweet sister." She turned and hollered up the stairs, "Temperance! Kathie's momma is here!" then glanced at Liz and rolled her eyes. "Like *that's* gonna do anything. . . . Y'all come on in."

Liz and Deb-Deb followed her down the short hallway, past a tiny living room dominated by a playpen and strewn with plastic-wheeled vehicles, noisemaking instruments, and dolls. In the kitchen Linnell Williams gave a quick stir to the stewish concoction simmering in a pot, hitched Dmitri up a notch on her hip, and pulled out a chair from the kitchen table for Liz.

"You want something to drink?" she asked. "Some sweet tea?"

"No, thank you," Liz said. "I should probably be getting home. My other two are going to be getting there soon."

She regretted the refusal as soon as it was out of her mouth; Linnell Williams looked startled by it, and even chagrined. But Temperance's mother said, amiably enough, "I hear that. I got two more still running around out there somewhere myself." She turned to the doorway again, plainly accommodating Liz's ungraceful haste. "*Temperance!*"

"Coming, Momma!" her daughter called, but the music continued to blare. They'd started the record over again.

Oh, you can't hurry love, no, you'll just have to wait—

The two mothers exchanged "What can you do?" smiles.

"They still working out that routine for the school talent show," Linnell said. "They calling themselves the Supremettes now."

"Oh, God, did I miss something?" Liz moaned. This was the first she'd heard of the Supremettes. "What talent show?"

"Oh, it ain't 'til next month sometime," Linnell reassured her. "You know how these girls are. Everything gotta be right away."

Liz was silent a moment, feeling embarrassingly out of the loop of her daughter's life, then shook her head at herself and regrouped. "I suppose Kathie's going to need some kind of glittery outfit. God, out comes the sewing machine again. I'm still trying to find the right material for her Bluebird uniform, much less figure out the pattern and the sash."

Temperance's mother gave Dmitri another hitch up and busied herself with the stew. "Uh-huh."

"Did you manage to get Temperance's together yet?"

"Oh, ain't no hurry on no glittery dress."

"No, I mean her Bluebird uniform."

Linnell Williams gave Liz an odd glance. "Temperance ain't in no Bluebirds."

"Well, neither is Kathie yet, until I get out the sewing machine. These people are uniform crazy, aren't they? Won't even let them walk in the door without the right outfit. I've seen shorter lists of requirements for an amphibious assault." Liz began to feel she was babbling, as Linnell's silence persisted. "Did I miss something else? Kathie said she and Temperance were joining together."

Linnell shrugged. "Temperance can say what she please, it ain't gonna happen."

"Well, granted, it's a pain in the butt. But the girls are so excited about it. I mean, if it's a matter of you having trouble getting Temperance there, I'm sure I could—" She broke off, at a sudden thought, then blurted, "Oh, God, this isn't about money, is it? Because if it is—"

"Now, now—" Linnell Williams said, a sharp, warning note. "None of that."

Liz shut up, feeling chastened, white, and very stupid. Temperance's mother eyed her for a moment, as if weighing how much she really had to spell out.

Finally, apparently opting to give Liz the benefit of the doubt, she said, more gently, "You ain't from around here, are you?" She seemed almost amused.

"Well, no," Liz conceded. "I'm from Detroit, originally. But—"

"Well, I don't know what things are like in Detroit. I never been up north. But down here, honey, the Bluebirds ain't blue. Just like the Brownies ain't brown."

Liz opened her mouth then closed it again, unable quite to believe Linnell Williams was saying what she seemed to be saying.

Upstairs, the record started over again. Temperance's mother shook her head.

"I wish you *could* hurry love," she said, and went to the doorway again. "Temperance Williams, if you are not down here in ten seconds I am going to whup your little fanny!"

"Oh, *Momma!*"

"*Now,* girl. Miz O'Reilly's gotta get going."

"Liz," Liz said, futilely. She really wished she'd taken that glass of tea.

CHAPTER 7

OCTOBER 1967

THE ANCIENT air conditioning system at St. Jude's had broken down again, and the pews were a desultory tumult of makeshift fans, row upon row of fluttering missals and weekly bulletins, like the wings of a thousand tethered doves. Father Winters's homily went on and on, the pop of the *p*'s in the microphone punctuating the priest's drone with little explosions.

From the chairs to the side of the altar, where Danny and Percy Killebrew sat garbed in their red altar-boys' cassocks and white surplices, it was clear that no one was listening to the sermon. The children were all squirming, and the faces of the adults who weren't trying to keep their children quiet had settled into expressions of patient endurance. High in the west wall of the church, where a new stained-glass window was to be installed, a raw hole gaped, hastily patched for the Sunday services by an old green tarp. One corner of the tarp had come loose, and a shaft of Indian summer sunlight, filled with lingering construction dust, sifted through the gap and fell across the area just behind the altar. It looked like an intruder, a bright weed in the meticulous garden of the candlelit sanctuary.

Danny checked his watch. It was already early evening in Vietnam. That seemed realer, somehow, than this endless mass. Beside him, Percy was quietly mangling key phrases from the sermon out of the side of his mouth, ventriloquist style—*the eugaradsic communillby, the laugh of faith, the gaggacy of our common ploptism*—and it was all Danny could do to keep from laughing out loud. In the third row, his mother sat with Angus, who kept trying to slip down under the pew, and Deb-Deb, who was placidly drawing otters in the margins of the program. Kathie was at her friend Temperance's church this morning, as she almost always was now. Danny could see that his mother's lips were set in the thin tight lines of what he had come to think of as her I-can't-stand-this look. He knew she thought Father Winters was an ass.

The Sunday service was different from the daily mass he had come to love, serving it with Father Germaine. On weekday mornings the altar area and first few rows were all that were lit; everything was sharp with crisp shadows, and the church was alive with what felt like holiness. Father Germaine said a brisk mass without flourishes; he often didn't give a sermon at all. Danny had the impression that it actually pained the priest to talk, sometimes. But Sundays were a different kind of mass, and Father Winters was a different kind of priest.

The sermon ended at last, and the congregation stirred and stood for the Nicene Creed, knelt for the prayers of the faithful, and sat for the preparation of the gifts. Everyone seemed relieved to be in ritual motion again. Danny and Percy brought the water and wine to the altar for Father Winters to mingle in the chalice, then returned with more water and the linen cloth for the ritual cleansing of the priest's hands. Father Winters wet his stubby fingers perfunctorily, dabbed them dry, and dropped the visibly soiled linen into Danny's hand.

It was unsettling to be privy to the theatrical underpinnings of the mass; beneath the green and gold silk chasuble and pristine linen alb,

Danny knew, Father Winters wore an aloha shirt with sweat stains at the armpits and polyester slacks crusted with recent spaghetti. Being an altar boy was like slipping behind the curtain of the Wizard of Oz; this magic show was run by a churlish, somewhat prissy man who picked his nose and kept a bottle of peach schnapps with his liturgical gear. It made it hard to maintain an attitude of awe.

The congregation stood for the preface to the Canon, then knelt for the Eucharistic Prayer. Danny and Percy moved to opposite sides of the sanctuary and knelt facing each other, with the sunlight from the construction gap puddled on the floor between them. As Father Winters turned to the altar and launched into the solemn business of the Eucharist, Percy gave Danny a wink and contorted his plastic features into a face that looked like Popeye. Danny ducked his head to keep from laughing and concentrated on Father Winters's obsequious monotone. He'd missed his cue the previous Sunday because of Percy's antics and rung the bells late at the sacramental hoisting of the bread, a mortifying lapse that Father Winters in his fury after the mass had seemed to think all but invalidated the Transubstantiation.

"*Lord, you are holy indeed, the fountain of all holiness. Let your Spirit come upon these gifts to make them holy, so that they may become for us the body and blood of our Lord, Jesus Christ. . . .*"

Angus took advantage of the general solemnity to slip under the pew, and Liz's head disappeared briefly as she retrieved him. Percy was still mugging; he looked like Herman Munster now. A baby began to scream in the back of the church. And suddenly none of it mattered, because this was it.

"*Before he was given up to death, a death he freely accepted, he took bread and gave you thanks . . .*"

The dust swam languidly in the renegade sunbeam, keeping its own slow time. Danny could feel the silence in that light, beyond the wailing babies and the coughs and fidgeting of the sweaty congregation, the silence that was the church's secret heartbeat, the silence nothing could mess up. He reached for the bells, lifting them gently to avoid any premature sound.

"He broke the bread, gave it to his disciples, and said: Take this, all of you, and eat it: this is my body, which will be given up for you."

Father Winters heaved the Host upward in his theatrically strenuous way, as if the body of Christ were pure dead weight and the sacrament culminated in a three count at the top of a clean and jerk. Danny timed the bells on the upswing, and their jangle resonated sharply, then faded as the priest held the wafer high, his fat arms trembling slightly beneath the burden of the Incarnation, and the dust motes stirred afresh in their shaft of silence, lighter than air, dancing in the hush that let the miracle in.

THE SOUTH VIETNAMESE Regional Forces battalion caught up with Hotel Company just before dawn. Mike could hear the RF coming from a quarter mile away. He'd thought his own company's noise discipline was loose, but half the Ruff Puffs had transistor radios stuck into their helmets, blaring jazzy Oriental music. Mike moved Hotel Company to the side of the trail to let them pass, and the Marines sat beside the railroad tracks and watched in amused astonishment as the column went by. It sounded like a Chinese disco on the move.

"Didi," Sergeant Thay, the RF liaison, told Mike proudly, obviously relieved that his people had gotten out of bed after all. "They move fast, hey?"

"Very fast," Mike agreed. The RF column was tightly bunched, with less than an arm's length separating each man. With all that music, it had the effect of a rumba line. The South Vietnamese were very relaxed, laughing and joking as if they were going on a picnic, trying their rudimentary English, mixed with the lingering colonial

French, out on the Marines, who answered cheerfully in even more rudimentary Vietnamese and the universal language of obscenity.

"Hey, Mah-reen, we kick boocoo VC ass you betcha!"

"*Bac-bac,* baby! Makee boo-coo boom-boom, you dinky dau motherfuckers!"

"Fuckin' A, Mah-reen! You got Lucky Strike? You got cigahrette?"

Mike saw that many of the Vietnamese soldiers' packs were stuffed with live animals, mostly cats and chickens, and the occasional pig. He could hear the cats yowling and clawing at the canvas, trying to get out.

"What are they carrying those animals for?" he asked his RF liaison.

"Lunch," Sergeant Thay said.

The RF command group approached, bristling with radio antennae like a porcupine. The battalion CO was a major wearing leopard-pattern camouflage and a jaunty bush hat with one side of the brim pinned up. He looked like he was about seventeen years old. He saluted Mike, bowed, and held up a sack with something wriggling inside.

"Major Ngai would like you to have this cat," Sergeant Thay told Mike.

"Oh, I couldn't possibly—" Mike began but caught himself at the looks on the faces of the South Vietnamese. "I'm honored," he amended. "Please thank the major for me."

He looked around for something to give to the RF CO in return. What did you give a guy who was leading a six-hundred-man conga line and half the livestock in the Quang Tri Province toward the DMZ in the dark? A flak jacket, maybe. A good helmet. But the major shook his head cheerfully and said something prolonged. Thay listened respectfully, then summarized, "He say, You shoot good today. Maybe get big cannon to shoot too."

"Okay," Mike said. "I'll do my best."

The Vietnamese major smiled, showing crooked, stained teeth. "O-kay," he said. "Numbah One."

"Ichi-ban," Mike agreed, and the Ruff Puff command group moved on, leaving him with the cat still clawing inside the sack. Mike glanced back for someone to hand the thing to, but Stinson had alertly found something crucial to do with the radio. Noting the quiet light in Sergeant Thay's eyes, Mike offered the sack to the RF liaison.

"Oh, I could not take your cat," Thay demurred.

"I had cat for breakfast, actually," Mike said.

LIZ STOOD BY the station wagon after mass, waiting for her older son and trying to keep Angus and Deb-Deb out of the traffic while the St. Jude's parking lot emptied hectically around them, as if the liberated congregation were fleeing a fire. She was feeling edgy and peevish; the morning had lost its crispness in the labor of getting the kids to church at all, and the afternoon seemed doomed to dissipate into the usual Sabbath torpor. Danny and Percy always took an incomprehensibly long time to disvest—or whatever they called taking off their liturgical whatchacallits, their smocks and robes—after serving mass, and Kathie still had to be picked up at Lynnhaven Pentecostal, where she was actually singing in the choir now, standing proudly between Temperance and her mother. By the time Liz had all her kids in one place, she'd have to begin thinking about dinner.

Angus, after several close calls with absconding vehicles, settled in the back of the station wagon. He rolled the window down and took his plastic M-16 out, sighting in on the church's side door, preparing to snipe at Danny and Percy when they came out. To Liz's immediate right, Deb-Deb was practicing her latest trick, an unnerving mock faint. She would stand normally for a time, then let her eyes roll back in her head and keel over without warning, falling straight backward, stiff as a board. Liz kept catching her daughter and propping her back upright, but she was afraid she'd miss sooner or later and have to add a trip to the Oceana emergency room to have Deb-Deb's head sewn up.

The church door opened and Angus's finger tightened on the plastic trigger, but it was Father Germaine who emerged, unvested now himself, a square peg in the round hole of his ill-fitting black street clothes, tugging at his white collar with one finger as if it were a too-tight tie. Liz said, "Hold your fire, Angus."

The priest noticed her across the parking lot and waved, then hesitated, blinking in the sunlight. Liz couldn't tell whether he wanted to come over and say hello or was trying to decide whether it was all right to simply flee.

His dilemma was solved when the door banged open behind him and Danny and Percy surged out into the fresh air on a wave of laughter. Germaine fell in with them for the walk across the parking lot, looking a little stiff and self-conscious. The boys had their usual unsettling postmass swagger and smirks. Liz suspected that Danny and Percy were doing something vaguely outrageous in the sacristy during the cleanup, like tippling the altar wine, but this was probably not the best time to confront them about it.

"You guys are dead," Angus said, safing his M-16 as Germaine and the boys reached the car. "I shot you the minute you got outside."

"No, I'm just wounded, I had my flak jacket on," Danny countered.

"I'm just wounded too, and this is a grenade!" Percy added, crumpling his church program into a ball and tossing it into Angus's sniper's nest through the open back window of the station wagon. "Kaaaaa-*boom!* Now you're dead."

"I am not!"

"Yes, you are, you're blown to bits!"

"Boys!" Liz said. "Can't you at least wait until we get home from church to start killing each other again?"

"Hello, Mrs. O'Reilly," Father Germaine said.

Liz turned to him, feeling a ridiculous pleasure that the man had remembered her name. "Hello, Father. How are you?"

"Just wounded, thanks."

Liz laughed uneasily, suspecting an implied critique of her parenting. "It's a beautiful day, isn't it?"

"I'm ready for some real fall, to tell you the truth. I don't do well in the heat."

"That must have made Vietnam tough for you."

"That, and all those young men dying."

So much for talking about the weather, Liz thought. Conversation with Germaine was like hiking on a glacier; things had a way of falling through the covering snow of small talk into dauntingly deep crevasses.

Danny, with Angus momentarily finished off by the grenade, piped up, "Father Germaine said Percy and me can quit studying Latin."

"Itquay atinlay," Percy seconded.

"Percy and *I*," Liz said.

"Yeah. Percy and I."

"Atinlay isway upidstay," Percy elaborated, and both boys giggled.

"I thought we agreed to keep that confidential," Germaine said.

"It's okay, Mom's cool," Danny said. "She won't tell Father Winters."

Liz raised an eyebrow at Germaine, who shrugged uneasily. "Father Winters believes Vatican II is a Communist plot doomed to fail," he said. "But it's ridiculous to have these kids memorizing a mass that isn't going to be said anymore."

"So you're subverting your pastor and corrupting the minds of these innocent altar boys."

"I see it more as fostering an independent liturgical understanding."

Danny and Percy turned their attention to Angus; having blown him up, they now enlisted Deb-Deb as a corpsman and began administering battlefield first aid. Danny called for a medevac chopper, using the car radio. Angus continued to deny that he was a casualty.

Germaine was also watching the boys. Liz met his eyes self-consciously, sure by now that he disapproved.

"Their father's sons," she said, but that sounded disloyal to Mike, and she added, "with my sense of drama thrown in to boot."

"They're good kids."

"Interesting, at least."

He gave her a sharp glance, saw that she was teasing, and conceded ruefully, "Which is better than good."

Liz felt another rush of peculiar joy, that he had remembered their conversation in the dentist's office. "No," she said. "It's just the reality of incarnation."

Germaine, to her delight, was left speechless.

"Father Zeke, could you give Angus last rites?" Danny called from the back of the station wagon, where they had laid Angus out to await the chopper.

"I do *not need* last rites!" Angus insisted. He did appear lively enough; it was all Percy could do to keep the younger boy on the beach towel that was serving as a medevac stretcher.

"Would you rather just go straight to hell when you die?" his brother demanded.

"Mom! Danny said I was going to hell!"

"*Danny*—" Liz began in exasperation, but Father Germaine interrupted firmly, "Nobody's going to hell."

Angus gave Danny a triumphant glance, and his brother, for once, had no reply; the older boys had been awed into silence by the priest's eschatological turn. Germaine stepped over to Angus and knelt beside him.

"It looks to me like Angus is going to make it anyway," he said.

"I *told* you," Angus said smugly.

"On the other hand, with the danger of infection, and so forth—" Germaine continued. "It couldn't hurt to give you the sacrament, Angus."

Angus looked freshly alarmed. "Does it mean I have to die, if you give it to me?"

"No, no. Whether you live or die is in God's hands. The last rites just covers all the bases. Makes sure you've got God's attention, whatever happens."

Angus weighed it out, then nodded his approval, relaxed back onto the blanket, and closed his eyes. Father Germaine took out his stole and looped it around his neck; he made the sign of the cross on Angus's forehead and began, "Go forth, beloved soul, from this world in the Name of God the Father Almighty, who created thee; in the Name of Jesus Christ, the Son of the living God, who suffered for thee; and in the Name of the Holy Spirit, who was poured out upon thee. . . ."

Liz watched, gooseflesh pimpling her arms, as first Danny, then Deb-Deb, and finally even Percy slipped to their knees on the pavement in a solemn semicircle around Angus and bowed their heads. Liz felt an urge to tell them all to get up, for God's sake, and quit all the nonsense; death was no game, and it was too easy to see her husband lying there beneath the priest's useless hand, waiting for the helicopter that would come too late. But it seemed worse to stop the play—it made it too real—and she held her tongue.

"Make speed to aid him, ye saints of God; come forth to meet him, ye angels of the Lord; receiving his soul, and presenting him before the face of the Most High. Rest eternal grant unto him, O Lord; and let perpetual light shine upon him. Amen."

"Amen," the children echoed, even Angus. And Liz whispered, past her tears, "Amen."

IT WAS ALMOST two hours before Mike reached the battleground himself, with Hotel's Second Platoon. The medevac helicopters were still landing, ferrying the Regional Forces' casualties out. Chopper space was at a premium, and the South Vietnamese were loading only the worst of their wounded; those who could walk back to Gio Linh would have to, and the dead were being wrapped in ponchos and lashed to carrying poles like deer. As the Hotel command group approached the RF battalion field CP, they passed clusters of South Vietnamese soldiers sitting around open fires, cooking their ration of small animals on spits; along with the lingering bite of cordite and blood, the air was thick with the smell of roasting pig and duck and cat. The Ruff Puff soldiers, even the walking wounded, all seemed business as usual; these men had been fighting for years, and their approach to battle was very blue-collar by now.

The circle of antennas marking the South Vietnamese battalion CP was much smaller than it had been that morning; a number of their radios had been destroyed in the fight. Several of the radio operators themselves, along with the other command group dead, lay to one side, bundled in a neat row of ponchos-*cum*-shrouds, looking horrifyingly like freshly wrapped cigars set out to dry.

Mike, with Sergeant Major Thay beside him, made his way to the edge of the RF command group, where Major Ngai lay on a litter, propped up slightly, smoking a cigarette. He had refused to be evacuated until all his wounded were out; in any case, it looked to Mike like the RF battalion commander would be going back to Gio Linh wrapped in a poncho. Ngai had a handful of field bandages stuffed into an abdominal wound, and the bright leopard pattern on his camouflage fatigues was submerged beneath a quiet tide of black-red blood. He looked like a soaked kitten who had been hit by a car, but he gave Mike a smile as he approached, and spoke.

"He say, Thank you for the howitsahs," Sergeant Major Thay supplied.

"I wish we could have done more, sooner," Mike said.

Thay translated. Major Ngai gave a weak, dismissive flip with the hand that held the cigarette. "*C'est la guerre*," he said, his accent making it sound like a Vietnamese proverb.

"*Oui*," Mike said, groping for his Jesuit high school French. "*Et à la guerre comme à la guerre. Mais je suis desolé néanmoins.*"

"It's hokay," Ngai said. He closed his eyes for a moment, and the cigarette slipped from his hand into the bloody mud beside the litter. Ngai opened his eyes again and looked woefully at the ruined butt. Sergeant Thay hastened to offer him a fresh one, and Mike dug a strike-anywhere match from his pocket, dragged it into flame across a rough spot on his helmet, and bent to light the cigarette for Ngai.

"*Merci*," the South Vietnamese major said.

"*De nada.*"

Ngai smiled weakly and closed his eyes again. Mike would have moved on, but as he turned to go, Ngai opened his eyes and said something softly, almost wistfully, in Vietnamese. Sergeant Thay leaned in to listen, then gave Mike an uneasy glance.

"He say, He hoped you have enjoy the cat."

Mike met Ngai's quiet, unfathomably dark eyes, the eyes of a dying man at peace, and smiled. Don't fucking cry now, he thought.

"Tell the major it was the best cat I ever had," Mike said. He touched his chest. "Tell him, Thank you, from my heart."

Thay looked relieved, and translated. Ngai, still holding Mike's gaze, winked.

"*De nada*," he said. "Numbah one." He closed his eyes, keeping a firm two-fingered grip on the Lucky Strike this time, though he did not raise it to his lips again. Mike waited until the cigarette melted into a long drooping ash and the ash dropped into the mud, then moved off, feeling his own eyes sting. But there was so much to do, if they weren't going to get their asses handed to them that night. It wasn't until he got Hotel Company back to Gio Linh the next day without further incident and learned that Major Ngai had died before the last helicopter went out, that he wept, alone in his bunker, looking at the empty cot across the dirt floor.

PART THREE

The first night of our marriage
He showed me forthwith how good a man he was
For he did attempt no violence
That might hurt me.
And before time to arise
He kissed me a hundred times, I remember
Without a single villainy
Ah, indeed, the sweet man is fond of me . . .

CHRISTINE DE PISAN,
"A SWEET THING IS MARRIAGE"
(TRANSLATED BY HELEN R. LANE)

CHAPTER 8

OCTOBER 1967

O N T H E F I R S T Saturday of October, Liz loaded the kids into the station wagon and drove north to Maryland, for Mike's parents' thirty-fifth wedding anniversary. It was a four-hour drive under the best of conditions, five with the weekend traffic, and then six with the cold, sloppy rain that began to fall near Richmond, and the whole time Liz grappled with the recurrent temptation to pull off the highway, claiming engine failure, and go home. She pictured herself on the truck stop pay phone, tearful, stressed, regretful. She was actress enough to pull it off easily. So sorry, car trouble, the kids are so upset, we're all upset, of course, but you know how it is. It was even possible to imagine Mike's parents being secretly relieved; the four O'Reilly children always hit their grandparents' tiny house like a storm.

In the end, though, she drove on. Because it was family, it was what you did. The Beltway was the usual nightmare, and by the time they reached the tidy gray house in suburban Silver Spring, she was exhausted, unable to imagine putting on a civil face. She pulled into the driveway and the kids all piled out and ran ahead to the door, and

Liz let them go, feeling a surge of despair. This was the visit on which she would have to announce her pregnancy, and she felt brittle and emptied in advance, incapable of the expected joy.

And lonely. Desperately lonely. With Mike along, these visits had their own bearable rhythm and their own subterranean rewards. He was as uncomfortable in his way here as she was, unsuited to the role of fond son, and there was a kind of camaraderie in watching him ease into cautious rapport with his father, in seeing the awkward tenderness he showed his mother and hearing him banter with his sister. She could ride it out, with Mike here, waiting for the subliminal joy in the amused glances he gave her at moments, the little looks and winks across the room at O'Reilly-isms. Without Mike, she was simply a dutiful fish out of water, delivering the brood for their dose of grandparenting. She tried to imagine making these ritual visits alone for the rest of her life, if Mike was killed. Seeing Mike like a shadow in his sister's face, in his father's quiet stubbornness, in his mother's eyes. She couldn't bear the thought.

She remembered her first visit here, about a month after she and Mike had begun to date. In retrospect, she'd been a sunshine-headed naïf, but she'd understood even at eighteen that she was a peace offering of sorts. Mike had fought savagely with his father for permission to join the Marine Corps early, at seventeen; Michael O'Reilly Senior believed he had raised a gifted scholar, not a warrior, and Mike's determination to fight for South Korea's freedom had been at least as much a war of independence against his parents' hopes and expectations as a battle against godless Communism. In the end, Mike Senior had grudgingly signed off on the enlistment papers only on the condition that Mike promise to come back from his mad crusade and finish college, and Mike had gone off to fight his war and duly come home to reenlist in academia. Along with a riotously witty paper on Kipling and empire, Liz was the first tangible evidence of his return to normality after his Korean service.

That first visit had been revelatory: as a peace offering, Liz had realized quickly that she amounted to a Trojan horse. She was not the woman Mike's parents had pictured for him; she was a flame to people who had been expecting flowers. Mike's father was a tall, dignified man steeped in Shakespeare and the Old Testament, a natural patrician with courtly manners, utterly placid in his ways. He had Mike's dry wit and marvelous offhand eloquence but none of Mike's refreshing irony. Mike's mother was a tiny, temperate woman who had never learned to drive, prepared to exchange recipes with Liz, to talk about the fine points of gravy and stuffing and leave the serious matters to the menfolk. It was an almost oppressively tranquil, if not complacent, household, and Liz felt too large from the moment she walked into the tiny living room: too loud, too vivid, and altogether too much, with all her jokes and comments going flat and clunking, like birds falling from air that somehow would not support their wings.

She and Mike had arrived fifteen minutes late that first day, to the silent displeasure of the elder O'Reillys. The assumption, blithely uncorrected by Mike, had been that it was Liz's fault, and the tension had eventually dissolved into indulgent nods to the inevitable vanity of a girl's prolonged preparations, which had infuriated Liz not only because of the condescension and sheer wrongness of the cliché, but because their tardiness had actually been entirely Mike's doing: they'd stopped in the park, three minutes from the house, to see the place along Sligo Creek where he had found a fox with a broken leg when he was a boy. Mike had shown Liz the tree where he'd carved his initials to mark the spot. The beech had healed around the wound of his memory, the blocky letters in Mike's already characteristic printing black with time, sunk deep in the bark, scars among other scars. He told Liz he had taken the fox home wrapped in his sweatshirt and been bitten several times in the process, but he'd never breathed a word to his parents. He'd splinted the fox's leg and kept it in the basement until it was well, then released it.

There was a self-conscious, almost furtive, passion in Mike's telling of the story, a sense of something shy and unused to exposure slipping from a mythlike depth. The moment had touched Liz deeply; she'd recognized that it was Mike's gift of himself to her, a glimpse of the crypto-Spartan in him emerging for the first time from the unlikely matrix of his moderate upbringing. She'd held her tongue with his parents to honor that secret sharing, but she couldn't help but feel dismay at the way he left her twisting in the wind in that smug little living room, exposed to the indignity of their pigeonholing.

The visit, on the whole, had proven a quiet disaster. Mike had told her that his father adored Shakespeare and led Liz to believe there would be a solid ground of early rapport there; and indeed, Mike Senior's thick volume of the collected works was soft and battered with rereading, with three thin stripes of dark gray along the page edges marking the locations of *Hamlet, The Tempest,* and *Romeo and Juliet.* But they'd run into trouble almost immediately on *Richard II,* whom the elder O'Reilly apparently considered a Christ figure and martyred philosopher. He'd quoted, without a trace of irony, ". . . if angels fight, / Weak men must fall, for heaven still guards the right." Liz had jumped in with both feet, typically, in spite of herself: "And nothing can we call our own but death; / And that small model of the barren earth / Which serves as paste and cover to our bones," to which Mike Senior had replied with an air of accepting insult with forbearance, "You may my glories and my state depose, / But not my griefs; still am I king of those." Mike had let them go at it, amused, noting only that at least in the end Richard had drawn his damned sword and gotten two of the bastards before they got him. Liz suspected Mike had seen both the argument and the stalemate coming, and even that he was pleased: she'd battled his father as an unsuspecting proxy on a kamikaze mission of sorts.

They'd had the first fight of their relationship in Mike's Chevy on the way back to D.C. that night, and Liz remembered her dismay at succumbing to petulance. Until then she and Mike had been free proud beings together, grown-ups trying the wings of their deepest hopes for themselves, and it was humiliating to see things degenerate so quickly into squabbling over family politics. Mike had finally stopped in Georgetown and bought her ice cream, and they'd laughed together over it in the end, but the damage was done, and the pattern set. Neither of their best selves would ever be at home in that, or any other, living room. She had fallen in love with the warrior in Mike: the fierceness of his integrity and his strange, easy willingness to die for the right thing. As he had loved her actor's vividness and fire. But those weren't qualities that promoted domestic peace.

The kids had disappeared long since into the house; the pale face of Mike's sister, Theresa, a Bethanite nun, appeared now at the tin screen of the outer door, looking concerned, her features a moon echo of Mike's, framed by a veil of soft blue cotton rather than her usual starched wimple. Her order was easing into the new climate of Vatican II by tentative degrees, and she wore a plain blue dress now rather than her former engulfing robe; the children had been thrilled, on their last visit, to discover that their aunt had ankles. Liz roused herself and got out of the car.

"Are you all right?" Theresa asked, opening the door as Liz reached the porch.

"Just peachy," Liz said. It was a Mike-ism, meaning, "Are you kidding?" and Theresa smiled in understanding. A year older than Liz, she shared Mike's subversive sense of humor, which was always a relief to Liz. The siblings were much alike, indeed, in many ways; Theresa had entered the convent straight out of high school, as Mike had gone to boot camp and to war: like watermelon seeds squeezed too tightly, both O'Reilly children had shot off into transcendent vocations at the first opportunity.

Theresa gave Liz a hug. "I'm afraid Angus broke the County Cork angel again," she said, with a warning note.

Liz groaned. "Jesus. Already?"

"The boy has a gift," Theresa agreed. "I've got a Manhattan made for you."

"You're a saint."

Theresa laughed. "As if that would do any good."

Liz smiled appreciatively. Her sister-in-law half-turned, ready to enter the house, but this was the moment, and Liz said, "Theresa—"

Theresa paused, with her hand on the door. "Yes?"

"I wanted to give you a heads-up, before I tell your parents: I'm pregnant."

"Ah!" Theresa said carefully. "Well . . . Hooray?"

"I'm working up to it. I really don't see any alternative."

Theresa glanced inside the door, then met her eyes and smiled. "Then 'Hooray' it is, I guess."

"Yahoo," Liz said.

"Do you still want the Manhattan?"

"I don't see how one can hurt."

"I'll make you a weak one."

"Don't you dare."

Theresa laughed and gave her a quick hug, then led the way into the house. Liz took a deep breath and followed, to find her mother-in-law fretting over the pieces of the shattered angel, with Angus a step behind her, looking abashed. The white Irish porcelain figure, hand painted with gold trim, shamrocks, and unsettling blue eyes, had been purchased in Cork City, Ireland, the year before Mike was born, on the great journey of his parents' lives. The sacred heirloom had survived more than thirty years undamaged before the coming of grandchildren, but Angus had broken it three years running now, though he had outdone himself this year and apparently knocked the Erin-go-bragh angel off the coffee table before he'd even removed his coat. Danny already had the traditional model airplane glue out and was trying to reaffix one of the wings of the angel, which was relentlessly playing "An Irish Lullaby" despite its damaged condition.

"Angus, for God's sake," Liz said.

"I said I was sorry!"

"Say it again, then."

"I'm sorry," Angus said. "I'm sorry, I'm sorry, I'm sorry."

"It's all right," Mike's mother said, though it clearly was not all right.

"I am *so* sorry," Liz told her.

"It's all right," Anna O'Reilly repeated, still sounding unconvinced. She offered a distracted cheek to her daughter-in-law, and Liz bent to give her a kiss and a hug. Her mother-in-law always reminded Liz of a bird: a sparrow, maybe, nothing but bones and air, with a will of quiet steel. Mike's mother ran her traditional household in the traditional way, almost invisibly. But at moments like this, there was no doubt that she ran it. No one was going to be happy until she officially lightened up.

"Do we need a chaplain?" Liz asked Danny, who was still attending to the angel.

"No," he said seriously. "It's a good clean break. It should stay together fine, once the glue dries."

"A million-dollar wound," Theresa offered, from the periphery. Angus giggled gratefully, and Liz shot him a warning look: too soon to celebrate, buster. He sobered at once, and she felt a pang of remorse. She actually felt like hugging him, her little bull in this grandparental china shop.

"Green Dragon, Green Dragon, this is Coffee Table," Danny said, in his radio voice. "We need a dust-off here, pronto, over."

"Copy that," Angus croaked, in his own version of the radio voice. He glanced at Liz, who glanced at Mike's mother, then nodded tentatively; released into action, Angus fled downstairs to the basement, where the boys kept their toys.

As the angel continued to tinkle "An Irish Lullaby," Mike Senior appeared, like the cavalry, from the kitchen, holding two Manhattans. He handed one to Liz and one to his wife, with a little extra flourish, which was exactly the right thing to do. O'Reilly family lore had it that Mike's father made the second-best Manhattans in the world. Theresa made the best. Anna O'Reilly accepted the drink a trifle grudgingly, unwilling to be entirely appeased yet, but she took a sip at once. Liz gave Mike's father an appreciative kiss on the cheek.

"Happy anniversary," she offered ruefully, and he smiled.

"War is never a pretty thing," he said.

Angus reappeared, holding a big green plastic Huey helicopter above his head, making subdued *whoomp-whoomp* sounds.

"Coffee Table, this is Green Dragon," he croaked, in his radio voice. "I have purple smoke, over."

"Affirmative, Green Dragon, goofy grape," Danny croaked back. "Come on in."

Angus brought the chopper in low and hovered above the battered nativity scene. Danny loaded the wounded angel, holding the reattached wing tenderly in place, and the two boys headed for the back bedroom, which in recent years had come to serve as Charlie Med for porcelain figurines wounded in action.

"*Sic transit gloria angelii,*" Mike Senior noted dryly, when the chopper noise had faded, and gave his wife a wink. She smiled back, mock-grimacing at first and then with an *oh, you!* twinkle in her eye. A good marriage at work, Liz thought: a sweet moment. She hoped Mike could still wink at her like that after thirty-five years.

WITH THE ANGEL evacuated, the decks were cleared for her announcement, and Liz duly made it. She gave it her best theatrical spin and felt that she sold it with appropriate cheer. Theresa was marvelous in her supporting actress role, and the senior O'Reillys were a receptive audience in any case; they loved her best, Liz had always known, as the vehicle of their grandchildren. Anna O'Reilly teared up briefly, then took the Manhattan out of Liz's hand and brought her a cream soda. Mike Senior settled back in his chair, beamed quiet satisfaction, and quoted something from Proverbs about a quiver full of children.

After the flurry of the news, the weekend routine resumed in merciful uneventfulness. Anna O'Reilly retreated to the kitchen with the single Manhattan she would nurse through the entire afternoon and busied herself with preparing the meal; Liz went in after her, to offer to help, and Mike's mother gently but firmly threw her out, as she always did. The other adults settled into the living room and consumed their drinks at the ritual O'Reilly rate of one per hour. The inevitable football game appeared on the TV, quietly monitored by Mike Senior from his deep stuffed chair by the fireplace, while Theresa and Liz bore the brunt of the conversation as always, discussing Liz's pregnancy and how the kids were doing at school and comparing notes from recent letters from Mike. Kathie, who had cried at not being able to spend the weekend with Temperance and her family, had brought music, and she disappeared into the attic bedroom, from which the sounds of Martha and the Vandellas emanated scratchily. Deb-Deb plopped down beside the coffee table to play with Anna O'Reilly's other prized porcelain figures and soon had the leprechaun chatting happily with the magic cows. After a few subdued missions with the plastic helicopter under the anxious eyes of the adults, Danny and Angus decided they preferred to play in the freer reaches of nearby Sligo Creek Park, and Liz let them go, despite the continued rain. Dealing with their eventual sogginess and even pneumonia seemed preferable to the vast potential for further misadventures inside. Angus could break something in his grandparents' house just by looking at it, and they were running low on model airplane glue.

By halftime, the small talk in the living room had been exhausted; they watched the rest of the Texas-Notre Dame game desultorily while warm cooking smells filled the house. It always seemed a kind of humiliation to Liz, to be reduced to watching images flicker on a screen. This was one of the times she missed Mike the most; the easy American male patter he exchanged with his father carried these barren afternoons.

Danny and Angus returned from the park, shockingly drenched; they had apparently gotten into the creek. Liz made them take off every article of clothing possible outside, to minimize drippage on the tidy rugs, and put them straight into the bathtub.

By the time the boys reappeared in fresh dry clothes from the stash in the extra bedroom, looking scrubbed and improbably pure, like the newly baptized, dinner was ready. Mike Senior said grace with his usual understated dignity, added a blessing on the baby-to-be, and followed this with an unprecedented prayer for Mike, which awed everyone into silence: for a moment, the deferred reality surfaced through the politeness and the strain. What they had in common, the reason they were together here, the father of these children, the husband of this wife, the son and brother of these parents and this sister, was at war. Liz met her father-in-law's eyes and was conscious, painfully, of their essential kinship: both of them had fought Mike on this, fought hard, and both of them had lost. He was out there defending freedom in spite of them.

She reached to touch her father-in-law's hand; Mike Senior took her hand in his and gave it a quiet squeeze, and Liz's eyes filled. She felt for an instant the man's almost elemental goodness, the sturdy, simple faithfulness of his heart. The deep, deep thing in him that in Mike had turned, goddammit, into heroism.

The moment passed; everyone dug in. The football game continued from the living room, a close game in the fourth quarter now, which Mike Senior kept one eye on over his shoulder. There was the usual food awkwardness: none of the children except Deb-Deb would eat the peas or the onions, and Anna O'Reilly's famous squash casserole was out of the question. Angus kept trying to say what the casserole looked like, in defense of his position, and Liz kept shushing him. She didn't know what he was going to say, but it didn't seem likely to her that Angus's grandmother would appreciate hearing one of her prize recipes, passed down from her own grandmother, compared to whatever Angus had in mind. Angus grew increasingly restive under the suppression but managed to hold his tongue until both grandparents were away from the table, at which point he muttered to Danny, with an air of having been unjustly denied his truth, "It looks like dog vomit."

"I know," said his brother, more seasoned in the ways of their grandparents' home. "But if you move it around on the plate a little, it looks like you ate some."

AFTER DINNER, the photograph albums came out. It was, Liz knew, partly an homage to her pregnancy, her father-in-law's way of asserting continuity. The O'Reilly style in general was fond but undemonstrative, but Mike Senior was a quietly passionate family chronicler and a secret sentimentalist, with a loving eye; much of his seldom-spoken love went into taking excellent pictures, and the albums he had assembled over the decades had the sweep and coherence of good novels. The kids particularly loved the black-and-white pictures of the early years of Mike and Liz's relationship.

"Look how small the bush beside the door is!" Danny exclaimed, over a photo of Mike and Liz three months into their marriage, embracing on the porch of this same house.

"I had just planted it," Mike Senior said. "That was the day your parents told us they were going to have *you*."

Danny, awed, bent over the photo with redeepened interest. Liz could see him trying to come to terms with the entwinement of his own life with that blue juniper's, the bafflingly twinned paths of growth. It blew her own mind too, actually. That bush was over eight feet tall now and had the aura of the eternal, of having always stood sentry beside the entrance. Liz wondered how she would feel about the pictures Mike Senior had taken today, when she looked back on them in ten years with her fifth child beside her, and she felt, for the first time, the flicker of sweet anticipation.

Across the living room, Deb-Deb sat happily with her grandmother at the coffee table, the two of them absorbed in the surviving Cork City figurines. Kathie and her Aunt Theresa were in the dining room, trying to rig a nun's habit for Kathie's Barbie from one of the blue cloth napkins. On the television screen, the muted nightly news flickered in black-and-white, some Vietnam footage, mercifully ignored by everyone.

"Danny's in Mom's *stomach* in that picture?" Angus asked.

"Yup," his grandfather said, amused. "Just like your new brother or sister is in her stomach right now."

Angus gave Liz's abdomen a frankly skeptical glance. Danny flipped the album pages back and found another photo of Mike and Liz on the porch, as newlyweds, pre-bush. He studied it intently, then flipped back to the photo with the bush, still trying to grasp a world in which he did not yet exist.

All those years ago, Liz thought, looking over her son's shoulder at her own bright, heartbreakingly fresh, young face, and Mike's, seeing again how they had loved each other. She felt a wave of gratitude to her difficult father-in-law for this gift of their shared history; she wanted her own grandchildren looking at these pictures someday. With Mike sitting beside her, God willing, their aged faces testifying to the mysteries of time and love, of what changed and what stayed the same. She was glad, as she always was in the end, that they had made the long trip north.

CHAPTER 9

OCTOBER 1967

from: Capt. M. F. O'Reilly
H Co., 2nd Bn., 29th Marines, 6th Mar Div FMF
c/o FPO San Francisco, Calif. 96602
Mon 2 Oct 1967
Dong Ha, RVN

My Dearest Lizzie,
   Well, here I am in Dong Ha, at the crossroads of scenic Highway
Nine and the Street Without Joy, the truck stop garden spot of
Southeast Asia. It seems like the lap of luxury after Gio Linh; the
rats in the bunkers are much better fed, for instance, and so are not
as aggressive. I usually keep them at bay with my .45, but I am
cautious with them, as word has it they charge when they are
wounded. So I only shoot when I can see the whites of their eyes.
   We have settled in here, apparently for a while, after our
adventures circa Gio Linh, and have managed to stagger through a
few Rough Riders convoy escort hops up to Con Thien and several
truly futile patrols in various hinterlands without anyone getting

killed, which definitely helps morale. The men call me "Lucky Mike," though that can't last and will no doubt come around to bite me on the ass at some point.

In fact, one of the main problems right now is that we've been too damned lucky. The company hasn't been shot at enough recently, and humping day after day along mud roads and up and down mountains with sixty or seventy pounds of equipment on your back, without ever having to fire your weapon, it's easy to lose the sense of ammunition as anything but dead weight. We've hit booby traps and been mortared, taken artillery fire, and had a few guys get bit by snakes; but there haven't been many opportunities to shoot back. Inevitably, the troops begin to cut corners and lighten up. But it only seems like good luck, to be so bored in a combat zone that you forget why you are carrying so many bullets.

Fortunately, we've also had some time to train, and I've been running all the platoons through Immediate Action drills and throwing good old-fashioned kick-shit-everywhere act-all-pissed inspections. My first sergeant, Ike Tibbetts, is a great help in this. He is very Old Corps, a huge black man with the Marine Corps motto tattooed across both his biceps. It is spelled wrong on his left arm, but if anyone points this out, Tibbetts bruises them severely. His teaching style is very simple: He goes around grabbing screwups and malingerers by the stacking-swivel and hollering, "YOU ARE FUCKING UP MY MARINE CORPS!" which has a pronounced motivational effect. In this gentle fashion, he has been schooling the men in such fundamental truths of military life as "Ambushes are murder, and murder is fun." (Don't tell Danny and Angus this, as I suspect it would not play well at school.)

I'm using that great waterproof pen you sent, which does in fact write wonderfully under monsoon conditions. Please send waterproof paper next.

Weird incident as we came in from our last patrol. Just outside this village, a little girl came toward the column. It is not unheard of here for a child to be booby-trapped, but this kid penetrated our perimeter pretty effortlessly and walked right up to me. Sweetest little face you ever saw, huge black eyes, bangs cut straight across. Maybe five years old, walking around on her own in a war zone. I thought of Deb-Deb, of course. I gave her all the candy I had, and all of Stinson's candy too, and then she said, "You got cig-ahrettes?" I did in fact have two packs of those Korean War–vintage C-ration Lucky Strikes, which I trade for Cold War–vintage C-ration pound cake, and I gave them to her. I assume she will trade them for the Vietnamese equivalent of pound cake. I hope she wasn't going to smoke them herself.

After she'd cleaned us out of all our sweets and cigarettes, she tottered off to wherever she had come from. I looked at Stinson and he looked at me, and I said, "Cute kid," and he resafed his rifle and said, "Skipper, I'm just glad she wasn't wired with grenades."

Your U.S. armed forces, building trust and goodwill one civilian at a time.

Give my love to Deb-Deb and the rest of the fearsome foursome, and tell them Daddy says they can have all the cig-ahrettes they want.

It's getting towards shower time. That means I trot down, turn today's dust into mud, mop off the mud, and pick up a fresh coat of dust en route to my cozy abode. I miss you so, my darling liz. I think of your skin, so clean and smooth. Thanks for sending that picture of Kathie in your wedding dress. She looks as beautiful in it as you did. Marrying you was the best thing I ever did.

> *Love, your*
> *Mike*

P.S. It doesn't sound like you, to let that Girl Scout shit pass; I assume you'll be going in soon to kick ass and take names. I don't know what the hell I'm fighting for over here, if Kathie's friend can't join the goddamn Bluebirds.

"THIS ONE? . . . Or this one?"

The lens before Danny's eyes rotated with a click, blurring the lettered chart. The eye exam had the flavor of a test, but the answers were so obvious it seemed like cheating. It was too easy: clear, not clear. He wondered if he was doing something wrong, if there was a catch.

He said, "The first one."

"Good," the optometrist said. "Now . . . This one? Or this one?"

"The second one."

"Good." He changed the settings. "This one? . . . Or this one?"

"The—I don't know, they're both blurry."

"Ah." The doctor made a note. "Well, which is less blurry?"

Danny felt a surge of anxiety. Perhaps his eyes were hopelessly flawed and no lenses would be able to correct them completely. The world would be blurry forever. He would have to stay in the front row, to which he'd recently been moved at school. He hated sitting up there like a sore thumb with all the teacher's pets. All his friends sat in the back.

"Could you show them to me again?" he asked.

"Sure. This one? . . . Or this one?"

Danny studied the alternating charts intently. Both images were terrible; it seemed a choice between greater and lesser evils. He hesitated, then conceded, "The first one." Maybe he could still get away with a seat somewhere in the middle, if he squinted.

"Good." The doctor changed the setting and the chart clicked suddenly into perfect focus. "This one? . . . Or this one?"

"The first one!" Danny exclaimed. "That's the clearest one yet."

"Good." The doctor turned the machine off and made another note on his clipboard. "You have a slight astigmatism."

"Is that bad?"

"It's correctable."

"Can I sit in the back row again at school?"

The doctor smiled. "Absolutely."

"I hate the front row."

"Yeah, the front row sucks," the doctor said.

ON THE DRIVE home, Danny could see the leaves on the trees. They were so beautiful. He'd never realized such intricacy existed, had lived with masses of indeterminate green. He wondered what else he'd been missing.

"I can see the leaves on the trees," he told Liz.

"Wonderful."

"I'll bet I can see a baseball way better too. Dad's going to be so surprised, how good I'll be hitting by the time he gets home."

"He sure is," Liz said.

LIZ WONDERED, as she often did, where the time went. Running a couple loads of laundry and peeking out the living room window every fifteen minutes to make sure a Marine Corps green sedan wasn't pulling into the driveway hardly qualified as productivity, but that often seemed the sum of her accomplishments by late afternoon.

She had spent an hour on the phone that morning with Maria Petroski, inevitably a good way to leave a day feeling gutted. Maria was at the stage of frankly wishing she was dead. Lately they had been getting deeper and deeper into their conversations before Maria conceded that she couldn't kill herself, of course, there were the boys to think of. But she was scarily lucid about the varying capacities of her relatives and friends to raise Chevy, Lejeune, and Ramada. Maria had been setting aside five pills from every bottle of what she called her "widow chokers," the generous sedatives the doctors had been prescribing to help her sleep; and this morning she had announced cheerfully that she had enough now to kill a rhinoceros. She'd hastened to add that there was no way she'd take them until she had enough to kill an elephant, and she was apparently far enough gone to believe that Liz would find this reassuring.

What *did* you say to a friend who was squirreling away lethal-to-a-large-mammal-sized overdoses for a rainy day? It was like watching a child play on railroad tracks and being unable to tell her to get off. Liz understood Maria's feelings perfectly; sometimes she wished she was dead too, even with a husband who was still alive and a baby on the way, but she never got further than the vision of the kids finding her body. Maria was well past the funeral, in her own mind, happily entombed beside Larry at Quantico National Cemetery, while her three boys languished in her sister's—disqualifyingly inept, thank God, in Maria's still-realistic judgment—care or Liz's own overloaded home or even, in certain completely morbid scenarios, in the custody of the state.

After a conversation like that, it was a little hard to worry about dusting the china shelves and the rest of the day's domestic to-do list. Liz had taken the vacuum cleaner out but never plugged it in, and it looked vaguely reproachful standing beside the dining room table with the uncoiled cord lying slack. They hadn't eaten in the dining room anyway, since Mike had left; Liz hadn't had the heart to set the formal table and leave the place at the head empty, and so they had taken to bolting down their meals from stools at the kitchen counter or eating off TV trays in the family room, accompanied by Walter Cronkite's lugubrious take on the war. The boys lived for the Vietnam reports and were always trying to spot Mike in the footage of Marines slogging chest-deep through rice paddies with small-arms fire plucking at the water, ducking incoming mortar rounds, or jamming the sodden heaps of the wounded into medevac choppers. Liz didn't know how to tell them that if they saw Daddy on the CBS evening news, it was almost certainly a very bad thing.

The little tin ship's clock given to Mike by his First Platoon in Okinawa tolled six bells on the afternoon watch: three o'clock. The kids would all be home by four, even with their various after-school activities. Dinner was going to be a problem, as it was too late, yet again, to get to the commissary, and everyone was sick of hamburger, canned peas, and macaroni and cheese. Liz had a sudden urge to call Miranda Simmons to babysit, leave a casserole in the oven, and drive up to Dumfries to hold Maria's hand and possibly take away some of the pills, leaving her with only enough to kill a chipmunk.

Instead, she went into the dining room, relooped the vacuum cleaner's cord around its handle, then put the machine back into the closet. It was an odd sort of non-accomplishment, granted, but it seemed better than doing nothing.

DANNY SLIPPED self-consciously among the trees, doing the heel-to-toe "Indian roll" step that Mike had taught him to advance quietly over the fallen leaves. He carried his BB gun in the ready position, safety off. The "island," as the kids called it, was actually a peninsula, a finger of soggy, wooded near-marsh that joined the suburban mainland not far from the elementary school. But it was big enough to feel like Indian country to a ten-year-old. Danny had rowed over, in lieu of being choppered in. Recon.

The new eyeglasses felt heavy on his nose, and he freed a hand briefly from the rifle to thumb them back into place. The leaves on the trees still seemed miraculously distinct to his freshly corrected vision, crisp edged and vivid now in autumn yellows, reds, and browns. He had chosen the heaviest black-rimmed frames, over Liz's objections that they were ugly and awkward. Danny thought they were ugly too; of course they were ugly, that was practically the point. And they did keep slipping down. But they were durable, made for combat; they were, he knew, the kind of frames the Marines wore in the field.

The late afternoon light was rich and already fading; twilight came early since the shift from Daylight Savings Time. Danny skirted a patch of poison ivy and caught a glimpse of movement in the branches of a pine tree just ahead. A jay, vivid blue and white and black, crested with lapis lazuli. He'd been amazed, since getting his glasses, at the beauty of birds.

Danny raised the BB gun instinctively. He already had a pellet chambered, and he snapped off a shot. He'd never hit anything before, firing into the blur, but this time the bird dropped instantly. Danny wavered, shocked at the effect, then moved forward uneasily and found the body beneath the tree. His shot had been perfect, to the heart: a single bead of bright blood stood out on the jay's breast like a ruby.

Danny safed his weapon and laid it on the ground, then knelt beside the dead jay, feeling the wet cold earth soaking through the knees of his jeans. The limp bird's exquisite feathers were undamaged, as fine as anything he had ever seen, but the blue seemed muted already, as if the color had died as well. He had never killed anything before, and it was not what he had imagined it would be. His nerves were electric with horror, and his stomach seized abruptly into a queasy ball of dismay and heaved. The bitter acid of the vomit in his mouth was strangely satisfying, the first taste of an unimaginable penance; and when he had finished throwing up, as the twilight settled in the woods, Danny sat beside the dead bird on the boggy ground and began to sob in shame.

CHAPTER 10

OCTOBER 1967

MIKE WOKE FROM a dream about Liz; she'd been running her hands through his hair. He loved his wife's hands, an actress's hands, elegant and expressive and eternally surprising. He could still remember slipping the wedding ring onto her slim tanned finger, the way the gold band transformed the wild bird of her hand into something infinitely richer, something still untamed but grounded, rooted and sacred, a precious trust that asked everything of him. He'd been so proud to be associated with a hand like that.

In the dream, there had been some kind of complication, duty had called, and Liz had gone somewhere to put on a play, something Greek, or maybe he had, and somehow by the dream's end the Parris Island barber was there, wielding his buzzing electric razor gleefully, handing Mike his sideburns in a little black heap.

The bunker was pitch-black. Mike could hear Ed Perrone snoring across the dirt floor and, in the lulls, Doug Parker's quieter breathing with its distinctive nasal whistle. Sometimes one of them woke up screaming. That was always unnerving, but it happened to almost everyone and no one made a big deal out of it. It was understood that you didn't talk about it in the morning. But tonight everyone had slept straight through.

By the green glow of Mike's watch, the twin of the one he'd given Danny, it was 0343. He hadn't bothered to set an alarm; his body's internal clock was infallible in a combat zone. He'd been up past midnight the night before, planning the mission out and then getting his personal battle gear in order, recleaning the M-16 he wasn't even supposed to be carrying, taping together ammo clips for easy changes after emptying one, finding some dry socks. Tucking the AK-47 round into his helmet band, per the Marine superstition that that was the bullet that wouldn't kill you; and making sure Larry Petroski's moldy rabbit's foot was at the bottom of his map pocket.

And, in case superstition didn't work, checking his *hasta la vista*, the good-bye letter for Liz he always left under the Lincoln Memorial paperweight, a honeymoon souvenir, on the crate beside his cot. He'd added a few lines to the letter the night before by candlelight, just tender stuff. The thing got longer before every mission and was turning into a mushy mess.

Mike lit the candle on the cot-side crate and swung his feet onto the bunker's cool dirt floor, hearing the rats scurry away in the darkness. He was already dressed in his combat dungarees, and his boots were right where he had left them, beside the M-16 under the cot, laces loose, ready to go on. He'd been using his flak jacket for a pillow. As the other officers stirred and started rousing themselves, Mike poured half an inch of water into his helmet, soaped his face, and scraped the dull razor through his stubble briskly, a ritual on battle days. It was too late to die young and leave a pretty corpse, but if he died before his five o'clock shadow came in by early afternoon, he could at least leave a clean-shaven one. Liz hated that three-day beard look.

He wiped his face and dumped the soapy water, wiped the helmet semidry with his shirttail, and put it on his head again. Parker and Perrone were good to go now, and the three men walked together through the thick wet blackness to the mess hall without a word.

Inside, the place was brightly lit and already starting to hum. Isaiah Tibbetts was sitting at a table by himself; most of the enlisted men in the company were too intimidated by the master sergeant to eat with him. Lieutenants Perrone and Parker, who were also too intimidated to eat with him, hurried by to get their own meals. Mike stopped and sat down.

"Morning, Skipper," Tibbetts said.

"Morning, Top. What the hell is that you're eating there?"

The sergeant grinned. "Steak and eggs, sir."

"Steak and fucking eggs," Mike marveled.

"Guess they think we're gonna get our asses handed to us today."

"Fattening us up for the slaughter," Mike agreed. He stood up. "Well, ours but to do and die. No sense wasting a good steak."

Tibbetts liberated another slab of meat with his K-bar, stabbed it with the knife point, and conveyed it to his mouth. "My sentiments exactly, sir."

"Save my spot, Top."

"Aye, aye, Skip. Ain't exactly no crowd forming here, though."

Mike gave him a wink. "It's lonely at the top, Ike."

Tibbetts laughed and devoted himself once more to savaging his steak. Mike moved toward the serving line.

More men were streaming into the mess hall now, all of them exclaiming over the unprecedented menu. Near the head of the line, planted attentively like a maître d', was the company supply sergeant, Bruno Bentano, who looked very pleased with himself.

"Sergeant Bentano, what is all this goddamned steak doing, going to waste in a line company's mess hall?" Mike demanded.

Bentano smiled smugly, ran a hand over his slicked-back hair, well past regulation length, and bounced a bit on the balls of his feet. He was a natural hustler from somewhere in Jersey who had chosen the Marine Corps over doing time for grand theft auto, and his exploits in the service of acquiring goods and luxuries for the company were the stuff of legend. But he had outdone himself today, and he knew it.

"Must have been a misdirected shipment, sir," he said modestly. "Probably supposed to end up at the Phu Bai Officers' Mess or something."

"Mistakes do get made in wartime, I suppose," Mike allowed.

"Sad but true, sir."

"Nice job, Sergeant."

"Thank you, sir."

When Mike got back to Tibbetts's table, Bill Savard, the company's Forward Air Controller, had joined the sergeant. Mike liked Savard, a grounded pilot who had an almost magical rapport with the Marine aviators and could often get the fast-movers to come in at treetop level for strikes that the Air Force pilots wouldn't touch from an altitude of a thousand feet. Savard's call sign had been "Billygoat," which probably explained a lot; scuttlebutt had it that he had broken his squadron CO's nose and accepted the infantry liaison position and a loss of grade rather than the brig.

"Good morning, Lieutenant," Mike said as he sat down.

"Morning, sir."

"Enjoying your breakfast?"

"Yes, sir. Primo stuff. I haven't had steak and eggs since I got grounded."

"It means they think we're going to die," Tibbetts informed him, past a mouthful of hash browns.

Savard glanced uneasily at Mike. "Really?"

"Pretty much," Mike conceded.

The FAC was silent for a moment.

"Well, shit," he said at last. "In that case, I'm sending this back and asking for medium rare."

KATHIE'S BLUEBIRD UNIFORM lay half finished beneath the frozen needle of the sewing machine, literally in midseam. Liz turned on the Singer and sat before it for a moment listening to its efficient little hum. It was time to either finish the outfit or acknowledge that the whole Bluebird thing wasn't going to happen. She had been putting off the inevitable crisis from week to week, finding reasons to delay actually getting Kathie signed up, but Kathie had been increasingly ardent lately. She and Temperance still believed they would be the belles of Bluebird Troop 232. They had reached the point where telling Kathie they were out of blue thread wasn't going to cut it.

Liz ran through a few desultory stitches, but her heart wasn't in it, and at last she turned the sewing machine off and crossed to the telephone. She knew the Williams' home number better than her own; she and Linnell talked several times a day, coordinating Kathie and Temperance's relentless sisterhood.

The phone rang six times, but Liz waited patiently, knowing that Linnell Williams was home from work by now and probably changing a diaper or something.

"Hello?" Temperance's mother said at last, sounding somewhat breathless.

"Hi, Linnell, it's me."

"Oh, hey, Miz O'Reilly. How are you today?"

"Fine, thank you." Liz had long since given up on trying to get Temperance's mother to call her Liz, but that "Miz O'Reilly" still felt like a defeat every time. "And you?"

"God help me, honey. DeeJay has figured out climbin'—"

"Uh-oh."

"But he ain't figured out gettin' down, except by landin' on his head."

"I remember when Danny got to that stage. He'd get halfway up the bookshelf and just hang there, pulling things off the shelves."

"Maybe he could teach DeeJay some of that hanging, 'cause that little boy's head ain't gonna hold up. I can't keep him on the ground, I swear. I turn my back for a second, and next thing I know I hear the *clunk*. Half the time he's just sitting there laughin', ready to start up again."

"Thank God they're so durable." Liz hesitated. "Listen, Linnell, there was something I wanted to talk about—"

"Oh, I know, honey. I *told* Temperance she had to give Kathie's lunch box back to her. But you know those girls—"

"No, no, it's not about the lunch box, that's just sweet. Kathie gave it to her and that's that. She already made me buy another one exactly like it so they'd be lunch box twins. No, it's this Bluebird thing."

There was a cool silence before Linnell Williams said, "I thought we were done with talking about that."

"You and I were, maybe. But Kathie and Temperance still think they're joining together."

Linnell was silent again, and Liz thought she understood the woman's dilemma. No mother wanted to tell her daughter something couldn't happen because of the color of her skin. Liz herself had been hard-pressed to explain the delay in the Bluebird registration to Kathie without invoking race and had taken refuge in her deficient sewing skills. But you could only delay the inevitable so long by pleading poor time management.

The silence on the other end of the phone showed no sign of relenting. Liz offered, awkwardly, "Linnell, maybe it's really not that big a deal. I'm sure if we just show up, if we just give everyone a chance, everything will—"

"Just show *up*."

"Well, I mean—"

"I know what you mean. You mean well. You think that's enough. But the thing is, honey, Temperance is a little girl, she ain't no battering ram. It's all fine for you, get on your high horse, do the good thing. We gonna change the bad bad world. But it's my little girl who gonna come home cryin' when those white girls call her 'nigger.' "

"I wouldn't let that happen."

"How you gonna stop it? You gonna get some of them whatchacallits, them National Guard troops from Alabama, with their rifles and helmets? Just walk my little girl up the sidewalk between 'em, make the news shows, let everybody see what a fine progressive white lady you are? I seen the looks on those children's faces on the TV, sitting on them buses lookin' out the windows. I don't want my girl lookin' like that."

"Then we've got to figure out what to tell the girls, because they aren't taking no for an answer, and I can't keep telling Kathie it's because I can't get her damned dress finished. She's already gone out with some of her own money and bought me more blue thread."

"That ain't my problem. All I gotta do is tell Temperance it ain't gonna happen."

"Well, you haven't done that yet, have you?" Liz said pointedly. Temperance, she knew, had been told that the main reason she couldn't join was the time lost for schoolwork, but Temperance and Kathie had responded to this by getting Danny to help them with their math homework, and both girls' grades had climbed from something near D to solid Bs. Money had also been invoked, but Temperance and Kathie now spent most of their afternoons combing the ditch along Little Neck Road for discarded bottles; cashing them in at two cents apiece, they had a working Bluebird fund of $21.85 at last report. They had drawn up a little chart, complete with a target sum, and were coloring in the rising column of money raised in red crayon. Liz would personally rather have had them rob a bank than spend so much time tempting fate near traffic, but she couldn't see any way to stop them short of offering to pay the fees and expenses herself. Which is what she wanted to do anyway. But here they were.

Liz realized that the silence on the phone had changed to a dull hum. Apparently she'd hit a nerve; Linnell Williams had hung up on her.

She thought about calling back and decided they'd probably both had enough for the moment. Instead, she went out to the car, checked both ways for incoming green sedans as she pulled out of the driveway, and drove to the church to light candles. It was something she'd taken to doing lately, and it worried her; her prayer, such as it was, seemed mostly to involve a concession of complete defeat.

OUTSIDE THE MESS HALL, the drizzle had turned into a hard rain. The company formed in the dark beside the trucks with a minimum of fuss, and the platoon sergeants moved through the ranks, more attentive than usual to checking the company roster. You didn't want to spend time later looking for the body of someone who hadn't shown up in the first place.

The sergeants gave the orders, and the platoons moved toward their trucks. As the men stood quietly waiting to board, the rain drumming audibly on their ponchos, someone in the depths of the Second Platoon began to sing.

> *Oh, my name is McNamara, I'm the builder of the Line,*
> *The grandest project in the land, a notion just divine—*

Other men took up the song, a low swelling.

> *A barrier impregnable, to seal the DMZ,*
> *And all I need to make it work is a thousand dead*
> *Marines!*

The song spread along the convoy as the men continued to clamber aboard the trucks one by one. Ike Tibbetts, the platoon's First Sergeant, gave Mike a questioning glance, and Mike shrugged: Let it go for now. The SecDef's ill-conceived scheme for a Maginot Line along the Demilitarized Zone was no more popular with the troops than it was with the officers, and he hated to quash the essentially healthy gallows humor and defiant spirit of these combat Marines; but there was a fine line between robust cynicism and demoralizing resentment, and he didn't want things to go too far.

> *Oh, the cannons boom and the wire's strung and the*
> *mine fields lie in wait;*
> *From Khe Sanh down to old Gio Linh we all await our*
> *fate:*
> *We're sitting ducks for every gun that Charlie brings on*
> *line:*
> *We're target practice dummies building McNamara's*
> *Line!*

The trucks were loaded now. Dermott Edmonds, whose Third Platoon was in the lead trucks, trotted up and said, "Good to go, Skipper."

"Let's roll, then," Mike said. Edmonds turned and hurried back up to the head of the convoy. As another verse of the song began, Mike told Ike Tibbetts, reluctantly, "Time to belay that shit, Top," and the sergeant roared, "*Company, shut UP! The singing light is OUT!*"

The singing ceased at once. In the silence, the lead truck's engine could be heard starting up, and the noise rippled along the convoy truck by truck as the big motors roared to life. By the time the last truck's engine had started, the lead truck was moving. Mike looked around one last time, like the conductor on the platform of a departing train; but you couldn't see shit in the rain and darkness, and there was nothing more he could do anyway; and finally he stepped up into the middle truck and settled in among his radio operators for the rough ride west and north.

THE PARKING LOT at St. Jude's was empty; no afternoon rosary group today, thank God, cranking out industrial-strength Hail Marys. Liz slipped in the side door, moving gingerly, self-conscious in the church's daunting silence; every noise she made seemed amplified by the emptiness into a kind of sin. The afternoon light through the stained-glass windows had a watery, chastened feel, suffusing the cool stillness with aquamarine and the deeper blues. She wet her fingers in the last drops of holy water in the shallow marble font, genuflected to the altar, and crossed to the doe-eyed Virgin in her arched stone niche in the west wall. Someone had left a fragrant sprig of Carolina jasmine at the statue's feet. Half a dozen candles flickered in the rack, old prayers, red and lonely in their crimson cups.

Liz knelt and tried to summon an appropriate emotion. Humility, maybe. Gratitude for God's unwavering goodness. Faith, and brotherly love. Compassion, a breadth of sympathy for the suffering world. But all she really wanted was for her husband not to be killed or maimed, for her children not to lose their father, for Maria not to eat her elephant dose of sedatives. For Kathie and Temperance to enjoy being little girls without having to reorganize society in the fleeting moments between their after-school play and their bedtime. For her baby to be born with ten fingers and ten toes. Pure personal greed, specific and local.

C'est la vie, Liz thought. Ask and ye shall receive; knock, and it shall be opened unto you. That was the promise. That was what she was here for. She closed her eyes. Help, God; please help. Help me, the helpless one. Help those I love, as I cannot.

CHAPTER 11

OCTOBER 1967

*A*ND THOU, *son of man, be not afraid of them . . .*

Zeke Germaine slipped into St. Jude's as he always did, like a rabbit testing the fringes of a grassy clearing, scanning the sky for hawks. It was an ugly thing, it amounted to an ongoing mortal sin, for a priest to dread his congregation so. But his first prayer was always that the church would be empty.

. . . neither be afraid of their words, though briars and thorns be with thee, and thou dost dwell among scorpions.

He could tell at once that someone else was there. The quality of silence was different. It took him a while to locate the lone woman kneeling at the shrine of the Virgin Mary, her head bowed. Germaine hesitated in the shadow of a pillar, tempted to just cut his losses and withdraw, but the woman seemed immersed enough in her prayer for the moment. If routine ruled, the minute he closed his own eyes, she would be tapping him on the shoulder and asking something about the bake sale.

And thou shalt speak My words unto them, whether they will hear, or whether they will forebear . . .

She truly did seem absorbed. Germaine stood for a long moment, feeling the quiet deepening again, in spite of himself, the silence opening like an emerald meadow in the sunlight, irresistibly; and finally he slipped into the back pew, eased the kneeler to the floor, and knelt, wincing at the bite of the shrapnel in his knee, the metal grinding on the bone. He crossed himself and closed his eyes, surrendered to what came.

But thou, son of man, hearing what I say unto thee: Be not rebellious like that rebellious house; but open thy mouth and eat what I give thee.

He breathed, slowing his respiration consciously at first, and then letting his breath be, letting the prayer be all he knew; he let go of everything, and sank into the peace that lay beneath it all. And into the dangerous lucidity: the country of prayer was so like the jungle, a still, vast realm of luminous green, the light uncannily placid beneath the triple canopy of vegetation, the silence steeped with the nearness of death and rent with the cries of strange birds and monkeys, that Germaine was never surprised to find himself beside the river again, with the dying Marine in his arms.

He couldn't even remember how they'd ended up in that shell crater on the muddy bank. He wasn't supposed to have been in the field at all that day, had clambered into the chopper at the last minute, almost on a whim, and the company's sergeant had laughed as he gave him his zip number, the tag that would identify him should he become a casualty, saying, "Padre, bring a gun this time." The combat Marines always treated him with rough affection and a certain maddening protectiveness, like a pet, like the company mascot. Before a mission they would turn gruff and sober for a moment and urge him to "Pray good," to use his supposed in with God, but that was more superstition than anything else, like rubbing a rabbit's foot or smacking a hockey goalie's pads before the game. Germaine knew that no one really took him seriously until they were hit. He often felt like Gunga Din among the troops, scorned and despised until the bullets began to fly. It was a point of what he knew to be unseemly pride.

> But if it comes to slaughter
> You will do your work on water,
> An' you'll lick the bloomin' boots of 'im that's got it.

They'd stumbled into a bunker complex that day and been pinned down for hours by a flesh-savaging cross fire, the enemy machine guns clipping off everything that stuck up more than eight inches from the ground. Late that afternoon, they'd been hit from the flank and driven toward the water, where they'd regrouped as twilight fell and made a stand.

Germaine hadn't registered many of the tactical details. He just ran when everyone ran and ducked when they ducked and did what he always did in combat—

> If we charged or broke or cut,
> You could bet your bloomin' nut,
> 'E'd be waitin' fifty paces right flank rear

—shadowing the corpsmen, making his way to the wounded, the dying, and the dead. He was already hit by that time: a bullet had creased his forehead and nipped his ear, which was bleeding inordinately, and a mortar round had made something like raw hamburger of his right leg. But all of them were bleeding one way or another by then, and Germaine was barely conscious of his shredded limb except as a hindrance to his movement.

He was terrified but strangely calm, as he often was under intense fire. Combat was the world, and he was in the world but not of it. There was even an exhilaration to the experience; he'd never felt so free, so true and so real. The blazing adrenaline made him simple as a flame, all radiance and quiet heat, a lit place where everything was clear and all he could see, in perfect focus, was the next man in front of him in need of care and comfort. He didn't think much about dying himself. Death came, in such a place, or it didn't. That was in God's hands.

The battle had been chaotic and their position desperate. Germaine had never seen Marines put bayonets on their rifles before, and he didn't register what that grim action meant until, as darkness fell, their ammo began to run out and the hand-thrown grenades fell among them and the open space between the river and the trees erupted into spectral shapes, a surge of shadows, the muzzle flashes of the AK-47s braiding the night with flickering necklaces of savage light. As the North Vietnamese reached the foxholes, the Marines leaped to meet them, and in the darkness Germaine could hear the unspeakable sound of blade meeting body, of rifle butt crashing into bone and flesh.

They'd been overrun twice, the hand-to-hand fighting ratcheting back and forth by terrible degrees. At one point a flare sizzled upward and burst into uncanny illumination, revealing a circle of hell more vivid than any imagined by Dante or Bosch, dozens of men beyond all but the most naked ferocity, grappling ferally.

And then the flare expired and the nightmare vision subsided once more into a rage and flux of desperate shadows, anonymous flashes and explosions, the sickening impact of unidentifiable woundings, and the screams.

Germaine had no recollection of how he'd tumbled—or plunged, or been shoved—into the shell crater. The battle had caught him up as a tornado would and whirled him until he knew nothing and finally flung him like debris into the arms of the wounded Marine.

The kid was shot through the abdomen. A teenager, thin and pale, his hollowed cheeks smeared with mud in an attempt at camouflage. His lips were moving, and Germaine recognized the rhythm of the "Our Father" and murmured his own prayer with the boy's. He did what he could, stuffing the kid's wounds with all that remained of his battle dressings and using up the kid's morphine, and then the last of his own.

The battle had moved on by then, a fitful, impersonal fireworks show now a few hundred meters to the south. As Germaine's night vision cleared, he became aware of figures moving quietly and methodically in the darkness around them: NVA with bayonets, finishing off the American wounded.

So that was how it would be, he thought. He realized how desperately he wanted to live, how unreconciled he was to dying here. *My God, if it be Your will, take this cup away from me.* So much for faith, the life surrendered wholly to God's work, the priestly Gunga Din bringing the water of life to those in desperate need. That all ran dry in the last moment, it turned to dust. He'd been offering phony comfort all along, and congratulating himself for the generosity of counterfeit gifts.

One of the dark figures approached. Germaine shifted his body, trying to shield the wounded Marine, but the North Vietnamese plunged his bayonet through the flesh of Germaine's shoulder into the young man's chest, brusquely, workmanlike. It took him a moment to work the blade free, but he yanked it clear at last, and it was Germaine's turn.

Thy will, not mine, be done.

Germaine was conscious suddenly of the stars, of the river's quiet murmur, of the fleshy weight of blood in the night air, and the tang of cordite, and of the warmth, the intimacy of the dying Marine beside him. Of the weird, deep beauty of it all, the way it touched a heart so easily stopped. It wasn't faith, he realized, nor hope; it was just the reality of an utterly superfluous and extravagant love. This peace had been here all along, occluded by everything he'd thought he was accomplishing, shut out by all the nonsense of what he'd believed he knew of God and life and service, of meaning and of truth.

An airburst somewhere to the south lit them for an instant, and Germaine saw the soldier's eyes register Germaine's collar and the cross on his armband. The Vietnamese stopped himself, then pulled his rifle back and shook his head at Germaine, almost playfully. He crossed himself, whether out of mockery or actual reverence, Germaine could not tell; then he waved a finger at the priest, in admonishment or benediction, turned, and moved away to continue with his brutal work.

In Germaine's arms, the young Marine's chest gurgled around the fresh bayonet wound. The kid's eyes were wide and pleading, baffled by the puzzlement that breathing had become. Germaine reached for the boy's hand and held it, wincing at his own slashed arm; there was nothing else he could do. He was beyond prayer. They lay together like that through the night, until the Marine was gone.

It was strange by then to hear no labored breathing; it was easy for Germaine to imagine that his own breath had ceased as well, and to feel the liberation in that quieting. As the heat of the expired life seeped into the bloody mud and the body stiffened in his arms, Germaine let his own pain settle into the stillness and listened to the river, watching the stars creep across the sky. Beyond prayer. Beyond, quite beyond, utterly beyond.

When he finally disentangled his own hand, the boy's arm remained upright, the fingers curled in their final gesture. And still Germaine held him, their bodies laced together, their blood commingled, and when the remnants of the demolished company returned near dawn the next day, as he had known they would—the Marines never left their dead behind—they found the two of them entwined like brothers in a grave and were startled by the frozen supplication of the dead man's hand under the flicker of a fading star.

LIZ CAME BACK to herself with a sense of almost unbearable poignancy, as if waking unwillingly from a dream so sweet and ethereal that daylight hurt. The silence of the church was like the atmosphere of a different planet, thick with the unfamiliar substance of alien air. She'd really lost track of time. She wondered if that was what happened to saints. They lost track of time and never quite found their way back, and the world turned as strange and holy to them all the time as it felt to her right now.

The candle she had lit for Mike flickered in its red cup. Liz was relieved to see that the church was still deserted; she felt naked and undone and needed time to ease back into being Mrs. Michael O'Reilly. She crossed herself and rose, feeling her knees creak, and would have passed before the altar again and left by the side door. But she realized suddenly that she was not alone after all. It took a moment to spot the single figure kneeling in the far back pew. The man was completely absorbed in his prayer; she had sensed him less because of the buzz of another presence in the church than than through the absence of the usual buzz, as if the quiet of St. Jude's intensified where he knelt.

It was Germaine, looking at home in his ill-fitting medieval black for the first time since she had known him. Liz stood uncertainly for a moment. It would have been easy enough to just slip out, but she found that she didn't want to. She even realized, with some chagrin, that she had been half hoping all along to find the priest at St. Jude's.

As she stood there, Germaine's eyes opened and met hers. Liz felt the shock of their gazes meeting in the hush and understood that he was as she had been, emerging from prayer, undone and naked. As she still was, apparently, because she felt none of the usual anxiety at holding someone's gaze.

After a moment that was much too long, Germaine stood up and moved toward her, limping more than she had seen him limp before. He smiled as he approached, in gentle recognition. It all felt frighteningly right and easy, as if they had arranged this in advance. But they hadn't, Liz assured herself. It was all on the up-and-up. Parishioner and priest, crossing paths by chance at church. A pastoral exchange.

"Hello," he said.

No "Mrs. O'Reilly," Liz noted. The greeting seemed thrillingly intimate, stripped of the formalities, and she answered, brightly, "Hello, Father Germaine," because anything else would have been way too much.

MIKE CALLED IN fixed-wing air strikes on Hill 93, and it was beautiful. The Marine F-4s coaxed in just above the treetops dropped "snake eyes" first, two-hundred-fifty-pound bombs of fiendish accuracy, winged with special tail fins that slowed their fall and gave the bombs themselves an oddly lyrical soaring quality in the air, like fat flying fish. The explosions blossomed upward, squat mushrooms of orange and black, showering dirt over Hotel Company in their positions at the base of the hill.

While the debris was still settling, the next wave of Phantoms roared in and loosed waves of napalm, and the air turned eerily cool for an instant and stank of gasoline before the hillside was swamped beneath a terrible tide of flame. Glancing up, ill-advisedly, Mike felt his eyebrows sear and his face scorched tender with the heat. A glimpse into the heart of hell, he thought, awed. And also, succinctly: Good. Better them than us.

He was on the radio before the flames stopped crackling, sending Dermott Edmonds's Third Platoon up the hill, charging them literally into the fire. The apocalyptic completeness of the air strikes was illusory, Mike knew. It was a truth close to the heart of this war: all the technological superiority and firepower in the world couldn't eradicate that final moment of naked human necessity when determined men with guns fought other determined men with guns for whatever piece of scorched earth was up for grabs, for whatever reasons had brought them there, and the most determined won.

"Hey diddle diddle, straight up the middle," Edmonds said before he took off. Too cocky, compensating with Basic School macho.

"Godspeed, Dermott," Mike told him, and thought, God help us all. It was way too late to fine-tune the young lieutenant's attitude. It was one of those sobering moments when Mike was painfully aware that he was playing God on the local level. He was sending Edmonds, his shakiest platoon leader, into the teeth of whatever the NVA had left to shoot because the Third was his best platoon and they needed this hill, and some of Edmonds's men were almost certainly going to die.

LIZ AND FATHER GERMAINE left the church together, pausing self-consciously on either side of the font to dip their fingers into the holy water and cross themselves before slipping out the door. The Indian summer sunlight and the brisk normality of the traffic on Little Neck Road came as a small shock; Liz felt as if she were emerging from a matinee double feature to the surprise of the world still solid in uninterrupted dailiness. She was conscious of the hush lingering even now from her prayer, of silence sifting from her like the fragrance of incense from clothing steeped with holy smoke.

They stood uncertainly for a moment on the step.

"Buy you a drink?" Germaine suggested, and it took Liz an unnerving instant to realize he was kidding. It was like him, she already understood, to both name the moment's dangerous dynamic and somehow to make it seem manageable through the suggestion that it was absurd. She wanted so much to talk, but she had no idea how to even begin. If they were to talk as she wanted to talk now, to carry the live egg of this extraordinary silence into the coarse country of words, she needed Germaine to be something more than merely a standard-issue priest. If he said something banal and reassuring about God right now, she might begin to scream. But she did not want to see him as a man, with all the hazards of that.

"It's a little early for cocktails," she said. "But it would be nice to sit and chat a bit."

Germaine glanced left and right, hesitated, then made his decision and nodded to her to follow. Liz had a sense that he'd had a spot in mind all along. They crossed the entry plaza, slipped between a pair of bedraggled camellias onto ground deep in spent flowers, and turned the corner of the building into the torn-up area beside the gap in the wall where the new stained-glass window was being installed.

Like two kids sneaking off to smoke, Liz thought uneasily. Or, God forbid, to make out. Leaving the sidewalk with Germaine felt a little outrageous. Standing in front of the church beneath the doleful statue of Jude, patron saint of hopeless causes, she was obviously a parishioner talking to her priest, even on a weekday afternoon. Crossing the churned dirt to sit together in the shade of the construction site, things got less clear-cut. Liz wanted nothing of what lonely men and women so easily blundered into; she'd seen enough as a military wife to know how quickly it happened. She didn't know what she wanted here, really. She had never spoken to anyone of her soul.

Germaine took out his handkerchief and, with a show of gallantry, dusted off the top of a pile of cinder blocks then bowed broadly, offering her a seat.

"I have a confession," Liz said preemptively, as they settled on the blocks.

"Ah."

"Seriously."

Germaine was silent a moment. She wondered if he was disappointed, if after all he had his hopes for something else. But then he reached into the inner pocket of his ridiculous jacket and drew out a white linen scarf with crosses embroidered at both ends. He kissed it, then draped it around his neck.

His priestly stole, Liz realized. She hadn't meant things quite so literally, but he'd taken her at her word. She couldn't help but notice the rusty stains on the vestment. Old blood. It must be the one he had used in Vietnam. She wondered whether there was some kind of weird canonical proscription against cleaning these things, then decided no, it just meant something to Germaine that way.

The priest was looking at her quietly, and Liz could feel the different quality of his attention. Waiting, simply.

"This counts?" she said. "I mean, you can just do it here, just like that?"

"Sure."

"Wow. Well, okay, then . . ." Liz hesitated, wondering what she'd gotten herself into. Maybe it would have been easier if he'd just made a pass at her. She gathered herself, made the sign of the cross, and said, "Bless me, Father, for I have sinned. It's been—Jesus, how long *has* it been?—call it a year or two, since my last confession, and these are my sins. . . ."

She trailed off, not certain where she was really going with all this. Germaine waited patiently. Liz realized she'd expected something different from him, some sort of wink at the process, but he was placid and steady and quite serious. A priest, who needed a shave.

"I'm afraid I'm a lousy wife," she blurted at last. "I'm afraid I'm a lousy mother."

Germaine smiled. "It's not a sin to be afraid."

"I'm afraid I'm a lousy human being."

He shrugged.

"*Seriously,*" she said.

"Lousy human beings are the state of the art. That's sort of the point, actually."

"Not like this. I'm appalling. My husband's off fighting a noble war I really couldn't care less if we won or lost. He's been training his whole adult life for this, and he's happy as a pig in shit. And I could just kill him. I'm in there praying for him to just dodge the god-damned bullet of history and get himself back in one piece, and part of me is just completely pissed off at him, and I'm thinking, Honey, you idiot, what are you *doing?* Come home, for Christ's sake. Be a father to your children. Fight the goddamned North Vietnamese when they land in North Carolina. And meanwhile here I am just running around in my station wagon. I'm nothing, I'm a cipher. I can't even fight racism in the local Bluebird troop. At least Mike's willing to die for something. I can't even *live* for something."

Germaine said nothing.

"Look, are we going to do this or not?" Liz demanded. "I'm a sinner, goddammit. I'm pouring out my heart here. Say something priestly. Peer into my soul. Give me a bone-breaking penance or something. Consign me to hell. Invoke higher powers. I don't know."

"I'm afraid you're going to have to be a little more specific. I haven't heard anything yet that can't be addressed with a long hot bath, some brandy, and chocolate." Germaine hesitated, then said, "I'm not sure this is what you wanted to talk about anyway."

Liz startled herself by beginning to cry. Germaine amazed her further by doing nothing. Any other man she knew would have panicked and tried to talk her down. Tears were way too scary, way too real. But he just sat there quietly. It was disorienting.

They sat side by side as she sobbed. When the wave had passed, Liz snuffled and said, "Christ, I'm a wreck." She rummaged in her bag, looking for a Kleenex.

Germaine offered her one end of his stole. The nonbloody end, she noted. What delicacy. She looked at him, saw that he was at least half serious, and laughed.

"God help me," she said. "I'm sorry. I don't know what the hell I wanted to talk about."

"That's no sin either," Germaine said.

CHAPTER 12

OCTOBER 1967

MIKE SAT BESIDE Dermott Edmonds on the truck ride back to Dong Ha. Every jounce on the rutted road hurt; Mike's rib cage was turning purple and green from a round that had slammed into his flak jacket, and he'd strained something badly in his right arm, throwing a grenade. So much for his major league pitching career. But Edmonds, who didn't have a mark on him, was in even worse shape. The young lieutenant had lost eleven men killed and fourteen wounded, almost half his platoon, because he'd walked into an ambush with his eyes wide open. He'd screwed up royally and he knew it, and he was sunk back into himself now like a collapsed cake.

Mike didn't rub it in; he just sat quietly beside Edmonds and offered what comfort companionship could provide, a stick of stale gum, and a swig from his canteen. There would be time later to go over the young lieutenant's mistakes with him, starting with the obvious, that "Hey diddle diddle, straight up the middle" was not the best approach to bunkered machine gun positions. Meanwhile, when they got back to base, the kid had eleven letters to write, informing eleven families that their loved ones had died under his command. That was penance enough for anyone.

At some point after the convoy made the turn onto the relative security of Highway 9 east of Cam Lo, someone in one of the trucks behind Mike's started singing.

> Oh, we lug our guns and ammo, from dawn to bloody
> dawn,
> But they tell us not to fire, unless we're fired on.
> It's a crazy way to fight a war but a wonderful way to die:
> We always let them shoot us first on McNamara's Line!

Isaiah Tibbetts had already sucked up a lungful of air, to shout a quashing command, but Mike stopped him. It wasn't like noise discipline was an issue, grinding along the most obvious road in the region in half a dozen vehicles that sounded like dinosaurs in heat. The men, he thought, had earned their black commentary.

More to the point, Mike realized that he just didn't give a damn tonight. His men had bled and died for a piece of ground and then been ordered to leave it to the enemy again before the sun went down on the battlefield. All Mike could see in his mind's eye was one of his PFCs, a kid named Hamilton, going down, and the look on Hamilton's buddy's face as he lingered over his dying friend with the bullets zinging past; and he could see the bodies of the men in Edmonds's platoon littering the hillside in front of the bunkers. He could see the fresh-faced corpse of one of his young PFCs, still clutching the jammed M-16 he'd died trying to shoot.

Good men pissed away, in Mike's mind. In a real war, you fought for ground, you took ground, and you held ground. In a real war, they'd have taken Hill 93 and used it to move toward the next hill to the north and taken that in turn, and then the next hill, and the next, until they took Hanoi and the goddamned war was over and the bad guys had lost. But this wasn't quite a real war, it seemed. The dead were real enough, though.

And so they rode home in the darkness, Charlie's darkness, the darkness they gave back at the end of every day, and Hotel Company sang.

> *Oh, you'll find us walking proudly in our uniforms of*
> *green,*
> *The finest men you'll ever know, United States Marines.*
> *We're here to serve our country, we're noble and sublime,*
> *So what the fuck are we doing, building McNamara's*
> *Line?*

BY THE TIME Liz got back from the church that afternoon, the kids had already come home from school, made snacks for themselves, and gotten on with their business. Danny and Angus were patrolling along the shore of the lake and preparing to repel an amphibious assault by undetermined forces; Deb-Deb was swimming, round and round the downstairs, out of the dining room, where she had built her otter's lodge beneath the table, and into the entryway, back up the hall through the family room, and past the kitchen into the dining room again, with various snacks and objects she had gathered along the way, which she deposited in her nest. Kathie and Temperance were in the garage, sorting and counting their latest haul of empty bottles, which meant a run to the grocery store later to cash their collection in. Everyone seemed perfectly content. Liz decided to leave well enough alone and went upstairs to her bedroom, where she lay down and looked for a while at the ceiling fan spinning lazily above her.

She felt wonderful, she realized, despite the relative incoherence of her confession to Germaine and the absurdity of the penance he had assigned: a good Act of Contrition, three Hail Marys and an Our

Father, and a long hot bath. Liz wondered how binding the bath decree was. She would rather he had told her to wear a hair shirt, on the whole.

She got the prayers said, but it was too early to climb into the tub. If she ran a bath now she'd be a sodden happy heap, useless for the nightly homework and bedtime battles. Still, she actually had time on her hands, a rare condition. No one was crying, no one was hurt, no one seemed in immediate danger. Dinner was pretty much set—an unambitious tuna casserole, one of the rare foods all the kids would eat. It was too early to start fighting about schoolwork or what TV programs would be allowed.

And so Liz just lay quietly for a time, in a state she recognized only with difficulty as peace of mind. She could feel the weight of the baby in her womb, unexpectedly, as warmth, as an intimate, vibrant pulse. She had been conscious, at the church, of not mentioning her pregnancy to Germaine; the omission had seemed dishonest at the time, more evidence of her iniquity; but she realized now that she had not confessed to the complexities of the child forming inside her because, when it had come down to it, reduced to the desperation of truth, she really hadn't felt that her condition was a sin. Not the life in her, and not the tortuous course of her coming to peace with that life.

Outside the window, the clouds were bathed in quiet gold and rose. Liz lay still until the sky had settled into indigo, then got up, moving gently, savoring the sense that her center of gravity had shifted. She crossed to the sewing machine, turned on the lamp, and sat down to finish Kathie's Bluebird uniform and to begin sewing Temperance's. She had no idea what she was going to tell Linnell Washington, but there would be time for that. All she knew was that she couldn't tell her daughter she wasn't letting her do something with her friend because her friend was black. If all these sacrifices meant anything, if Daddy's war meant anything, if her own life meant anything, they were fighting for that.

PART FOUR

And the threat of what is called hell is little or nothing to me;
And the lure of what is called heaven is little or nothing to me;
Dear camerado! I confess I have urged you onward with me, and still
urge you, without the least idea of what is our destination,
Or whether we shall be victorious, or utterly quelled and defeated.

WALT WHITMAN, "LEAVES OF GRASS"

CHAPTER 13

NOVEMBER 1967

from: Capt. M. F. O'Reilly
H Co., 2nd Bn., 29th Marines, 6th Mar Div FMF
c/o FPO San Francisco, Calif. 96602
Tue 7 Nov 1967
Khe Sanh, RVN

My Dearest Lizzie,
   So, here I am in scenic Khe Sanh (pronounced, by the Marines
here at least, like "caisson"), the mountain garden spot of Vietnam.
We're a long fly ball to left field away from the Laotian border here,
and North Vietnam is within easy artillery range, but it's pretty
much off the beaten track and no one seems to give much of a damn
about the place. The soil is a red clay that degrades into the most
clinging, pervading dust you have ever seen. The climate, however,
is marvelous. It seldom goes above 137° (in the shade) during the
day and cools down to a damp, soggy 33° or so at night, except
when it rains.

It must be good for the natives, for they seem to thrive on it. They are not Vietnamese here, but Bru tribesmen, kin to the Meo in Laos. They are a sturdy, robust people, averaging 4'2" in height and weighing at least 70 pounds. They all seem to smoke pipes, which I believe stunts their growth. They carry small but very powerful crossbows, which they use to shoot game, tax collectors, any and all lowlanders, unpleasant neighbors, or anyone else who catches their fancy. They are a sort of Oriental version of Snuffy Smith.

We have settled in here for a while, after our adventures circa Con Thien. Did I mention that "Con Thien" in Vietnamese means "Hill of Angels"? The men all get a kick out of that. I don't believe that's how they think of the place. We took a few too many flunks around that hill last month to think of it as particularly heavenly. The guys have taken to calling the DMZ the Dead Marine Zone. They have also stopped calling me Lucky Mike.

Ah, well, that's life in the Nam. Only place in the world where you can stand up to your knees in mud while dust blows in your eyes. If you don't like the way things are, wait a minute. They'll get worse.

Please forgive my jerky penmanship—Charlie Battery 1/13 is firing a mission. They're not really shooting at anybody, just making noise to keep some idiot happy. TDA: NFI, as they say hereabouts: Target Damage Assessment: No Fucking Idea. It just feels so good to go Boom-Boom-Boom.

They may even be shooting at elephants. Lots of elephants around here—the old emperor of Indochina used to hunt tigers and elephants hereabouts. Also, the Ho Chi Minh Trail runs just west of here, and the gooks use elephants to haul their ammo down from the north. But we have been sternly instructed not to kill any friendly elephants. You can tell the local elephants from the bad-guy elephants by their bellies—the Ho Chi Minh Trail elephants' bellies are all stained red from the clay soil farther north.

Pink elephants. Really. We shoot pink elephants on sight.

There's not much shooting going on here otherwise. Our strategy at Khe Sanh appears to be to let Ho Chi Minh die of old age. Their strategy appears to be to wait for the monsoon to come and hope we sink out of sight. It is conceivable that, if we wait long enough, both outcomes will occur simultaneously. We shoot a few rounds now and then, dig a little bit to improve our position, shoot a few rounds, and so forth. We annoy them, anyway. Sometimes. A few patrols, some recons, up and down the mountains through triple-canopy jungle with wait-a-minute vines grabbing your ankles and rock apes throwing things at you. We fish more than we hunt; we're walking bait, basically. But Charlie ain't biting much lately. Every once in a while, there will be actual fighting elsewhere and they haul us down to Dong Ha with much urgency and throw us on a truck or a chopper, but it's usually over before we get there.

There seems to be something wrong with my lightbulb or with the generator. The light keeps going out. I'm going to secure for the night, before the rats take advantage of the darkness to steal my cot. I love you, my dearest Lizzie. I miss you more than I can possibly say.

> *your loving*
> *Mike*

"MOM, WHAT'S A 'floonk'?" Angus asked, from the kitchen counter.

"I don't know, sweetie," Liz said distractedly. She was in the dining room, rummaging through the accumulation of miscellaneous debris on the table there. In the failure of regular dinners, the big walnut table she had inherited from her mother had come to serve as a staging area for all the neglected paperwork of her life—bank statements dating back to midsummer, birthday cards received and never acknowledged, birthday cards purchased and never sent. She had gotten stuck on the unfiled copy of the final papers on the purchase of their house, which Mike had signed just before leaving for Vietnam. The mortgage agreement made for ironic reading. This beautiful house with the lake out back, her long-awaited dream home, felt like a tent at this point.

"'We took a few too many floonks around that hill last month to think of it as par-part-partick-p-a-r-t-i-c-u-l-a-r-l-y . . .'"

Liz realized that her son, who was supposed to be doing his arithmetic, was reading Mike's latest letter, which she had absentmindedly left on the kitchen counter. She normally took pains to keep her husband's letters out of the children's reach, though she sometimes would read snatches of them aloud to the kids after dinner, taking the opportunity to edit out the sex, violence, and cynicism, which left remarkably little of substance. Mike's laconic "flunks," to characterize his unit's deaths in combat, was not a concept a first-grader should have to come to terms with.

"'Particularly,'" she supplied, setting the mortgage agreement down and moving into the kitchen. "*Particularly* means 'especially' or, uh, 'very.'"

"And 'floonk'?" her son persisted.

Liz took the pages from Angus as calmly as possible and scanned the paragraph in question, thanking God that Angus had not gotten to the sentence about the men calling the DMZ the Dead Marine Zone.

"It's pronounced 'flunk,'" she said, to buy time.

"Like flunking in school?"

"Yes." Liz could feel a bubble of rage forming in her belly, the gaseous fizz of an unreasonable resentment. It wasn't Mike's fault that war was terrible and that the men fighting wars had their cold ways of minimizing that emotionally. But such obscene flippancy was not something she would have imagined possible in the man she had married. And this was not a conversation she had ever wanted to be having with one of her children.

Angus was waiting, his hazel eyes innocent and alert. His math homework still lay before him. Eight minus three equals five. Two plus five equals seven. One flunk equals a failure, and the failures in war are dead.

Liz said, "It's sort of complicated, Angus."

"Uh-huh," Angus said carefully.

Liz could see that he was baffled by her subliminal anger, and suddenly she was tired of it all, tired of having to justify the indefensible ways of men to children, tired of being a good military mother, tired of trying to translate the world's madness, and her country's, and her husband's, into something her sons and daughters could salute.

She took a deep breath, folded the letter, and put it back into its blue and red airmail envelope.

"It's a Marine thing, sweetie," she said. "It's just a Marine thing." And, briskly, before Angus could say anything else, "Are you finished with your arithmetic?"

"Almost."

"What else do you have to do?"

"Reading."

See Dick run. See Dick flunk. See Jane grieve. It seemed to Liz that Angus had already read enough. She said, "Why don't you just take a break for a while and I'll help you finish up later?"

Angus looked startled, and then delighted at this unexpected reprieve. "Can I go watch TV?"

"Yes," Liz said resignedly. So much for Mother of the Year. But letting her son numb his brain with mindless entertainment seemed preferable at the moment to trying to find a way to explain to him that his father's humanity had passed into appalling eclipse.

Angus hopped off his stool and trotted into the family room, clearly intent on getting out of there before she changed her mind. Danny, who invariably finished his homework on the bus home from school, was already watching *Dark Shadows*.

Liz took a couple of deep breaths and returned to the dining room, where she went back to rummaging through the paper piles on the table, sifting desultorily through long-expired magazine subscriptions, unanswered birth announcements from obscure cousins, and newsletters for things she didn't give a damn about, until she finally excavated what she had been looking for, the copy of the *National Enquirer* she had found on the gas station floor in Detroit. She hadn't been sure she remembered correctly, but there was Jeanne Dixon's prediction for 1968, in bold black headline type: "1200 to Die Soon at Khe Sanh." Her husband's new address. Somehow it didn't help that the psychic had also predicted the emergence of incontrovertible evidence of a government cover-up of UFO landings in New Mexico.

In the family room, *Dark Shadows* had yielded briefly to a commercial, and Liz could hear her sons talking.

"Danny, what's a 'flunk'?"

"It's a KIA," his brother told him matter-of-factly.

"Oh," Angus said, and then the show came back on and they were silent again.

HOTEL COMPANY came in through the wire late that afternoon, moving through a thick mist that made the clayish red dirt treacherously slick. The main drag of the Khe Sanh combat base looked like Dodge City in its gunfighter days, a rutted dirt road running between the airstrip and a shanty row of green tents, sandbagged bunkers, and rickety shacks with tin roofs and open sides. The base was crowded with an assortment of grungy frontier types, the Seabees who were working on the airstrip, flyers and artillerymen, officers in relatively clean uniforms, and line company grunts with M-16s slung over their shoulders, but Hotel Company moved through them all like an alien tribe from a different world. They were a grim and furious crew, soggy, filthy, and exhausted, and no one wanted to meet their eyes.

They'd been out on patrol for five days, working northward along the Rao Quang River into what the Marines at Khe Sanh called "The Slot," the river valley between Dong Tri Mountain and the hills to the west. The valley led straight into North Vietnam and amounted to an invasion highway for the NVA, but Hotel Company hadn't seen a single enemy soldier the whole time they'd been out. The conventional wisdom had it that there weren't any in the area. But the conventional wisdom didn't spend much time in the field. Hotel Company had found many signs of the enemy's presence along the network of well-worn trails that threaded through the hills, from piles of freshly whittled punji sticks smeared with dung, the makings of the fiendish pit traps Charlie favored, to the still-warm ashes of cooking fires and a pot of slightly underdone rice. They'd even found two 122mm rocket launchers in a clearing, staked down with fresh-cut branches tied off with vines, aimed right at the Marine combat base on the Khe Sanh plateau. The earth of the site was scorched from recent firings, and the ground was littered with cigarette butts. Lucky Strikes, Mike had noted. The goddamned gooks were smoking Marine C-ration cigarettes.

They'd also lost a man, to a Bouncing Betty, a perversely clever mine that popped up to waist level before exploding. It had happened less than a klick from base, right about the time everyone was starting to feel like they'd made it, and so it was particularly galling. You wanted some payback after something like that, but there was nothing to do. The poor guy, a PFC named Thomas, just lay there in the mud, screaming for morphine and his mother while a medic tried to keep his intestines in his abdominal cavity and everyone else tried to find somewhere else to look. Mike called a dust-off, but by the time the chopper got there ten minutes later, Thomas had lapsed into merciful unconsciousness and died. Mike had sent the Huey back empty and picked up one end of the kid's litter himself. Hotel Company would carry its own dead home.

Mike hustled the men off to the showers and the mess hall, then went on to the helo pad with the corpsman and Ike Tibbetts to send Thomas's body home. They put the stretcher on the Huey and stood together as the chopper lifted off, watching it go in silence.

"See if you can find some beer for the men, Top," Mike told Tibbetts. "Steal some from the Seabees or something. Get Bentano on it."

"Aye, sir," Tibbetts said.

Their eyes met. It seemed pretty sad that a can or two of warm Miller was all they could offer their company on a night like this. But they both knew it was the best they could do, and after a moment Tibbetts turned away and got on it.

THE INTEGRATION OF Virginia Beach Bluebird Troop 232 proved surprisingly easy in practice. Liz and Linnell Williams accompanied their daughters to the first meeting on a Tuesday night and were greeted at the door by Brenda Hinton, the troop's leader. Brenda was a statuesque woman, with frosted blond hair piled medium high. She wore an impeccably tailored uniform of bluebird blue with a sash laden with badges and insignia, two-inch heels, and soft cherry-colored lipstick. Her eyes were bluebird blue as well. They widened at the sight of Linnell and Temperance in her crisp new uniform.

"Hello, I'm Liz O'Reilly," Liz said firmly. "This is my daughter, Kathie. And this is Linnell Williams and her daughter, Temperance. We talked on the phone about the girls joining the troop."

"Of course," Brenda said. She had not let them in the door yet. They all stood for a moment in silence. The Hinton home was old Virginia Beach, a two-story colonial painted soft yellow, with non-weight-bearing white pillars flanking the front door and massive azalea bushes surrounding the house. The yard was huge and lush and crowded with crepe myrtles still leaking pink flowers from their late summer bloom. Above the entrance, a hand-carved wooden sign read, AS FOR ME AND MY HOUSE, WE WILL SERVE THE LORD.

"Is there a problem?" Liz asked. "This is the right night, isn't it?"

"You're a little early," Brenda said. She hesitated a moment longer, and Liz took a deep breath, ready to let her have it. But Brenda said, "But please, come in. You can help set up the refreshments."

And that was that. It turned out that Kathie and Temperance already knew a number of the girls in the troop from school; there was some excited girl chatter, and the meeting proceeded without incident. On the way home, as the two girls practiced the Bluebird Oath, the Bluebird Sign, the Bluebird Law, and the Bluebird Promise in the backseat, Liz and Linnell Williams exchanged a wry look of shared amusement. Liz realized that she was actually a little let down by the failure of fireworks. But Brenda Hinton's indomitable Southern decorum had turned out to be the deciding factor. The woman would have died before allowing an awkward scene, Liz thought; Brenda wouldn't say "shit" if she had a mouthful. It was too bad, in a way. Liz had really been ready to wreak some havoc.

"BLESS ME, FATHER, for I have sinned. It has been a week since my last confession, and these are my sins. . . ."

Germaine relaxed, recognizing Danny O'Reilly's voice. Every time he slid open the window in the confessional, it was a fresh leap of faith, and a new opportunity to despise himself. The litany of a suburban parish's sins was humbling, inevitably; he knew himself to be worse than even the most tormented of his parishioners could imagine, as they poured out their hearts to him. It was easier, with the children: not easier to forgive them—that was God's job in any case—but easier to forgive himself.

"I was mean to my brother," Danny said. "Seven times."

"Seven times?" Germaine said, amused.

"Maybe eight."

"How many times were you nice to him?"

"Well, we play together a lot."

"An approximation."

Danny considered. "A hundred, maybe."

Germaine was silent a moment. "Do you love your brother?"

"Of course."

"Are you sorry you were mean to him?"

"Yes."

"What is a hundred divided by eight?"

There was a pause, but Germaine knew the kid could do it in his head; and after a moment Danny said, "Twelve, with four left over."

"That's a niceness-to-meanness ratio of more than twelve to one. You understand?"

"Yes."

"You let me know if it dips below ten to one. Okay?"

"Okay."

"Anything else?"

There was a pause, and then Danny said reluctantly, "I lied."

"Oh?"

"I told my mom I was sick, but I wasn't really sick."

"Because you wanted to stay home from school?"

"Yeah. I needed time to think."

"Uh-huh," Germaine said, and waited, sensing more to come.

There was a silence. And then, "I shot a bird."

"With your BB gun?"

"Yes." Danny began to sob. "I killed it."

Germaine said nothing, resisting an urge to cross to the other booth and take the boy in his arms. He was thinking of the PFC in Charlie Company who used to come to him for confession after every firefight. At first the kid had cried, confessing to killing enemy soldiers. In the end, though, he had wept because he no longer felt remorse.

Danny's sobs had quieted. Germaine said, "Danny, some things you can make up for. If you tell a lie, you can find the courage to go back and tell the truth. If you are mean to your brother, you can find the strength and compassion and humility to apologize and try harder to be nice. But with this bird, there is nothing to do but feel the pain of what you have done. To be truly sorry. Which you are. God sees that. And God has already forgiven you. Now you have to begin to try to forgive yourself."

The boy was silent, and Germaine felt the inadequacy of his own words. He said, "Danny, I know what I'm talking about. I killed a man once, myself."

"In the war?"

"Yes." He could still see the figure looming over the foxhole, on a night the Vietcong had broken through the wire. The wounded Marine beside him had given Germaine his M-16 earlier, and when the moment came Germaine had fired it. He'd told himself he did it to save the wounded Marine, but he knew he would have fired anyway. The enemy soldier had crumpled from the burst across his chest and fallen backward, but he had taken almost twenty minutes to die, five feet away, and the whole time Germaine lay in the hole, listening to the man begging for his mother in Vietnamese and wishing he had the moment back.

"It's different in a war, though," Danny said tentatively.

"No, it's not," Germaine said.

They were silent again. There was nothing left to say, Germaine felt; he suspected there had been nothing to say all along; and at last he began, "Oh, my God, I am heartily sorry—"

Danny joined in to the Act of Contrition, "—for having offended thee. And I detest all of my sins, because of thy just punishment. But most of all because they offend thee, my God, who art all good and deserving of all my love. I firmly resolve, with the help of thy grace, to sin no more and to avoid the near occasions of sin. Amen."

Germaine raised his hand and made the sign of the cross. "*Passio Domini nostri Jesu Christi, merita Beatae Mariae Virginis et omnium sanctorum, quidquid boni vel mail sustinueris sint tibi in remissionem peccatorum, augmentum gratiae et praemium vitae aeternae. Ego te absolvo a peccatis tuis in nomine Patris, et Filii, et Spiritu Sancti.*"

"Amen," Danny said, crossing himself.

"Amen . . . Your sins are forgiven. Now go in peace."

The boy rose, with a scrape of the kneeler, then stopped. "But— what about my penance, Father?"

"Danny, what you're feeling is already the penance. Do you understand?"

Danny said, after a pause, "Not really."

"You will," Germaine said.

BACK IN HIS bunker, Mike cleaned his rifle, in case the NVA decided tonight was the night to storm the wire, then lay down on his cot. He could hear the rats rummaging along the walls and the sound of music somewhere nearby, someone playing Laura Nyro. He was thinking he should write the letter to Thomas's mother, but he just didn't have it in him yet.

Instead, he took out one of the photographs he kept in a plastic bag in his map pocket, a picture Liz had sent of Kathie in Liz's wedding dress. His daughter looked so beautiful it almost hurt to look at her. Liz always said that Kathie looked like him, but Mike saw Liz in all the kids. Kathie had his eyes, but she had Liz's cheekbones and Liz's determined jaw. And she would cry at the fall of a sparrow, just like Liz. He wanted to protect that little girl's heart. On a night like this, it seemed like the only thing left worth doing, the only thing he had left of who he had been, back in the world. Someday he would be home, and this war would be nowhere but inside him, in a place that Kathie would never have to know, and everything he had seen would be wrapped in plastic like Thomas in his poncho, and Liz and Kathie would never have to see or know; none of them ever would.

After a while, Doug Parker came in.

"Plenty of good chow left, Skip," the lieutenant said. "Tibbetts came up with some beer too. The man's a genius."

"I'm not feeling much like eating," Mike said.

"Yeah. Me neither." Parker sat down on his cot, took off his helmet, boots, and flak jacket, and lay back. The two men were silent for a time.

"It's a fucked-up war, Skip," Parker said at last.

"All wars are fucked up," Mike said. "We've still got to fight them."

CHAPTER 14

NOVEMBER 1967

THE MARINE CORPS' birthday on November 10, traditionally an O'Reilly family holiday, was exceptionally subdued this year. The year before, with Mike egging them on, the kids had actually come up with 191 candles for the hideous green cake that Liz always made, and the resultant conflagration had rendered the cake inedible. But this year no one seemed particularly inspired. The green food coloring in the milk, the cookies cut out into the eagle, globe, and anchor of the Marine Corps emblem and frosted in red, black, and gold, the traditional meal of creamed beef on toast, which Mike had taught the kids to call SOS—none of it aroused much enthusiasm. Danny, who had been unaccountably subdued for days, disappeared upstairs before the serving of the green cake inscribed with "Semper Fidelis." Kathie had chosen to eat dinner at Temperance's house, where the celebration of the Marine Corps birthday might have been expected to be at least a small occasion, given that Temperance's uncle was also in the Marines. But when Liz mentioned the birthday to Linnell Williams,

Linnell had merely said, "Only Marine Corps holiday I know about is
the one when that boy gets his reckless ass home alive."

Deb-Deb's otter loyalties precluded much in the way of gung ho,
so in the end Liz and Angus lit the candles—a somewhat arbitrary
seven of them this year, the last loose ones in an old box—and sang
the "Marine Corps Hymn" alone.

"Since it's a holiday, do I have to do my homework?" Angus asked,
as he dug into the cake.

"Yes."

"Do Marines need to know subtraction?"

"Yes, Angus."

Angus considered this, then said, "How come?"

So that you'll know how many men are left in your platoon if
seven of them die, Liz thought, but she said, "Marines have to balance
their checkbooks just like everyone else, sweetheart."

She took a piece of cake upstairs to Danny and found him in the
top bunk in the boys' bedroom. He looked unnervingly like one of
Mike's second lieutenants, fresh out of Basic School, in the preposter-
ous black-framed glasses he had insisted on; and somehow he looked
sadder too. It hurt Liz's heart; she had a sudden sense of having lost
track of her older son.

"Are you all right?" she asked.

"Yeah."

"You seem awfully quiet lately."

Danny shrugged. "I'm okay."

Liz stood for a moment more in the doorway, feeling helpless.
Danny had gotten more and more like his father lately; she could feel
a kind of inarticulate darkness moving in him, something fiercely
inward and guarded. Her son was drawing something, but the pad
was shadowed and she couldn't see what the picture was. Six months

ago she would have walked right in and assumed the right to look. Now she felt that would be wrong somehow.

"I brought you some cake," she said at last. "Marine Corps birthday cake."

"I'm not really hungry, thanks." It was almost an outright dismissal, but Liz lingered, unhappily, and after a moment Danny lifted his head and gave her a melancholy smile, touched with rueful acknowledgment, also eerily Mike-like. "I'm fine, Mom. Really."

"I'm sure you miss your dad. Especially tonight."

"Yeah," Danny said.

Liz waited, but it looked like that was it. She was about to go, when her son said, "Mom?"

"Yes, honey?"

"Do you think Dad would mind if I became a priest?"

"A priest?"

"Like Father Zeke. A Marine priest."

"Father Zeke was in the Navy."

"But he was with the Marines. That kind of priest."

Liz took a couple of steps into the bedroom, still holding the cake. "I'm sure your father would be very supportive if you felt called to the priesthood," she said carefully.

"It's just something I've been thinking about."

"Uh-huh." Liz hesitated, then asked, "What made you start thinking about being a priest?"

Danny shrugged, already in retreat, and turned back to his sketch pad. He was drawing a bird, Liz saw now from her better vantage point.

"That's beautiful," she offered.

"It's a blue jay."

"I can tell."

"I can see the birds clearly now, with the glasses."

"That must be wonderful."

Danny shrugged. He actually looked a little pained, but there was nothing more forthcoming. Her oldest child ran frustratingly deep sometimes. Liz lingered a moment, watching him etch delicate feathers and fill in the jay's crest. She was always amazed by how well Danny could draw; he'd shown an obvious gift since he first picked up a crayon. Neither she nor Mike had any graphic talent at all; they were both word people.

LATER, AFTER THE KIDS were all asleep, Liz cleaned up the kitchen, took out the trash, and began to ready herself for bed. Mike's toothbrush was still in the rack, a black, stiff-bristled, minimalist thing, a Marine's ascetic toothbrush, dry now and a bit withered. Her own toothbrush was as soft as toothbrushes came, and colored light pink. The tube of Crest on the counter was set for a left-handed pickup and squeeze, her habitual mode. Mike was a right-handed squeezer, but after their honeymoon, and every night of their married life since, he had put the toothpaste down prepositioned for a left-handed pickup, making that little effort every time. That was love, Liz thought. When he got home this time, she planned to surprise him by having the toothpaste set up for right-handed squeezing.

She was restless, for some reason. Had Mike been home, they would have been at the Marine Corps Birthday Ball tonight. The year before she'd gotten a little drunk and insulted a general's wife somehow. But they usually had fun.

She opened the closet and found her husband's uniform in its plastic bag. Mike in his dress blues was a gorgeous stranger, severe and noble; usually so satirical, he was almost embarrassingly earnest about all the corny tradition surrounding the uniform. Mike's ceremonial sword was on the top shelf, a replica of the North African Mameluke scimitar presented to Marine Lieutenant Presley O'Bannon by an Arab desert chieftain in gratitude for whatever the Marines had done on the shores of Tripoli almost two centuries ago.

Happy birthday, you wretched institution, Liz thought. Here's health to you and to our Corps, which we are proud to serve. A hundred and ninety-two years of going overseas to fight for right and freedom, and to die for things that earned the gratitude of desert chieftains and left the families at home to grieve. She closed the closet door and went to find some paper to write her nightly letter. She wished it wasn't going to take anywhere from three weeks to a month to get Mike's take on the fact that their older son suddenly and inscrutably wanted to be a priest.

She was just starting to undress when the doorbell rang. Liz froze, feeling instantly ill, then glanced at the clock. 9:07. Did the Marines doing casualty calls work nine to five, or did they just come as soon as they got the news themselves, at any time of the day or night? All the wives she knew who had received the two grim messengers in uniform had gotten their visits midday. What time was it in Vietnam, anyway? Danny's watch was still set to Vietnam time. She had an insane urge to run into his room and check.

She finally made herself go to the window and peek out. A Volkswagen bug was parked out front. No Marine Corps green sedan. Liz relaxed and hurried downstairs, opening the front door just as Zeke Germaine started to walk away down the steps, apparently having given up after his single ring.

"Hello, Father," Liz said.

Germaine stopped. "Oh," he said, as if he were surprised to see her. "Hello, Mrs. O'Reilly."

"Is everything all right?"

The priest mulled this for much longer than seemed necessary, then said, "I suppose that depends on what you mean by all right."

It was such a Germaine-like answer that she laughed. "I have very low standards for 'all right,' at this point. You're not here to tell me my husband's dead, are you?"

"No."

"Then everything is all right."

Germaine nodded, conceding the existential point, and swayed slightly. They stood irresolutely for a moment, looking at each other. Liz realized that the priest was a little drunk. Or even a lot drunk. She wondered what the hell he was doing here. He didn't really seem to know himself.

"Would you—like to come in?" she offered.

Germaine considered this as if such a notion would never have occurred to him, then said tentatively, with an air of willingness to try a radical idea, "If that would be all right."

"It depends on what you mean by 'all right,'" Liz said, mock ponderous, and the priest laughed delightedly. He really was the oddest man.

LEADING GERMAINE into the house, Liz hesitated at the entrance to the living room, but the formality of that seemed unbearable. She couldn't really picture the two of them sitting stiffly on the unused furniture, making priest-parishioner small talk. The dining room table was still submerged in unprocessed life debris, and the TV room was knee-deep in toy soldiers, block forts, half-clad Barbies, and stuffed animals. In the end, she sat Germaine on one of the kids' stools at the kitchen counter. Liz moved to the counter's far side, feeling a little like the bartender at the last stop on the priest's pub crawl.

"Can I get you anything?" she asked, and, pointedly, "Coffee, maybe?"

Germaine looked dubious. Liz went on, "Apple juice, Kool-Aid, Tang, water, milk, beer, bourbon . . ."

"What kind of Kool-Aid?" Germaine asked.

"Grape, I think."

"What kind of bourbon?"

"Jack Daniel's. He's got a bottle of Jameson's in there too, I think."

"Faith and begorra," Germaine said approvingly, which Liz took as a yes to the Irish whiskey.

She slipped into the living room and opened the bar cabinet that Mike had brought back from Taiwan. A gift from a Chinese general, it was an elegant thing shellacked in black, with colorful dragons entwined on the front panels. The bar was well stocked with the liquors necessary to the alcohol-reliant dinner parties she was compelled to put on as an officer's wife, including the ingredients of Mike's infamous Artillery Punch, a sledgehammer concoction that regularly reduced full colonels to babbling idiots after three cups. But Mike's domestic drink of routine was a double shot of Jack Daniel's on the rocks, a beer chaser, and a bowl of peanuts. He was a moderate drinker, a quiet sipper, easing sometimes into hilarious deadpan eloquence as the bourbon level diminished. Liz loved the nights when her husband really settled in. She would read the signs early and get a casserole in the oven, then make herself a strong whiskey sour and join him in the family room. The kids knew to leave them alone at such times; the islands of their parents' cocktail hours were taboo, slightly awesome and mysterious. Grown-up stuff. She and Mike did some of their best talking then.

A quart of twelve-year-old Jameson's, Mike's special-occasion whiskey, stood behind the Jack Daniel's, untouched, like all the liquor, since July. Liz grabbed the bottle and a Third Marine Division shot glass and went back into the kitchen. Germaine was still at the counter, leafing through a pile of the kids' artwork. Deb-Deb's infinite variations on otters, Angus's airplane battles, Kathie's hearts and flowers.

Liz got a glass set up and twisted the top off the Jameson's. "How do you drink this?"

Germaine shrugged. "Out of a brown paper bag in the 7-Eleven parking lot, usually. But since it's the good stuff, you could drop an ice cube in it."

Liz fixed him the drink, slipping a second ice cube in for dilution's sake, then went back to the refrigerator to try to find something for herself. There were three Schlitzes in the back, left over from Mike's last six-pack. She hadn't had the heart to throw them out. She opened one now and came back to the counter.

Germaine had held off on his drink until she returned. Liz lifted her beer and said, wryly, "Semper Fi."

He raised his glass. "*Sangre Christi.*"

"Yikes," Liz said, but she tapped her drink against his. "Amen, I guess."

Germaine tossed the shot off in a single gulp and spit the ice cubes back into the glass. Liz hesitated, wary of contributing further to the delinquency of a priest. But there was no mistaking the way he set the empty glass down, and she poured him another. He still had the pile of the kids' art spread in front of him. Liz noted that he'd paused over one of Danny's recent drawings, a Marine carrying a wounded buddy across a stream.

"I feel like I should apologize for my children's lurid war pictures," she said. "I'm afraid the boys are a little obsessed right now."

"It's natural enough," Germaine said. "Actually, though, I think this is St. Christopher."

"Really?" Liz said, gratified.

"It looks like the new stained-glass window at the church, to me."

"Who knew?" She hesitated, then said, "He wants to be a priest, you know."

She'd thought he would be pleased, but Germaine looked pained. "No, I didn't know."

"A chaplain. 'Like Father Zeke,' he told me."

"Shit," Germaine said. He considered his drink, then said, "He'll grow out of it, God willing."

"You are a very strange man," Liz said.

Germaine shrugged, as if to say he'd heard it before. They sat for a moment without speaking. Liz was surprised by how comfortable the silence was. She went over the relationship in her mind, trying to remember how they had gotten to a point of such ease.

"You're probably wondering what I'm doing here," Germaine said at last.

"I assumed they threw you out of the last bar for getting theological or something while celebrating the Marines Corps birthday."

"Actually, I'm a very well behaved drunk, even on major holidays. I just get quiet and brood."

"And how is that different from you sober?"

He smiled ruefully. "Touché."

"I'm an obnoxious drunk," Liz said. "I get loud and satirical, especially when I hit overload on the duty, honor, country stuff. Mike always has to keep an eye on me at Marine Corps functions."

"What do you do, when you get loud and satirical?"

"I tend to start quoting Shakespeare. 'Seeking the bubble reputation even in the cannon's mouth.' 'Who hath honor? He that died o'Wednesday.' That sort of thing."

"'I like not such grinning honour as Sir Walter hath . . .'"

Liz gave him an appreciative look. "Exactly. Mike used to love that about me, actually. But it turns out that having a loose cannon for a wife is bad for a military officer's career."

"It's the same for priests," Germaine said, so deadpan that it took Liz a moment to get it and laugh.

"Do priests even *have* careers?" she asked.

"Most do," Germaine said. "I never did."

His glass was empty. Liz picked up the bottle to refill it, and their eyes met. It was a little unnerving. She felt invisible most of the time in her life, submerged into this role or that—mother, wife, daughter, supportive friend, or friend in need of support. But Germaine seemed to see her without the mask of a particular function. She felt like herself with Germaine, and that felt both exhilarating and dangerous in some vague way.

"What *are* you doing here?" she marveled.

"Damned if I know," Germaine said frankly, and this time they both laughed.

CHAPTER 15

NOVEMBER 1967

from: Capt. M. F. O'Reilly
H Co., 2nd Bn., 29th Marines, 6th Mar Div FMF
c/o FPO San Francisco, Calif. 96602
Mon 20 Nov 1967
Khe Sanh, RVN

My Dearest Lizzie,

*   If Jeanne Dixon says 1200 people are going to die at Khe Sanh, it must be true, as she certainly knows more than the people actually running the war do. She must mean bad guys, though, as there are not 1200 Marines here. Maybe she means 1200 elephants. We've been hell on those pink elephants lately. The Vietnamese SPCA is furious with us.*

*   This place is actually a backwater of sorts. If the North Vietnamese ever do decide to attack, we'll be a truck stop on the Ho Chi Minh Trail long before 1200 people have time to die, as our*

"defenses" at present consist of a single strand of triple concertina wire, some unmowed elephant grass, and a couple of No Trespassing signs. Fortunately, the bad guys seem to care even less about this place than we do. III MAF has consequently pulled out everybody but the cooks and bottle washers to fight where there's actual fighting, and at this point we're basically just a bunch of guys camping out beside the airstrip, which they've finally gotten around to improving recently through the addition of a billion tons of crushed rock and a layer of flattened beer cans. Hotel Company has done its part in emptying the beer cans, but otherwise we have not seen much action and don't expect to.

Don't worry about me, my darling Lizzie. Really. The war is elsewhere these days. Khe Sanh isn't on anybody's map.

> *your loving,*
> *Mike*

DEB-DEB'S SIXTH birthday fell three days before Thanksgiving. Liz worried that Deb-Deb hadn't made any new friends yet in kindergarten; her youngest daughter was not so much antisocial as socially oblivious, in her benign way, impervious to the usual dance of forming relationships. Most often she moved happily enough in a world of her own. But Deb-Deb had come up with a substantial guest list of half a dozen names, and Liz had duly sent her daughter off to school with a pile of pink invitations to an after-school tea party to be held at the O'Reilly house. On the afternoon of Deb-Deb's birthday, however, no other children arrived. Instead, the dining room table, cleared for the occasion, had seven exquisite place settings of tiny teaware, and at each place but one, a stuffed animal sat with an invitation propped neatly on its lap. The empty place was for Linkalink, Deb-Deb's very special friend, who was invisible.

Deb-Deb, apparently content with the gathering, took her place at the head of the table, just to Linkalink's left, and poured chocolate milk from the teapot for all the guests. Liz stood in the doorway, trying to decide how freaked out she should be. She'd long understood that her youngest child was a special case, but she'd hoped that the stringencies of kindergarten would have a moderating influence. It would have been nice to have at least one other actual human child present.

The party proceeded happily. Deb-Deb swam otter-style into the kitchen to refill the chocolate milk, blew out the candles after making God-knew-what sort of wish, and served the cake graciously to everyone present. She opened her presents, several from Liz, one from each set of grandparents, and one from Maria Petroski, her godmother. Danny had given her a sketchbook and a set of colored pencils; Kathie had cut out a huge pink heart and written "I love You" in the center of it, and Angus had given Deb-Deb a pine cone, for reasons of his own. There had been nothing from Mike, not even a card, which was understandable enough, Liz thought, given that her husband had a war to fight, but still upsetting. She'd bought a card and signed it with Mike's name, but Deb-Deb had recognized her handwriting. For a child hopelessly lost in a fantasy world of her own, she was remarkably acute.

THAT NIGHT, tucking Deb-Deb into bed, Liz took another shot at invoking Mike's presence.

"You know your daddy loves you," she told Deb-Deb.

"I know," her daughter said serenely. "He's just never home for my birthday."

Liz opened her mouth to protest, then, upon review, held her tongue. Mike must have been present for at least one of Deb-Deb's birthdays, but she couldn't remember any. For a long time, Liz had shown Deb-Deb pictures of Mike and told her daughter that was "Dada," but that hadn't worked any better than forging signatures on birthday cards: For years, Deb-Deb had thought a framed photograph was called a dada.

The previous year Mike had been in Puerto Rico on some kind of amphibious exercise; the year before that he'd been on a ship in the Mediterranean. It really was possible he hadn't celebrated a single one of his younger daughter's birthdays at home. He'd even been in Okinawa when Deb-Deb was born. Liz vividly remembered the loneliness and borderline despair of that last birth. Deb-Deb, like the other three O'Reilly children, had been conceived on the rhythm method, a good Catholic accident. Every pregnancy had thus started out feeling like a sort of defeat, but Deb-Deb in particular had strained Liz's sense of the balance between motherhood and simply having a life. She had just recovered from Angus's arrival, and had managed through sheer force of will to lose the usual forty pounds in record time and land a role in that summer's Quantico little theater production of *Joan of Arc*. The director had been okay with her bottle-feeding at rehearsals, but a pregnant Joan of Arc was too much, and the role had eventually gone to her understudy, a lithe, virginal second lieutenant's wife who was probably on the Pill. The night Deb-Deb was born, Liz's first thought was relief that she actually felt love for the poor kid, that the sight of her daughter's angelic little face and bright blue eyes did, thank God, make it all seem worth it; and her second thought was that if the pope thought birth control was wrong, the pope could jolly well have her next baby himself. She'd given Mike a box of condoms the day he got back from the Med, and they'd worked fine, as mortal sins went, until now. Apparently even the thought of getting back into theater was enough to make her pregnant.

She was just settling in to read Deb-Deb's bedtime story, *Harold and the Purple Crayon*, when Danny hollered from downstairs, "Mom! Telephone!"

"Take a message and tell them I'll call them back," Liz hollered back.

"It's Dad!"

Liz bolted to her feet, thinking, Ohmygod, he's hurt. He was calling to tell her he didn't have a left leg anymore, or something.

Deb-Deb's eyes were wide; no doubt her daughter's expression was mirroring her own. Liz willed her face into composure and found a smile. Just your run-of-the-mill weeknight phone call from a husband in a war zone. At least he was alive.

"I'll bet he's calling for your birthday," she said. "Do you want to talk to Daddy?"

Deb-Deb, relieved, beamed and nodded, and they hurried downstairs together. Danny was at the kitchen counter with the receiver pressed to his ear, fighting off Angus and Kathie, who were pressing for a turn.

"Here's Mom," he said, as Liz approached. "Over." And then, "I love you too. Over."

"'Over'?" Liz said as she took the receiver.

"He's on a radio."

"Mike?" Liz said into the crackle of static. There was an unnerving pause, an emptiness, and she could feel the thousands of miles, the continents and the ocean between them. At last she added, uncertainly, "Uh, over?"

There was a click of sorts and Mike said, "It's a radio-satellite hookup, sweetheart. You have to use radio procedure. Over."

"I love you. I love you. I miss you. I miss you terribly. Uh, over."

"Copy that," he said dryly. She thought he was being humorous, a typical Mike tweaking of the absurdity of it all, though it was hard to tell through the attenuated tonal quality of the transmission. "I love you too. I miss you like crazy. Over."

"Are you all right?" Again, the unforgiving static. "Over?"

"Just peachy," Mike said. "I've only got three minutes here. Over."

"I love you," she said. It seemed silly to waste their precious three minutes saying anything else. "I love you. I love you. It's Deb-Deb's birthday. Over."

"Roger that. You want to put her on? Over."

A disembodied voice came on the line just then and said, "One minute left, Captain."

"Copy that," Mike said, as Liz handed the phone to her younger daughter.

"You have to say 'over' when you're done talking," Liz told Deb-Deb. "Like a game, see? You say blah-blah, over, then he says, blah-blah, over. Back and forth."

Deb-Deb nodded solemnly and took possession of the receiver. "Daddy?"

"Over," Liz prompted.

"Over?" Deb-Deb listened for a moment, and her face lit up. Birthday greetings with a Deb-Deb twist, probably; Mike was actually very good with his younger daughter. Deb-Deb was nodding happily in response.

"He can't hear you nodding, sweetie," Liz said, and Deb-Deb said hurriedly, "Blah-blah, over." And then, "I love you too, Daddy. Here's Mommie. Blah-blah over."

"—fifteen seconds, over," Mike was saying, as Liz got back on the line.

"I love you," she said. "I love you. I love you, my beautiful man. Over."

"I love you too, darling," Mike said. "Over and out."

IT SHOULD HAVE been routine. The Hotel Company patrol had slogged out to the limit of the artillery cover from the 105mm howitzer batteries at the Khe Sanh base, about ten klicks, three days of hard travel out and three days back, working up and down the steep, slick slopes through triple-canopy jungle, bamboo, and vine thickets, picking off leeches and keeping an eye out for bamboo vipers, water buffalo, and even tigers. The jungle was beautiful, surprisingly cool and green and so quiet you could hear the crystalline burble of the streams snaking down toward the Rao Quang and the sound of twice-filtered raindrops hitting the big fronds of the ferns at ground level. But the silence and the beauty fooled no one; the next turn in the trail could hide an ambush, the next tree a sniper. The monkeys in the area had a distinctive cry that sounded eerily like "*Fuh kyoo,*" and they liked to throw rocks. One of the Third Platoon's point men had crapped in his pants one day when a fuck-you monkey threw a rock at him, though he had retained the presence of mind to blow the monkey away. No one begrudged him the overreaction. Everyone's nerves were pitched high.

Mike kept the men moving through the bush as much as possible, but in the end the only realistic way to cover any ground was to walk single file along the trails or streambeds. The company was about two klicks from the base, stretched out over half a mile of trail like a snake in a bent rain gutter, when the firing erupted at the head of the column. Two single shots, tiny, almost offhand cracks, delicate as ice shifting, followed by the roar of dozens of M-16s responding.

The Hotel Company column dissolved instantly as the Marines flattened and assumed firing positions. They lay along the trail, everyone's eyes wide, scanning. In the jungle all around them, nothing stirred. The shooting continued from the front, M-16s busting caps, an uninterrupted tumult, a mad moment. Stinson handed Mike the radio handset without being asked, and Mike heard Doug Parker hollering over the First Platoon net, "What are we shooting at? What are we shooting at? . . . Cease fire! Cease fire!"

Mike said, "Hotel One, this is Hotel Six. Whaddaya got?"

"Six, One. I think it was a sniper, Skipper. We've got a man down."

"Try to get the shooting under control. That's all outgoing fire, by the sound of it."

"No shit," Parker said, with a touch of exasperation, which Mike understood. One of Parker's men was hit, and the First Platoon was enraged. You didn't just turn off fifty furious Marines bent on payback by saying, "Please."

Mike had the other platoons send squads out to cover their flanks, then began working his way up to the front of the column, with Stinson in tow. Moving past a quarter-mile column of locked-and-loaded Marines was an American education all its own: face after dirty young face, black, white, Hispanic, each face its own story, but all of them kin in their expressions, uniformly wide-eyed and watchful and dead serious. It was oddly moving, and Mike felt a sort of love welling up. It wasn't something you could explain, not even something you particularly wanted to talk about. But it was very real. Combat made a kind of family as real and deep as anything he had ever known.

By the time Mike reached the front of the column, Parker had gotten the shooting stopped. Half the First Platoon was out in the bush now, sweeping for the sniper, and the rest of the platoon had set up a perimeter. Parker himself was fluttering like a mother quail near the heart of the protected space, where a corpsman was working on the wounded Marine. Mike recognized the kid who had choppered in with him on his first day with Hotel Company. Something-some-thingski. The kid's helmet had a rough calendar sketched on it, with August, September, and October x-ed off. And, on the back, mercifully, his name. Krzykrewski. Three months in-country had turned the nineteen-year-old's acne-scarred face leathery and lean. He looked like they all did now after a week or two of getting shot at, like a stone-cold killer; but his hazel eyes were still like Angus's, wide and gentle and a bit bewildered. He had a single wound, a neat little bullet hole in his right shoulder that didn't look like much.

Mike said, "How you doin', Ski?"

The kid gave him a weak grin. "Been better, sir. I feel like I've got a bad case of heartburn."

"That might just be the C-ration beans." Mike glanced at Parker. "What's up with the sniper?"

Parker shook his head angrily. "Fucking Lone Ranger hit-and-run piece of shit. Two shots and he fucking disappeared. We may even have hit him. We fired enough rounds to sink a fucking ship."

"Yeah, I heard."

Parker glanced at him sharply, to see if he was being given shit. Mike held his look, then raised one eyebrow, and Parker finally shook his head and laughed.

"Fucking goddamn sniper, Skipper," he said. "It pissed everybody off, when he shot Krzykrewski."

"Yeah." Mike turned to the corpsman, who was setting up an IV line. "How's it look?"

The man shrugged. "No exit wound. Fucking bullet must've bounced around in there and settled somewhere. But he seems okay."

"Lieutenant Parker said I can keep the slug as a souvenir," the kid offered happily.

"Fuckin' A," Mike said.

"Makes a nifty paperweight," the corpsman offered.

"Something to tell the grandkids," Parker seconded.

Mike told Krzykrewski, "That's a million-dollar bullet, Marine. We'll call in a dust-off and get you out of here, pronto."

"I already called it," Parker said.

"They'll fly you first-class to a hospital ship and on to scenic Japan, and beautiful nurses will feed you beer and ice cream."

"Copy that, sir," the kid said. "I'd settle for a cigarette at the moment."

"Can he smoke?" Mike asked the corpsman, who shrugged and said, "What the hell. If any smoke comes out the hole, we'll figure the bullet hit a lung."

Mike bummed a Salem from one of the men in Krzykrewski's squad, who were all hovering nearby, placed it between the kid's lips, and lit it for him.

"Thank you, sir."

"My pleasure. Hang in there, Marine."

"Thank you, sir. I'll do that."

The sweep for the sniper proved useless. Mike called for a meal break and left the company in a defensive posture, flankers out, while he took a team up to the ridge to find a place for the dust-off chopper to land. Krzykrewski's squad mates insisted on carrying his litter themselves, and they bore him up the treacherous slope as if they were carrying a load of spun glass. Krzykrewski himself seemed embarrassed by all the attention.

They emerged from the brush into the elephant grass of the hilltop just as the *whomp-whomp* of the helicopter became audible in the distance.

"Skip—" the corpsman said with subdued urgency from beside Krzykrewski's stretcher. Mike turned to him. The corpsman stood to meet him and lowered his voice. "His blood pressure's going through the floor. I'm afraid that bullet caught an artery or something in there. We gotta get him to a surgeon *didi*."

"Right, we're on it." Mike squatted beside Krzykrewski's litter. "How you doin', Ski?"

The kid's eyes were closed, but he opened them and mustered a smile. "Not so hot, sir."

"Hang in there, Marine. Your taxi home is on the way."

"Maybe you could write my mom."

Mike hesitated, then said firmly, "Nobody's going to need to write any letters for you, son. You'll have plenty of time in a nice clean bed to write all the letters you want."

"She always thought I was a fuckin' loser," Krzykrewski said wistfully. "Be nice if somebody said somethin' good about me."

The helicopter circled the hilltop, and they popped some purple smoke to mark a landing zone. As the Huey started down toward them, a single shot cracked, and everyone flattened.

"Fucking sniper," Krzykrewski's squad leader, a taciturn corporal named Smith, growled, and emptied his clip in the general direction the shot had come from.

The chopper had leveled off at about five hundred feet. The radio crackled, the helicopter pilot sounding peevish. "Hotel, this is Tango Angel. We're taking fire. Repeat, LZ is hot, over."

Another single shot popped, and this time Krzykrewski's whole squad, outraged at the interference, opened up.

"It's barely even warm, Tango Angel," Mike said. "It's just a sniper. We have a wounded Marine down here in need of immediate evacuation. Repeat, this is a critical medevac. Land your fucking chopper. Over." Mike released the mic key and looked incredulously at Stinson.

"Fucking candy-ass," his radioman said.

"Yeah," Mike said.

They waited as the Huey continued to waver; then both men let out their breath as it finally started down toward them. It got to within fifty feet, so close that the elephant grass flattened out from the prop wash. Mike and Smith squatted at either end of Krzykrewski's litter, ready to load him the moment the bird touched down. No one heard the shot this time over the chopper's din, but a sudden splay of cracks blossomed in the Huey's windshield as another round hit. At almost the same instant, a mortar round landed about fifty yards away. Their sniper had apparently found some friends.

"Oh, Jesus," Smith said.

The helicopter wavered. It was so close now that Mike could see the pilot, a mustachioed young man in a beat-up fatigue cap. The guy looked like a poor man's Errol Flynn, a real flying cowboy. His eyes met Mike's through the cracked windshield, and Mike could see him weighing it out: bolt, not bolt.

Come on, cowboy, show some balls, Mike thought; and finally the guy shrugged and gave Mike a what-the-hell, life-is-short, damn-the-torpedoes grin and started down again.

It all depended on the NVA's mortar tactics now, Mike knew. They were committed to being sitting ducks for the next thirty seconds. If the bad guys walked the rounds in ten meters at a time, by the book, they probably had time to get Krzykrewski on the chopper and out of here. If the gooks just guessed and bumped the range the right amount, they were fucked.

The chopper got to within five feet of the ground, and Mike and Smith straightened and heaved Krzykrewski's litter upward. They only got him to chest level on the first try, and two more of Krzykrewski's squad mates dropped their guns and leaped to help. The door gunner was firing his M-60 right over their heads, and the spent shells rained around them. With four men lifting, they got Krzykrewski aboard on the second try.

"Go, go, go!" Mike hollered, and the bird lifted away, just as the next mortar round hit. The gooks had guessed right, it turned out, and the sky slammed down on them.

He never heard the explosion. There was just a flash that was everything, the world evaporating into light. They always said of guys who bought it that they never knew what hit them, but it turned out that wasn't true. Mike knew; he had, indeed, a sense of immediate and infinite leisure: there was all the time in the world. Because time had turned to light, and the light was everything, was air and flesh and duty and memory, and everything was plunging as light into the heart of a deeper emptiness still. His life was present without sequence, not passing before his eyes, that old cliché, because there was no passing, and nowhere to pass to. It was just there, all of it, everything, Liz and the kids and his parents and his sister, the company and the Corps, gulls he had seen with sunset light on their wings and the wounded fox he'd found when he was eight and things he'd thought he'd only dreamed that turned out to have shaped everything and snow falling quietly through a streetlight: all of it, simply all. He'd loved it all completely, he saw, and he wished he could tell Liz how much, how beautiful their life looked in this instant of his dying. But there was no telling such things, there never had been, there was just this love that had made the flesh of every instant real, and that had always been so.

The air turned solid and savage, a wallop of needles and hot gravel suffused with a sudden red fog. Mike felt his body slammed away from him like a baseball leaping off a bat. But there was no pain, just a sense of distant impact, the ripple of faraway thunder after a lightning flash. All the pain had been sucked out of the world with its substance, and there was nothing left but this tenderness and this beauty and a sadness too deep and peaceful to be regret.

And then those were gone too, the labor of the specific abolished, and Mike felt free and clean and grateful, and he was floating, flying, rising forever into the embrace of the silence that was deeper even than the everything of untellable love, soaring without movement from somewhere to nowhere, from something to nothing, forever.

CHAPTER 16

NOVEMBER 1967

GERMAINE REGRETTED THE previous night's excess of bourbon; his head felt like an unripe cantaloupe. The morning mass should have been routine, but he had forgotten that today was the blessing of St. Jude's new stained-glass window, a depiction of St. Christopher donated by the parents of a young Marine recon sergeant killed in action the previous year in the Co Bi-Thanh Tan Valley near Hue.

The parents had been waiting outside in the dark when he had arrived that morning at 6:01 to open the church. Sergeant Martin Truman's father, Chet, was a small man with shoulders squared against the world's skew, a boxy jaw, and a gray crew cut like something hewn from raw silver. A former Marine himself, a World War II veteran of Tarawa and Iwo Jima, he had pushed hard for something gung ho on the plaque for the window. His first choice had been the classic Chester Nimitz line about the Marines in the Pacific: "Uncommon valor was a common virtue." He'd also considered the third verse of the "Marine Corps Hymn," in its awkward entirety, and the anonymous poem that ended,

And when he gets to heaven,
To St. Peter he will tell,
"One more Marine reporting, sir;
I've served my time in hell."

His wife, Wanda, trailed him by a step and a half at all times, like an adjutant. She was a sturdy, watchful woman, not entirely resigned, in brown Sears polyester slacks, handicapped by a bad haircut and a slightly crazed husband. Her cautious eyes, soft brown, kept flickering around as if she were looking for a place to hide and cry.

It felt like madness to Germaine, but he steered with the skid. Steering with the skid seemed like the whole of his priestly vocation these days. Danny O'Reilly was serving the mass, which was a break, because the kid had just the right mix of gravitas and attentive flexibility, and a good feel for the subtleties of ritual. The rest of the crowd was the usual suspects, six old women with rosaries, the widower who kept the church lawns mowed, and a middle-aged man of frighteningly earnest demeanor who was probably contemplating divorce or suicide.

Germaine did the best he could, though he found the scripture readings sticking in his throat. Chester Truman had chosen the Gospel text from Jesus's words in Matthew 16: "If any man will come after me, let him sacrifice himself, and take up his cross and follow me. For whosoever will save his life shall lose it; but whosoever will lose his life for my sake shall find it." As if Christ had died for his country, Germaine thought. The Son of God as a KIA in another splendid little war. He wondered again what he was doing on this altar.

In the end, he swallowed his bitterness one more time and raised the Host into the mystery. The tiny crowd filed up for communion. Germaine had saved the consecration of the window for the end of the mass, in case anyone needed to leave early to get to work, but the whole crowd stuck around and several of the old women put away their rosaries and came up with small American flags.

They gathered before the new window in the east wall. Danny O'Reilly got the incense going and stood to Germaine's right, holding the chain of the censer at arm's length, stoic with the smoke wafting into his face. Chet and Wanda Truman stood on the priest's other side, and the rest of the congregation clustered around behind them. The stained-glass image showed a burly St. Christopher with a live tree as a staff, wading across a stream with the Christ child on his broad shoulders. The window's colors were subdued in the predawn; they really should have done this ceremony midmorning, Germaine thought, when the light coming through would have made the mosaic properly translucent.

He sprinkled holy water on the window and began the benediction from the *Rituale Romanum: Benedic, Domine, hanc aquam* ... Beside him, Danny O'Reilly's eyes were streaming from the incense. Wanda Truman was weeping too, frankly, at last, and Chet Truman stood at parade rest with his shoulders hunched, his hands clenched behind him, and his head bowed as if against a wind. They all said an Our Father, and Wanda tugged the veil away from the window's plaque, tentatively, as if it might explode. In the end, Sergeant Martin Truman's parents had settled on the simplest of inscriptions, from Paul's second letter to Timothy: "*I have fought a good fight, I have finished my course, I have kept the faith.*" And just below it, "*Beloved Son.*"

When the ceremony was over, the church emptied quietly, as if after a funeral; but Germaine stayed long afterward, kneeling alone in the silence and the shadows until the sun was up and the window came alive. Perhaps it was best after all, the priest thought, that the ritual had ended before the image grew too vivid. To Germaine, the saint, thigh-deep in the water with his poncholike robe flaring, his staff at port arms, and the Christ child on his shoulders like a sixty-pound pack, looked way too much like a Marine in a rice paddy, wading toward a hamlet somewhere in the Co Bi-Thanh Tan Valley.

HE WAS CONSCIOUS first of a nagging sense of demands on his attention, of a persistent ruckus unraveling the peace. Like a Sunday morning, being awakened by the kids tumbling into bed with him and Liz and bouncing, laughing, only it wasn't Sunday, that much he knew, and it wasn't bed, and this wasn't kid tumult, it was something not good. It was more like being in a forest fire, at the center of a riot of flame. And there was something else going on, something that had been important.

Krzykrewski, right, getting him on the chopper. They had gotten him on, Mike was pretty sure of that: he could see the wounded Marine's boots in his mind's eye, muddy, splayed, and sad, as the litter slid in, and he remembered the clamor of the door gunner's M-60 and the hot brass rain of the spent shells clattering down on him and Smith. They'd gotten poor Ski on the bird and then gotten hit.

Accomplish your mission; take care of your people.

Mike could smell the powder of the mortar round; his nose burned with it, which meant he wasn't dead and he still had a nose. But he could see only the dimmest black shapes swimming in a blacker haze, and he couldn't hear and he couldn't find his body at first; and then he realized that his sense of encompassing conflagration was pain, a raw fire of undifferentiated agony, that his body was blazing with pain, everywhere, that everything he could feel was pain.

He was being handled, someone was wiping his eyes, a searing pressure across his face that swirled fresh flames of pain into prominence, and Mike's vision cleared into a working blur. It was Parker, with a handful of blood now, looking appalled. The lieutenant bent

close, hollering something, and Mike felt his urgency and, simultaneously, the concussion of explosions nearby. Incoming, mortar fire.
Right, there was a war going on, that hadn't stopped. He was on fire,
but he wasn't dead, he still had to deal with it. *Accomplish your mission; take care of your people.*

Mike nodded, which seemed to be the right response. Parker motioned, and two Marines bent down on either side of Mike to carry
him to cover, but both men recoiled as they reached for him, a simul-
taneous double take, almost comical. Mike looked down and saw that
he was covered in blood, his flesh unrecognizably roiled. He looked
like something in the catch tray of a badly calibrated meat grinder,
like one big wound, and the Marines didn't know where to grab him
to pick him up. Poor Liz, he thought: they're going to have to scrape
me up and send what's left of me home in a plastic bucket. He was a
closed-coffin funeral waiting to happen.

He tried to say something reassuring to the Marines, like, Latch on
anywhere, guys, it all hurts like hell anyway. Or even, Just leave me
here, I'm a waste of fucking time at this point. But his mouth wasn't
forming sentences, and all he could get out was, "'sokay . . . 'sokay."

The Marines, still tentative, steeled themselves to pick him up, and
suddenly Stinson was there, seizing Mike under the armpits, and the
other men took the hint and grabbed one leg each.

Everyone was in urgent motion now. Several Marines had grabbed
the other casualties; Mike saw at least two bodies, both limp and broken,
flopping in the heedless acquiescence of the dead. Another man stopped
to pick up the bottom part of someone's leg, the boot still on it; he set it
gently on the stomach of one of the bodies they were carrying. Mike
glanced down at his own body, almost idly curious: both legs still attached, he noted, pleased in spite of himself. A fucking miracle.

They set off for the brush line, everyone staying as low as they
could. Mike could hear explosions now with his left ear, muted to dull

thuds as if through layers of quilting. Every jounce and jerk hurt, his flesh sawing against steel in a hundred places; he was laced with burning razors. They'd have been better off just leaving him in the open to bleed out undisturbed. There was nowhere to go now but into the pain; he was flanked, surrounded, overrun.

They made the trees and found low cover, and the Marines set Mike down so gently he wanted to cry, then grabbed their rifles and found firing positions. Well trained, Mike thought. Good men. Parker was on the radio, calling for another dust-off, for artillery and air, and Stinson was kneeling beside Mike now, cradling his head and hollering, "*Corpsman! Corpsman!*" in that keening, outraged way the men screamed when it was too late for a medic to do anything anyway and the call for help was just the first wail of grieving. Mike was touched by his radioman's distress. Poor guy, so urgent and so solicitous, and it was such a waste. There was nothing to do now but die, and Mike just wanted a bit of quiet to get on with it.

"Did Krzykrewski get out okay?" he asked, or tried to ask, but the words came out as ruined as his body. Stinson bent closer, trying to understand, his face pained and tender, and Mike tried again, "Ski . . . okay?"

"Yeah, Skip," Stinson said. "He's on his way home."

Belanger, the corpsman, scurried up. He flinched when he saw Mike, confirming Mike's sense that he was fucked. It took a hell of a mess to make a battle-seasoned corpsman flinch. The kid started sorting through the gore, looking for the main holes. Mike wanted to tell him not to bother, to tend to the other wounded. But it was important to go through the motions. Belanger had shown a tendency early on to be excessively frank about the severity of people's wounds, and it had taken Mike a while to impress upon the corpsman the essential truth of battlefield diagnosis, which was that no wound was fatal. Everyone was going to make it. Period.

"Who . . . else?" he asked Stinson. "Hit?"

"Consalvo and Seretti are dead."

"Smitty?"

"He was standing between you and the shell," Stinson said. There were tears running down his face. He said to the corpsman, "Give him some morphine, for Christ's sake."

"He'd go into shock, and we'd lose him for sure," Belanger said.

"Already in shock," Mike said, and the two men looked at him, startled. "Joke," he said. "Ha-ha."

"You're a crack-up, Skipper," Stinson said. "You hang on. Chopper's coming."

A 105mm shell shrieked overhead just then, and Stinson and Belanger ducked instinctively. But it was outgoing fire from Charlie Battery at Khe Sanh, the artillery strike Parker was calling on the mortar position. Mike listened contentedly to the familiar rhythm of the Marine reply: one shot to find the range, tweak the coordinates, another on the money, and fire for effect. Within seconds, a dozen more howitzer shells screamed over them and a wave of explosions rippled across the face of the neighboring hill.

"Fry, you bastards," Stinson said.

Mike said, "Get . . . Parker."

"Sir, you don't need to be worrying about—"

"Just get him, goddammit."

"Aye, sir." Stinson laid Mike's head back gently and moved off to fetch the lieutenant. Mike looked at the corpsman, who had a handful of battle dressings out now but seemed at a loss as to which hole to plug first.

"All the king's horses—" Mike said.

"You're gonna be fine, Skipper," the kid said, and Mike smiled because it was exactly what Mike had trained him to say. It was, Mike realized now, a policy more for the living than for the dying. It kept the survivors focused on saving what could be saved and doing what they had to do. But he actually felt a little irritated by all these people pretending he wasn't toast.

Parker appeared at his side, with Stinson shadowing him. The lieutenant's face clouded, but he said, lightly enough, "Skipper, how ya doing?"

"Been better," Mike said. "Sitrep?"

"I think we got the sniper and the mortar. I've got a couple of fast-movers coming in with napalm. And there's a chopper on the way for you."

Mike tried to look at his watch, but his left arm wouldn't move. Parker, attending closely, looked baffled. Mike said, "Time?"

Parker, clearly humoring him, took his left hand gently, wavered, then wiped the blood off the face of the watch on Mike's wrist. The crystal was shattered, but the hands were discernible: twelve minutes after one in the afternoon. 1312 hours.

"Your company, now," Mike said. "Thirteen hundred hours."

"Aye, sir."

"Just . . . get them home. No hero shit."

"Copy that, Skipper. I'll get everyone back." Parker smiled. "I had a pretty good teacher."

"I stand relieved," Mike said. He closed his eyes and was instantly far away, somewhere cool and dark and quiet, as if the burning in his body were a bonfire on a beach and he had walked off into the night, as he and Liz had once sneaked away from a beach party with a blanket and made slow love on the dunes, then left their clothes in a heap on the sand and slipped together into the sea. Mike remembered the coolness of the water and the warmth of Lizzie's perfect body against his, and he thought of Major Ngai, dying on the litter north of Gio Linh. He knew now why the Vietnamese CO had seemed so bafflingly peaceful. You did what you could, and then you let it go. And there was such sweet relief in the letting go, and such unforeseen beauty.

When he opened his eyes again, Stinson was still with him, covered with blood now himself, holding Mike's head, weeping unashamedly. Fifty yards away, purple smoke billowed in the flattened elephant grass, marking the LZ for the dust-off; the chopper was coming in. Belanger had an IV bag out and was feeling around gingerly in the mess that was Mike's left arm, looking for a place to put the needle.

"Save it for someone else, Andy," Mike said. The corpsman looked startled, then chagrined: he'd been thinking the same thing himself, but he'd been determined to go through the motions. Mike met his eyes and smiled. "Just this once," he said.

Belanger managed a rueful smile in return. "Aye, aye, sir," he said. "God be with you, Captain."

Four Marines grabbed the corners of the stretcher, and they ran for the chopper, keeping low, though no one seemed to be shooting at them for the moment. Stinson stayed beside Mike all the way, holding his hand now, not letting go until they raised the litter to slide it into the Huey. Mike met his radioman's eyes and tried to give him a wink, but his face wasn't working that well and it felt more like a grimace.

They slid him into the bay with the three dead bodies, and the last thing he saw as the chopper lifted away was Stinson's grieving face, the two clean lines of tears running straight down through the mud and blood, and then that was gone and duty was done and Mike closed his eyes and thought of the sea on a summer night. He was out beyond the breakers now, and he could see moonlight on the vastness of the water beyond him and hear the soft waves crumpling like memories on the beach, and he could feel the warm nakedness of Liz's body, sleek as a dolphin's against his own, the two of them floating together quietly, looking back at the distant flicker of the bonfire.

THE SEDAN PULLED into the driveway just after the kids had gotten home from school on a Wednesday afternoon, and so its arrival went unnoticed until the doorbell rang. Liz thought it was probably Linnell Washington coming to pick up Temperance, who had taken the bus home from school with Kathie. She opened the door to find the two Marines standing there in their dark green winter dress uniforms and promptly slammed it shut.

She stood for a moment with her shoulder against the door, holding her breath. As a child, she had believed that if she held her breath she was invisible. She was furious with herself for answering the bell so casually, as if she'd somehow allowed the evil in by letting her guard down. She had also cut off most of her options for active denial. Plan A had long been to bolt without even answering the ring, but the children were in the kitchen, happily rummaging for snacks; she would have to get past them to get out the back door. Liz considered running upstairs and locking herself in the bathroom, but she knew Danny would answer the door then and she didn't want that. So she just stood there holding her breath until the Marines knocked again, and then a moment longer, feeling the blood in her face and her heart in her chest. At last, though, she was forced to let the held air out in a whoosh and gasp a fresh lungful. That was the catch, she remembered from childhood; eventually you had to breathe.

She opened the door a second time. Her initial wave of sustaining rage had already passed, and she felt empty and fragile, helpless as a soap bubble. All she could think of was the first time she had seen Mike's naked body, on their wedding night. Theirs had been an autumn-winter-colder-than-usual-spring Catholic courtship, movies and hamburgers, blues and jazz in Georgetown dives, chilly walks along the Potomac and through Rock Creek Park in layers of sweaters and coats, and reading Yeats and Synge on the floor beside the radiator, in lieu of a fireplace, in the apartment Mike shared with three other guys. No trips to the beach, and they'd never gotten past second base in the back of his old Chevy sedan; she'd never seen Mike with his shirt off. She'd never even seen his bare legs. When they finally shed their clothes, absurdly tentative in the sacred shyness of their first night together, Liz had been thrilled to discover that she loved her new husband's body; it was like unwrapping a mystery party gift that turned out to be a winner. Mike had a slim, mild physique, the shoulders strong but undaunting, the chest covered lushly in soft black hair, the delicious belly still Marine flat. The thought of that beloved body violated now, savaged, possibly even destroyed, made Liz feel as if her own belly had been torn open.

"Is he dead?" she demanded of the nearest Marine, a major. The other one was a first lieutenant. Both men stood at parade rest, their hands clasped in front of them and their covers under their arms, the left breasts of their uniform jackets gaudy with ribbons, including the yellow and red one for Vietnam service. They both had Purple Hearts too, Liz noted: initiates in the blood brotherhood. She wondered whether Marines had come to their wives' doors. She wondered what the hell their wives had done.

The major looked distressed. There was a script for these things. "Ma'am, maybe we should sit down and—"

"Just tell me whether my husband is dead or not, goddammit."

The major glanced pointedly at the lieutenant; rank had its privileges. The lieutenant, clearly unprepared for frankness, blurted, "No, ma'am, he's not dead. He's hit pretty bad, though."

Liz sat down on the floor, just plopped, before either of them could move to support her. In the hallway behind her, the kids had gathered, alerted somehow. Kathie was already crying. Angus, a beat slower, asked plaintively, "What happened? What's going on?"

"Shut up, birdbrain," Danny told him. "Dad got shot."

PART FIVE

Oh now, in you, no more in myself only
And God, I partly live, and seem to have died,
So given up, entered and entering wholly
(To cross the threshold is to be inside),
And wonder if at last, each through each far dispersed,
We shall die easily who loved this dying first.

E. J. SCOVELL

CHAPTER 17

NOVEMBER 1967

CHARLIE MED, THE Khe Sanh field hospital, was a bloody zoo. One of the companies of 3/26 had run into trouble near Hill 881S, and several helicopters loaded with casualties had arrived not long before the Hotel Company chopper came in. An informal triage was taking place in the medical tent, with the dead laid in a row along the far wall and those with minor wounds left more or less to their own devices, while the seriously wounded were hurried to the tables to be worked on. Mike returned to consciousness to find himself among the dead.

He didn't mind that; he'd figured as much himself. No sense moving his body twice. But if he was going to die, he'd had plenty of time to do so; and if he was going to confound God, the Fates, and the Marine Corps and live, it was probably time to start getting some actual attention.

He tried to raise his head and managed only to tilt his face slightly to the right. But everyone to his right was dead: Consalvo, Seretti, something mangled that was probably what was left of Smitty, and several other Marines he didn't know. Mike tried to get a good look at the other bodies, to see if they were from Hotel Company too, hoping nothing else had happened, something he didn't know about. But he didn't recognize any of the faces. And he didn't see Krzykrewski, which was a good sign.

Mike rested for a while with his head flopped to the right, watching the huge, metallic green blowflies landing indiscriminately on the faces of the dead men and on his own face. Everything hurt; everything. It was going to be a long road back. But he was pretty sure now that he was going to live, he hated those damned flies so much.

IN THE END, Liz served the Marines coffee. She was appalled at herself; it was humiliating. She had felt superior for so long, contemptuous of all those well-behaved Marine wives keeping stiff upper lips at the expense of their real feelings, taking devastation in docile stride. But she understood now. It had nothing to do with strength or weakness of character, with denial or truth or depth of feeling, with right or wrong or meaning or sacrifice or nobility. You just did what you did, when it came down to it. Two men came to the door to tell you that your husband had been blown up, and you collapsed on the floor for a little while, and then you got up and seated them in the living room and asked if they wanted cream or sugar. Because the children were there, wide-eyed, desperate for clues as to how shattered they should be. Because there were calls to be made, to Mike's sister, to his parents. Because the phone was going to start ringing soon, as word spread through the amazingly efficient tribal system of other Marine wives. Life went on. It seemed wrong, that it did; it seemed impossible, that it could. It even seemed outrageous. But it did.

Linnell Washington showed up like an angel about ten minutes after the Marines. It was she who actually made the coffee, after she had shepherded the kids upstairs to their rooms. Liz went into the kitchen to try to help, but Temperance's mother waved her off.

"You just take care of your own self, honey."

"I don't even know what that means right now," Liz said, but she leaned back against the counter gratefully.

Linnell opened one cupboard, then a second and a third, before she found the coffee cups. Liz watched her, thinking, I know where the coffee cups are. But by the time her brain caught up with what was going on, Linnell had found the cups and gone through all of the lower cupboards to come up with a tray.

I know where the trays are, Liz thought.

"I suppose them Marines drink it black," Linnell said, opening the refrigerator to consider the limited milk options.

"Mike does," Liz said, and she began to cry. She didn't want to; she was afraid she was never going to stop. Linnell put her arms around her.

"It's gonna be all right, Lizzie," she said, which only made Liz cry harder. Temperance's mother had never called her by her first name before, and in the subtlety and naturalness of the shift, Liz glimpsed the depths of her own secret arrogance. The barrier had been hers, not Linnell's. She had been working so hard to be benevolent, helpful, and generous in the friendship, as if from on high. As if she could afford to, as if the bad things, the real-life things, happened to other people.

"He's not dead," she said, when she could breathe again without sobbing.

Linnell patted her back. "Maybe he'll get to come home now," she said.

The thought had not occurred to Liz yet, and it cheered her instantly. She straightened to reach for the sugar bowl and placed it on the coffee tray, then took a deep breath, tore off a paper towel to wipe her face, and met Linnell's eyes.

"Would you mind going up and seeing how the kids are?" she said. "And hold their hands a bit. The girls, in particular. Tell them I'll be up there soon. And if you could possibly stick around for a while—?"

"Of course," Linnell said. Liz touched her arm, then picked up the coffee tray and went back into the living room. The Marines were sitting bolt upright on the sofa, side by side. They rose in unison as she came into the room, standing alertly, with identical glum, determined, sympathetic faces. She felt a surge of compassion for them, they were so obviously resigned to any emotional extravagance on her part and so plainly eager to be done with it.

Liz set the tray on the table and poured everyone a cup of coffee, trying to present a reassuringly unhysterical manner. Then she settled in to hear what the poor men had to say, stirring a double tablespoon of sugar into her cup. She'd been using saccharine since Deb-Deb had been born, figuring it was better to die of cancer than to be fat, but somehow having her husband blown up seemed to call for the real thing.

"YOU JUST COST ME fifty bucks," the doctor told him cheerfully as he cut Mike's bloody uniform off, after they had finally realized Mike wasn't going to die and gotten him up onto one of the plywood flats laid atop ammunition crates that served as the first line of operating tables in Charlie Med.

"Really?" Mike said, pleased.

"It was a split vote on whether to stick you in the corner. I was sure you were history."

"Who was betting on me?"

"Mackenzie." The doctor nodded at one of the men at another table, though all the doctors and nurses looked pretty much the same in their helmets and flak jackets.

"I hope he got odds," Mike said.

"Mackenzie always gets odds," the doc said. He dropped the bloody shreds of Mike's uniform in a heap behind him and reached for a sponge.

"There are some pictures in the pockets—" Mike said.

"Don't worry," the doctor said. "Some poor sergeant sorts it all out."

"I wouldn't want to lose those pictures. My wife and kids."

"We'll make sure you don't lose the pictures, Captain," the man told him gently, and Mike relaxed back onto the table. He could still smell the powder from the mortar round. He wondered if he was going to be able to smell the powder forever.

CHAPTER 18

NOVEMBER 1967

BETTY SIMMONS showed up at the O'Reillys' house on the first morning after the news of Mike's wounding, ringing the bell three times in her hypervivid way. Liz opened the door warily, half expecting to find two more Marines there. She felt she would never again be able to answer the bell without flinching. She was wearing her shabbiest bathrobe; she had intended to go back to bed after taking the kids to the church to light candles for Mike and then getting them off to school.

She had considered keeping the children home, then decided that was pointless. The boys would just spend the day playing toy soldiers, Deb-Deb would swim around in her otter world, and Kathie would cry all day. Better, Liz had finally decided, that they should feel the comfort of normality. She would dearly have loved to feel that herself. But here was Betty, holding a casserole covered in foil and wearing a brick-colored suit with black velvet buttons, two-inch heels, and a huge straw sun hat with a red ribbon, as if she had stopped off on the way to a polo game. It was 8:53 a.m.; Liz had the impression that Betty had felt she shouldn't arrive before nine but then had been unable to hold off.

"Oh, God, sweetheart," Betty breathed. "I heard about Mike last night, and I swear I couldn't sleep a *wink*."

"I slept like a baby," Liz said. "Woke up every two hours and cried."

Betty, relentless as a heat-seeking missile, persisted. "Honey, how *are* you?"

"God, I don't know. I don't care, really. Mike's alive; that seems like enough for the moment."

"No, no, honey-pie, that's no way to think. You've got to be strong for Mike, now more than ever. And for the kids."

Fuck off, honey-pie, Liz thought. She felt dangerously raw. Kneeling in the dim church that morning, watching her children light their solemn candles one by one, she had seen the awe on the faces of her sons, the dreadful pride in their father's heroism, and she had thought, I'm raising cannon fodder. This is not what I signed up for, all those years ago, when I married that beautiful black-haired man.

Betty pressed the casserole on her. The dish was still warm, almost to the point of burning her fingers. Liz considered pretending it was too hot and dropping it. She contented herself with not stepping aside to let Betty in. They stood for a moment in silence.

"I hope I'm not interrupting anything," Betty said.

"What the hell is there to interrupt?"

Betty blinked, then recovered to offer, "I talked to Dick last night."

"Uh-huh," Liz said noncommittally. Betty's insanely ambitious husband had already gone back to Vietnam for his second tour; as a bird colonel, he was in a staff position with the Sixth Marine Division, and the last Liz had heard, he was stationed somewhere cushy. Of course, in Vietnam, you could die somewhere cushy too.

"I told him about Mike, and he got on the horn and talked to a few people."

"'People'?" Liz said, wondering where Betty was going with this.

"The division CO, the 2/29 battalion commander, one of Mike's doctors—"

Liz came alert. "Dick talked to Mike's doctor?"

"Well, you know Dick. Once he's on the case—"

"What did he say?"

"Well, he had a few ideas, actually. For one thing—"

"Not Dick. The doctor, for God's sake." The two Marines the day before had been hopelessly vague about the extent of Mike's specific injuries; Liz had harassed them from every angle and finally concluded that they probably didn't really know anything.

Betty looked alarmed. She floundered for a moment, apparently rummaging for a benign approach to the information. Liz thought of herself with Maria Petroski, trying not to say anything about hair, teeth, and eyeballs. She could feel her heart, a sudden blunted thudding within her chest.

"Would you like to come in for a cup of coffee?" she asked, resigned to a protracted debriefing.

"I'd love some coffee," Betty said, with some relief.

HE WAS ALIVE, when you got right down to it, mainly because Smith was dead; standing between Mike and the mortar shell, the corporal had absorbed the worst of the blast, and the outline of his body was plainly discernible in the pattern of Mike's wounds. Like a tattoo, or a permanent shadow, Mike thought: the ghost of Smith's obliteration would linger in his own scars for the rest of his life. It didn't help to know that a meter's difference would have reversed the situation. It was just one of those things you had to live with.

Two beds down from Mike, a paraplegic was feeding a blinded man with no hands. In the bed beyond them, Krzykrewski dozed amid a tangle of IV lines. The star of the ward for the moment, the resident miracle. They'd cut the PFC's chest open on that plywood slab in Charlie Med and found the chest cavity full of blood. The docs said five more minutes and he'd have died. Everybody who'd gotten him on the chopper was up for a Bronze Star. Three of them posthumous, of course: Smitty, Consalvo, Seretti. Another one of those things you had to live with: they would do it again, under the same circumstances, every time. Marines died to save other Marines. It was simply what you did.

Mike shifted in the bed and sucked in his breath at the wave of pain. It was still hard to sort out exactly what hurt most, and where. He checked the wall clock: thirty-four minutes until his next Demerol shot. His left side was the worst; his arm and shoulder were a mess, as were his hip and left leg, and what remained of his left ear was going to look like a cauliflower. His flak jacket had stopped most of the shrapnel to his body, but what had gotten through had been enough to collapse his left lung and perforate his spleen. They weren't sure about his kidney; the nurses had been instructed to monitor his piss pan closely.

On the bedside table, a spent 105mm howitzer shell, fashioned into a jar of sorts, sat like the punch line to an obscure joke. A gift from the surgeons, it held eighty-seven pieces of good Soviet steel, including the little triangular chunk they'd plucked from deep in Mike's pectoral muscle, half an inch from his heart, and a piece that had been sticking out of his skull behind his ear like a sprouting antler. The docs, a remarkably jolly bunch, all things considered, had told him they hadn't gotten all of the debris, by a long shot; apparently a lot of the small pieces would be slowly working their way out of his body for years, like metal worms surfacing after a rainstorm.

A little something to look forward to, Mike thought. He'd be setting off metal detectors for the rest of his life. But better a living pincushion than a dead hero.

The clock had a red second hand, and he was conscious of how slowly it moved. Demerol, sweet Demerol, in thirty-three minutes and twenty-seven seconds. Twenty-six, twenty-five. Mike wasn't sure what day it was, and he didn't care that much about hours, but he knew that second hand's crawl like the plodding of his own improbable pulse. Thirty-three minutes and twenty-four seconds until the nurse came around with her magic syringe. Thirty-three minutes and twenty-three seconds. And twenty-two. And twenty-one.

SHE HADN'T WASHED anything since the Marines had shown up at the door, and the sink was full of dishes waiting to be rinsed and put into the dishwasher, which was full of clean dishes waiting to be put away. Liz started a fresh pot of coffee and looked for somewhere to put Betty Simmons's enormous sun hat. There was no place in her entire house for a hat like that. The thing required a different life: new furniture, months of a remodeling, a room of its own. Liz settled for tossing it on top of the heap of deferred obligations on the dining room table.

When she came back into the kitchen, Betty was still standing by the counter, at a loss for a place to sit. Every chair and stool had its own still life of child debris, jet fighters crashed amid stuffed animals, Barbies and G.I. Joes sprawled in disconcerting intimacy atop coloring books, miniature armored personnel carriers defending indeterminate piles of plastic and copies of Dr. Seuss. Betty's house, Liz knew, was an exquisite expanse of polished, unencumbered surfaces.

She swept a platoon of toy soldiers and a heap of crayons off the nearest stool into an Easter basket full of cracked-open plastic eggs, the chocolate long since hatched out. Betty ran her hand over the chair's surface, checking discreetly for stickiness, then eased onto the seat and crossed her legs. She was wearing nylons, Liz noted. Nylons, for God's sake, on a Wednesday morning.

The coffee had just started dripping into the pot, and Liz felt a surge of irrational despair at the thought of trying to get some straight answers out of Betty without a cup of something strong in her hand. She considered just plopping down on the floor and beginning to cry. But she had done that yesterday. And there really wasn't much free space on the floor either.

"I'm going to make myself a Bloody Mary," she said. "You interested?"

Betty looked distinctly interested but said dutifully, "Oh, God, it would wreck me, this early, and I've got so much to get done today."

"Not me," Liz said, and opened the cupboard under the sink, where she kept her bottle of emergency Smirnoff's with the cleaning supplies. There was no tomato juice in the refrigerator; she settled for the dregs of an old can of V8, and A1 sauce instead of Worcestershire.

"Are you sure you should be drinking, in your condition?" Betty said.

"To hell with my condition. My husband just got blown up."

Betty watched her fix the drink with a slightly woebegone air and finally said, "Oh, what the hell, just one. But make it weak."

Liz took down a second glass without a word and splashed in some vodka.

"Maybe a touch more," Betty said.

THE BLOODY MARYS helped. Betty with a couple of drinks in her was immediately a more pleasant person to be around; she was one of those alcoholics whose friends were forced to feel guilty because they liked her better drunk. You still had to wade through what a big shot her husband The Colonel was and how perfect her daughters were and how utterly marvelous was her life in general, but with the vodka flowing there was a light at the end of the tunnel. Liz waited patiently, nursing her own first drink and refilling Betty's quietly, until Betty grew a little sloshy and finally got around to being honest about how badly Mike was hurt.

"Dick didn't actually go in to see him," Betty said. "But he talked to the doctor and got the basic picture."

"Uh-huh," Liz said. The ideal wound was bad enough to get Mike sent home but not bad enough to leave him maimed, debilitated, or bitter. It was a fine line. She knew wives who had been delighted by their husbands losing only the lower part of their legs.

"Everything still attached," Betty said. "Everything still in working order. Except, um, his spleen. And a lung."

"A lung?"

"His left lung collapsed. I guess it's like a balloon or something."

"And they can blow it up again?"

"I guess," Betty said uncertainly. "There may be some nerve damage to his left arm too. They're not sure yet."

"He's right-handed," Liz said briskly, wanting to stay focused on the essentials. "So what does a spleen do? Does he need it?"

"They didn't have to take it out, Dick said. It's just, um, damaged."

"How damaged? Come-home damaged, lie-around-for-six-months-in-a-hospital damaged, or just be-miserable-while-getting-shot-at-again damaged?"

"I don't know," Betty said. "I mean, a spleen, right? That sounds pretty serious."

"Did anyone say how long he was going to be laid up?"

"A month, at least, Dick said."

"That goddamned Mike," Liz said. "It would be just like him to go trotting back into the fray with half a spleen. I give him two weeks."

"Dick said the family jewels are just fine," Betty offered.

"What a goddamned relief."

Both their glasses were empty now; medical issues did that. Liz made them fresh drinks. Betty dabbed delicately at her Bloody Mary with a limp celery stick, then took a no-nonsense slug and leaned forward.

"Here's the thing—" she said, with an air of getting down to business. "Dick is adjutant to the Sixth Division CO, now. He says that even if Mike doesn't come home, he can get him a staff job in Da Nang." She gave Liz a wink. "Which would also put him on a faster track for promotion."

Liz said nothing, but her heart hurt suddenly. She knew her man; Mike didn't give a damn about how fast his track to promotion was. Betty meant well, and she could only believe her news was good, but Liz could read between the lines. Mike's wounds were apparently severe enough that he had a chance to come home, if he played his cards right; and he could certainly get a safer job and no doubt further his career in the process. But none of that mattered. Betty, with her husband ensconced in his long-sought staff position, happily chummy with the generals, could never get drunk enough to understand that Mike wouldn't do anything that made that much sense. He was a goddamned Marine, a warrior, a believer. He would go back into battle while there were battles to be fought.

"Dick says Da Nang is safer than Chicago," Betty continued. "They have an Officers' Mess with table clothes. They have *ice cream.*"

Liz stood up to put away the vodka. She'd learned all she was going to learn, and it would be best to stop before Betty got truly sloppy and started talking about Dick in bed. Or before Liz herself started crying. She really wanted to wait until Betty was gone before she started crying.

"What kind of ice cream?" she asked.

Betty blinked, brought up short. "What?"

"Mike is very picky about his ice cream flavors," Liz said. "I doubt he'd stay back in Da Nang for anything less than Rocky Road."

MIKE SURFACED from his latest period of unconsciousness into the labyrinth his body had become, the maze of blocked passages, tortuous corridors, and blind alleys dead-ending in the same inescapable pain. He had a moment of the usual disorientation; in his drugged dreams he had been playing catch with Danny, and the baseball, spinning infinitely slowly toward him in the summer air, had turned into a mortar shell. He'd caught it and thought, for the thousandth time, I'm fucked.

The lights were on; it was early evening. Not that it mattered in the least. Mike flexed his right hand and lifted his arm tentatively, pleased by the mobility. Every physical effort was an adventure, at this point, but he was starting to explore what could move and what couldn't, like a newborn in a crib.

His movement set off a gentle clinking; there were three medals pinned to his pillow. Mike vaguely remembered some colonel in a pressed uniform coming in that morning and sweeping through the ward like the goddamned tooth fairy. Medals, for Christ's sake, in a place where no one gave a damn about anything but the next dose of pain medication: a Bronze Star, for being an idiot and getting three guys killed while loading a dying man onto a helicopter under mortar fire; a Purple Heart, for getting blown up while being an idiot; and something else, something silver and cross shaped, with a yellow and red ribbon, for some fine point of undetermined idiocy.

At the other end of the ward, a man was moaning every thirty seconds or so, a persistent keening, strangely methodical: "Oh, Jesus . . . Oh, Jesus . . ." Otherwise, the hospital was so quiet you could hear the *whoop-whoop* of the spinning blades of the ceiling fans.

Mike turned to his bedside table, which held the box with his personal effects, delivered by a brusque sergeant that afternoon. Like the medals, it had showed up at a bad moment in the medication cycle and Mike had just let it sit, but he reached for it now, moving slowly, feeling his way along the serrated edge of the pain. He had found that he had a period of about eight or ten minutes every two hours in which he was neither too groggy from the Demerol nor in too much pain to think straight, and he wanted to start using his windows of lucidity.

Everything in the box was bloodstained: his shattered watch, the hands still showing 1:12; Larry Petroski's rabbit's foot, soaked in blood, like a slaughtered mouse. The plastic bag with his photos of Liz and the kids had been torn open by the shell fragment that had found his spleen. You always heard the stories of old family Bibles in breast pockets stopping what would have been fatal bullets, of the St. Christopher medal that deflected the shrapnel and saved a guy's life. You never heard about the bullets that went right through every sentimental item and killed you.

Some of the photos seemed salvageable; Mike carefully laid them out to dry, smoothing them flat on the bedside table. Then he turned back to the carton and continued to sort through its contents until he found what he was looking for, the waterproof pen that Liz had sent him early in his tour.

All the activity had exhausted him. He set the pen carefully on his chest and lay back and rested for a while, listening to the hushed churning of the fans, like distant helicopters in a dream purged of urgency, and to the moans of the poor guy in bed fifteen. Somewhere in the distance, he could hear the rumble of artillery fire. Or maybe it was thunder.

His pain settled slowly, like silt from stirred waters. When his breath had steadied, Mike unpinned the medals from his pillow and dropped them into the howitzer-shell jar beside his bed, along with the eighty-seven other pieces of useless metal. Then he picked up the writing tablet he'd had the nurse leave earlier, flaked the dried blood from his pen, and started the letter to Smitty's wife.

CHAPTER 1 9

DECEMBER 1967

THE WEEKLY MEETING of the pastoral care committee had run long, as it always did. It was hot in Priscilla Starkey's parlor, where Prissy kept the central heating cranked up near eighty through the winter, right up until the moment she turned the central air down to sixty-five for the summer, and Germaine resisted an urge to undo his clerical collar. He had done that once, early in his time at St. Jude's, and never heard the end of it. Jesus had sent his disciples out without wallets, shoes, or extra coats, but St. Jude's wanted its divine representatives in uniform at all times.

He was sitting in the mauve Queen Anne chair by the window, which was in the sun but offered the advantage of being not quite entirely in the loop of the discussion, which for the last fifteen minutes had revolved around what to do with last week's altar flowers. Cynthia Abbott wanted to give them to Mabel Condotti, whose husband, James, had died the week before, which was fine with Germaine. It was all fine with Germaine. But Priscilla Starkey had other ideas for the lilies, and the two women were negotiating the fine points of the charitable dispersal with barely subliminal savagery.

"It seems to me that Mabel has plenty of flowers left over from the funeral," Priscilla said.

Germaine considered his empty coffee cup. It was impossible to get enough coffee at these meetings. Priscilla Starkey made a single pot of weak Jamaican Blue Mountain at 8:59, poured the first round at 9:05, and never offered more. She had a connection in Kingston and brought back smuggler-sized hauls of the beans from her regular jaunts to the Caribbean, but she always acted as if she bought the coffee retail and served it as a benevolence to the parish. Propriety demanded that everyone sip a single cup throughout the meeting and exclaim occasionally over how extraordinary it was. As a priest, Germaine was often allowed a second cup, but Priscilla's fine china cups were very small. It didn't help that he was hungover.

Wise as a serpent, Germaine reminded himself. And, more important in parish work, harmless as a dove. He sat tight.

"I think it's the least we can do," Cynthia Abbott persisted. "I mean, the poor woman—"

"The poor woman already has a house full of irises and carnations, and we've got half a dozen other situations. Portia Morgan's husband just went in for heart surgery. And what about some of our housebounds?"

"We could divide them up," one of the other women suggested.

"No, no," Cynthia said firmly. "We can't break up that beautiful arrangement, not after Peggy went to so much trouble putting it together."

Priscilla nodded her agreement: no feeble Christian compromises on the lilies. It was one of those all-or-nothing things. A surprising number of the pastoral care committee's issues were.

Beyond the window, a thrush was rummaging in Priscilla's freshly planted bed of autumn pansies. Germaine watched it idly, thinking of James Condotti. He hadn't known the man well, but he'd liked him. Jim and Mabel had shown up at mass together every Sunday for fifty years, sitting unobtrusively in a pew in the middle of the church, dropping their envelope in the collection basket, smiling over coffee afterward. The two of them would hold hands when they walked back to their car after mass, which always touched Germaine. A veteran of the third wave at Omaha Beach, who never mentioned his war experiences, Condotti had fathered four children who had bred true in their turn and given him a dozen grandchildren and three great-grandchildren, at last count, and even now it was a rare month at St. Jude's that did not include a Condotti marriage, baptism, or first communion. Jim Condotti had always been the one to notice when a lightbulb at the church needed changing and to change it without fuss; he'd been the one out there on Saturday mornings in the fall with a rake in his hand, the one who repainted the lines in the parking lot when they started to fade, with paint that he would buy himself. Asking nothing, and quietly giving much, an almost bafflingly good man. A miracle of decency, typical of his generation.

As was true in most of the parish's terminal cases, Germaine had been the one called to the hospital for James Condotti's last long night; Father Winters did not like deathbeds and avoided them when he could. Germaine arrived in late afternoon, as a beautiful autumn day turned to twilight. The doctors had already let the family know that Condotti would probably not last through the evening, and the grown children were there, two of them having flown in from out of state. Germaine said a mass in the crowded room and gave Jim his last rites as the sun went down in a damask blaze outside the window. Condotti had refused morphine and was lucid, though weak. His children made their good-byes, kissed him, and held his hand. From every corner of the room, the rosary beads rattled; a small altar had been set up on the bedside table, with a statue of the Virgin Mary that Condotti had brought back from France after the war. Mabel sat on James's right, holding his hand in both of hers. From time to time he would glance toward her, as if reassuring himself that she was still there; their eyes would meet and they would smile.

Just after eight o'clock, Condotti sent the children out. Germaine would have gone with them, but Mabel shook her head; her husband wanted the priest to stay. Germaine took the seat to Condotti's left and picked up his free hand, and the man squeezed his fingers once in greeting, then seemed to buckle down to the business at hand. His demeanor had changed the moment the door closed on his children, like someone taking off his tuxedo jacket after a party; he was now plainly in pain, his breathing ragged. He gave his wife a glance, lingering and tender, almost apologetic, then closed his eyes and sank into his suffering.

It was a terrible thing to see. Condotti fought, his body resisting its demise instinctively, his face contorting with the effort. Germaine could feel the agony of his every breath, the confounding depth of the misery within the man, rising wave by submerging wave like a tide, while everything in him struggled toward the surface. There was nothing to do for him, which was its own agony.

This was why Father Winters avoided the ministry of the dying, of course: the rector's muscular religion left no room for this helplessness. But Germaine felt the weird peace that came upon him at such times, the tranquillity of utter defeat, the same whether it came in a hospital room or lying in the bloody mud of a shell crater. It was, perversely, the only time he ever felt like a priest: here, just here, where every priestly comfort failed. Dying with the dying, he knew God's immediacy. It was only with the heedless living, in the kingdom of stopgap and denial that passed for most of life, that he felt despair.

He could see that same peace in Mabel Condotti's eyes across the bed, the helpless freedom of surrender; her face was calm, though her cheeks streamed with tears at her husband's agony. For an hour they sat in silence with Condotti, his increasingly labored breathing the only sound in the room. Condotti opened his eyes twice to meet his wife's gaze, disoriented now, his eyes wild with pain. Each time Mabel murmured something and brought his hand to her lips and kissed it; and Condotti settled himself, closed his eyes, and got back to dying.

"What do you think, Father Germaine?" Cynthia Abbott asked.

Germaine came back to himself: a futile man in clothes as black as a sewer grate, draining the heat from a room full of dangerously earnest women. "Excuse me?"

Cynthia exchanged an arch glance with the others; they all took Germaine's abstractions as a given by now, not entirely endearing but better than too much actual participation. "About the *flowers,* Father."

"Of course, the flowers."

Prissy reiterated, preemptively, "It's not that I don't feel for Mabel in her loss, deeply—"

"Of course," Germaine said again. The discussion, clearly, had reached an impasse. Like the vice president in the Senate, he was a ceremonial presence at these meetings, useless except to break ties.

"I still say it's the least we can do," Cynthia Abbott insisted.

The other women held their tongues; no one wanted to cross either Priscilla or Cynthia.

Germaine considered his empty coffee cup. James Condotti's last breath had been little different from the tortured breaths before it, a shallow exhalation like the last drip of a faucet, too weak to be a sigh but perfectly audible in the silent room. And then, simply, there had not been an in-breath, and Condotti's face relaxed and was still.

Mabel had raised her husband's hand to her lips and kissed his knuckle; she held his hand there, pressed against her lips, her eyes closed. For a long time neither she nor Germaine moved or spoke, and the silence was deep and sweet and full.

Finally, Mabel had opened her eyes and met Germaine's look, her gaze serene and spent. "Would you mind getting the children?"

He rose at once. "Of course."

"Thank you," she said. "It meant a lot to him, to have you here. And to me."

"I'm the one who is grateful," Germaine had said. And in the hushed expectancy of Prissy Starkey's parlor now, "Frankly, I think Mabel Condotti couldn't care less about the damn flowers."

The meeting broke up quickly after that. As everyone was getting their coats, Priscilla, still bright with triumph, sang out, "Oh, one more thing, ladies. Elizabeth O'Reilly's husband was wounded in Vietnam the other day, and someone should probably stop by there and express our sympathy. Any takers?"

There was a beat of irritated silence as half a dozen busy women recalculated their day's itineraries. Germaine said, "I'll go."

It was so unprecedented that everyone gaped briefly, but there was a general sense of relief as well, at one less thing to do, and they quickly went back to getting their coats on and getting out of Prissy's house before they began to sweat. Priscilla's eyes narrowed, lizardlike, into alertness, but all she said was, "Wonderful."

One for the gossip mill, Germaine thought. But he didn't care. He picked up his coat and started for the door, then paused by the vase of disputed lilies and plucked one flower from the sacred arrangement.

"For Mabel," he told Priscilla before she could object, and he took a moment's guilty pleasure in the flare of her nostrils.

"Of course, Father," she said.

• • •

GERMAINE DROVE STRAIGHT to the O'Reillys' house, already beginning to feel ashamed, and blatant in his eagerness. He felt like an idiot. And worse, remembering Prissy Starkey's knowing lizard look, an obvious idiot. To be at Elizabeth O'Reilly's side in this hour of her pain was the only pastoral duty he had actually been eager to perform since he had arrived at the parish. This struck Germaine as a devastating judgment on his life.

His second thoughts peaked as he approached the house, and he drove past it instead. Pulling to the curb a hundred yards farther down the road, beside one of the subdivision's lakes, he turned off the VW's engine. The sunlight glittering on the lake hurt his eyes; his head and his heart were both pounding. He opened the glove compartment and took out a bottle of aspirin and a pint of Jack Daniel's, his emergency stash. The bourbon and the aspirin both burned going down. So much for his head.

He took a second shot of the whiskey, to clear the aspirin taste. And then another shot, just because. Because the day was already ruined by what he'd seen in himself. Because he could either get out of the car now and walk the hundred yards back to the O'Reilly house as one more skirt-chasing priest, or he could sit here and do nothing, and let a decent woman grieve alone, because he was a burnout and a human husk.

He wanted to be with Elizabeth O'Reilly. Not to comfort her, that cheap thing, but to be with her in her suffering, to suffer with her, as helpless in it as she was. To keep vigil, to wait with her for the glimmer of God at the root of everything, for the grace that came only through being torn open. He wanted to tell her that he understood, both her wound and her husband's; that he had been wounded too, and was wounded still; that everyone was wounded, finally, and that wisdom came with learning to live with your wounds. Humility came with that, and compassion. That was truth, God's truth, hard-won.

But the deeper truth here was that anything of wisdom, humility, and compassion he had to offer Liz O'Reilly was false, was poisoned with hope and longing, and with a secret joy.

He had not been prepared for the loneliness, Germaine thought, watching a raft of mallards duck and bob near the shore, as the alcohol began to blunt the edge of his self-contempt. For sacrifice, yes; but what was commonly viewed as sacrifice was easy for him. He had never wanted status, security, material goods, the soothing and absorbing whirl of family and friends; the conventional protections against the abyss, the things most people could not imagine living without, had never appealed to him in the first place. All that had turned to dust too early for him. What had drawn him along, what had sustained him all these decades now, was the simplest, weightless brightness: the moment, always a surprise, when the world turned clear and lucid and holy in the light of God.

It seemed absurd to think of that now, sitting here without a destination in a car that might not start when he turned the key, watching ducks through a whiskey haze while the world groaned and labored. The lily lay beside him on the seat, already beginning to wilt. He had known, Germaine realized now, even when he snatched it out from under Priscilla Starkey's nose, that he wanted to give it to Liz O'Reilly. But that would be a giving that undid the gift, made it a lie and a theft.

Take up your cross and follow me. Well, he had. He had the cross down cold; he was even a specialist of sorts. A man perversely good at dying, at home only when he was nailed into hopelessness between two thieves. It was the resurrection, the path back into the world of the living, that baffled him. Like Lazarus, Germaine thought, called back by Jesus after three days among the dead: dressed in the ragged black of the grave, he still stank of the tomb. He had set out to live in the light and found his way through infinite effort only into deeper darkness, largely of his own making. He was an empty clerical costume, a wasted grace, a drunk among fools. The real sacrifice, for someone like him, was knowing that.

Germaine took one more hit from the Jack Daniel's, then recapped the pint, half empty now, and laid it in the glove compartment, beside the half-empty bottle of aspirin. The VW's engine caught on the third try, with a cough and roar that startled the ducks. As they swam away, bobbing fastidiously, Germaine coaxed the car into gear and headed up the road to the Condotti house, to give Mabel her flower.

CHAPTER 20

DECEMBER 1967

O N THURSDAY AFTERNOON, a week and a half after Mike was
wounded, the principal of King's Grant Elementary School
called Liz to inform her that Danny, Kathie, and Angus were all in his
office after getting into what he characterized as "a rumble" in the
school cafeteria.

She rushed to the school at once and found her children sitting together on a wooden bench in the school's outer office. The three of
them had a chastened but embattled air, like an outnumbered platoon dug in against overwhelming odds. The bench was big enough
for half a dozen children, but the O'Reilly siblings were tightly
bunched, their shoulders pressed against each other, sealing the
perimeter. Kathie had been crying. Both boys had wads of paper
towels pressed to bloody noses, though Angus's efforts to stem the
flow had failed and the front of his yellow shirt was streaked unnervingly with blood.

Kathie began crying again as soon as she saw Liz. Liz hurried to hug her.

"What *happened*, Danny?" she asked as she took Kathie into her arms.

Her oldest son gave a Mike-like shrug. His face was stony with defiance.

"We got in a fight with the Bentleys," Angus said.

"With Tony and Mark?" The Bentley boys were both enormous; Tony, a fourth grader in Danny's class, was a year older, having been kept back once, and Mark was an oversized fifth grader, also repeating his grade. The two were notorious bullies.

Angus nodded. He had taken the paper towels from his nose to talk and was bleeding again. Liz took the gory wad and reformed it so that an unbloody spot was facing up, then pressed the paper gently beneath her son's nose.

"Hold it right there," she said.

Principal Evans emerged from his office. He was an earnest man in his midthirties, with thinning brown hair swirling toward his collar, in the fashion of the times, and a tendency toward stockiness, ill served by a pair of olive bell-bottoms with light lavender stripes and half-boots that zipped up the inside of the ankle.

"Mrs. O'Reilly, thank you for getting here so quickly."

"What in the world happened?"

He glanced at the children and said, "Perhaps we could discuss this in my office."

"Of course. Kids—"

The three O'Reilly children rose at once.

"I meant, the two of us," Evans said.

Kathie and Angus took the hint and sat back down. Danny, stubbornly, remained standing, clutching the bloody paper towels to his nose. He was near tears, but he was furious, and everything in his demeanor said he considered Principal Evans an idiot. Evans gave him an exasperated glance, then looked at Liz, his eyebrows raised, as if to say, You see what I've had to deal with here.

Liz sought her oldest son's eyes, but he would not meet her gaze. Whatever had happened, he believed he was in the right.

She said to Evans, "I'm sure that whatever you have to say, the kids need to hear it too."

Evans seemed inclined to dispute the point, then shrugged a reluctant concession. Liz nodded to the children, and Kathie and Angus rose again, like overworked puppets. They all trooped into the principal's office. Evans moved at once to sit behind his big steel desk. The children arrayed themselves on a threadbare couch with an incongruous rose pattern. Liz took the stuffed chair directly in front of the desk, with a sense of sinking into ineffectuality. The thing was much too low for dignity, which was, perhaps, the point.

"So what actually happened?" she said.

"There was some kind of argument in the cafeteria between your boys and the Bentley boys, which, unfortunately, um, escalated, I suppose you could say. Into a brawl."

"What were they fighting about?"

"No one seems able to say," Evans said, with a pointed glance at Danny, who glared back. "But the facts are clear enough. One of the lunchroom monitors saw the whole thing. Your boys—well, attacked, is really the only word for it, the other boys. Just started hitting."

"Unprovoked," Liz said dryly.

"I'm sure there were unpleasantries exchanged prior to the fight," Evans said. "Boys will be boys. But the point is, Danny started it. He hit Tony, and the thing took off from there. No one is disputing that."

Liz glanced over at her children, but it was true, they were not objecting. Even Angus, on whose tendency to spill the beans she generally relied, had his mouth firmly closed, though it was clearly requiring an effort.

Name, rank, and serial number, Liz thought, impressed in spite of herself. A united front. Whatever was going on, they had decided not to talk about it here, in what they clearly considered hostile territory.

"I find it absolutely impossible to believe that my kids jumped two much larger and older boys for no good reason at all," she said. "The Bentley boys are bullies. You know that as well as I do."

"Nevertheless," Evans said. "Your boys started the actual fighting. Under normal circumstances, in a case this clear-cut, I would have no choice but to suspend the fight's instigator—"

"Meaning, Danny?"

"Yes. For three days, and everyone else involved, for one day. But I understand that there are, um, special circumstances in their lives right now, what with their father, uh—"

Getting blown up, Liz thought. But she realized that wasn't what the principal meant. His tone was off; he clearly didn't know Mike had been wounded. He meant simply that her husband was a Marine in Vietnam. Warmongering father, violent sons. She thought she understood something of Danny's fury now. This chubby little peacenik twerp in his bell-bottoms fancied himself a psychologist. She let him fumble.

"—with his situation overseas, I suppose you could say," Evans managed at last. "With the family's situation." He paused, savoring his own delicacy, then went on, "Given that, and the children's otherwise excellent records, I'm inclined to forgo the suspensions in this case and ask you to simply keep them home for a day or two. In a spirit of, shall we say, self-examination."

"A day or two," Liz said.

"I'll let you be the judge of that," Evans said magnanimously.

THEY WALKED to the car in silence. Kathie was in tears again, and Liz put her arm around her. In the parking lot, Liz unlocked the station wagon and opened the door. Kathie climbed into the backseat, followed by Angus and then Danny. About to shut the door, Liz paused, seeking her older son's eyes. To her relief, he met her look.

"You really hit Tony Bentley first?" she said. It was very hard to picture; Tony was at least six inches taller than Danny and twenty pounds heavier, and his brother Mark was bigger still.

"I hit them both first," Danny said. Both he and Angus had stopped pressing the paper towels to their faces, and their lips and chins were smeared with half-dried blood, as were their shirts, but Liz decided not to try to clean them up yet. She just wanted to get her children home.

BACK AT THE HOUSE, Danny went straight to his room without a word. Liz let him go; she knew her older son. Like Mike, he would talk when he was ready. She debriefed Kathie first, but Kathie, it turned out, did not know what had started the ruckus. She had simply jumped in, on principle, when she saw her brothers fighting with the Bentleys. Apparently she had blindsided Mark Bentley with a cafeteria tray that still had a plate of spaghetti on it, and she seemed pleased, on the whole, with her performance. Liz, still at a loss as to what sort of disciplinary measures were going to be appropriate, considered sending her daughter to her room, but in truth, she could not feel too upset with Kathie for what amounted to sibling solidarity. And there was a secret, guilty pleasure in the image of that bully Mark Bentley with spaghetti sauce all over him. She ended up giving her daughter a glass of milk and some cookies and letting her watch the afternoon soaps. Kathie loved soap operas.

Liz finally got the whole story out of Angus while she was sponging the blood off his face. The Bentley boys, he said, had come over while he was eating his lunch and taken his Twinkies. Angus had started crying, Danny had hurried over to defend him, Tony Bentley had "said something," and Danny had hit him.

"What did Tony say?" Liz asked.

Angus hesitated.

"Come on, Angus."

"He said that Marines are baby killers."

God help me, Liz thought. She felt sick, instantly and literally nauseated. And furious. But at whom? Tony Bentley had not arrived at that formulation himself; he'd heard it somewhere, probably from his parents. He could have gotten it off the evening news, for that matter, from one of the increasingly frequent film clips of college students waving signs and chanting, "Hey, hey, LBJ, how many kids did you kill today?"

She said, "Why didn't you tell any of this to Principal Evans?"

Angus shrugged. "Danny said it was none of his business."

Liz was silent. She suspected that Danny's take on Evans was accurate; the man was probably out there waving a sign himself on weekends. She had a sudden sense of embattlement, of a net of hostile forces tightening around her and her family. If her children had to fight every kid whose parents thought the war was dubious, it was going to be a long haul through grade school.

"Daddy would never kill a baby," Angus declared, with a trace of tentativeness that hurt her heart.

"Of course not, sweetheart."

"He only kills bad guys."

Liz dabbed the wet washcloth at her son's upper lip. Angus's soft peach skin was raw from all the scrubbing, but at least he didn't look like someone requiring a medevac helicopter anymore. She felt completely inadequate as a parent, as a communicator of values and principles: defeated, by complexity, by vicious circumstance, by history itself. She had wanted to raise her children on poetry, beauty, and the subtlety of the world's glorious grays, and here she was, reduced to cleaning the blood off them while they defended a painfully simple white against an even more idiotic black.

What *did* you tell a seven-year-old who had just had his nose bloodied fighting with someone who had called his father a murderer? She wished that Mike was here to help her deal with this. Though if Mike were here, he would probably have been laughing and giving the kids pointers on combat technique. He would have been proud of his children, pure and simple. Liz felt perversely proud of them herself; there was a quixotic nobility in them taking on the Bentley boys that came straight from their father. Mike was fighting this war because he believed, essentially, that Communist bullies were trying to take the South Vietnamese's Twinkies.

Angus was as cleaned up as she was going to be able to get him. Liz took his bloody shirt off and found him a clean shirt in the pile of unsorted clothes on top of the dryer. Since she had already given Kathie milk and cookies and let her watch the soaps, further discipline was out of the question at this point. She found the last package of Twinkies in the cupboard, to replace the loss to the Bentleys, and left her younger son at the table with a glass of milk while she went upstairs to try to talk to Danny.

The door to the boys' bedroom was locked, as she had known it would be. Danny, she noted, had put his bloodied shirt in the dirty clothes hamper at the end of the hall. For some reason, that small fidelity tore at her heart, and Liz sat down on the top of the stairs, put her face in her hands, and finally began to cry.

IT WAS TWELVE STEPS, on crutches, to the double doors that led onto the hallway, and twenty-three steps down the hallway to the courtyard. It took Mike a week to get to the hall doors, and another week to build up enough stamina to reach the courtyard exit. By that time he had stopped using the crutches and had to recount: twenty-one hobbling steps to get off the ward, and another forty steps to get down the hall to the door. His left leg wouldn't bend much yet, but it held his weight now and that would have to do. He carried the crutches with him anyway, partly because he wanted to make sure he could still carry a gun but mostly because the doctors seemed to think he needed them and he was trying to keep the doctors happy. The happier his doctors were with him, the sooner he was out of this place.

The courtyard was a lush leftover from the days of the French, overgrown now but still incongruously beautiful. You couldn't even hear the Da Nang traffic. It felt like a secret; the only other patient who came out there was a lieutenant in a wheelchair, who had taken an AK-47 round through his hip. The guy was a brooder and never spoke, just nodded politely and rolled himself to the farthest corner possible. He would smoke two cigarettes with metronomic regularity, lighting the second off the butt of the first, then nod once more and wheel back inside. Otherwise, the garden was deserted and Mike savored its silence, the odd birds flickering through the flowering shrubs, the sweet, alien fragrance of the heavy white blooms. He could feel parts of himself stirring and stretching, in inner openings blocked off too long by bustle and blare. It was like water after a long parching; in a weird way, more even than warm food, clean, dry clothes, and not getting shot at, solitude was what he missed the most. You were almost never alone in a war zone.

He had Liz's latest letter with him; he'd been saving it up since the morning mail call. The envelope was heavy and promised photographs. Mike gave it a discreet sniff and smiled at Liz's faithful dab of Chanel No. 5, then tore the flap open carefully, conscious of still relearning the mechanics of his left arm. It was like working a puppet with a couple busted strings; the hand was intact, but the fingers were numb, and something had happened deep inside his shoulder that would have made it impossible to comb his hair, if he'd had enough hair to need combing. But he didn't, and the hell with it.

There were three photographs, a welcome haul, one of the kids in their Halloween costumes, one of Kathie and her friend Temperance in their Bluebird uniforms, and an old black-and-white of Liz on the front steps of his parents' house. She was wearing a sundress, and Mike studied her shoulders closely. He loved his wife's shoulders: smooth, strong, and firm. Proud shoulders, and luscious. Sometimes in bed with her, he would just put his nose against her nearest shoulder and breathe. She would laugh at him for that and call him a cheap date, and he would just smile into her perfect skin.

The letter was disheartening, as so many of the recent letters were. The kids had gotten into some kind of scuffle at school; Danny had punched a bully after he made an antiwar crack and had ended up taking the fall with the school's authorities. It sounded to Mike like the next time it happened, Danny should just skip punching the bully and go straight to punching the principal. It tore at Mike's heart to picture his older son being put in a spot like that. It was like sending Edmonds up Hill 93 with the Third Platoon: the poor kid had been thrown in over his head, sink or swim, and he was just doing the best he could. But of course Liz didn't see it that way. All she saw was that Danny was in trouble and needed his father home, which was true enough. In a perfect world, Mike would have been there, of course he would have been there; he would have had his son's back come hell or high water, as in a perfect world he would have had somebody running the Third Platoon who wasn't getting his on-the-job training by running head-on into fortified bunker positions. But in a perfect world you didn't need to be at war in the first place.

The thing was, Liz was still mad at him for getting wounded, though she couldn't say so. Mike had told the goddamned doctors not to bother with a notification, or at most to just send a telegram, but of course the Marine Corps in its wisdom had sent two guys in uniform to the door and made the whole thing into an unnecessarily big deal. Then they'd given him the damn medals to boot, so she thought he'd done something crazy. It wasn't his fault the goddamn Marine Corps gave you medals for just doing what Marines did.

He'd tried several times to call and say something reassuring, but the radio-telephone hookup was hit-or-miss and he hadn't been able to get through. And even if he had, those harried radio conversations tended to leave them both feeling worse anyway; with the time limit, the necessity of using radio procedure, and the knowledge that pretty much anyone in I Corps could be listening in, it was hard to get very real or deep. It left a bad taste. You just ended up feeling frustrated, and lonelier than ever.

What could he say to her, anyway? His country was at war. It was his job to fight his country's wars. It wasn't like he was some clueless cowboy with his six-shooter strapped on. He knew the score. You started out shiny and certain, but that didn't last. He remembered getting off the boat in Hungnam, North Korea, in late October 1950, bright eyed and bushy tailed, fresh out of Parris Island, not knowing a damn thing. The wind was straight out of Manchuria, and the thermometers were sticking at twenty below, and suddenly they weren't fighting the North Koreans anymore, they were fighting the Chinese. There were two Marine regiments trapped in the mountains around the Changjin Reservoir, which on the Japanese maps they were using then was called the Chosin, and Mike's company had climbed an icy ridge above the main supply route to try to keep the road to Hagaru-ri open for them.

The first night on the hill, it seemed like the whole slope below them turned into Chinese, like the snow just gathered itself into a thousand moving shapes. Mike remembered the bugles, the eeriness of their tinny toot-toot sounding suddenly in the darkness. The bugles, and whistles, and the Chinese screaming as they came: *MAH-rine, you die tonight.*

And the next night was the same, and the next; he'd just become an animal, they'd all settled into savage simplicity: try not to freeze to death, kill Chinese. And every night there came that point at 3:00 a.m. when everybody in the company knew exactly how many bullets he had left, and you fixed your bayonet and figured that this was your night to die, because the Chinese just kept coming and you just couldn't kill them all. There were a million of them, like the stars in the sky. And it wasn't noble, it wasn't John Wayne at Iwo Jima and people dying in well-behaved movie ways in one take. Mike had killed one man with his knife, and it had taken what seemed like hours, just the two of them in that frozen hole in the ground, in the pitch-black, closer than lovers, trying to stab or choke or bludgeon each other through all those winter layers. When he finally got the knife in under the guy's ribs and held it deep inside him, keeping the pressure up, he had felt the warmth of the man's blood spreading over his hand and smelled the shit as the man's bowels let go. That wasn't something you did for freedom and democracy.

They'd given out medals like Halloween candy afterward, but Mike knew he hadn't been a hero. He'd just been a freezing animal in a hole, doing what he had to, what they all had to do, on an endless night no one expected to survive. But it had meant something, in the end, watching the Marines of the Fifth and Seventh Regiments file past on the road below, the road they'd kept open for them. Not something you wanted to wave a flag about, not even something you wanted to talk about. Just something so deep it changed you completely inside. And then you came home and everyone thought they knew something, everyone had their glorious opinion on war and why and the price of tea, and you just wanted to tell them to shut the fuck up. No one could ever know who wasn't there.

MIKE REALIZED he was sweating; the late morning sun had cleared the roof line. He looked at the photographs one more time, lingering over the Halloween picture. Danny and Angus had gone as Marines, wearing his old dungarees and field jackets, their faces blackened with burned cork. Kathie had dressed up as a nurse, and Deb-Deb had gone as some kind of animal. God, they were all getting big.

He'd be there for them next year. He'd play catch with the boys, go fishing, get them out to the ballpark and eat too many hot dogs with them. He'd take the girls to ballet and Girl Scouts and birthday parties and sit in the back row trying not to tear up when they sang in school shows. He'd do his job here, take his lumps, and go home to his family.

Meanwhile, it was time for his noon nap. He might as well enjoy the clean sheets while he could; they were the last ones he was going to see for a while. He'd walked two hundred steps today, and he would walk three hundred tomorrow, and by God, by Friday he was walking out of this damn hospital and getting on a chopper back to Khe Sanh before they gave his company to someone else. He just hoped Liz would understand.

PART SIX

To surrender now is to pay the expensive ogre twice.
Ancient woods of my blood, dash down to the nut of the seas
If I take to burn or return this world which is each man's work.

DYLAN THOMAS, "ON NO WORK OF WORDS"

CHAPTER 21

DECEMBER 1967

from: Capt. M. F. O'Reilly
H Co., 2nd Bn., 29th Marines, 6th Mar Div FMF
c/o FPO San Francisco, Calif. 96602
Fri 15 Dec 1967
Khe Sanh, RVN

My Dearest Lizzie,
Well, here I am, recovered from my so-called wounds and back safe and sound in the world's best-armed mountain vacation spot. Much safer than the Da Nang hospital, which is besieged by mad generals jabbing medals into people's chests and hurrying back to the base for happy hour.
In my absence, the company somehow acquired a parrot. Hotel Henry—Hank, for short. He is in the Second Platoon, rank as yet undetermined. He doesn't speak much English yet, except for a few typical Marine obscenities, but is fluent in French and Vietnamese. He is quite fussy, won't touch birdseed, or anything of a typical bird

nature. Having been raised on John Wayne crackers (C-rations), he won't eat anything else. If he's starving and there are no John Waynes available, he'll eat a Saltine or two. He also smokes—Salems only—and I believe they have stunted his growth.

Meanwhile, the rats are teaching their next generation to run up and down inside the tin inner roof of my bunker. The rats over here are a constant threat to anything smaller than an elephant. After seeing them, I figured out why there are no cats around. The rats eat them. The Third Platoon positions have one slightly smaller than a St. Bernard. They've caught him four times in a regular rat trap, but he just pulls his head out and leaves. The First Platoon has given up trying to catch theirs. They've named them instead.

Other than that, you wouldn't know there's a war on. The reason Khe Sanh isn't on the map is that nobody knows where it is except a few Bru tribesmen, and they can't read. Also, nobody except a few idiot Marines even cares where it is. It has little strategic value, is actually a liability, and is a complete and total loss aesthetically. Outside of that, it's a pretty nice place.

The weather continues steady—it rains daily. Chances of a white Christmas extremely poor. No new developments otherwise. The bad guys have clearly decided this place isn't worth bothering with, an opinion in which I concur. I think we ought to let them have it. They would go crazy figuring out what to do with it, and how to keep the rain from washing it away.

I love you, my darling Liz. With all my heart. Thanks for the pictures of the kids, and especially for the picture featuring your shoulders, which I have been savoring on a constant basis. I would marry you again in a second, just for those all-universe shoulders of yours. Please don't waste any more time fretting about my continued well-being. This place is safer than Nebraska, in many ways. And not half as exciting. Plus, my men are more determined

than ever to keep me alive, as there is a great loss of face involved in
a company losing its CO. I'll do my unheroic stint here and be home
in no time, in one slightly scuffed-up piece. I'll be where I belong, in
your arms, happy and grateful for our beautiful life. I love you.
     your loving,
     Mike

LIZ DIDN'T TRUST the letters anymore. Mike's blithe reports of a war safer than Nebraska had already continued to arrive for a week and a half after he'd been blown up once. If it was all so goddamned safe, why did he have to keep telling her how safe it was? She knew her man. She'd seen him break an ankle once playing touch football, about six months after they were married. He'd jumped right up and tried to walk it off, assuring her it was just a little sprain. She would probably have believed him, at that point in their relationship, if she hadn't seen the bone sticking through the skin.

And now the bone was sticking through the skin of their life, and she was still supposed to pretend it was just a little sprain. It would have been so much better—not easier, but better, truer—if he had just been honest with her. She could handle living with the possibility of his death, minute by minute; she *was* handling it. She could handle the goddamn empty bed. What she missed was the reality of her husband, the depth of shared life that had disappeared from his letters lately. One of the strengths of their marriage had always been their mutual realism, their capacity to talk things through, to acknowledge the obstacles, problems, and even absurdities in any situation and find a way through together. She missed the late-night conversations at the kitchen table, fretting frankly about money or the kids' latest phases; she missed lying in bed with Mike's arms around her, talking about the latest difficulties with her mother or his father or what an ass his new CO was. She missed the man who could look at her when the car's tire went flat on an empty highway in the rain at two in the morning and raise one eyebrow so eloquently that it made the whole thing a shared adventure, the man who could get back in the car soaked to the skin and turn the key and have the ignition click once and die, and say, "Do we still have that blanket in the trunk?" She could share anything with Mike, she would, she had, willingly and happily. Except the lie that everything was fine.

These letters were unreal now, was the thing, cheerful little tours de force from a stranger caught up in a role. The war had gotten to him, somehow. He didn't trust her with the reality of his life. She'd turned into the little woman in his mind; she'd turned, Liz thought, into his mother. That hurt. But there was a Mike in her heart, a Mike she remembered perfectly, a partner, comrade, lover, and friend; and she would let nothing in the world take that real man from her, not the Marine Corps, not the war, not history, not even his own maddening need to protect her from the truth. He would make it home to her or he would not, and that was in God's hands. But she would not forget who she was waiting for.

IT WAS ONE of those years when Christmas felt like heaving a dead weight. While the other houses in the neighborhood sparkled with strings of lights, and reindeer and manger scenes blossomed in every yard, the O'Reilly home remained dim. The kids kept bringing home charming little craft items from school; Kathie dropped increasingly pointed hints, and the Christmas cards piled up on the mantel over the cold fireplace, but Liz couldn't make herself go out to the garage and find the box of ornaments and seasonal paraphernalia and just get down to work. It didn't feel like a holiday, and it certainly didn't feel like the advent of our dear Savior; it just felt like another cold

month with her husband away at war. She was amazed at how cheerful the rest of the world was, celebrating the ordeal of a pregnant
woman forced to travel in the dead of winter by a governmental di-
rective, unable to find decent shelter on a frozen December night.
How did all these people manage to feel so festive on cue? Didn't they
have lives?

She finally bought a tree on the Wednesday before Christmas, but
the thing was too big to get off the station wagon by herself, and she
let it sit on top of the car for three days before she finally mustered
the boys and they all dragged it inside and wrestled it into position in
the living room. Kathie had already given up on her, rummaged
through the garage, and found the Christmas box herself by then, and
Liz let her older daughter take charge of the decoration. She sat on
the couch with a cup of hot chocolate while the children hung the ornaments and strung the lights and draped the tree with so much
tinsel that it looked like the aftermath of an ice storm. Kathie had the
kids all singing carols, and Liz sang along as best she could and tried
not to cry.

After the children were in bed, Liz went back to the couch and
plopped down on it. She could feel the baby fidgeting, as if it had
picked up on its siblings' excitement. She was exhausted, though she
hadn't really done a thing. She reached over to turn off the lamp and
sat for a time in the quiet colored glow of the tree's lights. No angels,
she thought; no Magi, not a shepherd to be seen. She felt fat, sad, and
lonely, but she couldn't stop humming "Away in a Manger."

TWO DAYS BEFORE Christmas, someone at Battalion Headquarters
decided that Hill 851 needed someone on it, and Hotel Company was
dispatched to occupy it the next day. The mountain was about three
kilometers due west of the combat base, a crooked peak jutting out of

the jungle like a shark's fin, and was more or less useless, on the whole; but it had an unobstructed line of sight to the main Khe Sanh runway and had been popular recently with NVA mortar and rocket teams.

It was almost noon before the fog burned off enough for the company to chopper in on eight CH-46 transport helicopters. Mike had everyone locked and loaded, but the landing zone wasn't hot, which came as a relief. No one wanted to die on Christmas Eve.

They strung a ring of concertina wire and secured a perimeter, set up some Claymore mine booby traps and noisemakers on the fringes, then started to dig in. There were a number of old foxholes and bunkers and scatterings of typical combat troop trash; Marines had already died once for this hilltop, the previous May. The trees were so full of shrapnel from that battle that the Marines' chain saws had all broken on them within half an hour of starting to try to cut them down. They would have to live with the jungle a bit too close for comfort for a while.

Mike got a shovel and started working with everyone else, digging a command bunker. It wasn't raining, which was a glorious break, and the air was crisp and pleasantly cool. The sun came out for about fifteen minutes, midafternoon, and the sea of jungle below them turned into a kingdom of jewel green, an exquisite wonderland, surreally beautiful.

By early evening, everyone's holes were deep enough for Mike to give the order to stand down for the night. The Christmas cease-fire was set to begin at 1800 hours, and at 5:57 some joker on the next hill over shot a 120mm rocket at them. Everyone heard the *whoosh*, and the entire population of the hilltop disappeared instantly into their freshly excavated holes. The rocket went high, but it enraged the company, and there was a mad moment as everyone in Hotel Company shot everything they had at the neighboring hill.

Mike let the firing go on for precisely two and a half minutes and called for a stop as the second hand on his brand-new watch from the Da Nang PX went straight up at six o'clock. They all waited tensely; the sudden silence seemed to have a weight of its own. Mike had the fire control center of Charlie Battery 1/13 on the radio, and if there had been one more shot fired from the other hill, if someone had even lit a cigarette over there, then fuck the cease-fire, he would have called in every howitzer available and told anyone who cared that his watch was slow. But apparently the rocket had been a whim, and there was no more hostile fire.

The Welcome Wagon, Mike thought. Just a little note to say we're glad to have you in the neighborhood. He would have preferred a fruit basket.

As the quiet lengthened and firmed up, someone in the Second Platoon perimeter began to sing "Silent Night" in a high, sweet tenor. Other voices joined in, and soon the whole company was singing. To Mike's astonishment, these bad-ass Marines even knew the second verse. His arms prickled into gooseflesh.

To the west, the sun was going down behind the massive sawtooth of Co Roc Mountain in Laos; to the east, a full moon floated over the Khe Sanh plateau. The Marines at the main base would have hot meals tonight, actual turkey, cranberry sauce, mashed potatoes, and real vegetables, but Hotel Company would have to make their Christmas feast of C-rations. Mike had saved up two cans of his favorite, Meal, Combat, Individual, Beef, Spiced With Sauce, Cookies, Cocoa, White Bread, Canned. Add a little carefully hoarded Tabasco, and it was almost edible. Liz had sent a special Christmas care package that included an entire case of Kathie's Girl Scout cookies, and Mike set one box aside for himself and had Ike Tibbetts distribute the rest to the troops.

Liz had also sent a plastic baby bottle filled with Jack Daniel's. God, he loved that woman. Mike ate his tinned beef and sopped the sauce out of the can with the bread, then sat on the edge of his fox-hole and sipped the bourbon gratefully. The moon was so bright in the cloudless sky that you could make out individual trees on the company's perimeter, and the spikes of the mountains cast deep shadows in the valleys, where the NVA were no doubt using the cease-fire to move everything they could into better position. Across the dark gulf of jungle to the east, dozens of campfires burned openly at the combat base, an unprecedented sight. To the north, beyond the Rao Quang River, something was going on around Hill 950; he could see the green and red arcs of tracer bullets and the occasional flash of a grenade or mortar explosion. So much for the cease-fire and good-will to men. It looked like a probing attack—not big, but nasty enough.

Sleep in heavenly peace, indeed, Mike thought. It was a very strange feeling. They were singing around the campfires in Khe Sanh, and he was sitting here eating Girl Scout cookies and sipping Ten-nessee bourbon, but men were dying in plain sight on Hill 950. Merry Christmas to all, and good fucking night.

GERMAINE LIFTED the Host for the consecration and felt the tug of the old bayonet wound in his shoulder, skewing the elevation slightly to the left like a kind of gravity. St. Jude's was packed, as always, for the midnight mass on Christmas Eve, but for a moment he felt per-fectly alone in the church. Emptied, stripped, finished. And grateful, to be spent, to be done. All the roads of his life led uphill to this, to the place of the skull and the place of the birth, to the eternally re-peated last meal of a man born in a manger to die on a cross. This was the moment it was made new, if there was such a moment any-more. If there ever had been, if there ever would be. Not omens and magic, not angels singing and gifts from alien kings. Just this bit of bread, dry as cardboard, and the silence that lifted it into holiness, or made it nothing. *This is my body, which will be given up for you. Take, eat; do this in remembrance of me.* This, just this, and a sip of blood red wine to wash it down. He wondered what Elizabeth O'Reilly was doing tonight.

CHAPTER 22

JANUARY 1968

L IZ HAD BARELY gotten the tree up in time for Christmas, and
now she couldn't get it down. It stood in the living room, dropping needles day by day. The children had long since stopped com-
menting on its protracted presence and were treating the thing as
furniture.

Liz knew she should take the tree down, just put the ornaments
away and drag the thing out to the curb. But somehow she couldn't
find the energy. She took to sitting in the living room at night, after
the kids were in bed, with no lights burning but the tree's strings of
red and green, nursing half a glass of red wine and considering the
impossibility of normality.

She often caught herself addressing Mike, in her mind. *You could
have come home, sweetheart.* Much of her inner life now was an ongoing letter, one long unanswered conversation with her husband. *You
were wounded badly enough to come home with honor, duty done, and
you refused the gift. I hope one day you can tell me what it was, beyond*

honor and duty, that kept you there to fight your goddamned war some more.

The baby would stir and thrust, then settle, and Liz would feel the weight of its presence, the neglected miracle growing in her, day by day. There was a sweetness in the mystery of that movement, the haunting flavor of an irreducible truth. Some things didn't have to make sense, she thought. Maybe even most things, in the end. Like her husband, turned toward battle like a plant toward the sun. Like this life inside her, stretching its limbs, blind and insistent. And this tree, this relic, this ghost of a gutted celebration, casting its web of shadows in the quiet like a sentinel guarding an abandoned outpost in a war long since lost. It was what it was, when you got right down to it. And tomorrow was another day.

ON SATURDAY, the thirteenth of January, an unprecedented series of supply planes began landing at the Khe Sanh combat base. Hotel Company watched from their hilltop, fascinated, and then awed, by the C-130s, C-123s, and cargo choppers landing one after another on the plateau below. The sleepy Khe Sanh airstrip suddenly looked like O'Hare on a busy day.

"What the hell is going on?" Ike Tibbetts growled.

"Damned if I know," Mike said. "Looks like somebody in Da Nang decided we don't have enough toilet paper."

"I hope they're bringing beer," Stinson said. "All that cargo space, there must be some beer in there somewhere."

"Ain't no beer gonna get to this fucking hilltop, no way," Tibbetts told him. "Those fuckers at the base will drink it all themselves. We'll be lucky to get bullets."

"We're going to need bullets more than beer for a while, it looks like," Mike said. "Ike, tell the guys to start digging their holes deeper."

from: Capt. M. F. O'Reilly
H Co., 2nd Bn., 29th Marines, 6th Mar Div FMF
c/o FPO San Francisco, Calif. 96602
Thur 18 Jan 1968
Hill 851, circa Khe Sanh, RVN

My Dearest Lizzie,

I'm sitting here eating a meatball sandwich, getting crumbs all over my flak jacket, in my brand-new, two-room, subterranean dwelling. Located on a choice hilltop site with a view of such scenic splendors as Hill 1015, the KSCB runway and ammo dump, and Laos, the bunker has all the comforts of home, except electricity and running water. The only real drawbacks are the lousy climate and noisy neighbors. However, be it ever so humble, etc. Let's face it, you can't beat the price.

Things hereabouts appear to be taking a slight turn toward the semiserious, finally. The latest scuttlebutt from various recon sources and intelligence wonks has "masses" of NVA crossing the DMZ. (A "mass" is defined as three or more hordes.) They have even identified some of the horde-sized units. (A horde consists of five unruly mobs.) In many instances, these are broken into the smallest unit of intelligence terminology, "beaucoup VC." Translated into English, this becomes "many, many," or "a whole bunch," if one is talking to a senior staff officer. (A "bunch," of course, is a subunit of a "mob"; the normal mob consisting of several bunches, according to its mission.)

I see that the fog has rolled in to our little aerie, yet again, and my fingers are getting numb. Back to the stove. At least it's warm, like you. But not as shapely, and the conversation tends to drag. I miss you, my precious wife.

> *your loving,*
> *Mike*

INSPIRED BY the latest letters, Danny occupied the high ground in the backyard, a small rise above the lake dominated by twin oak trees, and began to dig a bunker for himself. Angus wanted his own bunker, but there was only one shovel. The bickering got so intense that Liz finally went out and bought a second shovel.

She also bought a case of beanie-weenies, as the boys suddenly wanted to eat all their food cold, C-ration style, out of cans. Danny and Angus had already coaxed a loud green parrot out of her, for Christmas, after many promises to care for it responsibly. They named it Hotel Henry, after the already-legendary bird mentioned in Mike's letters, and were trying to teach it to say "Semper Fi."

Standing at the kitchen window, watching her sons dig their fortifications, with the birdcage sitting on top of the case of stockpiled beanie-weenies between the trees, Liz thought, I am insane. I have been going crazy for months now and have finally gone over the line. I am insane, my sons are insane, my husband is insane, and my country is insane. I am a madwoman in a world gone absolutely nuts.

JUST AFTER midnight, on January 21, a single flare sizzled upward and burst into bright red above Hill 851. In the eerie glow that suffused the fog enshrouding the hilltop, Mike could hear the *thunk* of mortar tubes firing from down the slope. The mortars were very close; he just had time to dive for the trench in front of his command bunker and cover up before the first salvo hit.

Instantly, all was chaos. The mortar shells kept coming, landing in clusters of three like weird rain, and some 12.7mm machine guns opened up from the neighboring ridge, lacing the fog with green tracer trails. A rocket-propelled grenade hit the bunker roof behind Mike and took out the radio antennas, and the first cries of "*Corpsman!*" went up. More flares lit the sky, the red NVA lights mingling now with white illumination rounds as the Marines tried to see what the hell was going on.

In the swimming light, through a break in the fog, Mike caught a glimpse of the north slope in front of the First Platoon's positions. It was swarming with dark figures scrambling upward, right into their own mortar fire. The clotted mass of enemy soldiers seemed almost comically hectic, as if there were too many teams on the field for a rugby scrum. As Mike watched, the red streaks of Marine tracer rounds began to stipple the enemy ranks.

Bring it on, you bastards, he thought. They'd been stuck on this damned hilltop for almost a month by now, doing nothing but dig and take incoming mortar rounds and listen to the latest rehashed rumors. It felt good to finally just be able to fight.

CHAPTER 23

JANUARY 1968

"MOM, DAD'S ON TV."

Liz's nerves flared, an electric crackle like a jolt from a frayed wire, but she made herself check the roast before she went to the door of the kitchen. She had summoned all her resources and had a real dinner in motion for once, roast beef, mashed potatoes, and fresh green beans, which none of the kids would eat without complaint. It had felt like a cosmic statement when she started it, a message to the universe: Life goes on. I can do this. Now she wondered if it had seemed like hubris to the gods of war.

Having allowed five seconds for defiant dignity, she hurried to the family room, where Danny and Angus were glued to the nightly news, as usual. Liz had found she couldn't stand to watch the war footage on TV, and she relied on her sons for headlines and updates. Tonight, CBS had led with the usual Vietnam story. On the black-and-white television set, a pillar of black smoke rose over some bleak landscape.

"The ammunition dump blew up," Danny informed her excitedly.

"What ammunition dump?"

"At Khe Sanh. That's where Dad is, right?"

"*. . . a spectacular explosion in a rocket attack just before dawn. . . .*"

"Yeah," Liz said. "That's where Dad is."

"*. . . heavy fighting through the night as a number of the Marine positions on hilltops north and west of the combat base came under intense attack,*" a reporter in a helmet and flak jacket, hunched in a trench, was saying into the camera now. Behind him, Marines scuttled against the backdrop of the burning dump, their heads low.

"What hills?" Liz asked. "Has he said what hills?"

"No," Danny said. He was excited, pure and simple, as if an interesting development had occurred in a football game. His father was where the action was. That was cool.

"*. . . facing a critical ammunition shortage. The problem of resupply is complicated by the weather and heavy North Vietnamese mortar fire on any aircraft landing. . . .*"

Liz could feel something solid in the pit of her stomach, like a large, dull knife. She wanted to sit down, but to do so seemed to be conceding too much importance to all this. She had a dinner in the oven, for God's sake. She had potatoes to mash.

The breathless guy in the helmet yielded to a map and the soothing overview of Walter Cronkite. Liz had not really had a solid image of where in South Vietnam her husband actually was. Gio Linh, Dong Ha, Phu Bai—they were all the same to her, obscure places with alien names, details at the tops of letters, each as vague and dangerous as the last. But here was Khe Sanh on a neat CBS graphic, a tiny spot in the extreme northwest corner of South Vietnam, framed by Laos and the DMZ, emblazoned on the map with a jagged red dingbat that was probably supposed to look like an explosion but resembled a spattered blood drop. The dot was encircled by thick black arcs representing bad guys.

"... *reports of at least two divisions of North Vietnamese regulars surrounding the base,*" Walter Cronkite was saying. General Westmoreland was assuring everyone that the Marines intended to hold. Khe Sanh would not be another Dien Bien Phu. Blah blah blah. Walter Cronkite seemed dubious. The parallels were ominous. And blah blah blah.

Liz asked Danny, "What's Dien Bien Phu?"

"I don't know," he said, which meant that whatever it was, it hadn't happened to Marines.

The phone rang. Liz considered letting it go but picked up after three nerve-jangling rings, in case the two guys in the sedan were overloaded tonight and the Marine Corps had decided to just telephone the news that Mike was dead. But it was Maria Petroski.

"Are you watching the news?"

"Yeah," Liz said.

"Isn't Mike—?"

"Yeah."

"Shit."

They were silent for a moment. Liz could hear the Petroski boys squabbling in the background at Maria's end, over the same TV sound track as her own. Someone in Washington was also insisting that Khe Sanh would not be another Dien Bien Phu.

"What the hell is Dien Bien Phu?" Maria said.

"Damned if I know," Liz said. The Vietnam report ended, and Walter Cronkite moved on soberly to other matters. The world's fourth heart-transplant patient had died, two weeks after receiving his new heart.

"Everything looks worse on TV, you know," Maria said.

"Does it?"

"Way worse."

"So this is actually only really, really terrible, not completely cata-strophic."

"Maybe just terrible," Maria said. "Really terrible, at worst."

Liz stared at the TV screen. According to the FDA, IUDs were a safe and effective means of birth control. A little late for that, Liz thought. The pain in her stomach was sharpening, and she had a sudden sense that her bowels might let go. "Listen, I've got a roast in the oven and I think I have to go throw up. I'll talk to you later, okay?"

"*Illegitimi non carborundum,*" Maria said. Marine Corps Latin, an old favorite of Larry's and Mike's: don't let the bastards get you down.

"Love you too," Liz said.

SHE BARELY MADE IT to the bathroom, trying not to double over until she was out of sight of the kids. She closed the door and fumbled at the buttons on her slacks, but she was already so crumpled from the pain that she couldn't get onto the toilet, and she sank to the floor with her slacks at her knees. She was still hoping it was something di-gestive, something she'd eaten, but her underwear was soaked with blood. The pain was not labor pain, it was more like a deep cramp with a knife edge, and the blood was bright red. Fresh blood, hemor-rhage blood.

Not here, not now, Liz thought, trying to breathe. Jesus, God, no. She would rather die than lose this baby here, on the goddamned bathroom floor. But the blood kept coming. She groped for a place in her body free of pain, some point of leverage, like a mountain climber who had slipped on a sheer slope of ice, stabbing at the surface with an ax, trying to dig the point in somewhere and arrest the slide to ruin. But nothing held; there was only the pain, like the cold of the mountain itself, and she was lost in it.

Time must have passed, because someone was knocking at the

bathroom door. Liz could smell the roast in the oven, just starting to burn. So it had been half an hour at least.

It was Danny, sounding concerned. "Mom, are you all right?"

Liz tried to find her voice, and failed at first. The blood had puddled between her legs, sopping, liquid, shocking. Life spilled, life lost, the color and substance of failure and defeat. But she was not beaten yet. She could still feel the baby inside her; it was exactly the size of the pain.

She tried again to speak and found a stranger's weighted voice, weirdly compressed. "Danny, call—" *Your father,* she had been about to say. *Call your father, for God's sake.* "—Mrs. Williams, okay? Ask her. If she can. Get over here right away."

"What's wrong?"

"Nothing. It's okay. But tell her to hurry. And . . . turn off the oven."

"Okay. What about the potatoes?"

"What?"

"The potatoes. They're turning brown from sitting out. Do you want me to finish mashing them, or—?"

"Never mind. About the potatoes, sweetie," Liz said.

AT FIRST LIGHT on the morning after the attack on Hill 851, Hotel Company started to sort the wounded from the dead. There were bodies everywhere. The NVA had broken through the wire during the night and overrun the First Platoon's positions on the Hump, but for the most part the Marines had stayed in their trenches and just fought from where they were. It had been chaos for several hours, shadows fighting shadows, until Dermott Edmonds's Third Platoon had finally counterattacked at about 4:00 a.m. and retaken the Hump just before dawn.

Mike picked his way among the shell holes through the devastated positions, his M-16 unsafed. The hilltop was still engulfed in fog, and visibility was about ten feet, which made it quite an adventure moving among the dead and dying. He was looking for Doug Parker, without much hope of finding him alive. Parker had stayed on the radio the night before when his platoon's position was overrun, and when it was clear that almost everyone on the Hump was enemy soldiers, he had begun calling in mortar rounds on his own location, watching the shells landing around him and adjusting the fire in increments of less than ten meters, until he went off the radio net at about three in the morning. They'd heard nothing from him since then.

Mike squatted to check two bodies sprawled side by side in the red dirt, but both were NVA. One of the dead men carried a stack of pamphlets in English, promising the Americans decent treatment as POWs and laying down some rules of behavior. Apparently the enemy had expected to prevail the night before. The other man had a vivid blue tattoo on his upper arm, partially obscured by the wound that had killed him. The tattoo's inscription was familiar to Mike; he'd seen it on half a dozen other painfully young North Vietnamese dead already: BORN IN THE NORTH TO DIE IN THE SOUTH.

"Skipper—" Stinson called, from the edge of a foxhole nearby. Mike went over to find Doug Parker curled up in the hole, with his radio operator beside him. A mortar round had landed between them, killing both men instantly. Parker was still clutching the radio handset he'd been calling in the fire with. Stinson bent to take the mic out of the lieutenant's hand, but it was frozen there, and he finally cut the wire and left the mic there rather than breaking Parker's fingers to get it out.

Mike felt the loss, but there wasn't time to dwell on anything but getting ready for the next assault. They had almost no ammunition left, and he had everyone shamelessly foraging among the dead and wounded to take what bullets and grenades they could find. With the fog, there were no choppers coming in, and so no reinforcements, no resupply, no ammo, no food, no water. They had wounded men who should have been off the hill eight hours before, just lying there to live or die, bleeding on stretchers in a makeshift bunker with nothing but a sheet of plywood overhead.

The crunch of shovels could be heard everywhere in the fog. Almost every bunker on the hilltop had been destroyed. Hotel Company was somewhere near half strength at the moment, defending a hilltop they hadn't had enough men to cover in the first place. If they come now, Mike thought, they might take us. He had a clip and a half of M-16 ammo left, one grenade, and seven shots in his .45. Six for them, one for him, if it came to that.

The fog lifted for a moment, and he could see down the hill to the wire. The hillside was strewn with NVA dead, like crumpled sacks, soggy now with dew. A number of enemy soldiers dangled from the concertina wire, frozen in the shape of assault or flight. The Marines who were visible were milling around like it was a piss-and-cigarette stop on the Quang Tri Day Tour and they were wondering where to buy postcards. It was a bad time for a fucking Chinese fire drill in a bad, bad place, and Mike already had a sick feeling in his stomach when he heard the first *swoosh* of a rocket being fired from somewhere in the brush to the northwest. And, a beat later, *swoosh-swoosh-swoosh.* And again, just before the first one hit, in that eerie clarity that came upon you instantly under fire, *swoosh-swoosh.*

"*Incoming! Incoming!*"

Time slowed, as it always did when the shit hit the fan, and everything got very clear. Everyone went into motion, looking for the nearest hole. Mike dived into the foxhole where Parker's body still lay, and

Stinson slammed in beside him. The first rocket hit the command bunker, and the second found one of the surviving gun positions, which blew up twice. Fifty-caliber machine gun rounds started cooking off, adding to the chaos.

The screams of "*Corpsman! Corpsman!*" began. Several of the company's Navy medics were already up and scurrying toward the wounded, extraordinarily, but they all dropped flat again as another salvo of rockets hit, and another. There was really nothing to do for the moment but survive. Mike pressed his helmet down on his head with his free hand and tried to burrow and blend with the mud, even as he was conscious of Doug Parker's body beside him, cold and imperturbable.

On his other side, Stinson began to pray, in a steady, unhurried murmur, "Hail Mary, full of grace . . ." Mike was surprised; he wouldn't have pegged his radioman as a religious sort. He was also impressed; his own mind was completely incapable of articulating sentences at the moment. The ground heaved palpably beneath him with every impact, the concussions slammed at him from above like blows, and he could feel his bowels on the verge of release.

More rockets hit. He'd lost count, long since, of how many; the noise of the individual blasts had fused into a single overwhelming roar, like a sea too stormy to distinguish individual waves. One of the mortar positions took a direct hit, then exploded again as its ammunition went up, and rounds of 60mm shells splayed everywhere like deadly fireworks. There was no sign of any of the crew escaping. Another salvo of the 140mm rockets came, and then another, and in the brief silences between the salvos the cries for corpsmen came, rendingly, from all around the hilltop.

Mike raised his head during a pause and spotted Bill Savard, his forward air controller, in the trench about ten yards in front of him. "Billy, get us some air!"

"My radioman's hit!"

"Just get us some fucking air!" Mike turned to Stinson, to call in artillery support, but just then another salvo of rockets began to land and he buried his face in the mud again and rode the bucking earth.

". . . Holy Mary, mother of God, pray for us sinners, now, and at the hour of our death. Amen. . . . Hail Mary, full of grace . . ."

CHAPTER 24

JANUARY 1968

THE GLARE of the hospital lights hurt her: too bright, too cold, a suffusing, almost chemical atmosphere that seemed to fix you forever in whatever painful posture you were caught in, like a fetus in a jar. Hospital lights should be soft, Liz thought. They could blow up cities with broken atoms, track submarines a mile beneath the sea by the sound of someone's disquieted heartbeat, and orbit the earth in tin cans. Why couldn't they make hospital lights that were soft and warm?

She lay on a gurney in a curtained niche of the emergency room, with a rood of IV bags canted above her, including a plump red sack of blood that looked like a swollen tick, while three doctors argued matter-of-factly over how to kill her baby. Two of them wanted to induce labor, and the other one thought they should do a cesarean. They all agreed it was probably too soon for the baby to be viable.

"Guys—" Liz said. It came out as a croak, and none of them turned. She felt a moment's ridiculous compunction, as if it were rude to interrupt. God, she was her mother's daughter. Just another woman, politely bleeding to death. "Hello? Hello? . . . *Hey!*"

The three men turned to her at last. Liz drew the deepest breath she could manage. She hadn't been given any pain medication yet, and it still felt like she had swallowed a guillotine blade. She said, as calmly as she could, "I would like to be included in this discussion."

All three of them looked dubious; the two pushing for the induction of labor actually exchanged a glance of collegial annoyance while the one advocating the cesarean said, a trifle grudgingly, "Of course."

His name tag read Levine. The best of a bad lot, Liz decided at once. I'll work with this one. She met his eyes and said, "So what's the deal?"

"There's been what we call a placental abruption, which is, uh, a tearing, of the placenta away from the uterine wall. That's what's causing the hemorrhaging. So our first concern here is to deal with the blood loss, and with getting the bleeding stopped."

"What about the baby?"

Levine looked pained, which by now seemed like the height of compassion. One of his colleagues said, "I'm afraid there isn't really anything we can do for the baby at this point, ma'am."

"Not if you cut me open and scrape the kid out like something from a broken garbage disposal, obviously."

The man opened his mouth angrily then shut it and shrugged, his meaning clear enough: it's your funeral, sweetheart. The third doctor seemed inclined to weigh in, but before he could say anything Liz looked at Levine and said, "Could we have a few less cooks in this kitchen, please?"

Levine just looked at his shoes, stuck between a patient's rock and a professional hard place. In the long moment of awkward silence, Liz's head began to swim, a wave of dizziness and unreality, as if the room might wash away and leave some nightmare flotsam behind like wreckage on a beach. She could feel the wet heat between her legs as fresh blood started to seep through the gauze they had plugged her with. She took a deep breath and sank back into her body as far as she could, finding the edge of the pain and letting it keep her lucid. It was all she could do not to just close her eyes and moan.

Finally the second doctor turned and went to the sink. He ran the hot water and soaped up perfunctorily, literally washing his hands of her, then yanked a handful of paper towels down and left. The third man, who clearly did not like controversy, said to Levine, "Let me know what procedure you decide on, Doctor," and hurried out too.

"Sorry about that," Liz told Levine, when they were gone.

He shrugged: all in a day's work. "We're faced with very limited options, Mrs. O'Reilly. The hemorrhaging is serious and needs to be addressed immediately." He hesitated, then said, "You could die. That's what we're talking about here. You have to understand that."

"And what about the baby?"

"I really think it's unlikely the baby will be viable at this point. Frankly. I'm sorry."

"I thought you wanted to try to save it. That's why I'm still listening to you at all."

"The cesarean would give it the best chance, certainly. But—" He trailed off, frankly appealing for reason. Liz said nothing. Levine took a breath and said, "Mrs. O'Reilly, the baby has to come out, one way or another, or there is a real chance we're going to lose you. It really comes down to that."

Why couldn't this have happened last July? Liz thought. It would have been almost painless, at that point; it would have been an actual relief. A nice spontaneous first trimester miscarriage, a bad day on the toilet. No one but Mike would even have known; she'd learned, after a miscarriage between Danny and Kathie, to hold off on announcements until the second trimester. It was just too ironic. She'd never been an unambivalent mother, but she'd made her tenuous peace with the goddamn war, with the idiocy of her husband shipping off to protect God and family at the expense of his actual wife and kids, and with the wreckage, yet again, of her own dreams of getting back into the theater. She'd lived with the loneliness and doubt, with the discomfort and exhaustion, and she'd come to love the daily miracle of the child developing within her, even with no one to share it with.

She said, "The baby's still alive, right?"

Levine sighed. "Yes. But—"

"So what would it take for it to be . . . viable? For it to live?"

He shook his head. "At least another two weeks in the womb, assuming the disruption of the placenta is not already fatal. I'd prefer a month."

"I thought babies were viable after six months."

"Ideally, and with luck. This one seems underdeveloped to me. When was your last regular checkup?"

Liz tried to recall. It seemed like forever. She'd had an appointment scheduled for some time during the week after Mike was wounded, but she'd blown it off. She wondered now if that had doomed her baby. She'd taken her eye off the dot.

Levine said gently, "Maybe we should get your husband in here and—"

"My husband's in Vietnam."

"Ah."

"He was wounded last fall, putting a man who had less chance than this baby of surviving onto a helicopter, under mortar fire. He'd back me on this."

Levine was silent for a moment, then said, "Mrs. O'Reilly, if it were my wife, I would already have induced labor."

The problem was, this kid had a name: Anna Marie, if it was a girl, for Mike's mother, and Lawrence Charles, after Larry Petroski, if it was a boy. She'd been playing old cassettes of Mike reading Yeats to her womb so that the child would know its father's voice.

Liz said, "Dr. Levine, I appreciate that. But I'm not your wife. So tell me what we have to do to give this baby another month inside me."

HOTEL COMPANY had cleaned up most of the enemy dead, but there were still three North Vietnamese soldiers hanging in the concertina wire surrounding the Hump. The NVA had registered mortars on the spots and had snipers watching the bodies; there was no question at this point of removing them, and so they all had to live with the stench.

Otherwise, things had settled in to a bizarre routine of sorts. It was like living on the black dot at the center of a target. The daily mortar barrages were relentless; you couldn't take a crap without drawing fire, and everyone moved around with one ear cocked for the sound of incoming. Mike had most of Hotel Company sleeping in their holes during the day, to keep casualties to a minimum; at night they were on 100 percent alert, just waiting to get hit.

They were still undermanned and undersupplied. It had been almost two days before the weather broke enough for choppers to get in, and the first helicopter landing on the hilltop had promptly been bracketed by 120mm mortar shells that killed three of the men loading the wounded onto it. Mike was losing a dozen or more men a day just receiving bullets and water, and they still didn't have enough of either.

The worst of it was, there was no end in sight. Mike's instinct, the basic Marine way, was to take the fight to the enemy, to get down off this hill and go kick some ass, but the higher-ups seemed perfectly happy with the Khe Sanh Marines' defensive posture.

Mine not to reason why, Mike reminded himself. In Korea he'd just been a rifleman, a grunt; he went where they pointed him, tried to kill bad guys, and then went to the next place, and all the places were the same and it all seemed like a cluster fuck. Now he was an officer and they let him see the maps, so he knew the numbers of the hills they were dying for and knew a little more about tactics, and he even had an occasional sense of a larger strategy. And it was still, generally speaking, a cluster fuck. But he did think he could discern some method in the madness of six thousand Marines defending to the death in a place there was really no sense being in the first place. The first B-52 strikes had started, and they were turning the jungle around the base into a moonscape with a Niagara of five-hundred-pound bombs. The sky was full of planes waiting for targets. The heavy guns at Camp Carroll and the Rockpile were all pointed west, and the motto of the artillery batteries was "Be Generous." The Marines at Khe Sanh were here as bait, pure and simple; Hotel Company was staked out on this hilltop like a goat on a tether, to draw the wolves out of the woods.

Well, so far, so good, Mike thought. There were at least two North Vietnamese divisions out there now, twenty thousand or more guys with "Born in the North to Die in the South" tattooed on their arms and "For Nation—Forget Self" written on their helmets. Maybe they could kill all the wolves they had drawn, and maybe not. Maybe the wolves would eat the goat. But in any case they were in for one hell of a fight. He could handle that, that was his job. He just wished he had more ammo and enough water to refill his goddamn canteen. It would be nice to start getting some mail again. And Lord, those bodies in the wire stank.

PART SEVEN

I balanced all, brought all to mind,
The years to come seemed waste of breath,
A waste of breath the years behind
In balance with this life, this death.

W. B. YEATS,
"AN IRISH AIRMAN FORESEES HIS DEATH"

CHAPTER 25

JANUARY 1968

L IZ WAS BORED long before she was beyond the immediate
danger of dying. The worst thing was not being able to go home,
and the second worst was not being allowed to get out of the bed. It
was much like war, she supposed. She understood Mike's maddening,
nerveless nonchalance much better now. You really could get used to
anything, including being a heartbeat or two away from death at any
given moment, and after a while what you were going to eat for your
next meal became much more interesting than the imminence of
mortality. Marines, at least, got medals, for the occasional adventure
of crawling around under fire to save a comrade; and Marines got to
shoot back. All an embattled mother got was four walls and a little
plastic name tag on her wrist.

She had spent three days in the ICU, and even now, in a regular
room with a view of the parking lot, she was wired to a BP monitor
that seemed to go off every hour or two just on principle, screaming
abruptly like a wounded robotic cat when the numbers drifted too
low. The nurses would rush in, there would be a flurry of activity,

they'd put something else in her IV or change the flow rate. Later one of the doctors would come in and look at the clipboard at the end of the bed without ever meeting her eyes, mumble something, then shake his head at her continued recalcitrance and leave. Dr. Levine in particular was short with her; Liz had been given to understand that he'd stuck his neck way out on her behalf and that it would be a professional embarrassment to him if she died. She suspected he had set the blood pressure alarm needlessly high just to impress upon her the seriousness of the situation.

Liz felt sufficiently impressed. She was not allowed to get out of the bed. A catheter had been inserted to keep her from having to get up to go to the bathroom. She was on some kind of drug to mature the baby's lungs, and with her belly wired up to track the baby's heartbeat, she looked like a pregnant time bomb. Levine had told her ominously that if there were prolonged signs of fetal distress, there would be nothing to do but a cesarean, but the baby's pulse was steady and strong. The doctors all seemed vaguely annoyed by that, as if the kid were thriving just to spite them.

The nurses were with her, though, thank God. Liz could feel their quiet support. They did all the little extras, including cheerfully putting up with the visits from the kids. It amounted to unspoken sisterhood. They wouldn't turn off the blood pressure alarm, though. Sisterhood only went so far.

She hadn't said anything to Mike about what was going on. Liz understood her husband's letters much better now, indeed. There was a gray zone of life-danger it simply didn't pay to express. Mike couldn't do anything for her right now, he would just worry and hurt and feel helpless, and she wanted to spare him that until there was some real news. Like, Sweetheart, you have a new daughter, despite a few complications. Or, Darling, our child is dead. Meanwhile, she kept her letters chipper and blithe while the blood pressure Klaxon blared, as her husband kept his letters chipper and droll with two divisions of the North Vietnamese Army at his doorstep. What a chipper pair they were. What a couple of stone-cold liars.

Mike's parents and his sister came down from Maryland to take care of the kids. The elder O'Reillys were also behind her all the way, though Liz knew it had never occurred to them that she would consider anything but saving the baby. She remembered how happy—and how utterly relieved—they had been the first time she had gotten pregnant and how uneasy they had been at the notion that she wouldn't immediately drop all her school and theater nonsense and just settle in to being a mother.

And here she was, after all these years of trying to swim against the stream, doing exactly what a good Catholic wife should. The irony of that nearly overwhelmed Liz at times, but she was grateful for the senior O'Reillys' presence. The kids, after a period of anxiousness, were delighted to have their grandparents around; it was almost like summer vacation, a series of museums, amusement parks, and special meals out. Only Danny really seemed to grasp what was going on.

The baby stirred inside Liz, a gratifyingly firm kick, and then a delicate series of taps. The child had wonderful rhythm; Liz was sure by now that it was a girl and that she would be a dancer. The heartbeat on the fetal monitor was steady at 113 beats per minute, at the low end of normal. If it went below 110, the damned bells and whistles sounded, but it hadn't gone below 110 since Tuesday.

They also serve who only stand and wait, Liz told herself. It was a Mike-ism, a Marine-flavored variant on something from Milton. The phrase was usually applied to a tedious posting in some obscure place and tended to be spiced with cynicism or obscenity. But waiting seemed holy, here. Waiting was all she had to do; it was her only work now. Everything was covered, and everything was out of her hands, except the time this baby needed. She would wait, and wait some more. And wait some more, until waiting seemed like dying; and wait more still, until the dying finally seemed sweet.

GIVEN SO MANY empty hours, Liz found herself spending way too much time watching the room's black-and-white TV. The world seemed to be falling apart out there, day by day, even aside from the fact that her husband's current address was surrounded by twenty thousand North Vietnamese soldiers. North Korea had seized a U.S. ship, the *Pueblo,* and a B-52 loaded with hydrogen bombs had crashed in Greenland. The Vietcong had just attacked in hundreds of places throughout South Vietnam, launching a countrywide offensive during what was supposed to be the Tet holiday cease-fire. But Liz found herself impatient with all the crises; all she wanted at this point was news of Khe Sanh. She hadn't been able to stand it when her husband's foxhole was the lead story on every news show, and now she couldn't stand it that it wasn't.

The door to the hospital room swung open, and Betty Simmons breezed in, wearing a blue suit-skirt combo with black piping, the shoulder seams squared off to razor sharpness, and carrying a bouquet of daisies.

"How's our girl?" she chirped.

Liz shifted in the bed to make sure the sheet was covering her legs, which had swollen with retained water and looked like giant sausages.

"Bloated, terrified, and trapped here for the duration, in constant pain," she said. "But otherwise great."

"That's the spirit," Betty said. She waved the daisies, which Liz acknowledged with a nod. Betty had been bringing flowers every day, and the room was starting to seem a little crowded. She'd also been bringing books, a relentless blend of the lurid and the sappily inspirational: Jacqueline Susann, Rod McKuen, *In Cold Blood,* and *Please Don't Eat the Daisies.* Liz just let both the flowers and the books pile up. She was actually reading *The Golden Notebook* and Virginia Woolf.

Betty spent a moment looking for somewhere to put the latest blooms and finally settled on a spot by the window. Then she came back to the bedside, pulled up a chair, and peered at the ruins of Liz's lunch. "You didn't eat your vegetables, sweetie."

"I'm on a hunger fast until they give me a color TV."

Betty made a little *tsk-tsk* sound. "You've got to keep your strength up, honey."

"I just want to wash my hair."

On the muted TV screen, the afternoon news footage of the shattered U.S. embassy building, with bodies in the courtyard, had just given way to a South Vietnamese policeman putting a pistol to the head of a Vietcong prisoner on a street in Saigon and pulling the trigger. God help us all, Liz thought, and closed her eyes, to concentrate on the pulsing heart inside her. God help us all. But especially my husband and my baby.

"I wish they'd stop showing that," Betty said. "You'd think that one ridiculous VC was the only person who had died in the whole damned country." She caught herself. "Oops, sorry."

"Mike's still alive, last I heard," Liz said dryly.

"Thank God."

"God's on probation, as far as I'm concerned," Liz said. "I'm just hoping Mike keeps his head down." She had finally found out what Dien Bien Phu was. Danny had gone to the library and found a fat, grim book, by some Frenchman, called *Hell in a Very Small Place.* The book had a distinctive poppy red cover, and Danny's math teacher had already sent a note home saying that he was reading it during class and would have to leave it home. Danny had solved this by re-covering the book in brown so that it looked like his math text. Liz would have liked to back the math teacher, but she counted too much on Danny's briefings. Dien Bien Phu turned out to be the place in the mountains of northern Vietnam where, in the spring of 1954, thirteen thousand French defenders had suffered through a terrible fifty-six-day siege by the Communist-Nationalist guerrillas then called the Viet Minh. The garrison had finally fallen, and the defeat had marked the end of the French colonial rule in Indochina.

The parallels to Khe Sanh were obvious, as Walter Cronkite kept pointing out gloomily. The French had invited the fight at Dien Bien Phu, hoping to finally get the Viet Minh to mass in one place, and had gotten more than they had bargained for. Danny said that the Marines had infinitely better air support, more and better artillery, and that they were holding the high ground around the base. Also, the Khe Sanh airstrip was still open, while the French had been reduced to parachute drops for their resupply. Liz would have felt much better about her son's analysis if it had not been so obvious that Danny felt the crucial difference in the two situations was that the Viet Minh had been dealing with a French army, not United States Marines. Walter Cronkite, not as schooled as her son in the myth of Marine invincibility, seemed much less sanguine.

The fetal monitor showed the baby's pulse at 115, as high as it had been in a week. Probably a response to maternal stress, Liz thought. But the doctors had been fretting over the child's low heart rate, so any elevation was a good thing. Maybe she should have Betty come by more often.

"So, do you need anything, sweetie?" Betty asked. "Anything I can get for you? Anything I can do?"

"I'm fine, Betty, thanks. I feel very well looked out for. But thank you."

The formalities completed, there was a beat of silence. The specter of more small talk loomed, but to Liz's relief the phone on the bedside table rang just then, as it did almost every day at this time. Mike's mother, no doubt, checking on what vegetables the kids could be persuaded to eat, or Linnell Washington with some fresh plan from Temperance and Kathie. Liz reached for the receiver. "Hello?"

"Mrs. O'Reilly? This is Miranda Simmons."

"Oh, hello, Miranda." Liz liked Betty's daughter, almost in spite of herself. Miranda was a crisp, no-nonsense girl, as energetically good-hearted as her mother but somehow without Betty's need to rub your nose in it.

"I told her she could reach me here, if she needed to," Betty said. "I hope that's okay."

Liz nodded, no problem. "How are you, Miranda? Congratulations on the scholarship."

"Thank you, Mrs. O'Reilly. We've all been praying for you and the baby."

"Thank you, honey. That means a lot right now."

"I'm so sorry to disturb you, but—is my mom there?"

The hair went up on Liz's forearms, as if she'd been licked by a cold wind. "Of course, sweetheart. She's right here, I'll put her on."

"Hi, honey," Betty said cheerfully as she took the phone, but her face clouded instantly. After listening a moment, she said, "Are they still there?"

No, God, no, Liz thought.

"Well, just have them wait in the living room, sweetheart. . . . No, tell them I'll be right there. . . . Oh, and Miranda—ask them if they would like something to drink. . . . No, nothing alcoholic. Coffee, tea, whatever. And some finger food, cookies or something. Use the platter with the flowers around the edge. . . . Okay, sweetie. I'll see you soon."

Betty hung up and looked at the phone for a moment, then composed herself and met Liz's eyes. She was dry-eyed, and even managed a thin smile of sorts, and for an instant Liz's hopes went up. But Betty said, "We have visitors, it seems. Two Marines."

"Oh God, Betty—"

"They won't tell Miranda anything."

Liz groped for words, and found nothing. She had a sudden sense what it might mean, under fire, to have the person beside you get hit. One moment you were talking, one moment life went on, however madly, and then there was blood. And even as you moved to help, there was that inescapable instant you would hate yourself for, when you thought, Thank God, it wasn't me.

In spite of herself, she glanced over at the fetal monitor. The baby's heart rate was steady at 113.

"He said Da Nang was safe," Betty said. "He was afraid we'd win the war before he got a regiment."

CHAPTER 26

from: Capt. M. F. O'Reilly
H Co., 2nd Bn., 29th Marines, 6th Mar Div FMF
c/o FPO San Francisco, Calif. 96602
Wed 14 Feb 1968
Hill 851, circa Khe Sanh, RVN

My Dearest Lizzie,
   *Reports of our demise here are greatly exaggerated. From what I
can glean from recent copies of* Stars and Stripes, *everyone back
home, including our beloved commander-in-chief, has gotten a little
hysterical about this siege, but here on the ground at Siege Central
it's actually no big deal. We take a few hundred rounds of incoming
a day, definitely an attention getter, but let's face it, when you've
seen one incoming mortar round, you've seen them all. Once you're
in your hole, it really doesn't matter how many they shoot. Unless
one lands on you, of course. And if one lands on you, it really
doesn't matter how many other ones they shoot.*

Having gotten their asses handed to them the first time, the NVA don't seem inclined to charge up the hill again and try to take us, so essentially we're just waiting them out. They shoot at us, we shoot back, then our planes come in and ruin their day. I sure wouldn't want to be on the other side of our wire when those B-52s drop a load. We've got them right where they want us, and it's just a matter of time before they run out of ammunition and people. We've actually got some loudspeakers set up down at the Khe Sanh Combat Base, to try to talk the NVA into surrendering, though I don't know what we'll do if all 20,000 of them chieu-hoi at once, as we really have nowhere to put them.

Meanwhile, the C-ration trade is brisk. In the Marine Corps, every day is a holiday and every meal's a feast, even on one-third rations. The beef and potatoes meals are going at a premium, with pork slices a close second. The spaghetti and meatballs are tolerable, but ham and lima beans are out of the question. With the ham-and-eggs meals, so-called, we take out the cigarettes, instant coffee, toilet paper, and pound cake, and throw the cans down the hill unopened, in hopes that the bad guys try to eat them. This is probably some kind of Geneva Convention violation. But war is hell.

Aside from the unending array of culinary delights, our days are fairly routine. Every day at dawn, we have a little colors ceremony, which consists of two insane Marines running out with a flag and attaching it to the radio antenna. This really pisses the bad guys off—as soon as our guys are out in the open, you can hear the mortar tubes pop. We've got it down to a science, at this point: you've got twenty-three seconds to get the flag up, salute, and get back in your hole before the rounds land. Strangely enough, everyone wants to do it—there's a waiting list for who gets to raise the colors every morning. No casualties yet, except Charlie's pride.

The rest of the day is more of the same—mortar barrages at ten and two, rocket attacks for lunch and dinner. At four o'clock every afternoon, some skinny little gook with a rifle he seems to have stolen from Daniel Boone pops up on our neighboring hill and cranks off a couple of ineffective rounds. We call him Sixteen-Hundred Charlie, a.k.a. Luke the Gook. Luke is an endearingly bad shot, and no one has the heart to kill him. Besides, we're afraid his replacement might be a better shot. So we just leave him alone.

In the absence of water, no one has shaved or bathed for about a month at this point. I look a little like Ernest Hemingway with my beard, if I do say so myself, except that the beard is full of beans and bread crumbs. You can easily tell the new arrivals on our little hilltop, not just because they do not smell and are clean shaven, but because their uniforms are green. Anyone who's been here more than a day and a half is colored orange-red, the precise shade of the Khe Sanh dirt. An upside of the nonbathing is that we stink too much even for the rats—no one has been bitten in weeks. No wonder the NVA won't attack.

That's about all the news that's fit to print from us history makers here. The Third Platoon's mortars are firing, and I guess I'd better do the Khe Sanh Shuffle and go see who is the lucky recipient of our attentions. I love you, my precious Lizzie. More every day, more every minute. I promise to have showered before I see you again.

> *your loving,*
> *Mike*

P.S. One recent casualty of note: Hotel Henry, our company parrot, unfortunately bought the farm the other day. His cage took a mortar hit, nothing left but three green feathers and a claw. Poor bastard. I've put him in for a Bronze Star. Hotel Henry's indomitable courage, selfless devotion to duty, and ability to swear fluently in three languages were an inspiration to all who served with him and upheld the highest traditions of the Marine Corps and the United States Naval Service. He gallantly gave his life for his country. Don't tell the kids.

THE RESUPPLY CHOPPER was hit by a rocket and 12.7mm machine gun fire just as it started its run toward 851, and it dropped like a rock in Indian country, about two hundred meters down the hill. There was an almost palpable collective groan from the Marines in the trenches, and everyone in Hotel Company opened up with everything they had, to cover the crew, and out of sheer frustration. The hill had been socked in by bad weather for three days, nothing coming in or going out, and men were foraging in the garbage dump, looking for the little containers of jelly and cheese left in discarded rations. They were sneaking out to the wire at night in the hope of finding rice bags on the dead bodies of the NVA. A can of spaghetti and meatballs could bring you as much as fifty dollars, but no one was selling.

The pilots and the door gunner made it in through the wire, to cheers; and moments later two fast-movers came in low and dropped bombs and napalm on the downed Huey. The men of Hotel Company watched in silence as the chopper burned.

"I hope it was all just ham-and-motherfuckers," Ike Tibbetts said. "I hope there weren't no cake or somethin' in there."

"It's probably just Valentine's cards," Mike said, but he was thinking of the three dead Marines and the half dozen wounded men he had at the landing zone waiting to get out on that chopper. The dead men were wrapped in ponchos because they were out of body bags, and the wounded men lay on ponchos because they were out of stretchers. Soon they would be out of ponchos. And they were out of socks. Everyone's socks had rotted off their feet, and half the company had trench foot. Mike had been begging the battalion logistics officer for socks every day, to no avail. The guy had told him to have his men wash the socks they had, which was a joke, because they didn't have enough water to brush their teeth, much less do laundry. Everyone knew by now that Lyndon Johnson had a scale model of Khe Sanh set up in the White House basement, that their commander in chief was obsessed with the siege and following every detail of the battle closely. Mike just wondered if the president knew how much they needed socks.

"I don't want them goddamned gooks reading my Valentine's cards," Tibbetts said. "Ain't none of their motherfuckin' business what my baby say to me."

WHEN THEY HAD EATEN, *Jesus said to Simon Peter, "Simon, son of Jonas, lovest thou me more than these?" And Peter answered, "Yea, Lord; thou knowest that I love thee." And Jesus said unto him, "Feed my lambs."*

"B–7," Father Germaine said. He sneaked a look at Mrs. Malewich, in the back row. The old woman was squinting dutifully at her array of three cards, her dauber poised, but she made no mark. This meant nothing; Mrs. Malewich seldom heard the call clearly, and her marking patterns tended toward the random.

"B–7," Priscilla Starkey echoed. "God's in heaven."

She posted the number on the big board. All through the parish hall, gray heads bent over cards laid out in lucky patterns, and daubers danced. It was Wednesday evening, and St. Jude's weekly Bingo Night was in full swing on Game 14. Beside Mrs. Malewich, Donna Palmer marked at least half of her ten cards. Donna was looking a bit smug at this point, Germaine noted, and would probably win again. She had two rosaries, a St. Anthony medal, a small statue of the Virgin Mary, and a bit of bone purported to be from the tibia of St. Paul surrounding her cards, which were arranged in a Celtic cross. Germaine thought the bone was overkill, but there was no denying Donna Palmer's methods. The woman won three or four times a night.

He turned to the air blower and touched the button, and the balls whirled within the glass case like a swarm of bloated white locusts. The state-of-the-art machine played a rousing version of "When the Saints Go Marching In" and delivered the next numbered ball into a tray precisely on the exclamation point. It had cost several thousand dollars, but Wednesday nights were the parish's money cow and no one begrudged the expense. Nothing but the best, for St. Jude's Bingo.

And Jesus said to him again a second time, "Simon son of Jonas, lovest thou me?" And again Peter answered, "Yea, Lord; thou knowest that I love thee." And Jesus said unto him, "Feed my sheep."

"I–23," Germaine said.

"I–23," Priscilla intoned. "The Lord is my shepherd."

She posted the number. Mrs. Malewich made a mark and then tried to erase it, with consequent smearing. That card would be useless. In the second row, Mr. Shoenfelder was peering at his single card as if the numbers might change, his USS *Pennsylvania* cap slightly askew. Mr. Shoenfelder always played card number 12741, the date of Pearl Harbor, and he liked to make a little whistling noise, ending in an explosion, as his marks landed. Somehow this kept him happy, despite the fact that he had not won a single game in the year and a half since Germaine had been calling on Bingo nights. It was not about winning, for Mr. Shoenfelder.

"O–76," Germaine said.

"O–76," Priscilla said. "Trombones."

Mrs. Malewich sang out, "Bingo!" and everyone relaxed. Mrs. Malewich's bingos amounted to a break, as they never held up.

Priscilla went to check the old woman's card. Germaine waited re-signedly. He had used to check the cards himself, until he had vali-dated one of Mrs. Malewich's fanciful bingos the previous October out of uncontrollable compassion and gotten caught. He had argued at the time that the occasional mercy bingo should be allowed, that the last should be first at least once in a while, and blessed were the poor in spirit, but all that New Testament reasoning had accom-plished was that he'd been relieved of his validation duties and now had Priscilla Starkey permanently attached to him to check the num-bers he called. Bingo was Old Testament.

Priscilla spoke sternly with Mrs. Malewich, who looked duly chas-tened and leaned back in her wheelchair dispiritedly. She would make no more marks this game, Germaine knew. Mrs. Malewich always lost faith in her hearing for a while after a false bingo.

And a third time, Jesus said unto him, "Simon son of Jonas, lovest thou me?" And Peter was grieved, that he had asked him a third time. And he said unto Jesus, "Lord, thou knowest all things; thou knowest that I love thee." And Jesus said unto him, "Feed my sheep."

Priscilla returned to her post, and the balls milled in the blower.

"I–28," Germaine said.

Verily, verily, Simon Peter, I say unto you, "When thou wast young, thou girdest thyself, and walkedst wither thou wouldst; but when thou shalt be old, thou shalt stretch forth thy hands, and another shall gird thee, and carry thee whither thou wouldst not."

"I–28," Priscilla said. "Heaven's gate."

Donna Palmer covered half a dozen cards in a flurry, pecking her marks like a hungry chicken snapping up grain. Everyone held their breath in anticipation, but Donna didn't call out.

It didn't matter; they all knew she had this one in hand. It was just a matter of time. Germaine punched the button and the white balls whirled.

THE FEBRUARY NIGHT was chill and crisp, a relief after the stuffiness of the parish hall. Many of the Bingo regulars were relentless smokers, and Germaine always emerged with his lungs raw and the smell of smoke on his clothes. It was strangely like coming out of combat, though his battlefield ministry at this point amounted to praying for Mrs. Malewich to get a card right; he bore steadfast witness to the reality of God under a weekly mortar barrage of plastic balls and laid his life on the line to the carnival blare of "When the Saints Go Marching In," comforting the obsessed, the lonely, and the disappointed through the carnage of the progressive jackpot, amid the savage haze from Mr. Shoenfelder's cigar.

Germaine sat down in front of the church, on the stone rim of the shrine beneath the statue of St. Jude. It was too early to go back to the rectory, and much too early to go back sober. It was his birthday, and he suspected that Sarah, the rectory housekeeper, had arranged a celebration. Blowing out pink candles and eating birthday cake with Father Winters struck Germaine as too much to ask, even of a religious professional. The vows of poverty, chastity, and obedience only went so far. He was thirty-five years old, halfway through his threescore and ten, two years older than Christ had been when he died. Germaine wondered, yet again, why God had let him live so long.

A crash from the side of the church startled him. Germaine hurried around the corner in time to spot a dark figure running across the parking lot. In the weak light from the bulb above the side entrance, a jagged hole gaped in one of the stained-glass windows. The new St. Christopher panel, Germaine noted with a pang, the memorial to Sergeant Martin Truman.

He went into the darkened church and swept up the glass by the light from the rack of candles beside the memorial plaque, his heart hurting with every crunch. The stone that had shattered the glass had a note attached, *Fuck the war,* which Germaine tore into small pieces and discarded with the rest of the rubble. It seemed to him that it would hurt Martin Truman's parents less to believe the act had been simple vandalism.

SURE ENOUGH, Sarah had made a chocolate cake, which looked oddly liturgical, ablaze with six squat votive candles and a thin purple taper left over from the Advent wreath. Apparently they were out of regular birthday candles. The housekeeper and Father Winters sang "Happy Birthday," a little painfully, and Germaine feigned surprise, if not delight. He dutifully donned the shiny party hat Sarah had provided as he and Winters sat down and blew out the candles, wishing the ceremony over swiftly.

Sarah poured them coffee, with a discreet birthday shot of Jameson's in Germaine's and a splash of schnapps in Father Winters's. The woman knew her priests.

Germaine gave the housekeeper a wink, then settled in to the ordeal of time at the table with his pastor. Winters reacted with predictable outrage to the news of the broken window, which he clearly felt to be symptomatic of a more general societal breakdown. He wanted to call the police, but it was almost time for *Green Acres,* and in the end the pastor decided to let it go. Winters had a thing for Eva Gabor.

"How did Bingo go?" he asked Germaine, one eye on the clock as he helped himself to a second piece of cake.

"Donna Palmer hit the Coverall Jackpot on a purple card."

"Damn that woman," Father Winters said, and signaled Sarah for more schnapps. Purple cards paid double; Winters monitored the house take on St. Jude's Bingo as closely as any casino manager, and he was no doubt already thinking about how much it would cost to replace the stained-glass window.

As the two men finished their cake in silence, the phone rang.

"Father Germaine, it's for you," Sarah called.

Germaine excused himself and took the call in the kitchen. His relief was mingled with guilt; a call at this hour usually meant either that someone had died or that someone was afire with some urgent fine point on the spring open house. But it was Danny O'Reilly, calling from the hospital, and Germaine felt his heart in his chest, abruptly, as if someone had yanked a corset tight.

"Is your mother all right?" he asked.

"I think so," Danny said. "She had the baby. It's a girl. Anna."

"Uh-huh," Germaine said carefully.

"She told me to call you and ask if you would do a baptism."

"Tonight?"

"Yes, sir." Danny hesitated. "Can you do a baptism at a hospital?"

Germaine relaxed a little. "Of course, Danny. I mean, normally we would wait and have the ceremony at the church, but—"

"She also wanted me to ask if you could bring the stuff to do the last rites."

Germaine was conscious suddenly that he was still wearing the cardboard party hat. He took it off and set it on the counter.

"Of course, Danny," he said. "Tell your mother I'll be right there."

CHAPTER 27

FEBRUARY 1968

S HE HELD THE BABY in her arms, careful not to pull the child's IV lines loose or entangle them with her own. Anna's face, pale gold from lack of air, was engulfed in a transparent plastic oxygen cup that looked like some obscenely premature Halloween mask. Liz wished the two of them could be on the same lines, that they could just run the tubes from her own body to the baby's, that her blood could move the child's blood and the breath in her lungs feed her baby's breathing. But it was too late for that. Her body had given this child everything it was ever going to give.

Her wheeled bed was canted at a maddening angle of thirty degrees, the most elevation the doctors would allow her so soon after the cesarean, and all Liz could see was the ceiling, an alien country of acoustic tiles, ventilation grates, and water stains, and those hellish fluorescent tubes above everyone's heads, their light as cold as the smoke off dry ice. But she wasn't seeing anything anyway except the baby's face. Anna's eyes were squeezed shut, and her brow was knit into a seam of delicate determination as she worked for every breath.

She looked, Liz thought, like Mike. They all had looked like Mike to her, from the moment they were born. But this baby looked like Mike in pain.

The curtains had been drawn around their crowded corner of the neonatal ICU. Germaine stood beside her, laying out the trappings for the baptism. To her left, Danny was holding Deb-Deb's hand, and Angus mingled with the Washington children, while Kathie and Temperance stood arm in arm with Linnell Washington at the end of the bed, weeping quietly like the Marys at the foot of the cross. Liz had asked Linnell to be the baby's godmother, which probably broke half a dozen Catholic rules. Danny would be the godfather, which no doubt violated several more. But Germaine hadn't blinked at any of the unorthodox arrangements. She had known he wouldn't; she had counted on him for that.

Germaine gave her a nod: good to go. He wore a long purple stole embroidered in gold, but he hadn't shaved and his deep brown eyes were sunk back in his skull, shadowed with sorrow. Liz hadn't given a moment's thought to what she looked like at this point. She could feel her hair dangling in limp, sweaty strands, and her eyes hurt from crying; wrung out like a bloody washcloth, gutted, and spent, she knew she looked like hell. And she didn't give a damn. She wondered if she would ever give a damn about anything again.

She nodded back to Germaine. He gestured, and Danny and Linnell stepped forward. The priest said something, and then something else, and then something addressed to Linnell and Danny. It was all said in the quiet matter-of-fact tones of ancient ritual, but Liz realized that she wasn't registering the words. She wondered for a moment if Germaine was speaking Latin; but Linnell and Danny both responded to their cues in English, answering for the baby. Linnell had her own baby, Luther, on her hip, and Dee Jay was clinging to her other leg, a little overwhelmed by all the solemnity.

Germaine turned to Liz. He took off the purple stole and draped a white one around his neck, then leaned in to gently lift Anna from Liz's arms. He handed the baby to Danny, since Linnell had her hands full. Liz wanted to weep all over again at the look on her son's face, grave and intent and tender, and the way he held his sister, like an egg, like a beating heart, careful of the dangling array of tubes. But it seemed she was all cried out.

Germaine picked up the cruet of holy water.

"Anna Marie, I baptize thee in the name of the Father—"

"How come they rubbin' that baby's head?" Dee Jay asked his mother. "What's that they pourin' on that baby's head?"

"That's water from God, child," Linnell told him. "That baby's going to heaven soon."

"—and of the Son, and of the Holy Ghost. . . ."

Liz watched the water dribbling from Anna's forehead onto Danny's arms and chest and thought, involuntarily, of tears. There was more, something with oil, and then more oil, but Liz was drifting again, seeing only her baby's face, and at last the child was in her arms again, a white veil draped on her head now, and Germaine was saying something about eternal life, and life everlasting, forever and ever, Amen.

And then it was done, and it was time for the children to go.

"Say good-bye to your sister," Liz said, and in turn Kathie, Angus, and Deb-Deb stepped forward and kissed the baby, and turned to leave with Linnell. But Danny hung back.

"I want to stay," he said.

Liz recognized the look on his face, that Mike look, no argument possible. She hesitated, then looked helplessly at Germaine, who raised one eyebrow and shrugged. Her call.

"Dad would stay," Danny said. "You need someone here."

"I need someone to stay with the other kids too, Danny."

"I'll watch the kids," Linnell said, and Germaine immediately seconded, gently, "Linnell can watch the kids, Liz."

It was the first time he had ever called her by her first name. So this is what it takes, Liz thought, to make a priest a human being.

"Okay, Danny," she said. "You can stay."

IT WAS INSTANTLY quiet with the other children gone. Liz opened her gown so that the baby lay against her skin. At a nod from her, Dr. Levine moved to unhook the baby's IV lines, with a tenderness that brought fresh tears to Liz's eyes. He left the oxygen mask for her to remove, as she had asked. Before he left, he paused beside her and said, "I am so sorry."

"Thank you for giving us a chance," Liz said.

He shook his head. There had been no note of I-told-you-so from him, at any point. Levine had harbored his own secret hopes for a miracle, Liz knew. This one had gotten to him.

"So sorry," he said again, and left the alcove. The night nurse, her face streaming with tears, hovered close and gave Liz a questioning look, prepared to stay or go. Liz sent her away with a touch to her arm.

And now it was just her and the baby, and Germaine and Danny, and the deepest quiet she had ever known. She could hear the false breath of the oxygen in the baby's mask. Anna had not cried a single time; her lungs were too weak even for that. It had been that silence, more even than the baby's eerie golden color and cloak of blood, that had made her fate real to Liz from the moment Levine had eased the child from the slash of the cesarean. There was no way to live in this world without crying.

Liz looked at the baby's face, screwed into effort beneath the mask. She hadn't seen Anna's eyes open yet; she didn't even know what color they were. Dr. Levine had said they probably had five minutes at most, after the mask was removed. Liz thought of Mike, of his story of the morning colors ceremony on the hill, of the men running out with the flag, knowing they had twenty-three seconds to get the colors up and get in a hole before the mortar rounds began to fall. But this was not quite like that. It was more like Mike himself, loading the wounded man onto the helicopter in the moment between explosions. There was no hole to jump into here; there never had been. There was only what you had to do, even as the falling round whistled in the air.

In any case, time meant nothing anymore. The month behind her, and the years ahead, meant no more than any moment's breath or breeze, and five minutes were enough for eternity. Liz met Germaine's eyes, and then Danny's, and took the mask from the baby's face.

Germaine, wearing the purple stole again, began the murmured rite, but Liz was beyond the words now. It all was wind and breath. Danny was holding the oil for the unction, his face wet with tears. Liz held her son's eyes for a moment and gave him a smile. She was glad now, grateful that he had stayed. They would all have to live with this.

And then they were done, and the five minutes passed, and five more, in silence broken only by the soft gasp of the baby's breath. It went on, and impossibly on: an O'Reilly baby, stubborn to the end. And then the gasp made no sound at all, and Anna's face relaxed and her eyes opened, easily, naturally, a baffled look, her glimpse of a world without sufficient air. Brown eyes, Liz saw. Like Mike's, like Kathie's.

The little girl looked at her for a long moment, expectant and helpless; and then she gave a tiny sigh and was gone. And still Liz held her, in the silence and the stillness that had no end.

CHAPTER 28

FEBRUARY 1968

S TINSON WAS SHORT. His thirteen-month tour of duty ended on
March 1, but it was a leap year, and Stinson was sure he wasn't
going to survive the extra day. He'd been bemoaning his fate all
month, passionately and profanely, but as his departure date approached he grew quiet and resigned. He gave Mike a packet of letters, already addressed and stamped, to send for him when he was
killed, and paid off his poker debts.

"You can have my mustard," Stinson told Mike mournfully. The
radioman's #10 can of spicy Dijonnaise had been the envy of everyone
throughout the siege. He doled out the mustard in portions the size
of dimes.

"You're not going to die, you fucking moron," Mike said. But he
accepted the mustard happily enough. The stuff was pure gold in the
Khe Sanh food economy.

He tried to get his radioman out early, to avoid the fatal twenty-
ninth altogether, but the weather settled in and nothing went in or

out from the hilltop for several days. And so Mike found himself in a trench fifty yards from Hill 851's single chopper LZ with Stinson, three walking wounded, the tactical-air-control radio operator and his "bodyguard," and a dead Marine wrapped in a poncho, on the last day of February.

Stinson had his pack on and his helmet strapped under his chin and was muttering a Hail Mary under his breath. On the horizon, a dozen CH-46 cargo choppers with external loads dangling from slings circled desultorily, chasing tail and waiting for their moment.

The TAC guy was on the radio, making his cryptic coordinations; with the cargo choppers on station, it was time to call in the fixed-wing air strikes. One of the wounded men was fretting about his leg, afraid it wouldn't hold up during the dash to the chopper. But they all knew he was better off trying to run than going out on a stretcher. You were a sitting duck on a goddamned stretcher when the shells began to fall.

Stinson handed Mike a tarnished silver flask. "I want you to have this."

Mike twisted the flask's top off and sniffed, smelling bourbon. The flask was ornately monogrammed with leafy entwined letters like climbing vines, *TIS,* and looked like it was about a thousand years old.

"It was my great-great-grandfather's," Stinson said. "Maybe three greats. Tobias Stinson. He was from Kentucky, and the story is he drank whiskey from that flask with Daniel Boone. Or was it Davy Crockett? One of those coon-tailed cap guys."

"You can't give me this," Mike said. "This is for your kids. For your grandkids. For all those future generations of Stinson alcoholics."

"I want you to have it," Stinson insisted.

A burst of 12.7mm machine fire made them all duck; but the NVA gunner on the next hill was just getting his range down for when the chopper landed. Mike put the flask back into his radioman's pocket and closed the flap over it. Stinson's fatalism was starting to get to him. He'd seen too many Marines sure they were going to die, who had, and he'd be damned if Stinson was going to be one of them.

"You stupid superstitious motherfucker," he said. "Just get your ass on that chopper. Have an extra drink at Dashiell Hammett's bar in San Francisco and tell John to put it on my tab."

The TAC guy gave them a warning nod and settled his helmet on his head; the jets were coming in. Everyone hunkered down, and a moment later six Marine A-4 Skyhawks screamed fifty meters to either side of the hilltop, streaming clouds of smoke and tear gas like the world's loudest crop dusters. The bombs tumbled in the air and the valley, and neighboring hills erupted into antiaircraft fire. As the bombs hit, the CH-46 supply chopper made its run to Hill 851, and as it swooped close, everyone in Hotel Company opened fire, trying to keep the NVA gunners' heads down.

"Go, go, go," the TAC operator hollered through the din, and Stinson and the three wounded men grabbed one corner each of the dead Marine's poncho and scrambled out of the trench for the fifty-yard dash to the LZ as the chopper touched down.

Mike watched them go, his eyes stinging from the smoke and drifting tear gas and his ears ringing from the bombs. The stretch of open red dirt between the trench and the chopper looked weirdly vast, like some kind of endless demented prairie from hell painted by Bosch, and the Marines lugging the body across it seemed to be moving in nightmare slow motion. He could see puffs of orange-pink dust being kicked up just to the four Marines' left as the 12.7mm machine fire started in earnest, and he realized he was counting to himself: *four-Mississippi, five-Mississippi* . . . It was too loud to hear the mortar tubes pop, but he knew the rounds were already in the air. The twenty-three-second limit was absolute. Four Marines with a stretcher case had taken twenty-five seconds on a recent emergency medevac, and they'd had to call in a second chopper for them and send out four more stretchers, each carried by four new targets. The guy on the original stretcher had died of his wounds by then; they'd transferred him to a poncho, to save the stretcher, and he'd gone out on a later flight.

... *twelve-Mississippi, thirteen-Mississippi* ... The men making for the chopper passed the replacements who had just jumped off it and were on their way to the trench, a bit of a Keystone Kops moment. The outgoing Khe Sanh vets were hobbling and filthy and so low to the ground that they looked like a different species, while the new guys were ridiculously upright, moving much more slowly than they should have been, their heads ducked slightly, more on principle than from any real sense of danger, as if they were uncertain about the decorum in a new church. In their startling green uniforms, they looked like unripe fruit.

Halfway to the chopper, the man who had been fretting about his wounded leg stumbled, then fell, and the other three men lugging the body went down with him. They sprawled in the dust, then scrambled to their feet again, with the two less-wounded Marines supporting the guy with the bad leg now. Stinson, his hands free, hesitated for an instant, then grabbed two corners of the poncho and starting dragging the body alone.

"*Leave it, Toby!*" Mike hollered, but there was no way Stinson could hear him, over all the firing. "*Goddammit, Stinson, leave the fucking body!*"

... *eighteen-Mississippi, nineteen-Mississippi* ... The other three men made the chopper, heaving the guy with the wounded leg in first and then diving in after him. Stinson was still ten steps away, dragging the corpse like an ant with a raisin. He wasn't going to make it, Mike saw. The chopper pilot was counting too, and he would take off at twenty-three seconds if he had a lick of sense. It was that or get blown up.

The poncho tore off at the corners, and Stinson stopped and got a fresh grip. Mike stopped counting. *Dear Mrs. Stinson,* he thought. *It is my sad duty to tell you that your son died today because he was a total fucking idiot and one of the finest Marines I ever knew.* He remembered a moment in Dong Ha, not long after Stinson had become his radioman. A group of the men had been sitting around a bunker on ammo boxes, drinking warm beer, talking story and swapping the usual bullshit tales of who was the fastest gun in the Far East. One of the guys had one of those little toy pianos that he'd picked up as a joke in Japan, the kind that Schroeder played in *Peanuts,* and people were horsing around on it, playing "Chopsticks" and ditties about Okinawan whores. At some point the piano had ended up beside Stinson, and the kid had tapped out a few idle notes, checking the tuning, then started playing quietly, using only his right hand, because the thing was too small to play the left-hand part. You couldn't even hear the music at first, as the palaver went on all around him, but it was relentless and complex, and gradually the talk faded and all you could hear in the bunker was the surge of the sonata, tinny and tinkling and surreally magnificent, like a stream of light in a muddy ditch.

The first mortar rounds landed about twenty meters from the chopper, which meant there was some wind blowing aloft. Pure luck, pure dumb luck. Stinson reached the door, and some idiot jumped out and helped him heave the body into the bay. The chopper went up like a loosed balloon just as both men dived in after the corpse. Mike could see their four legs still dangling over the side, could see Stinson's dirty white ass through a tear in his dungarees, hanging out in the Khe Sanh breeze as the bird lifted away, inadvertently mooning two divisions of the North Vietnamese Army.

And then the mortar rounds were falling in earnest and the new arrivals had reached the trench and were standing there looking around as if they were waiting for their tour guide to issue passes to the museum. It was almost impossible to grasp the realities of Hill 851 right away; often men came in as reinforcements on one chopper, only to leave on the next one out as casualties.

"Get in the fucking hole!" Mike screamed, and the new guys dived dutifully into the trench and covered up as the mortar rounds walked in toward them. They all burrowed into the dirt and held their helmets on. The trench was bracketed, explosions left and right, front and back, dirt and shrapnel flying everywhere; and then the second wave of fast-movers came in and loosed their wave of bombs and the world just shook for a while.

When things finally settled down a bit, everyone's heads eased up. One of the new arrivals looked down at his nice new uniform, smeared now in good old Khe Sanh orange.

"Jesus H. Christ," he said. "Who's running this cluster fuck?"

Mike could feel something against his chest, sharp, thick, and heavy, not quite an ache. He wondered for a moment if he'd taken a piece of shrapnel. But it was Stinson's flask; the kid had managed to slip it into his breast pocket.

"Just some standard-issue idiot," he told the new guy. "Welcome, gentlemen, to Hill Eight-Five-One."

THE NEW MEN were given shovels; everyone at Khe Sanh dug constantly—it was a way of life by now. The fresh supplies were squirreled through the maze of trenches: cases of grenades and 60mm mortar shells, M-16 ammo, C-rats, and even some new empty bags for sandbags. Not a bad haul. There was even, miraculously, a case of socks, a dirty cardboard box with one corner caved in, labeled prominently in black stencil, U.S. ARMY REJECTS. Nothing but the best for our boys in harm's way, Mike thought. But he grabbed a pair of the things before they all disappeared.

There was mail too, blessed mail, the first in almost a week. Mike took his precious handful of letters to his bunker, closed the blast door and lit a candle, and settled back on his cot. The best moment of any day.

There was only one letter from Liz, which was a disappointment after such a long stretch. But any letter was priceless. Mike sniffed and hefted the envelope—no perfume this time, and apparently no photographs—and slit it open carefully with his K-bar.

My dearest Mike . . .

HE'D HAD MEN DIE beside him and been splattered with their deaths; he'd had men he cared about die in his arms. He'd looked death in the face a hundred times, and he'd had death's arms close around him more than once and had surrendered to its embrace. But this was different. He hadn't known death at all, it turned out. All the deaths you thought you knew meant nothing, in the end. It was the one you didn't see coming that really took you out.

Mike read the letter through a second time, slowly; and then, because there was nothing else to do, he read it a third time, testing every word as if it were a tooth that might come out.

He was sitting upright by now on the edge of the cot, his feet on the dirt floor. The bunker was cool, and quiet as a tomb. No scurrying rats, no radio crackling, no one screaming for a corpsman. Something must have been exploding somewhere, but he couldn't hear it.

As if the war had ended, Mike thought. Abruptly, impossibly: all quiet on the western front. Piss on the fires and call in the dogs, boys, the show's over. Let the politicians and the journalists get to work, figuring out what the fuck it all meant.

But that was not quite it. You fought your war and you lived or died, and the men you loved and fought with lived or died beside you, and when it was over it was over and it was what it was. There might even have been some joy in that somewhere, like diamonds scattered in the mud of irony, if only in the knowledge that you had been a good Marine and done your job.

But this was different. This was the thing he could never have seen coming. It felt like the war had ended, yeah; but what it really felt like was that he'd lost.

PART EIGHT

All night beneath the ruins, then, . . .

. . . .

Where the son of fire in his eastern cloud, while the morning
*   plumes her golden breast,*
Spurning the clouds written with curses, stamps the stony law to
*   dust, loosing the eternal horses from the dens of night, crying*
Empire is no more! And now the lion & wolf shall cease. . . .

. . . .

For every thing that lives is Holy.

WILLIAM BLAKE,
"THE MARRIAGE OF HEAVEN AND HELL"

CHAPTER 29

APRIL 1968

GERMAINE DROVE UP to the O'Reilly house on Thursday afternoon of the week before Easter. It was strangely easy: he pulled
right into the driveway behind the O'Reillys' big green station wagon
with no compunction whatsoever. He dropped by several times a
week now, and it was hard to really remember what it had felt like to
drive past the house all those times and stop a hundred yards down
the road, wrestling with his demons and fretting over fine points of
divine timing, social repercussions, and dubious motivation. His
demons, such as they were, seemed so irrelevant these days. They
were like weather: some days stormy, some days clear. You got wet, or
you didn't; you sweated, or shivered. You still had to get your work
done.

He unfolded himself out of the VW and stood for a moment on
the concrete, waiting for the pain in his knee to settle. The grass in the
yard was calf-deep, and he made a mental note to try to drop by on
Saturday and get it cut. And do some weeding: in the border in front
of the porch, daffodils bloomed in the unkempt bed, their yellow

heads bobbing above the green tangle like life-jacketed sailors in a churned sea.

He would have gone up the sidewalk to the front door, but a call from the yard stopped him. "Father Zeke!"

Germaine peered into the side yard, toward the rise dominated by two oak trees, but saw no one. The knoll was riddled with an impressive maze of trenches and sandbagged holes, some of them covered with cardboard to achieve a bunker effect. Danny and Angus had been digging in to Firebase Fox for months now.

Germaine started walking toward the fortifications. As he approached, he called, "Fox Base, this is Saint Jude. I am inbound on your seven o'clock. Over."

"Saint Jude, Fox Six," came Danny's laconic reply. "Roger that. Hold your position. We will mark LZ, over."

Germaine paused in the deeper grass. The boys were still out of sight, but he knew the drill by now. He waited patiently, and a moment later a flare of red smoke blossomed from the nearest trench.

"Fox Six, Saint Jude," he called. "I have red smoke, repeat, red smoke. Over."

"Jude, Six, roger that. Choo-choo cherry. You are cleared for landing. LZ is hot. Repeat, LZ is hot. Over."

"Copy that," Germaine said. "Tallyho."

He made for the trench, keeping his head low. Landings at Firebase Fox often involved barrages of acorns and even the heavier ordnance of 122mm pinecones. Today he cleared the LZ unscathed except for some shrapnel from a handful of twigs.

Slipping in to the surprisingly deep hole, he found Danny and Angus squatted in a blast recess dug off to the side of the trench, holding plastic helmets tight to their heads. They had a mock mortar set up beside them, a jury-rigged contraption made up of tin cans duct-taped at the joints, leaning on a tripod of spliced-together tennis rackets. As Germaine settled in gingerly, easing his bad knee into as much of a bend as he could, Angus made an explosion noise and tossed a handful of dirt into the air, which duly showered them.

"Whew," Germaine said, as the dust settled.

"We've been taking fire all afternoon," Danny told him. "But we've got their position spotted."

"Where are they?"

Danny pointed across the lake. "In the tree line over there."

"Ah," Germaine said.

"Do you want some beanie-weenies, Father?" Angus asked.

"No, thank you, Angus. I had a big lunch in, uh, Saigon." Both boys looked dubious. "Da Nang?" Germaine tried.

"Dong Ha, maybe," Danny allowed.

"Dong Ha, then."

"Did you bring any potatoes?" Angus asked.

Germaine smiled. "No. Are you low on food?"

"Low on ammo," Danny said, and gestured to the mortar. "We were just about to fire a mission."

"I'll bring potatoes next time."

"Or apples," Angus said.

"Potatoes are better," Danny said. "Heavier." He and Angus turned to the mortar, and Angus took a potato out of the sack beside it. They were down to less than half a dozen spuds, Germaine noted. The mortar was a new twist.

Angus stuffed the potato into the open end of the beer-can tube, and Danny pushed it down into the tube with the end of a baseball bat. The bottom of the mortar was rigged with some kind of plumbing joint, from which Danny unscrewed the seal. Angus took an aerosol can—hair spray, Germaine noted, amused—and sprayed it into the chamber, then Danny screwed the cap back into place.

"Good to go," he said. "Get the FAO on the horn."

Angus picked up a pair of toy binoculars and peered over the top of the trench toward the island. Germaine leaned back against the dirt wall of the trench and watched their play, keeping his right leg as straight as he could. His heart hurt. There was no way around that. Danny, he knew, still wanted to be a priest. They had talked about it after morning mass just the week before, sitting in the back row of the silent church after everyone else had left. A priest, or a painter. But clearly duty called, in the afternoons after school. Danny apparently wanted to be a priest who fired mortars.

"Fox Six, I have the target in sight," Angus said. "Fire your mission, over."

"Roger that." Danny reached to the base of the mortar and clicked something that looked like the flint sparker from a lantern lighter. Germaine flinched involuntarily, but nothing happened. Danny, unperturbed, waited a moment, then pressed the button again.

Boom!

Germaine jumped at the surprisingly loud explosion. He hadn't quite believed the thing would go off. He stuck his head up above the trench line, expecting to see potato fragments strewn across the yard, but there was nothing.

"Shot," Danny said, and, a moment later, "Splash."

Across the lake, the potato landed in the shallow water by the shoreline, raising a distinct explosive plume.

"Does your mother know about this?" Germaine asked.

"Yeah," Danny said. "She only lets us shoot at the lake and the island. The houses are a no-fire zone." He sounded a little disgruntled at such constraints.

"War is hell," Germaine said.

Angus was still looking through the binoculars. "Fox Six, Lakeview here," he said. "Adjust fire. Right five meters, add five meters. Fire for effect. Over."

"Copy that," Danny said. "Right five, add five, fire for effect."

He crammed another potato into the mortar and went through the hair spray routine again, and this time when he hit the button Germaine had the sense to cover his ears.

THERE WERE STILL three potatoes left when Germaine left the trench and made his way to the back door of the O'Reilly house, but the boys were taking a break from their fire mission to eat some beanie-weenies and let the mortar cool down. Apparently the firing chamber had a tendency to explode if it got too hot.

Germaine knocked on the sliding glass door. Inside, he could see Elizabeth O'Reilly at the kitchen counter. She was on the telephone, but she gestured him in.

As the priest stepped inside, Deb-Deb walked up to him, carrying a doll. "Hello, Father Zeke."

"Hello, little otter," Germaine said. "How are you today?"

"I'm not an otter anymore," she informed him.

"No?"

"No. I have a baby now."

"Ah." Germaine bent close as she showed him the doll. "And what's her name?"

"Anna."

He felt his eyes sting and straightened to keep them from spilling. "She's beautiful. I'll bet you're a wonderful mother."

"I think she's hungry," Deb-Deb said.

He rummaged in his pocket and came up with half a pack of gum. Deb-Deb took it, gave him a smile, and wandered off into the living room cradling the doll. It was strange, Germaine realized, after so many months of getting used to her distinctive otter locomotion, to see Deb-Deb simply walking.

Liz was off the phone. "Hello, Father."

"Hi, Liz. You didn't have to get off the phone for me."

"That's okay, it was just my usual cocktail hour check-in with Betty Simmons." She glanced with amusement at Germaine's dirty pants. "I see you dropped in at Firebase Fox."

"They were shooting potatoes across the lake. That mortar is scary."

"They keep taking all my hair spray," Liz said. "You've got to use steel cans for the tube. It turns out that aluminum cans blow apart."

"Imagine that."

Their eyes met, briefly, and Liz smiled. "Do you want a beer?"

"Thanks." Germaine sat down at the counter as she went to the refrigerator. She brought back two Schlitzes, popped the tops, and handed him one.

"How is Betty doing?" Germaine asked as she sat down.

Liz shrugged. "She's a drunken wreck after 5:00 p.m. But otherwise holding up pretty well. I think she's going to go back to school in the fall." She sipped her beer. "She's turned out to be way tougher than I thought."

"Funny how that is."

He had meant it, obliquely, as a compliment of sorts, but Liz gave him a sharp glance and said nothing. Her eyes drifted to the window, and Germaine wondered if he had blundered. After a moment, though, Liz said, mildly enough, "It's like an archeology dig, I think. I've seen it in Maria too. You're sitting there in the ruins of everything you built your life around, and eventually, to get anywhere, you have to dig back down through all the trash and dirt and wreckage of previous civilizations, to who you were at eighteen. Or twenty, or whatever, whenever it was that you put yourself on hold to become a wife and a mother and an all-around solid citizen. And so you dig, and cry, and cry and dig, and eventually, there it is, under all those layers of debris."

"The road not taken?"

"Something like that. The self you never got to be, maybe. And you think, Jesus Christ, who was I all those years when I wasn't me? And who the hell does that make me now?"

Germaine had no answer for that and didn't even try to find one. They were silent for a time, a comfortable silence, sipping at their Schlitzes. Deb-Deb came through briefly with her doll, glanced disapprovingly at the beer cans, and walked back out with a handful of graham crackers. Aretha Franklin was playing on the turntable upstairs, accompanied by a rhythm of light footfalls as Kathie and Temperance worked out a new dance routine.

"Have you heard from Mike?" Germaine asked.

"Yeah. He was in Australia last week, on his R & R, telephones and everything—he called five nights in a row. So I've been able to relax. I mean, at least in Australia nobody was shooting at him, as far as I know. Not that he would tell me if they were."

"I can see how that would be a relief."

"We had originally planned to meet in Hawaii. But I told him I didn't feel ready to travel yet. I blamed it on the doctors, but I think it still hurt his feelings." She hesitated, then met his eyes. "I'm just not ready to see him yet. I'm not sure if I could stand it."

"Sure," Germaine said.

"I'll be ready by August," Liz said. "I hope."

From the side yard, the boom of the potato mortar sounded. Apparently the firing chamber had cooled sufficiently for further barrages of the island. Liz and Germaine exchanged a smile.

"Another beer?" she asked.

"Actually, I should probably get going," he said. "It wouldn't do for me to show up late for Bingo with beer on my breath."

"Again."

He laughed. "Besides, I want to get there in time to try to rig the machine to come up with a winner for Mrs. Malewich."

"God bless you, Father. It's a life of true service you lead."

"Yeah," Germaine said as he stood up. "Poverty, chastity, obedience, and attempted fraud." He hesitated, then drew a packet of photographs from his pocket. "I, uh, finally got these developed."

"Ah," Liz said.

They stood in silence for a moment, looking at the package. It had been almost eight weeks since she had handed him the Brownie camera when he walked into the hospital room and asked him to take pictures of her and the baby. Germaine hadn't had the heart to get the pictures developed right away; and for a long time after he had gotten them developed, he had found he didn't have the heart to give them to Liz.

"Did you . . . look at them?" Liz asked at last. "Did any of them come out?"

"Yes."

"Were her eyes open in any of them?"

It would do no good to lie, he knew. Germaine said, "No."

"I suppose that was too much to hope for."

"She is beautiful. That comes through."

"Yeah," Liz said.

He was still holding the packet out to her, but she made no move to take it. After a moment, she said, "Why don't you just hang on to them for me, for a while?"

"Of course," Germaine said.

"I mean, put them in a safe place, and all. I'm going to want them. Just . . . not yet."

"Of course," Germaine said again.

"And—could you send one to Mike?"

"What?"

"He should have one. I mean, I want him to have one. I just think . . . it would be easier, somehow, for him—for me, for us—if it came from you."

"I'm really not sure—"

"Please," Liz said.

Germaine tried to put himself in Mike's place, receiving a photograph of his dead child from a stranger. And then he tried to put himself in Liz's place, sending a photo of their dead daughter to her husband. And then he gave up entirely and thought, *Thy will, not mine, be done,* and put the photographs back in his pocket.

"Of course," he said.

AT THE FRONT door there was, as there always was, the pause at the good-bye. The instant fraught with danger, the moment Germaine used to crave and dread. Because he had always wanted to kiss her, and because that wanting hurt so much.

"I might come by on Saturday," he said. "That lawn could use mowing."

"That would be wonderful," Liz said. "Danny tries, bless his heart, but he can't get the mower running for more than five minutes at a time. And the boys are starting to fret that the grass is giving too much cover to the NVA."

Germaine smiled. He still wanted to kiss her. He probably always would. The only difference now was that he knew it would never happen. Something had changed between them, in that hospital room. He was, forever, the man who had given the last rites to her daughter. And soon enough would be the man who had sent the picture of her dead baby to her husband.

And he thought, So this is what it takes to make a human being into a priest.

"Okay, then," he said. "I'll see you Saturday."

ON EASTER SUNDAY morning, Hotel Company climbed out of its holes, stuck bayonets in all the sandbags, dumped the dirt into the trenches and bunkers, and walked down off Hill 851 under their own power, as if the place were just one more night defensive position and it was time to move on. Someone had decided that the siege was over and that the good guys had won. Mike hoped somebody had told the NVA. He didn't want any of his men getting killed in defense of an anticlimax.

They walked in through the wire of the combat base just before noon the next day. The base was a shocking mess, riddled with trenches, foxholes, and shell craters, with nothing left above ground but piles of Marine trash and the hulks of blasted machines. It looked, Mike thought, like a garbage dump that had been bombed, which was not far off the truth. There had never been a particularly good reason for them to be here in the first place. Khe Sanh's only redeeming tactical feature was that it was a very good place for a lot of people to die.

Hotel Company went straight to the airfield, but there had been some kind of fuckup, the typical bullshit, someone else had gone out on their choppers, and so the company waited in shallow trenches in the broiling heat for a couple of hours. The men broke out their cards and cigarettes and hoarded cans of peaches and played Back Alley. Some of them started writing letters. The general mood was upbeat and celebratory; they were almost out. Mike just sat and fretted. After all those months on their cozy hilltop, the base on the broad plateau seemed vast, and the vastness seemed very dangerous.

He felt like a cockroach, caught in the middle of a kitchen floor as the light came on.

The CH-46s finally showed up, and the men began loading. Mike kept everyone moving, hollering and kicking ass, his ears cocked for the pop of mortars or the boom of artillery, for the sudden scream of a rocket in the air. It was just going to be too much for him, somehow, if anyone got killed at the goddamned airstrip waiting for his evac. But everyone got aboard without incident, in good order, and the choppers lifted off one after another.

Mike clambered onto the last chopper, with the Third Platoon command group and the corpsman Mike had made stay until everyone was out. Dermott Edmonds was ecstatic as the chopper left the ground.

"Fuckin' A!" he hollered into Mike's ear, over the engine's din. "Fuckin' A, Skipper!"

"Fuckin' A," Mike agreed, and settled back against a stanchion. He was sitting on his flak jacket; the last thing he wanted was to lose the family jewels on the chopper ride out. But it was really starting to feel like they had made it.

As they gained altitude, the whole plateau came into view. Mike could still remember how, when he had first flown in the previous fall, he had been struck by the quiet green beauty of the place, the lushness of the mountains and the clear lines of the waterfalls, the gentle way the fog crept along the valleys in the morning. It looked like the moon down there now, a cratered landscape blasted clear of vegetation, with hundreds of burned-black scars carved into the red Khe Sanh clay and broad swaths of particular devastation stamped along the paths of the B-52 strikes. It looked, he thought, like there'd been a war down there.

"They say we killed more than ten thousand of them!" Edmonds hollered in Mike's ear.

The kid sounded almost giddy. Mike wondered if he'd ever been that gung ho himself. "That's what they say."

"I wonder how they figured that out?"

Mike shrugged. He knew exactly how they had figured it out. The grunts at the sharp tip of things had knocked some bad guys over and called them dead, and their squad leaders had passed the KIA figures on to the platoon leaders, who had inflated the count and passed them on to the company commanders, who had added a few more for good measure and forwarded the count to battalion, where it had been doubled by some pogue with a business degree. By the time the estimated KIA number got to the highest levels, they had wiped out two or three NVA divisions and generally depopulated North Vietnam.

In any case, they'd killed a lot of bad guys, any way you looked at it. Which was, he supposed, the point. If there had been a point. Mike said, "I guess somebody just counted up the arms and legs and divided by four."

Edmonds seemed happy enough with that answer and turned to pass it on to his first sergeant. The sergeant just nodded, leaned his head back against the vibrating chopper wall, and closed his eyes, with an air of long-suffering.

Mike settled back and took the letter from his inner pocket. He remembered Father Ezekiel Germaine of St. Jude's parish only vaguely. They'd never met formally that Mike could remember. The guy had been ex-Navy, but he always looked like a stone-cold Jesuit to Mike, a pre–Vatican II hard-ass, and his sermons were terse, almost grudging things, as sparing of words as a casualty telegram.

The priest's handwriting was oddly lyrical, lit with little swoops and scruples. Mike could appreciate the letter's gutsiness and its delicacy; as a company CO, he had written more than his share of this kind of thing. He knew he shouldn't hate the guy. He was glad someone had been there for Liz, someone of that quality. But it hurt so much that it hadn't been him. It was like the shrapnel in his knee, too deep in his working nerves and bones to be removed. It would hurt forever.

The picture was the killer. Liz with Anna in her arms, the two of them snagged in a web of half a dozen IV lines looping in and out, so many you couldn't sort out what went where, just a tangle of connections. Liz looked so drained that Mike could hardly bear to look at her. The baby's hair was wispy brown, like Liz's, and her eyes were squeezed closed tight. Mike wondered if he'd ever be able to ask Liz what color their daughter's eyes had been.

"We kicked their ass, Skipper," Edmonds hollered, still celebrating, and Mike came back to himself. They were crossing Highway 9, and the mountains were green again. On the horizon, the Khe Sanh combat base had faded to a single torn patch of blasted red, like a fresh wound, beneath a huge blue sky.

Just like that, Mike thought. He wondered if he would really be able to remember what it had been. Not what it had meant, not what it would become in the stories later, nothing lit by phony glory and phonier coherence: just what it had actually been. Just to be there, just to do it, day by day and moment by moment, wound by wound, and death by death. To pass beyond understanding any of it and to be more sure every hour that there was no way out of the thing alive while the world got smaller and smaller in the shrinking interval between the fall of the shells that were walking toward you, until finally you were infinitely patient and everything was quiet inside you because there was nothing left that you could do but take what came; and you were fearless, not because you were brave, but because you were at the empty bottom of yourself, and there was nothing left to lose.

Mike slipped the photograph into the envelope, put the letter back into his pocket, and took out Stinson's flask.

"Yeah," he said. "I guess we did."

He twisted the top off, took a shot, and handed the flask to Edmonds. Edmonds grinned, raised the flask in a brief salute, and drank.

Beside him, his first sergeant was eyeing the flask with an unmistakable air. Edmonds hesitated, then gave Mike a hopeful look. Mike nodded, and Edmonds handed the sergeant the flask with some relief. The kid might make a decent Marine yet, Mike thought, if he lived.

The first sergeant met Mike's eyes, raised the flask, and nodded. A moment, a simple moment between men. Mike nodded back, feeling the gooseflesh rise along his arms. The sergeant took his shot, then wiped his mouth on his sleeve, leaving a smear of orange Khe Sanh dirt, and passed the flask on down the line.

CHAPTER 30

APRIL 1968

IT WAS STRANGE being out alone at night. Liz tried to remember the last time she had been in the car after dark without children or Mike, and couldn't. She had the nagging sense of having forgotten something crucial, something no doubt child-related. But the kids were in good hands tonight. Liz had left them with Betty Simmons's daughter Miranda, which should have felt like some kind of defeat but somehow didn't. Miranda had shown up with her calculus homework, some Beatles albums, and a copy of *The Electric Kool-Aid Acid Test*. She'd told Liz that she planned to spend the summer working for the McCarthy campaign, and Liz had not failed to notice the round plastic compact of birth control pills in Miranda's purse, along with what certainly looked like a pipe. Liz wondered what poor Betty made of all that. But Miranda was wonderful with the kids, who adored her. When Liz had left, all of them, plus Temperance, had been singing along to "I Am the Walrus" and playing Parcheesi. Liz even had the sense that Miranda was going to find a way to let Deb-Deb win.

The April night was clear and balmy. They'd been in the grip of a spring heat wave, but it had broken on a thunderstorm that afternoon, and when Liz got off the toll road near the oceanfront, the sea-cooled air smelled of honeysuckle. It was Shakespeare's birthday, which Liz had fought an uphill battle throughout her marriage to make a sort of family holiday. It had always been like keeping a promise to herself to celebrate the day. One year, just after the miscarriage between Danny and Kathie, she and Mike had even made it to England in April and had walked hand in hand up the avenue of lime trees to the Holy Trinity Church in Stratford-upon-Avon.

It had been two days after St. George's Day; Mike had insisted on missing the crowds celebrating Shakespeare's traditional birthday, which had proved a brilliant call. They had the church almost to themselves on a gray, drizzly afternoon. The two of them had ducked through the comically low stone entryway and stood in the nave, looking through the pillars into the weeping chancel, tilted, it was said, at the angle of Christ's head on the cross. They'd knelt in the chapel of St. Peter—they'd still been praying together, then—and finally paid their pounds and entered the chancel, beneath which the playwright was buried. The room was still overflowing with flowers left by the local schoolchildren on St. George's Day. Liz had been awed but also oddly disappointed—the stiff, slightly pompous bust, the gilt crosses, the inescapable sense of a managed asset; it all seemed just a bit off somehow.

The real moment had come the next night at a performance of *King Lear*. When Paul Schofield's Lear had told Cordelia, played by Diana Rigg, "Come, let's away to prison: / We two alone will sing like birds i' the cage," Liz had found herself in tears. For everything, simply for everything. Afterward, walking back to their room beneath the slanted, centuries-old rooftops, she had continued to cry and Mike had put his arm around her and she had known he understood, and she had never loved him more.

When thou dost ask me blessing I'll kneel down
And ask of thee forgiveness: so we'll live,
And pray, and sing, and tell old tales, and laugh
At gilded butterflies. . . .

The narrow side street near Birdneck Road was badly lit, its pot-holed shoulder crowded with cars. Liz thought for a moment that she wouldn't be able to find a place to park and that it was a message from God, a cosmic discouragement. She was about to take the hint and turn around and go home and call the whole thing a stupid idea, a fantasy, but a pickup truck pulled out just ahead of her and left a gaping space. So much for God.

She settled the station wagon into the spot and turned off the engine and the lights. She took a deep breath and thought, Okay. Okay. Now. But it was almost ten minutes before she finally got herself out of the car and walked to the door, and another moment or two before she actually went in, past the sign with the quote from Kafka—"The great theater of Oklahoma calls you! Today only and never again! If you miss your chance now you miss it forever!" and, beneath that: "Virginia Beach Little Theater: open auditions tonight for John Millington Synge's *Riders to the Sea.*"

SHE HADN'T BEEN inside a theater since she'd tried to play Joan of Arc in Quantico while she was pregnant with Deb-Deb, but the whole feeling came back instantly the moment she was through the door: a surge of joy, the sense of a suddenly firm ground, of a place to work where the work would not be wasted. People often thought acting was about glamour, about spotlights and curtain calls, the crowded theater of an opening night, but it had never been the applause side of things that appealed to Liz. It was something much more blue-collar for her, something about the lighting, the spaciousness, and the quality of sound in a theater on a weeknight, when the real work was done: the house lights on low, the seats folded up, and the echoes amplifying everything anyone said, turning it plastic and framing it with possibility. The working emptiness of a theater in rehearsal felt like a church to Liz. More than a church, she thought: it felt like she'd always thought a church should feel, felt more like a church than any church she'd ever been in.

The auditions were already in progress—three women stood on the stage, two young and one older, keening through the first big grief chorus after the announcement of Michael's death.

CATHLEEN: *It's destroyed we are from this day. It's destroyed, surely.*
NORA: *Didn't the young priest say the Almighty God wouldn't leave her destitute with no son living?*
MAURYA: *It's little the like of him knows of the sea. . . .*

Liz skirted the back row of seats and walked slowly down the gently curving side aisle, along the wall, taking the measure of the place as she went. The women on the stage presented no problem; their accents were too self-conscious, their emotions Big and completely hollow. They'd end up village women at best, kneeling at the door, doing their gassy Weeping. Clustered throughout the theater like lily pads, half a dozen other groups of three or four sat poring over scripts, waiting their turns to read. Mostly women: the drama students from the local colleges, with savage eye shadow, wearing black; the song-and-dancers in sweatpants and leggings; the hopeful matrons, slightly chubby, and the first-timers, and the wishful thinkers; and, here and there, more or less transparently, the little theater veterans, some wearing T-shirts from previous productions, like advertising signs, some just quietly at home. It didn't seem to Liz that any of them was a factor. But no doubt she seemed the same to them.

A housewife, a first-timer. A wishful thinker. Maybe she should have done something savage with her eye shadow.

She slipped into the third row, where a woman in an Ashland Shakespeare Festival sweatshirt wielded a clipboard with a slightly officious air.

"Name? Role?" she said briskly.

"Elizabeth O'Reilly. I'd like to read for Maurya."

The woman gave her a frankly impatient look. "Maurya's the old woman. That's the old woman's role."

"Yup," Liz said. It was a Mike-ism, pure and simple; she realized that she had learned a lot since the last time she'd been in a theater. In the past, she'd have given the young woman a long speech on the art of acting or told her that she'd played Lady Macbeth twelve years ago at Catholic U., with nothing to age her but bad hair and a tremble in her voice. Now she just stood there until the woman finally shrugged and handed her the script.

"You'll be in the G group," she said, pointing to a cluster of women toward the back of the hall. "The parts are marked in yellow."

THE SCENE was a good one, the meatiest, the moments after the last son's body was carried in on a dripping piece of sail. Maliciously or not, the woman with the clipboard had grouped Liz with two daughters who were older than she was. The woman reading for Nora was a sturdy housewife in her midthirties, completely wrong for the role, while the woman reading the Cathleen part, a bespectacled, slightly horse-faced woman named Sally, with her auburn hair pinned up into a tight bun, looked to be pushing forty.

They read through the scene together quietly. Neither of the other two women showed Liz much, but she was keeping it low-key too, just walking her tongue through the words, playing a little with the accent. Liz actually liked Sally right away, and she suspected that the woman could act. The Nora wannabe, however, Barbara, was bad enough to take them all down with her. Barbara told them she had done *Oklahoma!* in high school, so maybe she could sing. Or maybe she just specialized in Bright. Her Nora was remarkably peppy.

After a couple of dry runs Liz felt like she had the text, and she settled back in her chair while Sally and Barbara continued to quietly work their lines. On the stage, the F group had just collapsed into giggles after blowing several lines in a row and were starting over, to the obvious displeasure of the director. A lean man in his midthirties, dressed in worn jeans, sneakers, and a sweatshirt with the sleeves cut off, he sat in the second row with his feet up on the chair in front of him, making low comments to an earnest note-taking woman beside him, not his wife, though they were certainly sleeping together. His dark brown hair was long enough for an incongruously mellow ponytail; his beard, trimmed crisply to a Mephistophelian point, seemed closer to characteristic. He had a mild Southern drawl in normal discourse, but when he grew impatient the accent steeled into uninflected diction.

Group F finally got through their scene without laughing and were hurried off the stage. The woman with the clipboard called for G, and Liz, Sally, and Barbara climbed the steps onto the stage.

"Who the hell is reading Maurya?" the director said. "Jesus, there's not a Maurya in this group. Elaine! What the hell are you doing, giving me three daughters?"

"The brunette is reading for Maurya," the woman with the clipboard said defensively. "She insisted."

"Shit," the guy said. His accent was long gone. Of course, he'd been peevish to start with, after the gigglers.

"Just let me try it," Liz said, uncomfortably conscious of her voice evaporating into the theater's empty spaces. She took a breath and found her diaphragm. "One time through. I promise not to laugh, at least, when they bring in the body."

The man just looked at her. She tried to meet his gaze steadily, a tricky thing with the footlights in her eyes. He hadn't taken his feet off the back of the chair in front of him, which left him looking impossible to please. An asshole, Liz thought, a perfectionist trying to fake a softer edge, and a bit of a megalomaniac. They'd probably end up friends.

Finally the guy shrugged and made a what-the-hell, the-night-is-circling-the-drain-anyway motion with his hand.

"Go," he said.

AND SUDDENLY it was simple. It was amazing, how instantly it all came back. The desultory onlookers scattered through the dimness of the seats beyond the footlights, the smell of the varnish and the floor wax and the must of the heavy burgundy curtain, the peeling tape on the floor marking the forgotten points of old productions—it all disappeared, and she was there, simply, in the close stone cottage lit by lamps, above a thrashing sea with waves shattering on the rocks below, with her last son wrapped in a piece of sail on the rough table, dripping still, while the neighbors knelt and crossed themselves and keened, and her daughters wavered, torn between their own grief and their fears for the final thread of their mother's sanity.

The accent was easy. Mike's father slipped into a brogue after two Manhattans, and Liz had always had a precise ear and the gift of echo. It wasn't a matter of inflecting every word, in any case, it was just the music of it, and a few crucial vowels. The emotions were the same, really—there was no need to make anything, or do anything, no need for elaborate imaginings and cunning technique. You just let go and sank into the unspeakable reality of it. You just got raw and real and waited for the line to rise on its own broken wings.

She knelt at the table that wasn't there, beside the daughters older than herself, on a spring night in Virginia, and grieved her dead son, and his dead brothers, and their lost father, her husband, and that father's father before him.

They're all gone now, and there's nothing more the sea can do to me. . . .

Barbara, as Cathleen, let out a piercing shriek and began to sob, a bit petulantly, as if she'd spilled something on her prom dress. Liz heard titters from the dim seats. Sally, as Nora, was playing it closer to the ground but still fluttering distractingly, crossing herself and muttering a Hail Mary that wasn't in the script.

And it didn't matter. They would do what they would do, as the world would, as the sea itself would, and it was out of her hands, as it had always been. She was ancient, and she was forever, and soon enough she'd be in the white pine coffin herself, with the last of the wood they'd saved up for their men. She was broken finally and at last and completely, and the peace beneath the suffering began to glow and sing.

I'll have no call now to be up crying and praying when the wind breaks from the south, and you can hear the surf is in the east, and the surf is in the west, making a great stir with the two noises, and they hitting the one on the other. I'll have no call now to be going down and getting Holy Water in the dark nights after Samhain, and I won't care what way the sea is when the other women will be keening. . . .

The theater had grown quiet. The director's feet were finally off the back of the chair in front of him, and the women chattering in the back of the auditorium went silent. In the wings of the stage, the women in group H stopped their own muttered rehearsals and attended, as Barbara's Cathleen keened on, ridiculously, and Liz went on, low and strong and spent.

> It isn't that I haven't said prayers in the dark night till you wouldn't know what I'd be saying; but it's a great rest I'll have now, and it's time, surely. It's a great rest I'll have now, and great sleeping in the long nights after Samhain, if it's only a bit of wet flour we do have to eat, and maybe a fish that would be stinking.

WHEN THEY WERE FINISHED there was the usual polite smattering of applause. Group H had hurried in from the wings before Barbara, Sally, and Liz were even off the stage, and the woman playing Nora was earnestly explaining something complicated to the director, some brilliant twist. The director was ignoring her.

"Thank you, ladies, very well done," he said to the trio of Group G. "We'll be in touch with you by Thursday, one way or the other. Make sure Elaine has got your numbers." And he put his feet back up on the seat and gestured to the group on the stage: Go.

"Asshole," Sally muttered as they went up the aisle toward the exit.

"You get the sense he likes his small pond," Liz agreed.

Barbara stopped to get her purse and blow her nose, and Liz and Sally both gave her a smile and then, in tacit understanding, went on without her.

"The Hail Marys were a nice touch," Liz said.

"Thanks," Sally said. "You were great. I wish I'd had the guts to read for Maurya."

"It's not guts," Liz said.

They passed through the doors and into the night. The balmy air was a surprise; Liz realized she had half-expected a cold wind with the teeth of the sea in it.

"I can't believe I've got to sit by the goddamned phone until Thursday," Sally said.

"He's not going to call us," Liz said. "The one he's sleeping with will be Cathleen, the one he wants to sleep with will be Nora, and the old pro in the red sweatshirt will be Maurya."

"Maybe he'll let us carry the damned guy in on the sail or something," Sally said. "I'd play one of the dead bodies, I swear, if they weren't all guys. I'm just trying to get my foot back in the door, for Christ's sake."

"Me too."

"You want to stop for a drink or something? My babysitter's good till eleven."

"Mine too," Liz said. "I'd love to have a drink."

PART NINE

In the evening of life,
you will be examined in love.

JOHN OF THE CROSS

CHAPTER 31

LABOR DAY 1968

T HEY HAD TAKEN the high ground, and the flanks were covered. To the east, beyond a line of dunes, lay the ocean, which they would leave to the Navy. With marsh to the west and impassable shrubbery to the north, the only viable approach to the main campsite was from the south, and they had dug a series of foxholes and established clear lines of fire and an FPL. The supply line was tenuous, a half-mile walk to the little general store, which could be brutal if you forgot your flip-flops and had to skitter barefoot along the hot pavement; but there were always beanie-weenies. On the whole, Mike thought, their situation at the Cape Hatteras National Park campground was reasonably secure, and he thought he could risk having a beer.

"Looks good," he told his platoon COs, Danny and Chevy Petroski. "Call in the sergeants and squad leaders for a briefing. We'll figure out the watches and LPs and secure for the night."

"Aye, sir," both boys said, and Danny saluted.

"Don't ever salute anyone in the field," Mike said automatically. "It just makes them a target." His son looked so distressed at this that Mike added gently, "A salute is a sign of respect, and the way you show respect in the field is by paying attention to each other, keeping each other alive, and getting the job done. You see?"

Danny nodded. Chevy said, "Are you allowed to say 'sir'?"

"Yes sir," Mike said. Chevy grinned, but Danny still seemed a little downcast, and Mike felt his heart hurt. His older son had developed some baffling depths over the last year, places he went inside himself where Mike couldn't find him yet. They were still feeling each other out.

He said, "Did you guys hear the one about the kangaroo?" They shook their heads. "Kangaroo hops into a beer joint, hops up to the bar, and orders a drink. Bartender says, 'That'll be twenty bucks.' It seems a little steep to the kangaroo, but he's thirsty and he reaches into his pouch and pulls out a twenty, and the bartender pours him a cold one. The kangaroo starts drinking the beer, and after a while the bartender says, 'You know, we don't get many kangaroos in here.' And the roo says, 'At twenty bucks a beer, I'm surprised you get any.'"

The boys laughed. "Now go get your brothers," Mike said. "It must be about time for chow."

The two ran off in separate directions. Angus was on patrol somewhere toward the swamp, and probably in it by now; Lejeune was in the fire control bunker near the shrub line, arranging and rearranging the fireworks they'd bought at the traditional roadside stand near Barco, and shooting off the occasional bottle rocket at a target of opportunity. Ramada had unfortunately been killed in the first assault on the main dune, but he'd taken it well and was off somewhere now playing with Deb-Deb.

Mike, who had been squatting in the command foxhole while they talked, took the opportunity to stand up and stretch his leg. The left knee was never going to be the same. He could feel rain coming now, by the ache in it. He'd always thought that was an old wives' tale. So maybe he was an old wife now.

He walked back toward their campsite, taking it slow on the sandy path. If he walked with particular attention, he didn't have to limp. He could feel the action in his knee with every step, steel on bone; if it was very quiet, he could even hear it sometimes. Like a squirrel in a cage, spinning its wheel in a tiny creaking circle of pain.

Chevy and Lejeune came running in from the left flank and fell in on either side of him. Mike put a hand on each boy's shoulder, and they walked on together. The two of them were excited about the fireworks; Lejeune had everything set up in some particular sequence, to be fired as soon as it got dark enough, and they were working out who was going to get to shoot off what. It all seemed fair enough so far, unless the girls wanted to get in on it, which seemed unlikely, and Mike let the boys plan it out on their own, nodding at the coolest ideas. He'd stay close once the shooting started and make sure they did it right.

He hadn't been prepared for what it felt like to be with Larry's sons; that loss was finally real. Every time one of them grinned or made a crack, every time one of them did something outrageous and then just stood there looking at you when he got nailed for it, with that placid, slightly wicked Petroski gleam that said it had been worth it and he was prepared to take whatever the consequences were, Mike thought of all the times Larry and he had promised each other that if one of them bought it, the other would step up with the kids. He was the godfather to each of these boys, as Larry was the godfather of all his children. Except Anna. And if there was a heaven beyond the flowers and the crap, Larry was more than a godfather to Anna now.

Mike shook his head, wondering if he was getting soft. Thinking of heaven, for Christ's sake. Taking comfort in such a notion. But there was no place else to go, with certain deaths. It was that, or turn to stone, or drink yourself to death. Larry would have understood. *One more Marine reporting, sir; I've served my time in hell.*

They rounded the corner, and the campsite came into view. Liz and Maria were sitting at the picnic table beneath a sprawling ocean cypress, drinking something pink. Lejeune ran ahead toward the women, but Chevy stayed close, and Mike firmed up his touch on the boy's shoulder. He wanted to say something. Chevy had flunked fourth grade, spectacularly, and then flunked summer school without ever completing an assignment, and Maria was close to despair. But Mike knew the kid was all right. He was just pissed off, and he had Larry's complete and utter disdain for bullshit. He would be fine. And it was no tragedy, to be a year back, on the whole. It would help him when the school sports started up; he'd have an edge.

Mike said, "Do you remember that time at the obstacle course in Quantico, when Lejeune fell off the rope and broke his ankle?"

"Yeah," Chevy said, a bit uneasily, prepared to be defensive. That Saturday on the Marine physical training course had passed into both families' lore: Larry and Mike had gone on ahead, blithely, racing each other, leaving the older boys with their younger brothers on one of the manageable obstacles, the short platform leading to a sandpit, for practicing parachute landings. Chevy had been eight years old then; Danny had been seven, Lejeune six, and Angus four. The sandpit hadn't held the boys' attention long, and they inevitably had moved on to tougher obstacles. Somehow Lejeune had gotten himself twenty feet up the big climbing rope, the one without the knots, and then had panicked and let go. A cluster fuck, any way you looked at it; a classic boys-will-be-boys episode, from the command level on down. Maria and Liz had given everyone hell that evening when they all got home from the emergency room.

"You kept your head that day," Mike said. "You got your brother's leg stabilized and kept everyone calm, and you sent Danny for help while you stayed with the younger boys. You kept your cool."

Chevy nodded, still not sure where he was going with it.

"And we all got in a bunch of trouble," Mike said. Chevy laughed, relieved. Mike said, "But your dad was so proud of you that day. Did he tell you?"

"I don't remember," Chevy said. "I don't think so."

"He told me," Mike said. They were close to the campsite now, and he stopped and squatted down to get his eyes level with Chevy's, feeling his knee scream, getting past that.

They were silent a moment. Chevy was looking down at his bare feet, digging his toes deeper into the loose sand. He looked pained and defiant, as he always did when Larry came up. Like nobody understood but him. There was probably some truth to that, Mike thought.

He said, "How do you think Lejeune is doing right now, with your dad gone?"

"He's sad," Chevy said. "He cries a bunch, like, *all* the time. Not just about Dad, either. Stupid stuff. And it's like he's gotten scared of everything. He's scared at the pool, he won't go in the deep end. And we have to have a light on now when we go to bed. I can't sleep with the light on, but we have to leave it on because Lejeune is scared. And if I do *any*thing, he tells Mom."

"What about Ramada?"

"Ramada doesn't get it," Chevy said contemptuously. "He's just a little kid. He's sad, but he still thinks Dad is going to come home."

"And your mom?"

"She's sad too. And mad, a lot of the time." He met Mike's eyes, a flare of the old Petroski defiance, and said frankly, "Mostly at me, because I keep screwing up."

Mike said nothing. He could feel his heart, or maybe it was that place half an inch away, the scar tissue in his pectoral muscle that was as far as the shrapnel had gotten. He could find his heart in his chest now by following the wounds.

He said, "There was this poem your dad loved, by a guy named Kipling. I guess I'm thinking of it because he quoted it to me that day you kept your cool with Lejeune getting hurt. I don't know the whole thing by heart, like your dad did, but I remember the lines he said that day he was so proud of you. He said, 'If you can keep your head when all about you / Are losing theirs and blaming it on you; / If you can trust yourself when all men doubt you, / But make allowance for their doubting too . . .'"

Chevy was silent for a moment, then said, "Then what?"

Then, Yours is the Earth and everything that's in it, and—which is more—you'll be a Man, my son!

"I can't remember the whole thing, like your dad could," Mike said. "I know he had the book somewhere. I'm sure you could find it."

BACK AT THE PICNIC TABLE, the tribe was gathering for supper. Kathie and Temperance were showing Lejeune the mass of shells they had collected, both girls flirting wildly and then giggling between themselves. Ramada and Deb-Deb were bent over two bottles of soda and a row of paper cups, like chemists, using their straws to mix different proportions of the strawberry and the grape. It was all coming out more or less brown, but they seemed happy enough with the results.

Chevy ran to the cooler for a drink of his own. Maria, who had seen them stopped up the trail, gave Mike a questioning look, and he smiled back, All good.

Liz had a beer already out for him, with his evening pills laid out neatly beside it. Two aspirin for the low-grade pain, though he was trying to ease off the pain medication entirely and just suck it up;

penicillin because his damned spleen was still screwed up; and anti-malaria pill, antipneumonia pill, and antimeningococcus pill, because the penicillin didn't cover everything.

Mike picked up the beer, leaving the pills in the cup, and went to stand beside his wife.

"Where are *our* boys?" Liz asked.

"Angus has gotten into the swamp, I'm afraid." She gave him a sharp look, and he laughed. "Danny's on it. They'll be back soon."

She still looked dubious, but he put his hand on her tanned shoulder and she snuggled in close under his arm. She was wearing an orange one-piece bathing suit with red vertical stripes; she wouldn't wear a two-piece any more because of the scar. It had taken weeks, this time, before she was willing to let him see her body at all. Not like his previous deployments, when she would farm out the kids to a friend for his return and they would have sex in the front hall the moment they were through the door, and sex halfway up the stairs, and sex in the kitchen, and in the shower, and their clothes would be scattered around the house wherever they had managed to get them off each other. They'd been like virgins this time. Liz had cried every time he took his shirt off—she still did—and kissed the scars, the new ones first, and then the old ones; and when Mike had finally gotten to her naked belly one night with all the lights out, he had found her cesarean scar by touch, and kissed it, and felt the smooth deep groove fill with his own tears, like a dry riverbed after a rain.

Chevy came back with his drink and plopped in close beside Maria at the table. She looked a little startled by this—the two of them had been tense with each other for most of the trip—then put her arm around him and kissed his head. He was telling her something, and she bent close to listen.

Liz was watching them too. "What were you and Chevy talking about?" she asked.

"Just guy stuff," Mike said, and he put his nose into her hair behind her ear. She smelled of salt and sun and something vaguely floral.

Danny came around the turn on the trail just then, slogging through the sand with Angus over his shoulder in a fireman's carry. Angus was coated with sticky brown mud almost to his waist, and his arms and face were smeared brown too. Mike felt his heart leap, but then he caught a glimpse of Angus's face. His younger son looked pleased enough and even a little proud. Mike relaxed.

"Angus is hit!" Danny called, and Chevy and Lejeune both jumped up and ran to help.

"Jesus God in heaven help us," Liz said.

"He's okay," Mike said. "Just dirty." He almost said, Boys will be boys, but he caught himself. He could feel the tension in her shoulder beneath his hand; and in any case, that old formula had changed while he was gone. It fell flat now, most of the time, when he said it; and when Liz said it, as she still did, it had a sharp edge and a hook.

Danny, aided now by Chevy and Lejeune, staggered up, and they managed to get Angus laid down along the picnic table's bench without doing any damage. Danny's face was bright red; it was really sort of amazing he'd managed to carry his brother all that way through deep sand. He looked over at Mike and rolled his eyes and let his tongue hang out, miming exhaustion. Mike gave him a wink and a quiet nod: Good job. Marines didn't leave Marines in swamps.

He said, "Chevy, keep his airway clear and apply pressure to the wound. Danny, go get the hose. And somebody get him a soda. We need to keep him hydrated."

"Is there any root beer left?" Angus said, perking up.

"I got the last root beer, but you can have it," Lejeune said. "I'm going to try the strawberry-grape mix."

"I want the strawberry-grape mix too," Angus said.

MIKE HAD GOTTEN the fire going earlier in the grill, and the coals were ready now. Liz brought him a second beer as he cooked the hamburgers and hot dogs. Kathie, Temperance, and Lejeune were dispatched to the store down the road for more strawberry and grape soda, as the exotic mix Ramada and Deb-Deb were concocting had suddenly become irresistible to all the kids.

As everyone settled in to eat, Chevy once more sat down beside Maria. She put her arm around him right away this time, and he gave her a bite of his hot dog. There wasn't room at the table for everyone to have a seat, so Deb-Deb sat on Liz's lap while Ramada clambered up on Mike's.

"That drink mix of yours is a big hit," Mike told Ramada.

"I figured it out myself, with Deb-Deb."

"I know you did."

"Do you want some?"

"As soon as I finish this beer."

"Uncle Mike—" Chevy called from down the table, and Mike stuck his head around Ramada to look.

"Yeah?"

"What was that poet guy's name?"

"Kipling," Mike said.

"Are you sure we've got the book?" Maria asked, frankly dubious. "I mean, I'd hate for him to get all—"

"It—Yeah, I'm pretty sure. It was in his seabag."

Liz and Maria exchanged a look, inscrutably, and Mike ducked his head. When in danger or in doubt, jump in a hole and wait it out. It was unnerving, how hard the women had gotten to read. Maybe it had always been that way, though.

"I'm going to mix mustard and jelly and see if it's good," Ramada told him.

"What kind of jelly?" Mike asked.

"Red."

"Should be interesting," Mike said, and attended to his hamburger before the kid wanted him to try the mix. Larry would have eaten it without hesitation, he knew, and said Yum-yum and asked for seconds. But Larry had been something special.

AFTER DINNER most of the kids walked up to the store with Liz and Maria for ice cream. Mike and Danny passed and walked west instead, to watch the sunset from the edge of the marsh.

They found a good spot and sat down on a fallen tree. Beyond the swamp, the sound glittered, alive with the long-angled sunlight. The sun, about a hand over the horizon, was turning orange, and the scattered cumulus clouds were starting to be fringed with pink.

"I'm sorry about saluting you earlier," Danny told Mike.

Mike's heart panged. The kid took everything so hard. He said, "It's no big deal, it's just something everybody has to learn. We had a lieutenant once, green as a head of lettuce. Nobody quite knew what to make of him, he was sort of stiff and bossy and full of himself. He loved to wear his nice shiny bars on his collar and to be saluted, and by golly, everybody saluted him all the time and nobody ever told him different. Until one day there was this little fight, and he did okay in it, kept his head, took care of his people. And that night somebody painted over his bars with shoe polish for him. And they stopped saluting him. That was the real sign of respect."

"That's cool," Danny said.

"The closer you get to the real thing, the less rank matters anyway," Mike said. "Everybody's a rifleman when the shooting starts."

Danny nodded and they were silent again. In the marsh, a fish jumped. A heron was stalking not far from them, poised on one leg, its blue head cocked. The mosquitoes buzzed, and Mike waved a hand desultorily. But he really didn't mind mosquitoes that much anymore.

"Are you still thinking of being a priest?" he asked Danny.

His son shrugged. "Maybe."

"I like that guy, Germaine. My kind of priest."

"Yeah. Father Zeke's cool." Danny hesitated. "Did you pray, in Vietnam?"

"All the time," Mike said.

"I was praying so much I thought maybe I should be a priest, because they pray just about all the time."

"You don't have to be a priest to pray all the time," Mike said. "Just about anybody paying attention is going to end up praying just about all the time. Because so much is out of your control."

"Yeah," Danny said.

The sun touched the edge of the horizon. The western sky was a quiet blaze of orange, rose, and gold. Somewhere across the marsh, a plover screed.

A moment, Mike thought. A forever. The thing he had promised himself he would never miss again. He put his arm around his son's shoulders.

"We don't get many kangaroos in here," he said.

Danny smiled and leaned back into his hand. He said, "At twenty bucks a beer, I'm surprised you get any."

CHAPTER 32

LABOR DAY 1968

THE BIG WAVES rolled in, one after another, swelling silently from the night sea, cresting white in the darkness, and breaking in a frothy crash. It was like thunder without clouds in the sky; the ocean itself was utterly placid, glittering beneath a three-quarters moon. But there was a hurricane somewhere far to the southeast, churning unimaginably, sending these long silent swells in a steady pattern like coded pulses, like telegrams, deceptively succinct and bland unless you happened to be in the water and got caught by one and tumbled, and felt the crush of the storm that had sent it.

Liz tried to remember the last time she and Mike had walked alone, hand in hand, on a beach at night. It would have been June of the year before, she was sure. The family had rented a cottage in Kitty Hawk not long before Mike deployed. That had almost certainly been where Anna was conceived; Liz remembered the nights in the flimsy bedroom with the watercolors of lighthouses on the walls and the shells lining every available flat surface: conscious of the kids beyond the thin walls, trying to keep quiet. She had felt torn open, like a plowed field; it made perfect sense to her that she had gotten pregnant despite all their precautions.

There had been a hurricane coming then too, though that storm was much closer, close enough to churn the sea into ragged gray, close enough to thicken the sky, close enough for them to have to leave early, to the disappointment of the children, especially the boys, who had wanted to batten down the hatches and ride it out.

Less than a year and a half ago, Liz realized, doing the math. But time meant nothing anymore; or, worse, it meant something entirely different, something fluid, fitful, and a bit capricious. It had been lifetimes and it had been moments, a grueling time that seemed it would never pass or an instant as fleeting as a dream. But everything was touched with forever now. She'd never wanted to be one of those people who got old and started blathering about how your sense of things changed, but here she was, thinking about forever and the way it undermined the clocks and calendars like a storm tide scouring the sand from the foundations of a beach cottage. It was probably possible to keep living in the thing, for a while at least. But you could feel it wobble.

She was holding Mike's right hand, which was new, and a little disorienting. She'd always held his left hand before; they'd spent twelve years learning each other's rhythms with her right hand in his left, partly because you walked facing the traffic with the man on the street side, the way he had been raised; and partly, Liz knew, because Mike wanted his right hand free in case he had to do something heroic, like hit somebody or snatch a spear from the air. He'd never said as much, but she knew her man. Just as she knew now, without him ever saying so, that his left arm hurt him, somehow, that that was what was behind the switch.

A particularly big swell made its eerily silent approach, gathered itself, and toppled with a crunch. The foamy water churned and thinned into swiftness, sizzling across the sand to run over their feet.

"God, those waves are huge," Liz said.

"Yeah," Mike said. "It'll be a yellow-flag day tomorrow, for sure. Perfect for body surfing. The boys will love it."

It was, in its way, precisely the opposite of what she'd meant. Liz repeated, trying for lightness, "*Huge*, Mike."

He laughed. "I'll be out there with them, Lizzie. We'll be okay."

"Not Ramada. And not Angus."

"Angus swims like a fish," Mike said, which was true. Angus had swum before he'd walked and had jumped off the low diving board into Mike's arms at the Officers' Club pool when he was two years old. He'd gotten caught by a riptide once, in a sea worse than this, at five years old, and Mike had just swum along beside him, talking him through it, teaching him to not try to swim straight back to shore, to swim sideways, across the current, until he was out of it. They were a hundred and fifty yards offshore by that time, and Liz had already screamed her throat out for a lifeguard and started planning the funerals, but when the two of them got back to shore, they'd both been elated and Angus had wanted to jump back in and do it again, as if it were a carnival ride.

"He'll be fine, sweetie," Mike said, and, as she hesitated, "I'll stay close."

"Lejeune won't want to go out," Liz said, conscious of insisting, of reaching for straws.

Mike shrugged. "I won't push him. But it might be the best thing in the world, right now, for Lejeune to go out."

This was almost certainly true as well; even Maria was starting to be concerned about Lejeune's gun-shyness of late; but still Liz resisted, feeling peevish suddenly, and more than a little ornery. Mike finally picked up on her tension, and they walked for a time in silence.

"What was that look you and Maria gave each other earlier?" he asked at last. "About the Kipling?"

It was a typical Mike move, connecting such disparate dots, and a touch of their old style together as well, frankly opening the can of worms. Liz felt a little leap of joy.

"It wasn't about the Kipling," she said. "It was about the seabag. She hasn't opened it."

"Jesus. Really?"

"Really."

"Jesus," he said again; and, after another few steps, "There are presents in there for her, and for the boys. His *wedding ring* is in there."

"I'm sure Maria knows that."

"Then why—?"

"For God's sake, Mike. It's the last thing left. She opens it, and he's dead, all the way, completely."

"Well, isn't he?"

She shook her head, disgusted: nowhere to go, with that tone. Another wave slammed in, slapping at their feet with more punch this time, running up their calves. Mike steered them a few steps higher on the beach and said, "The tide's coming in. We should head back now, or we'll have to walk back in the loose sand."

"I don't want to go back yet," Liz said stubbornly, and then realized that he probably meant his knee hurt already and that walking in the loose sand would hurt it more. But she kept silent anyway because she was mad now and they could jolly well deal with it, one way or the other. They'd been way too goddamned nice to each other since he'd been back, and they were overdue for a sorting out.

Mike hesitated, and Liz recognized the familiar chess-move mulling typical of the early stages of their fights. He could flank her easily, she knew, take the low road and insist on going back, but to do so would mean acknowledging somehow that he had come back so damaged that they'd had to change the way they held hands, that he couldn't raise his left arm enough to put it around her shoulder, that they couldn't walk on the beach unless the goddamned tide was going out and the sand was packed just so. She let him deal with it, feeling mean, and at last he said, "How about we just sit down for a while?"

It was a nice compromise: he was willing to have it out but not to admit his leg hurt. Liz said, "That would be great. I wish we'd brought a blanket."

"The sand's still warm. It will feel good."

It did. They settled on a slight rise just beyond the band of debris along the high tide line, and the sand felt like a lap. The moon was well over the ocean now, and the long band of its light on the surface ran straight toward them like a highway until the surf chewed it into impassability. Mike sat on Liz's left, which was still disorienting, and took her hand in his. They were silent for a moment, neither of them quite sure how much they really wanted to push it. Like two boxers after an early flurry of blows, backing off, circling, regrouping.

Mike was absently fingering his calf. Liz reached for the leg and found the scar beneath his hand.

"What's this from?" she asked. Her husband's damaged body shocked her still—this changed, scourged, compromised thing he had brought home to her, flesh of her flesh. She had a sense of ongoing violation and even, strangely, of jealousy, at his wounds, at the violent intimacies of them, in which she had played no part. She was still trying to sort the injuries out, to map his scars into some kind of coherent history. But it was hard to keep track. Her husband had scars on his scars, at this point.

Mike shrugged. "Shrapnel."

"From the mortar shell?"

"A grenade."

"I don't think I heard about the grenade."

"Wasn't much to hear about."

Liz was silent for a moment. There had been a telegram in May, informing her of Mike's second official wound, some splinters from a mine that had killed his radio operator. She had actually almost welcomed that one: the second one had not been as bad as the first, and she had been reduced by then to hoping for a not-too-bad third wound that would have gotten him sent home. But apparently Mike had not bothered to report his third wound.

Mike read her silence and said, reluctantly, "It was friendly fire. One of our guys got hit as he was throwing a grenade, and the damned thing just plopped down right there in front of us." And, as she still said nothing, "Really, it was no big deal."

"That would have been three," Liz said. "Three and out."

"It was our own grenade, for Christ's sake. It was more embarrassing than anything else."

"God forbid you should get an embarrassing oak leaf cluster on your overloaded Purple Heart and just come home." Her husband shrugged, stubbornly, maddeningly. Liz said, "Goddammit, Mike, you promised not to be a hero."

"I wasn't being a hero. I was just doing my job. And trying to keep my men from getting killed in the process. And trying to stay alive myself. Which I did. And here I am."

Liz noted how far down the list of his priorities his own survival had been, a distant third at best, but she said nothing. It was useless to fight about this, she knew. But it was so close to the fight they needed to have that she said, "Do you have any idea what it felt like, having Khe Sanh on the front page of the newspapers for three months?"

"It's not my fault those reporters needed something to write about."

"Goddammit, Mike!"

"It really wasn't that big a deal, Lizzie. They shot at us, we shot at them. It was a war."

Liz shook her head. Every time she tried to have this conversation, it dead-ended here: it was a war. Maybe it really was that simple to him; maybe that was all he would ever be able to articulate of what the last year had meant to him, and all he would be able to give her to try to grapple with what it had meant to her. It was a war. And Anna was a dead baby.

Her hand was still on his calf. Liz dug her fingernails in, sharply, along the soft smooth flesh of the scar. She had worked for a month before Mike's return, growing them long and shaping them, painting them soft pink. The skin of the recently healed wound gave beneath the point of her nail, and she tore at it, and Mike yelped and slapped her hand away.

"Jesus, Lizzie!"

She said nothing; she had shocked herself too. He gaped at her, then touched his fingers tentatively to his leg. They came away dark with blood in the moonlight.

"Jesus, Lizzie," Mike said again, more softly; and, trying to make a joke out of it, "You're worse than the NVA."

"Friendly fire," Liz said. She stood up and started walking south. Away from the campsite, away from him. Mike was slow to get to his feet, and she got a good head start, and it took him a long time to catch her. By the time he did, he was frankly limping in the loose sand.

He reached for her shoulder to slow her, and she shook his hand off. She was striding hard, almost trotting, and he really couldn't keep up. She wondered how the hell he had managed it, slogging through all those patrols with a pack and a weapon, leading the company up and down hills, through brush and jungle and rice paddies. But he wasn't going to talk about that.

Ahead of her there were no lights at all. If you looked north, you could see the lights of several piers, but looking south there was only darkness, the pale beach and the blackness of the grass-covered dunes, the white churn of the surf and the endless night sea beyond.

Mike caught her again, got a step ahead, and faced her, gripping both her shoulders, stopping her.

"Lizzie," he said. "For God's sake."

She tried to get by him, but he held her firm, and after a moment she stopped struggling. Mike let her go and stood facing her, panting but still alert, in case she tried to bolt again.

"We're not going to make it, are we?" Liz said. "You're not going to be able to talk about it. I'm not going to be able to talk about it. And it's going to kill us. It's going to take us down."

"I don't know," Mike said. "I reckon it's a little soon to say. We've hardly even started trying, the way I see it."

She shook her head.

"Let's sit down again," he said. "Okay? Please? My fucking leg is killing me."

"Imagine that," Liz said, but she turned and moved toward the dry sand. Mike paused to rinse the blood from his calf in an incoming wave, then limped after her. They sat down side by side in silence, not touching, and looked out at the ocean. Mike took a handkerchief from his pocket—he'd been carrying handkerchiefs everywhere they went since his return because Liz was crying so much—and pressed it to the wound on his leg. Liz saw the white cotton go dark, instantly. She'd really torn him open.

"Ask me one question," Mike said.

Liz blinked, caught off guard, then gave him a grudging smile. It had been one of the little rituals of their courtship, their private version of truth or dare. One question each, for all the marbles, no waffling allowed. The last time they had played it had been more than a dozen years ago. She had asked Mike, "Do you love me?" and he had said, simply, yes. And he had asked her if she would marry him.

She thought for a moment now, then said, "How did you feel, when you heard that Khe Sanh had been closed down?"

Mike shrugged. The Khe Sanh combat base had been quietly abandoned in June, the airstrip torn up, the bunkers filled in, the whole thing packed up and hauled away, like a carnival, leaving only the trash and the roiled dirt behind. The government had tried to keep it out of the headlines, but some reporter had gotten wind of the closing, and it had been a pretty big deal for a while, after all that talk about having to hold the damned place.

"One other rule," Liz said. "You're not allowed to say the words 'not that big a deal.'"

"I wasn't even there by then," Mike said. "We were somewhere northwest of Hue, by that time."

"You must have felt something."

"We'd fought, and bled, and a lot of good, good men had died for the damn place," Mike said. "We fought and bled and died and won, and while we were doing that, our country decided somehow that we'd lost, and gave it all away. How did I feel? I felt stabbed in the fucking back. Is that what you want to hear?"

"I want to hear the truth," Liz said. "That's the point. I just want to hear the truth." Her husband shook his head, fiercely. She said, feeling relentless, "Did you know that Danny asked me, the other day, how to spell *Pyrrhic?*"

"Ouch," Mike said.

"He's too young, don't you think, to know what a Pyrrhic victory is?"

"How the fuck old do you have to be?"

Liz conceded the point with a shrug. They sat in silence for another moment, and then Mike said, "My turn?"

Liz considered. It had been a start. That was all she had wanted, a start. She said, "Your turn."

"What color were her eyes?"

Liz opened her mouth to answer and found that her breath was gone. Like Anna, she thought: that little mouth, gaping, gasping for air with lungs that would never be enough.

"They were brown," she said. "They looked just like yours."

Mike nodded and looked at the ocean, and after a moment his shoulders began to shake. She reached for him, laying her hand on his back, wincing at the shuddering. It was like touching a live wire, electric with pain. But he never made a sound. He shook and shook and finally subsided, and she left her hand on his back.

They were silent for a long time. Liz realized that the waves were still rolling in, that the moonlight glittered on the water, that the night was cool and peaceful. It only seemed like everything had been on fire for a while; it only seemed that the world should be charred and ruined.

"I love you," she said softly. Mike didn't respond, and Liz thought for a terrifying moment that he was ignoring her. Then she remembered that his right ear was his bad ear, that he probably hadn't heard anything but the eternal ringing of the mortar round.

"I love you," she repeated, clear and firm this time, and he reached for her hand, brought it to his lips, and kissed it, leaving his head bowed over it, holding his lips there.

"Do you remember that time on the beach in Maryland?" he asked. "That one bonfire party, the year we got married?"

"The one where Larry had just gotten his bongos?"

"Maria sang 'Amazing Grace,' a cappella. And later, you and I—"

"I remember," Liz said.

"When I got hit—" Mike said, "I was thinking of that night."

He raised his head at last, his eyes dark in the moonlight. Liz wondered if she would ever be able to meet those eyes again without thinking of Anna. And then she thought, as he kissed her and her own eyes closed over the image, That's not such a bad thing.

They moved into lovemaking slowly. He eased her T-shirt over her head, eased her back onto the warm sand, and found the cesarean scar in the moonlight. Liz winced as he traced it with his finger, but he persisted, tenderly, and finally she relaxed and he kissed the length of the cut, then raised his eyes to meet hers. She held his look, and he straightened and slipped his own T-shirt off, and she touched the baffling legion of scars, the old ones first, and then the new ones, one by one. Her breathing had slowed and grown peaceful, and she felt Mike's calm and peace, their edges melting at last, and when he entered her it was almost imperceptible, a deeper caress, merely, a firmer communion.

Afterward, they lay together in each other's arms, and she felt him smiling.

"What?" Liz asked.

"We have to go in the water now," Mike said.

"No way."

"Oh, yes. It's part of the, uh—"

"Ritual?"

"I was going to say 'tradition.'"

"It's part of the tradition to drown?"

"Once you're past the breakers, it's like a lake out there."

"Your leg is probably still bleeding. What about sharks?"

"Sharks are stupid, not foolish," Mike said. "If any come around, I'll just establish an atmosphere of mutual respect."

Liz laughed. That was her man: prepared to reason with sharks on their own terms. "You're a madman, Michael Francis O'Reilly."

"You knew that when you married me," he smiled. He stood up and held out his hand.

"I didn't know anything when I married you," Liz said, but she took his hand.

The late-summer water was cool at first touch and then warm. They waded in hand in hand, and as the first breaker approached and curled over them, they dived through it together, and Liz felt the thrum and churn and surfaced on the other side. A second wave swelled, and then a third, and they dived under both of them, and then they were beyond them, and the avenue of moonlight stretched untroubled to the horizon. Liz felt the sea buoying her and remembered, with a thrill, how much she loved to swim. It was amazing what you forgot.

She reached for Mike's hand, and he eased her toward him and put his arms around her, holding her up, treading water in that tireless, effortless way of his. She had forgotten that too. They floated together, quietly, as if they could float together forever, and she kissed him, tasting salt, her tears, perhaps, or his, or maybe it was just the sea.

ACKNOWLEDGMENTS

I AM DEEPLY GRATEFUL to Renée Sedliar of Harper San Francisco, a writers' editor if ever there was one, for her guts and smarts, her road-tested sense of humor, and her marvelous ear. Thank you, Miki Terasawa, for all the poetry and the Sacred Rothko. Thanks also to Margery Buchanan, Terri Leonard, Carolyn Allison-Holland, to Priscilla Stuckey, Michael Maudlin, and Mark Tauber, and to Steve Hanselman and the rest of the awesome team at Harper San Francisco.

I owe a profound debt of gratitude to the veterans in my life: to my father especially, and to Col. Howard Lee and all the Marines of my childhood, for making service and heroism a daily reality to me from the beginning; and to the vets at St. Aidan's, especially Fred Boze, who have so generously shared their lives and experience with me. Thanks for all the sessions with Dr. Jim and Dr. Jack, Fred, and for the trip to the Wall.

A special thank-you to Elizabeth Letts, for lending both her fine novelist's eye and her obstetric expertise to a reading and repair of the relevant chapters. Any remaining medical discrepancies are my own damn fault.

Thanks too to Anne Poole for keeping me laughing throughout; to my Aunt Mary Ann and the rest of my family for all their love and support, and for keeping the "fun" in dysfunctionality; and to Andrea Marks, the Diamonds and Springers, the Waides, and the rest of my church "family," who make it all worthwhile.

I am grateful to the always-refreshing Laurie Horowitz, and to Matthew Snyder of CAA, for their intermedial labors.

Heartfelt thanks, as ever, to Linda Chester, of the Linda Chester Literary Agency, for steadfast friendship and elegant support. And my agent, Laurie Fox, remains my truest literary friend and comrade, an inspiration and a joy. Thank you, Laurie.